D0195018

LETTER
TO A KING

LETTER TO A KING

A Peruvian Chief's Account of Life Under the Incas and Under Spanish Rule

by

HUAMÁN POMA
(Don Felipe Huamán Poma de Ayala)

Arranged and Edited
with an Introduction by
CHRISTOPHER DILKE
and translated from
Nueva Corónica y Buen Gobierno

E. P. DUTTON • NEW YORK

This work was probably written between 1567 and 1615, and the original manuscript is held by the Royal Library of Copenhagen, by whose permission we reproduce the illustrations. A facsimile edition was published by the Institute of Ethnology in Paris in 1936.

This edition published by E. P. Dutton, a Division of Sequoia-Elsevier Publishing Company, Inc., New York.

First published 1978 by George Allen & Unwin, Great Britain.

For information contact:
E. P. Dutton, 2 Park Avenue, New York, N.Y. 10016

Library of Congress Catalog Card Number: 77-93243
ISBN: 0-525-14480-3

10 9 8 7 6 5 4 3 2 1

CONTENTS

THE FIRST PART OF THIS CHRONICLE
The Indians of Peru

THE SECOND PART OF THIS CHRONICLE
Conquest and Spanish Rule

ILLUSTRATIONS

TRANSLATOR'S INTRODUCTION

For me this book began as a personal adventure. A journey to South America had given me the opportunity of following up a long-standing interest in the Inca Empire. I travelled from Lima to the old capital of Cuzco, visited the cliff-top city of Machu Picchu and then crossed Lake Titicaca into Bolivia. The train to La Paz stopped close to the mysterious ruins of Tiahuanaco, which impress the spectator by their immense scale at such a high altitude. Two days later, in La Paz, I was introduced to a Bolivian scholar of Inca ancestry and was immediately fascinated by his views about the nature of Inca rule.

It was taken for granted by my new acquaintance that my knowledge of the Incas rested largely on W. H. Prescott's *History of the Conquest of Peru*, which is more than a century old. I said that I was also familiar with the *Royal Commentaries of the Incas* by the half-caste Garcilaso de la Vega, who was one of Prescott's main sources. Garcilaso's account, I was told, was to a certain degree misleading since he had been educated under Spanish custom, had left Peru as a very young man, had lived in Spain for the rest of his life and had written his book at an advanced age. In spite of his descent through his mother from the Inca rulers, he could be considered as a Spanish source rather than a Peruvian one.

The importance of a genuine source-book arises from the fact that the Inca Empire, which possessed no written system of language, was instantaneously destroyed on 16 November 1532 by the Spanish conquerors under Francisco Pizarro. The Inca ruler in his power and majesty was encountered only on two occasions by the invaders from Europe: once when he received a delegation at his camp and once during his capture and overthrow on the following day. Thereafter Pizarro was the ruler and the rule was Spanish. By the time learned men arrived and tried to piece together the Inca civilisation from reminiscences and from its records kept on knotted and coloured cords called the *quipu*, the trail was already growing faint. The scholars from Spain made mistakes of interpretation, even if they were able to discover most of the facts.

But there existed a source-book, I was informed in La Paz, which was discovered long after Prescott's time and which still remained unpublished in the Anglo-Saxon world although known to experts on the period. The name of the author was Huaman Poma, which means 'falcon puma' in the native language. He was a Peruvian chief who claimed membership of a noble family with a record of service in high positions under the Incas. According to Huaman Poma's account, his father was Viceroy to Inca

Huascar but then became a loyal officer of Spain and saved the life of a Spanish Captain in battle. Thenceforward the family borrowed the additional name of de Ayala from the rescued Captain, and Huaman Poma called himself in the Spanish style Don Felipe Huamán Poma de Ayala. He claimed to be of pure indigenous descent himself, but he had a half-brother who was an educated half-caste.

I questioned the Bolivian scholar about the precise nature of Huaman Poma's originality and difference from other sources. The answer was that Huaman Poma demonstrates how the Inca ruler was the prisoner of a complex set of superstitions. He was not free to act according to notions of prudence or self-protection, as some foreign writers have imagined, but was immobilised by his function as the interpreter of tradition. Also, by illustrating his work with drawings, Huaman Poma solves many problems which have puzzled historians about the secular and religious life of the ancient Peruvians.

My informant told me that he himself possessed a copy of Huaman Poma's work, which is entitled 'The First New Chronicle and Good Government', but this copy was at his home near Potosí. He gave me the name of the publisher, Arturo Posnansky, and I spent the next days trying to find a copy for myself, but without success.

Some days later, in Buenos Aires, a friend discovered an abridged Argentine version for me. This not only confirmed my interest by demonstrating the quality of the text and pictures. It also gave details about the original manuscript and about a facsimile edition published in 1936 by the Institute of Ethnology in Paris. The actual manuscript, I discovered, reposes in the Royal Library of Copenhagen. The facsimiles are distributed among places of learning and I was told that I was bound to find one in London.

Accordingly I went to the reading-room of the British Museum on my return and was soon supplied with a thick, squat, handwritten, copiously illustrated volume of more than 1,400 pages. It was prefaced by an account of the discovery of the manuscript by the discoverer himself, a German called Richard Pietschmann. In 1908 Dr Pietschmann, who was the Librarian of the University of Göttingen and an historical scholar of distinction, was attending a congress in Copenhagen. He was made free of the manuscripts in the Royal Library and among them came upon Huaman Poma's forgotten work. Evidently he was greatly excited by this find, which fitted into the picture of his own historical researches. He wrote his account, a concise and masterly one, and intended to edit and publish the whole book, but died before he could carry out his intention.

I was interested to discover in the British Museum what the contemporary reaction in England to Dr Pietschmann's discovery had been. The leading authority of that period was Sir Clements Markham, who had paid a visit as a young man to W. H. Prescott and had been inspired to carry on the American's life-work. Markham had indeed noticed the appearance of the manuscript, which he regarded as 'the most remarkable production of native genius that has come down to our time'. He was specially impressed by the courage and compassion of the Peruvian writer, who had dared to be the spokesman of his race against Spanish injustice. It was Markham's impression that the manuscript, the 'illustrated Peruvian codex' as it is called, would shortly appear in print in England. Another contemporary authority, the American Philip Ainsworth Means, was almost equally impressed. Books in French and Spanish were also written around it and explored its contribution to the existing knowledge of the Incas.

My next step was to visit the Royal Library in Christiansborg Castle in Copenhagen. The manuscript was exhibited there in a locked glass case. Once I had provided proof of my respectability I was allowed closer access. An attendant brought a big bundle of keys, of which the last but one unlocked the case. A few minutes later I was turning the pages, which until re-discovery had been lying untouched for 300 years, and were as thin and light as a spider's web. The ink, originally black in colour, had turned to a reddish-brown and had 'eaten' the paper in large, irregular blotches.

But this was nothing compared with the difficulty of interpreting the actual text. I began to read:

CARTADELAUTOR
CARTADEDO[n]
fe guaman poma de ayala asu
magd el rey phelipo – muchas
ueses dude S.C.R.M. azeptar
esta dha yn presa

The author made designs with his letters at the top of the page. If he reached the end of the line before the end of a word he either tucked the superfluous letter or letters on to a higher level in small writing, or else simply carried on without any hyphen into a new line. There were constant abbreviations of the type of 'dho' or 'dha' for 'the said'. The break between words was often made in the wrong place. Mis-spelling and faulty syntax, characteristic of Creole Spanish, often rendered the sense doubtful. Worst of all, several lines at a time would be inserted in the native languages of Quechua or Aymará. There were also long lists of names which might or might not have any importance. One such list ran:

nina quiro mallco rumisongo mallco
rumi naui mallco manacutana mallco
uizatomamallco apocuri mallco scapana hila

Here it was valuable to pick out the name of the General Rumiñavi, who played a dramatic part in the history of the Conquest.

Even with the aid of dictionaries the task of interpreting the manuscript would have been almost hopelessly difficult for me, had I not been told by the Librarian in Copenhagen of a 'crib' published by the Ministry of War in Lima, in which the original text is matched with a version in modern Spanish. The author of this three-volume work, who appears to have submerged himself in it for a full decade, is Lt-Col Luis F. Bustíos Gálvez. His knowledge and research have unlocked many mysteries, but I nevertheless found it necessary to translate or adapt directly from the original after reading his version. The Colonel sometimes, and very understandably, changed the text because of an error of fact or of religious doctrine. I have tended to leave such errors in being, as a clue to the writer's character and education, but have sometimes compromised over dates and ages. It has been my impression that Huaman Poma usually doubled figures relating to time, for whatever cause, and I have sometimes translated an unrealistic age as 'very old'. I have also, unlike the Colonel, omitted a lot of redundant passages and combined other passages together. Huaman Poma had something in common with the old *quipucamayoc*, the keeper of the knotted cords, who was the official recorder of the Inca civilisation. When in his writing he reached a point at which certain facts or memories became more or less relevant, he always set them down regardless of whether he had done so in a preceding chapter or not. He also had the habit of using unrealistic and repetitious phrases to describe his heroes, as when he says of some legendary Inca that 'his helmet was blue'. I have tried to use tact in conveying the flavour of this habit without the excessive repetition.

In all I have spent five and a half years of continuous effort on the manuscript. I first eliminated passages which seemed to be of no conceivable interest to the reader, such as recitals of details of Roman Catholic teaching imperfectly comprehended by the author, who was an adoptive Christian. Then I translated the remainder of the quarter of a million or so words, groping always for the thought in the author's mind and trying to clothe it in clearer and more graceful language. Next I indexed the passages in which Huaman Poma described the same set of facts in different words. Between these various versions I chose the best one and inserted any telling details from the others. I then re-shaped the whole work in what seemed to be a more logical order. For instance I combined a section of the Inca Kings with one on their Queens and another on their military campaigns. I put the whole work, instead of just parts of it as in the original manuscript, into the form of a letter to the King of Spain, for whose attention it was written. I followed the Peruvian Colonel Bustíos Gálvez in breaking the book into three parts instead of two and I gave these parts new descriptive titles. I also re-arranged the order of chapters and combined two sections in order to form a connected story under the heading of 'The Author's Travels', which concludes the book. I believe I can truthfully say that I inserted nothing new or alien into Huaman Poma's work. I took as my guiding principle a sentence from a Peruvian study of the author: 'If it were possible to extract from the chronicle its innumerable repetitions, litanies of facts and insistent trivialities, the torment of reading it would be greatly alleviated.' Indeed, it ceased to be a torment and became a rare experience. Often the narrative was strangely compelling and half-forgotten mysteries gleamed in the text. I tried to throw nothing of value away, whilst shortening the text to a third of its length. As an outcome the book cannot be regarded as a pure translation and any detailed criticism of my rendering would need to be answered by reference to the criss-crossing of the 23 notebooks which I filled during my task.

The purpose of Huaman Poma's work was to bring to the attention of the Spanish Court the great merits and the sufferings under Spanish rule of the Peruvian people. The full version is prefaced by an invocation to the Holy Trinity, a letter to the Pope and two letters to the King of Spain, one purporting to be written by the author's father and one by himself. The dating of these letters and other clues provide some evidence that the work was written between 1567 and 1615, when the author was nearly 90 years old. At the latter date King Philip III was on the throne of Spain and the manuscript, the fruit of half a lifetime, was intended for his eyes. But though it was sent off from Lima and evidently arrived in Madrid, it is unlikely that the King ever saw it. At best it may have been scrutinised by a favourite, thereafter coming into the hands of a Danish Ambassador to Spain, who took it home with him. This Ambassador, Cornelius Pederson Lerche, probably bought the manuscript in the 1650s.

In addressing his foreign overlord, Huaman Poma was eager to comply with the proper forms and to show a decent respect. He also thought fit to inflate his own claim to a hearing. With this in mind, he emphasised his membership of the Yarovilca dynasty, which had ruled the province of Chinchaysuyu before the coming of the Incas. He almost certainly resorted to false pretences in describing the title and position of his father. No other evidence bears out that the elder Huaman Mallqui was ever a Viceroy, although a Spanish account confirms that this 'Big Ears of royal blood' was indeed sent as an ambassador to Pizarro, as the younger Huaman Poma claims.

The truth is that Huaman Poma carried a double 'chip on the shoulder'. In the first place he was conscious of not belonging to the Inca caste and of being identified with a category of local chieftains whom it had been the Inca policy to pacify and keep in comparatively minor office, and whom the Spaniards had largely discarded. In the second place no Peruvian could fail to be impressed by the superior importance and power of the Spanish Crown, for the Spaniards were not only the new rulers of the country but were believed to have a mystical connection with the god Viracocha. Up to a point, Huaman Poma was ready to fit into this framework of divine and human power, but on numerous occasions some contrary influence in his own personality made him kick against the pricks. His respect became tinged with criticism and sarcasm. Admittedly, he wrote, the Incas had long been the ruling dynasty but the Yarovilcas were older and so the Incas were *parvenus*. Spanish institutions were important, but lacked the discipline and humanity of Peruvian ones. Christian principles were admirable, but did not justify the seduction of young girls by Spanish priests in the guise of religious instruction.

Thus, if the King of Spain had ever read this letter from a humble subject, he would have been far more insulted by the insinuations than flattered by the outward show of loyalty. Success in his attempt to communicate with the fount of justice could only have brought the writer to punishment, perhaps on the scaffold. Moreover, this inherent risk in his undertaking was too obvious to be unperceived by Huaman Poma himself. When he set out on his arduous travels, accompanied by his son, his horse and his two dogs, as one of the pictures shows, he was determined to record at whatever price the injustices being perpetrated by the Spanish settlers.

The manuscript falls into three main sections: the ancient history of Peru, the events of the Conquest and the bondage of the Indians under Spanish rule. At the same time the task of description is carried out by two separate functions of the pen: writing and drawing. The manuscript is truly a pictorial one. The drawings explain what is sometimes obscure in the text and text is used in the form of annotations to the drawings.

Many passages in the writing have an amazing authenticity and effectiveness. One example is the account of prehistoric battles, in which the leading personalities on either side adopted the disguise and names of ferocious beasts and birds. Or there is the touching description of the Inca ruler singing a song at a festival, when he mingled in his voice the cry of the llama and the sound of running water.

The pictures are of no less importance and power. Although lacking in sophisticated skills, such as moulding and perspective, they often display a high sense of composition which was no doubt borrowed from Christian patterns. Huaman Poma also possessed a knack for a likeness, so that the protagonists of the Conquest are set before us in a credible and consistent style. But the main service rendered by these drawings is to reveal particularities of dress, custom and religion which would otherwise have to be guessed at. The dress of the Inca ruler, for instance, is exactly portrayed: we are able to see how the imperial fringe was worn and how the feathers stuck up from the head. The burial customs of those times, according to which the dead were given a periodic outing, are shown in macabre detail. Most importantly, perhaps, the spirit world with its gods and demons is rendered exactly as it existed in the depths of the Peruvian mind. The German scholar Dr Pietschmann, as one instance, drew attention to the depiction in the manuscript of the *pituciray*, the nature of which had hitherto been obscure. Huaman Poma's drawing shows this divinity as two figures, somewhere between the human and animal, squatting on twin mountain-tops of the Andes.

Huaman Poma was not interested in making pictures for their own sake. His art is a means of exposition. He seems, like Goya, always to be saying: 'This is how it was. I saw this. This is what was done.' Often the drawings are lamentably cruel. There is one which portrays a couple of young lovers suspended by their hair and left to die as a punishment under Inca law for their love. In his text the author gives the words of their dying song: 'Take me with you, father condor. Guide me, brother falcon. Tell my mother that for days I have eaten or drunk nothing. Father and messenger, who can remove all troubles, take my grief and my affection to my mother and my father. Tell them what has happened to me.'

Thus poetry enters into the wretched victims' predicament, but the author and artist is still in favour of punishments, because they enforce a discipline which he believes to be necessary in society. He is stern and restrictive, but possessed at the same time of a strong sense of pity. When the punishment is not merited, but an example of oppression by the ruling race, his pity turns to an implacable anger, tinged by irony and contempt.

Huaman Poma's chronicle has already taken its place as an important source-book for modern histories such as Luis E. Valcarcel's *The History of Ancient Peru*. It is true, another historian has accused the work of naïveté. But even the passages to which this criticism fittingly applies have their charm, like 'Our Lord may have been poor, but he was well-born' or 'Everybody, from the Sun and Moon down to the poorest Indian, received enough to live on.' And there are judgements which are the reverse of naïve, as when this Peruvian author writes: 'The people with most influence in the Christian world are often light in body, thin and narrow-chested. These are the ones who become learned doctors, or men of great wealth and position, because of their energy.' Huaman Poma is capable of insight and commonsense, as well as of voyaging, as he does in his unforgettable last chapter, on the frontier of hallucination and reality. He begins by amusing with his credulity and his trappings of Christianity. But his strong purpose, his courage and his scorn for injustice gradually impose themselves until at last he can be seen as a folk-hero of the old Peru, who is still travelling into our times with a message of protest.

1 *Title page from* 'Nueva Corónica y Buen Gobierno', *showing the Pope on his throne and the King of Spain and the author kneeling*

AUTHOR'S LETTER
Don Felipe Huamán Poma de Ayala to
H.M. King Philip III of Spain

Your Majesty, I hesitated for a long while before writing this letter. Even after beginning, I wanted to retract my words. I decided that my intention was a rash one and that, once started upon my story, I would never be able to complete it in the way in which a proper history ought to be written. For I lacked all written evidence and had to rely on the coloured and knotted cords,* on which we Indians of Peru used to keep our records. Among our people I also sought out the oldest and most intelligent, on whom I could rely as witnesses of the truth.

In weighing, cataloguing and setting in order the various accounts I passed a great number of days, indeed many years, without coming to a decision. At last I overcame my timidity and began the task which I had aspired to for so long. I looked for illumination in the darkness of my under-standing, in my very blindness and ignorance. For I am no doctor or Latin scholar, like some others in this country. But I make bold to think myself the first person of Indian race able to render such a service to Your Majesty.

In short I determined to write this history, which describes the lineage and the famous deeds of the Kings, lords and officers who were our grand-parents; the life of our Indians and their descent over many generations; the idolatrous and heretical Incas with their Queens and concubines; and the great nobles who could be compared with the Dukes, Counts and Marquísses of Spain.

My story continues with the rivalry between Huascar, the legitimate Inca, and his bastard brother Atahuallpa and the generals Challcuchima, Quizquiz and others. It tells of Manco Inca's struggle to defend himself against the Spaniards after the conquest of our country, in the time of the Emperor Charles V; the revolts against the Crown of Don Francisco Pizarro, Don Diego de Almagro, Gonzalo Pizarro, Carbajal and Girón;

---

* *The* quipu *is a means of recording numbers. Many specimens have survived into our times, and these vary considerably from one another. In essence they consist of a large number of parallel strings depending from a thicker rope or other support. Being variously coloured, the strings can be used to represent different commodities, such as maize or potato. The absence of any knot in a string indicates zero. Numbers and quantities are represented by knots tied at certain points in the string. Different strings can be made to convey progressive decimal units. Thus a* quipu *could efficiently record the contents of a warehouse. It could also be used for astronomical and other purposes, including to a limited extent the recording of historical events.*

and the succession of the Spanish Viceroys from Don Blasco Nuñez de Vela onwards.

It recounts the life of the officials, the notaries, the deputies, the proprietors of Indian labour, the priests, the miners and the Spaniards who travel from post to post along the roads and rivers of Peru; the visitors, the judges, the Indian chiefs and their subjects, including the very poor.

In my work I have always tried to obtain the most truthful accounts, accepting those which seemed to be substantial and which were confirmed from various sources. I have only reported those facts which several people agreed upon as being true.

I chose the Castilian tongue for the writing of my work, as our Indians of Peru are without letters or writing of any kind, and I had to translate into Spanish the phrases of the different languages and dialects which we speak, such as Aymará and Quechua.

My work as a historian has been inspired by the wish to present to Your Majesty this book called 'The First New Chronicle and Good Government'. It is for the benefit of all faithful Christians and is written and drawn by my own hand, with those talents which I possess. I have given greater clarity to the text by means of pictures and drawings, knowing Your Majesty to be greatly addicted to these. I have also wished to alleviate the dullness and annoyance likely to be caused by reading a work so lacking in ornament and polished style, such as more distinguished writers devote to the preservation of the Catholic faith, the correction of errors and the salvation of souls.

Your Majesty, for the benefit of both Indian and Spanish Christians in Peru I ask you to accept in your goodness of heart this trifling and humble service. Such acceptance will bring me happiness, relief and a reward for all my work.

On 1 January 1613 in the Province of Lucanas, from your humble servant

Don Felipe de Ayala, the author

LETTER
TO A KING

THE FIRST PART
OF THIS CHRONICLE
The Indians of Peru

AUTHOR'S FAMILY

My history begins with the exemplary life which was led by my father Huaman Mallqui and my mother Curi Ocllo Coya, daughter of Tupac Inca Yupanqui, the Peruvian ruler.

My father interested himself in the education of his adopted son Martín de Ayala, a half-caste of mixed Spanish and Indian blood. He caused this boy to enter the service of God and take the habit of a Christian friar when only 12 years old. This was a happy chance for myself. For my half-brother Martín, once he had grown into a man, gave instruction to his brothers including myself. Thus I came to be able to write my 'First New Chronicle', having been taught my letters at an early age.

As one of the principal Indians of Peru, my father had duly presented himself to the envoy of the Emperor Charles V, Don Francisco Pizarro, and other Spaniards in order to kiss their hands and offer peace and friendship to the Emperor. He was received by them at the port of Tumbes before their march to Caxamarca. My father was on the side of Inca Huascar, the legitimate ruler, whom he served as Viceroy. After his reception by the Christians he returned to his province.

My father served in an important capacity during all the wars, battles and revolts against the Spanish Crown. In one of these wars he was in the service of a loyal Captain named Luis de Avalos de Ayala, the father of the half-caste Martín about whom I have written, and they both took part in the bloody battle of Huarina. The Captain was unhorsed by a lance-thrust while fighting against the partisans of Gonzalo Pizarro. He was defended and saved from certain death by my father, who knocked down and killed Martín de Olmos, one of the rebel side. The Captain, on rising from the ground, acknowledged his debt and declared that my father, even though an Indian, deserved a grant of land from the Crown. Thus my father, having gained some honour from this service, thenceforward took the name of Ayala and adopted the style of Don Martín de Ayala.*

THE HISTORY OF THE WORLD

Our Lord and Saviour Jesus Christ was born in the time of Caesar. In this kingdom of the Incas, in the same age, the first Inca Manco Capac began to reign over the city of Cuzco, which was called Aca Mama or 'mother of the fermented maize'. On his death Manco Capac left the government to his son Sinchi Roca, who extended his rule to Collao and Potosí by conquering the tribes.

The Roman Empire was founded and its rulers have succeeded one another until the present day. During the reign of Robert† the existence of our kingdom of the Indies became known, and how our land was rich in gold and silver, and how we possessed beasts of burden like small camels.

The discovery of the Indies and the discovery of Peru were events which transformed many of the ideas held at the time in Castile and Rome. The roundness of the world was proved. While the people of Castile, Rome and Turkey were hidden by night in the lower part of the world, the Indians of Peru were in broad daylight in the upper part. The name of India is derived from the Castilian words 'en día', in day.

Philosophers, astrologers and poets are aware of the relation between height and riches in the world and they know that everything is created by God, who is the Sun. So the greatest wealth is found in the part nearest to the Sun. It is important for astrologers to know that our King called himself the son of the Sun, and called the Sun his father. Our King, the Inca, was right in considering himself the richest of the rich.

There was excitement in the whole of Castile, caused by rumours about the gold and silver of the Indies. Don Diego de Almagro and Don Francisco Pizarro, with a schoolmaster named Fernando de Luque, succeeded in recruiting soldiers in Castile. Felipe, a Peruvian Indian, was engaged as an interpreter of the Quechua language. The Holy Father was represented by Friar Vicente.

The Spaniards first conquered Panama, Nombre de Dios and Santo

---

* *This story, in the precise form in which it is told, appears improbable or indeed impossible. Ayala arrived in Spain a year after the battle of Huarina in 1547. In other battles he fought on the same side as Martin de Olmos, who survived to be mayor of Cuzco in 1573.*

† *Probably Rupert II Clemens (1352–1410) is intended.*

EL PRIMER MVNDO
ADAN·EVA

adan

eua

en el mundo

2 *Adam and Eve*

Domingo. Then, during the Papacy of Marcellus II,* they embarked in their ships and landed at the port of Tumbes. The first person to greet them was my father in his capacity as envoy and second person in the State after Huascar Inca, the lawful ruler. As a sign of his peaceful mission my father kissed the hands of the newcomers and thus indirectly of the Emperor. Later, the Spaniards received the envoy of Huascar's brother, the bastard Atahuallpa Inca.

When they landed at Tumbes the Spanish captains only had it in mind to play the peaceful part of ambassadors, charged with the duty of kissing the hand of the Peruvian King. But when they saw with their own eyes all the riches of gold and silver which were to be had, greed awoke in them and they did not hesitate to seize and kill Atahuallpa.

THE FOUR AGES
AMONG THE INDIANS

1 *Gods and White People*

The first white people in the world were brought by God to this country. They were descended from those who survived the Flood in Noah's Ark. It is said that they were born in pairs, male and female, and therefore multiplied rapidly.

These people were incapable of useful work. They could not make proper clothes, so they wore garments of leaves and straw. Not knowing how to build houses, they lived in caves and under rocks. They worshipped God with a constant outpouring of sound like the twitter of birds, saying: 'Lord, how long shall I cry and not be heard? How long shall I speak and not be answered?' With the little understanding which they possessed they adored their Creator, and not idols or demons. They wandered like lost souls in a world which they did not understand. In this world, in early times, there were serpents, large and small bears, tigers, pumas, foxes and deer, which were often killed or made captive.

The white people knew the institution of marriage and lived peacefully with one another. They learnt the skills of ploughing and sowing, in the simple way in which these had been practised by Adam and Eve. The gods of the white people were Viracocha and Pachacamac and their manner of worship was on bended knees, their hands joined and their faces turned

---

* *The Pope was Clement VII.*

upwards to the sky. Their prayers were for health and mercy and they asked aloud: 'Where are you, my father?'

In their turn these first people were succeeded by the two castes: the great lords, who were the ancestors of our Incas, and the common people who were descended from bastards and multiplied rapidly in number.

However barbarous they may have been, our ancestors had some glimmer of understanding of God. Even the mere saying of the name Pachacamac is a sign of faith and an important step forward. Christians have much to learn from our people's good way of life.

2 Primitive People

The Indians began to work the virgin soil. As yet they had no houses, but built small dwellings of stone which had the look of ovens or kilns. They still could not make clothes, but learnt the art of softening the skins of animals, so that they could wear them as a covering.

They did not worship demons any more than their first ancestors had done, but kept faith with their God and prayed to him: 'O Lord, where are you? In the sky or on earth? Here in this place or somewhere beyond? Where are you? Hear me, creator of the world and mankind. Hear me, O God!'

They kept the law, respected their parents and their masters and helped one another. Having no houses or possessions, they did not make war but lived in peace. Their effort was spent in cutting out terraces in the ravines and rocky hillsides where they lived. They began to pick out the small stones from the soil, so that it would bear better crops. Apart from this, and the work of irrigation, their sole occupation was in eating and sleeping. But they were sure of God, the creator Viracocha who made men out of clay, and of a place of rest in the sky, and another place of affliction, hunger and punishment. Sometimes they called their God Illapa; and in later times the Incas made sacrifices to this deity, which stood for the lightning-flash and the thunder.

3 Wandering People

The Indians multiplied like ants or like the sands of the sea until they could no longer find room to live. Then they populated the lower levels of the land, where the climate was temperate or warm. They built houses and farms and made villages with open squares. The roads which they constructed still exist at the present day. Since they were not yet able to handle mud-bricks, they always built in stone. Their roofs were thatched with straw.

Clothing was now made of woven materials. Either coarse, thick threads or very fine ones were used, in order to vary the quality. The wool, which came from the growing flocks of llamas and alpacas, was dyed and woven in bands of different colours. The artistry of the Indians extended to tapestries and ornaments made of feathers. They also mined gold and silver, which they worked into diadems, brooches, bracelets and other jewellery, vases and decanters, drums, tunics and ceremonial clothes gleaming with straw-coloured plates of the precious metal. The baser metals which they found a use for were copper, bronze, lead, tin and pyrites.

The rulers and military leaders were chosen from among the legitimate children of nobility. Their laws were exemplary. The boundaries between the property of one lord and another, or one village and another, were marked by piles of stones and were constantly defended. Pastures and watercourses had their ownership indicated in the same manner.

Qualities of courage and resolution were shown whenever an armed struggle broke out, but the Indian way of life was generally mild and charitable. The good relationship of the people with one another was demonstrated by the communal meals held in the open air, at which there was singing and dancing to the music of drums and fifes. Drunkenness was admittedly common, particularly when the Indians gathered together to listen to songs or poems. But there was an absence of quarrels or of grave misconduct, and fights to the death were unknown. The people somehow succeeded in enjoying themselves without going to extremes.

A dowry was paid when women were taken in marriage. They were not addicted to adultery and there were no male or female prostitutes. Loose morals were avoided by keeping the women away from highly seasoned food and strong drink.

It was usual for the girls to remain virgins until marriage, which often did not take place until the age of 30.

As the people increased in numbers, differences arose between them and there were quarrels over firewood, straw, land, seed-beds, irrigation channels, pastures and enclosures for beasts. Attempts were sometimes made to procure more than the just entitlement of water for a property. Sometimes, owing to greed of this sort, it came to a state of war between villages, and raids were made with the object of carrying off clothing or gold and silver.

The population was so numerous that it was able to survive a plague which once raged for six months throughout the kingdom. During this period the condors gorged themselves on the human corpses scattered about the fields and villages.

Because of the mountainous nature of the country, in which one community was cut off from the next by deep ravines, a variety of different tribes came into being. Each of these tended to have its own dialect, style of clothing and way of life.

Since the people could neither read nor write, they stumbled in their blindness and ignorance into certain errors. They declared that human life had come out of the caves, lakes, stones, hills and rivers, rather than from God.

4 *Warlike People*

3 *Auca runa, warlike people*

The Indians abandoned the pleasant valleys and took to the high mountains again because of their fear of war and risings and disputes between one tribe and another. They began to build fortresses among the most inaccessible and rocky hills in order to defend themselves. The walls were stoutly built of stone, and inside were their living-quarters with cisterns to ensure a plentiful supply of water.

At first there were simply quarrels between the tribes, but these gradually turned into battles and then wars, with much loss of life. Each side was led by its own King in person.

The bravest and most outstanding of the warriors distinguished themselves by the use of arms such as pronged forks, lances, gauntlets, maces and cudgels, slings, axes, hatchets and shields. They wore helmets or masks and crests made from plumage. The blare of shell trumpets and the shrilling of pipes inspired them to a furious courage, so that their wars became more and more bloody. Those of the enemy who escaped death were taken into captivity.

They carried off women and children, captured farms and pastures and cut off the water from other communities. Often they resorted to extreme cruelty. Once they were victorious, they sacked and looted the defeated settlements, taking clothes, gold ornaments, silver, copper and also millstones of various sorts, which were considered as valuable property. Those who were most warlike and treacherous amassed enormous riches.

The leaders in these wars adopted the custom of disguising themselves on the battlefield as beasts and birds of legendary ferocity such as lions, tigers, foxes, mountain cats, condors, sparrow-hawks, swallows and snakes; and sometimes as powerful winds. They took their own names from these disguises and passed them down to their descendants as a mark of the glory they had won. In this way they resembled the grandees of Spain. And above all of them, comparable with the Holy Roman Emperor, was the King known as Great Cruel Unyielding Sacred Falcon, who was my own ancestor.[*] Our country was named the Four Quarters of the World,[†] which were respectively Chinchaysuyu in the north, Antisuyu in the east, Collasuyu in the south and Cuntisuyu in the west.

Each of the four quarters had its own King. Under him there were lords over 10,000 Indians, over 1,000, 500, 100, 50, 10 and 5.

A privileged caste was formed by those whom the King singled out for his favour, whether on account of victory in battle, loyalty or wisdom in council. But the highest offices still went to those who could trace their legitimate descent from the old rulers.

These Indians were domineering, fierce and courageous. They fought among themselves like lions. When they succeeded in killing their enemy

---

[*] *Falcon in the Quechua language is* Huaman, *the author's first name.*
[†] *Tahuantinsuyu.*

they cut out his heart and ate it in order to show their fitness for command.

Sometimes they showed kindness and pity for their neighbours, for they gave feasts to which all the poor and needy and the sick were invited. After the meal the broken meats were collected and distributed to those who had not been able to attend. This was a charitable custom which is unmatched, as far as I know, in any country of the world.

The dowries which were given at the time of marriage consisted of beasts, clothing or jewellery. Sometimes a tool such as an adze was presented; or the gift might take the form of a mace or an axe, jars, pitchers and cooking-pots, or even land and buildings. In fact the people, however grinding their poverty, were ready to give away anything which they had. It was also usual to improve such occasions with homilies and good advice to the young couples.

There were heavy penalties, including death, for those who committed adultery or incest.

The marriage ceremony consisted of an exchange of vows by the spoken word. The bride and bridegroom kissed each other on the mouth. From that moment contact with the woman was forbidden to all other men.

The naming of children was also carried out by the spoken word. A male child received the name of the father; a female that of the mother. A feast was held so that the friend who had spoken the name could be accepted into the family and saluted by everyone in turn.

Lazy people and liars were punished just as severely as thieves, highwaymen, cut-throats, adulterers and rapists. For all such offenders of whatever rank the punishment was execution by stoning or hurling over cliffs.

It was usual for the rulers to arrange a truce among themselves at intervals, which might last for six months or a year or even more. Their one preoccupation during these lulls in the otherwise constant warfare was to build houses and fortresses, put the farms in order and irrigate the land.

Those who lived to a great age were appointed as teachers and judges and instructed the young with the severity of Cato in ancient Rome. And there were also wise men who could foresee coming events by observation of the heavenly bodies and the flight of birds, although they were unable to read or write. War, famine, drought, plague and other calamities could be foretold by these seers.

Boys and girls were not allowed to eat fat or grease, honey, vinegar, hot condiments or sweets, or to drink fermented maize. The object was to make the men fit for battle and hard work of all kinds, and particularly for various exercises in which they were required to skip like young bucks and even fly through the air. They were made to work on the roads in the intervals between fighting. At all costs they were to be kept from becoming soft, undisciplined and complacent, with the consequent risk to society.

Their usual diet consisted of maize, potatoes and other tubers; cress, sorrel and lupin; pond-weed, laver and a grass with yellow flowers; leaves for chewing; fungi; edible grubs, shells, shrimps, crab and various sorts of fish; birds' eggs; pigeon, duck and partridge; the local rabbit; venison; and mutton from the different Peruvian sheep.* Other known foods included sweet potato, yacca, cucumber, kidney-beans, peanuts, green and red chilli and chilli pepper, watermelon, banana, avocado pear and plum.

The burial of the dead was conducted with dignity but without undue ceremony in vaults constructed for the purpose. There were separate vaults, which were whitewashed and painted, for people of high rank. The Indians believed that after death they would have to endure hard labour, torture, hunger, thirst and fire. Thus they had their own conception of Hell, which they called the place under the earth or the abode of demons. They provided the corpses with food, drink, clothing, silver and sometimes even women, so that they would be well looked after in the next world. Many tears were shed, because of the wretched fate which was thought to await those whose life was at an end.

The roads and bridges were not well built or formed into a connected system, so that each King was more or less isolated in his own territory. The greater this natural isolation, the less was the need for warlike preparations.

People of quality were carried in litters when they left their houses. There were regulations governing the type of litter which could be used by a person of any particular rank. Important people also had many wives and concubines, who bore them children and thus increased the numbers of the nobility.

It was the Indian custom to carry out a purge every month. The medicine which was used consisted of a measured quantity of lupin mixed into cakes of powdered limestone, and the whole then moistened with urine. Half of this was drunk and the other half squirted into the bowels with a syringe. The treatment was good for fighting men and improved their health and appetite. Life was often prolonged to a remarkable age. Although such purges were common, bleeding was seldom practised except accidentally as a result of falls and blows. The bravery of the men sometimes took the extreme form of fighting wild cats with their bare hands and tearing them to pieces.

---

* *Peruvian sheep is a generalised description of various sorts of animal, of which the Incas possessed immense herds. These were largely slaughtered by the Spaniards. They can be used as beasts of burden, for their wool and as meat. They stand taller than European sheep because of their long vertical necks, and they can move with a feathery lightness. The llama is much used for burden. The alpaca is prized for its wool. The vicuña has an exceptionally fine fleece. Other varieties are the taruga and the huanaco.*

The year was divided into weeks of ten days each. Each month had thirty days. The Indians observed the course of the Sun and the rotation of the Sun and Moon in order to know when to sow their fields. Over matters such as the right time for fruit-picking, pruning, ploughing and watering they were guided by their astrologers. The knowledge of these wise old men has survived into the present time.

Although they were illiterate, our Indians had the ability of poets and writers to record all that happened over the years. They used for this purpose their knotted and coloured cords.

There were serpents surviving from before the time of the first Indians. In the place called Quichicalla, among the lakes and thorn-trees, snakes can still be found which hurl themselves at a man from the distance which a bolt from a crossbow can travel and make a similar sound to the bolt as they fly through the air. Once they reach the victim, they wind themselves round his body and hold him in such a way that they cannot be detached or cut away with a knife. They have a bite which penetrates through clothing to the flesh and causes death unless the only effective antidote, which is the egg of the serpent itself, is applied to the wound immediately. Death can also be caused by lizards; and on the plains of the high Andes there are vipers and rattlesnakes, as well as wild animals, which will attack a man.

The Yarovilca Kings of the tribe of Allauca Huanuco in Old Huanuco, where they built their houses, followed one another in this order: First Yarovilca King, White Lion,* Yellow Lion and Noble Primitive People, Shining White Falcon, Lion as Agile as Lightning and Noble Primitive People, Origin of the Primitive People, Origin of the Condor, Origin of Fire, Origin of the Playful Lion and Origin of the White Conqueror.

The Kings and lords of the succeeding age of warlike people were as follows: Great Lord Battling Lion, Lion Darting Tongues of Fire, Shining Lion, Golden Lion, Cruel Unyielding Condor, Godlike Lion, Crimson Lion, Blue Lion, Prince of the Lions, Cunning Falcon, Captain of the Lions, Powerful Lion, Old Lion, Lion of Castile, Cruel Unyielding Lion, Roaring Lion, Falcon with the Burning Beak and Swift Lion. Then followed the twins, First Twin Falcon and Lesser Twin Falcon. Then came Cruel Unyielding Falcon, Rapacious as the Sparrow-Hawk, Powerful Condor, Powerful with Teeth of Fire, Powerful Sparrow, Flashing Lion, Powerful Earthquake and once again Cruel Unyielding Falcon. All of these were absolute rulers over the Indians and other peoples.

---

* The lion and tiger are not indigenous to America, but the jaguar and puma, which are, became linguistically confused with them at the time of the Conquest. In mythical or heraldic passages 'lion' and 'tiger' seem a better rendering of the text.

THE ORIGIN OF THE INCAS
AND THE TWELVE INCA RULERS

4 *First heraldic arms of the Incas*

The Kings of an earlier dynasty of Peru, the last of whom was called Tocay Capac Pinahua Capac, had their own coat-of-arms specially drawn to illustrate their legitimate descent from the Sun. These rulers were called *Intip churin*, which means 'children of the Sun'.

The founder of the Inca dynasty declared that his father was the Sun, his mother the Moon, and his brother the Day-Star. The idol which he worshipped was called Huanacauri. He and his family were supposed to have come from the place called Tampu Toco which means 'lodging with openings or windows'. This place was also named Pacari Tampu, indicating that it was where divine apparitions occurred. The worship of idols began in the time of the mother and wife of the founder of the dynasty, whose name was Manco Capac. Mother and son both belonged to the caste of the Serpents. This account which I have given is the true history of the origin of the Incas and all other accounts are false.

Manco Capac was not descended from the previous dynasty and had no inherited property. The name of his father was unknown. This was the reason why he called himself the son of the Sun and Moon. The truth is that his mother was Mama Huaco. This woman was a sorceress and a witch who was on close terms with demons. She was able to talk to sticks and stones, and even mountains and lakes, for they answered her in the voices of the demons. She succeeded in deluding the Indians of Cuzco and then of the whole country. Regarding her powers as miraculous, the people were content to obey and serve her. According to all accounts, she slept with the men whom she fancied, regardless of their rank.

When she discovered that she was pregnant with a son, she was advised by her demons to hide the child away and confide it to the care of a nurse called Pillco Ziza. This nurse was to take the child to one of the caves of Tampu Toco and keep it there for two years, while remaining silent about the birth. In the meantime it was to be made known that a King called Manco Capac Inca would appear and rule over the country.

In the course of time the mother became the wife of her son and assumed the title of Queen of Cuzco. In the beginning she had been named simply Mama. As a lady she had become Mama Huaco. Finally, as Queen to her own son, she was called Mama Huaco Coya. She was extremely beautiful, dark of skin over the whole of her body and handsomely built. She usually dressed in pink and wore large silver ornamental pins. She was friendly with the most important nobles, and indeed with a wide range of people, and thus wielded more power than her husband Manco Capac. As well as being uncommonly wise, she was known for her charity to the poor of Cuzco and the rest of the country. She survived her husband and died at Cuzco during the reign of her son by him, Sinchi Roca Inca.

The coat-of-arms of the dynasty founded by Manco Capac contains a sacred bird in the first quarter; in the second quarter a tree with a tiger behind it; in the third quarter the fringe which was the emblem of sovereignty; and in the fourth quarter two serpents with fringes in their mouths. Thus the arms depict the ceremonial dress of the ruler, the bird responsible for his ornamental crest and the dynastic name of Tiger Serpent Inca.

According to one legend, the Incas originally came from Tiahuanaco on the farther side of Lake Titicaca. There were four brothers, one of whom was Manco Capac, and four sisters. After reaching Pacari Tampu and in due course emerging from there again, they returned as a gesture of piety to the shrine of Huanacauri on the road from the lake. The city of Cuzco, where they settled down, was at first called Aca Mama. The later name of Cuzco means 'navel'. From the beginning, the Incas insisted on sacrifices to their own idols whose shrines were situated among the rocks, caves and mountains.

The Incas distinguished themselves by enlarging their ears, so as not to be mistaken for the common people. Only one of them, Manco Capac himself, bore the title of King.

The rulers of Collasuyu in the south followed the custom of the Incas in wearing bone earrings, head-cloths of fine wool and birds' feathers, and in piercing their flesh, but they were not considered true nobles. This was because they were lazy and failed to arrive at Tampu Toco in time for the distribution of ear ornaments which the Incas arranged in order to be able to identify their own caste. These Colla nobles were referred to as 'people with ears of white wool'.

The Huancavilca rulers wore gold rings in their noses and beards. They did not belong to the Inca race, but called themselves Incas.

During the reign of Manco Capac a certain Ancaullo, chief of the Chanca Indians, advanced from his lakeside province with a huge army of Indians but without any women, old people or children, in an attempt to claim the Inca throne. But the Inca sent him as a gift one of his sisters. This lady treacherously murdered Ancaullo and many of the Chanca Indians submitted to the Inca. The remainder fled towards the north and went on and on over the cold, harsh mountain country until they reached the sea-coast. There they have stayed ever since, keeping to their own forms of government and their own different kinds of dress. They make war against each other, as Indians often do. Gold and silver are found in abundance. The land is fertile and great herds of animals graze along the shore of the northern sea.

The First Inca

Manco Capac, the father of the Inca dynasty, adorned himself with a head-cloth of wool and a feathered crest. His ears were pierced to carry ornaments of fine gold. He wore the imperial fringe and also a woven flower. He carried an axe in his right hand and a sunshade in his left.

This Inca ruled over the city of Cuzco without seeking to extend his rule by battle or war. He was the builder of Coricancha, the 'temple of the Sun'. When he married his own mother he gave a dowry to the Sun and Moon.

DE IИGAS
MAИGOCAPAC:IИG

SEGVИDO IИGA ·6A·
CIИCHEROCAИ

esk ynga reayno sobeluz acamama

conquisto hasta hatun colla aniquipa

5 (a) *Manco Capac, the first Inca*

(b) *Sinchi Roca, the second Inca*

ELSESTO IИGA ·SVHIIA·
IИGAROCA·COИ

ELИOVEИOIИGA
PACHACVTI·IИG

IVPAИQVI

Reyno hasta andesuyo-

Reynohasta chile y se to basucor sellera

(c) *Inca Roca, the sixth Inca*

(d) *Pachacuti Yupanqui, the ninth Inca*

He lived to the age of 160, was wise and courteous in his dealings and possessed many accomplishments. In spite of his shrewdness he remained a poor man. His legitimate children were Sinchi Roca Inca, Chimbo Urma Coya, Inca Yupanqui and Pachacuti Inca.

The two latter sons did not make any conquests or do anything of any note. For them the whole of life consisted of sleeping, eating, drinking and whoring. They loafed about, gave parties and banquets and strolled in the city with their friends.

Apart from these legitimate children, Manco Capac fathered a large number of bastards of both sexes.

The Second Inca

Sinchi Roca Inca, who succeeded to the throne on his father's death, was strong and kindly in character, dark in complexion and outstandingly brave.

He was married to his sister Chimbo Urma Coya, who was very slender and beautiful and as dark-skinned as her mother. Chimbo Urma liked to hold clusters of blue flowers, or single flowers, in her hands. She grew these flowers, called *inquilcuna*, in her garden. She was loved by her husband and was very jealous of other women.

She was gentle and gay in her relationship with the people, who adored her. She was very rich and left part of her fortune to the Sun and the Moon when she died at Cuzco. On her deathbed she gave good advice to those whom she was leaving behind. Her children by Sinchi Roca Inca were Mama Cora Ocllo Coya, Lloqui Yupanqui Inca, Huari Titu Inca and Tupac Amaru Inca.

The last two were brave Captains who accompanied their father in his war of conquest against Collasuyu. They massacred the Colla Indians and also sometimes plucked out their eyes while they were alive. Their victories were won with quite small forces against adversaries, some of whom had never before been dominated. In general the Colla Indians, being lazy and cowardly, gave up easily and allowed the Inca laws and religion to be imposed on them. But the Colla ruler Tocay Capac Pinahua Capac succeeded in checking the advance of the two brothers Tupac Amaru and Huari Titu and putting them to death. In this way he fixed the farthest limits reached by the conquerors. From then on, the remaining Colla provinces defended themselves stoutly and did not allow the armies of the Inca to advance the frontier any more.

Sinchi Roca Inca, like his Queen, became rich and was able to increase the treasures of the temple of the Sun and other shrines.

When he was 80 years of age, Our Saviour Jesus Christ was born in Bethlehem.*

When Our Saviour ascended into Heaven, He caused the Holy Ghost to enter into His Apostles, so that they would go out and preach the Gospel in all the countries of the World. It fell to St Bartholomew to visit Peru, where he remained for many years under the sway of the Incas. As a proof of his presence among the Colla Indians he left behind him the miraculous Cross of Carabuco, which is still preserved.

The Third Inca

On the death of Sinchi Roca Inca, his legitimate son Lloqui Yupanqui Inca succeeded to the throne. The new ruler's insignia consisted of a mace representing a falcon in the right hand and a shield in the left.

He had a hooked nose, large eyes and small lips and mouth. He was swarthy, undersized and stooping; ugly and miserable-looking. He had the reputation of being worthless and so was avoided by his subjects whenever possible.

His wife was his sister Mama Cora Ocllo Coya. She was not entirely ill-favoured, but rather too tall. In character she was mean and disagreeable. She ate practically nothing but drank a good deal of maize spirit. On the slightest excuse she burst into tears. Everything which she possessed was kept locked up, including stores of food which rotted away and became unusable. Because she was such a melancholy and timid person, she did not have maids-of-honour or enjoy the other privileges of being a Queen. A meal of crude spirit and vegetables would be served up and she would say to those around her: 'Let us enjoy ourselves, princesses!' She made a bad impression on the ordinary people and was despised by the nobles. During the course of her reign, her irritable manners caused a great deal of trouble and annoyance.

Her children by Lloqui Yupanqui Inca included Mayta Capac Inca and Chimbo Urma Mama Yachi. She had other children as well, but they were killed by her husband's order to prevent them from trying to usurp the throne. Her sad existence lasted until about the end of her surviving son's reign.

With his sons, Lloqui Yupanqui Inca conquered the town of Maras from Tocay Capac Pinahua Capac, the ruler of the Colla Indians.

One of these sons, Cuci Huanan Chire Inca, was a courageous leader who, before going into battle, invariably drank a toast to his ancestor the

---

* *If Sinchi Roca was indeed an historical person, his reign is likely to have taken place about 1200.*

Sun. He was keen to settle a score with Tocay Capac Pinahua Capac, who had broken two of his grandfather's teeth with a sling-shot. Not only were the Colla chief's teeth broken in revenge, but he was defeated and killed; and his remaining territories came under the sway of the Incas.

When Lloqui Yupanqui Inca died at Cuzco, he was succeeded by his son Mayta Capac Inca, who with his bastard brothers had made a name for himself in many raids and battles.

The Fourth Inca

Mayta Capac was exceedingly ugly, not only in face but in all parts of his body, very thin and cold-blooded. Yet the impression which he made was highly courageous as well as melancholy.

With the help of his sons Apo Maytac Inca and Bilcac Inca he captured the Charca province, Potosí with its silver mines and Carabaya, where gold of twenty-four carats is found. Destruction and death were spread far and wide, and everywhere new shrines and temples were erected. Collasuyu was entirely subjected, but the rulers of Chinchaysuyu in the north succeeded in holding their ground and repulsing any attack.

According to Inca custom, Mayta Capac's sister Chimbo Urma Mama Yachi became his wife.

She was rather ugly and dark-skinned, with bright, clear eyes. Her appearance was distinguished and high-spirited and her reputation blameless. She liked paying social visits and amusing herself with music and dinners. It is said that she took part of her husband's wealth and distributed it to the old and the poor, whom she preferred to the rich. When she died at the age of 45 she left all her property to her mother Mama Cora Ocllo.

She and her husband Mayta Capac were the parents, in addition to the children already mentioned, of Chimbo Ocllo Mama Cava, Curi Ocllo and Capac Yupanqui Inca, who succeeded to the throne. During his lifetime Mayta Capac Inca was deeply fond of one of his bastard daughters, whose name was Inquillay Coya. He died at Cuzco, leaving his great treasures to the idol Huanacauri.

The Fifth Inca

Capac Yupanqui Inca was average in size, with a long face. He was miserly and stupid. It was his custom to serve meals to his idols. With a similar idea in mind, he caused implements for eating to be buried with the dead. He was responsible for the discovery of mines from which gold, silver, quicksilver, copper, tin and variously coloured earth were extracted.

His first marriage was to his sister Chimbo Ocllo Mama Cava, a lady of great beauty, peaceful disposition and much humility of heart. Soon after the wedding, however, her reason became disturbed. About three times a day she had violent attacks, in the course of which she uttered loud cries, assaulted and bit people, lacerated her face and tore out her hair. As a result of this illness she became extremely ugly. According to legend she also ate her own son, to whom she had just given birth.

Since she was incapable of carrying out her duties as Queen, the Inca sought the permission of the Sun to marry his younger sister Curi Ocllo. This lady was greatly esteemed and honoured throughout the country as his second wife, while the former Queen died at an early age and without leaving a will, as she had no possessions.

The children of the second marriage were Auqui Tupac Inca, Inca Yupanqui, Cuci Chimbo Mama Micay Coya, Inca Roca, Inti Auqui Inca and Illapa Tupac Inca.

Of these, Auqui Tupac Inca was a brave soldier who vanquished many enemy chiefs and brought the Quechua and Aymará provinces under Inca rule. It was his custom to cut off the heads of his prisoners and present them to his father, Capac Yupanqui Inca, so that the King could take pleasure in these victories.

Capac Yupanqui Inca was passionately fond of women and made a collection of virgins of noble birth. He left many bastards behind him when he died. His legitimate son Inca Roca succeeded him on the throne.

The Sixth Inca

Inca Roca is usually represented as holding his young son with his right hand, while in his left he has an axe and shield. The son was called Huaman Capac and was particularly dear to him.

The Inca was a tall, strong, corpulent man with a voice like thunder, a great gambler and whoremonger, who levied severe taxes on the poor.

Extending his father's conquests further still, he made himself master of the whole Antisuyu. The story goes that he and one of his sons changed themselves into tigers and in this form subjugated the Chuncho tribe.

This son, Apo Camac Inca, was also known as Uturuncu* Achachi because of his animal disguise. He lived in the conquered Antisuyu until his death and had a son by a Chuncho girl. This son took the name and armorial device of Old Puma Serpent Inca.

* Uturuncu *means 'tiger' or 'jaguar'.*

Inca Roca and his son introduced the coca leaf into their empire and were the first to adopt the custom of chewing it. Until then it was unknown in the high Andes, but the use of it became established as a habit or vice. Like tobacco it is only held in the mouth, not swallowed, and serves no useful physical purpose.

The wife of Inca Roca, Cuci Chimbo Mama Micay, was pale in complexion and very beautiful, with a slim figure and a high-spirited way of carrying herself. Smiling and gay, fond of singing and music, she particularly liked to play the drum and to hold clusters of flowers in her hands. It was her pleasure to give parties and banquets.

At her death the Queen left her great wealth in three parts: one for the Sun, one for the Moon and one for her children. She had a great quantity of fine clothes and also gold-and silverware and other treasures.

The Seventh Inca

Yahuar Huacac Inca was short in stature, broad, robust and powerful. His eyes were unusually large. A man of learning, he was peaceful by temperament and fond of music. He made friends with the poor and oppressed the rich.

The Inca led his people in fasting and penitence during the time when they were suffering from the plague. He arranged vigils at all the shrines and also processions with the object of ridding the people of their sickness. On his orders the houses in all the towns and villages were bombarded and purified by fire.

He married his sister Ipahuaco Mama Machi Coya, who could be recognised by her sky-blue cloak. She was an ugly woman with a long nose and longer face. Her body was thin and dried-up. She enjoyed breeding and domesticating small birds, parrots, macaws, apes and monkeys. Songbirds and woodpigeons were her special friends. She was charitable towards the poor, enjoyed the company of men and disliked women.

When the Queen died at Cuzco she left her fortune in two parts. One part was to provide refreshment for herself and her mother in the after life; and the other part was for her children and servants. She also remembered the Sun in her will.

The children of Yahuar Huacac Inca were Mama Yunto Cayan Coya, Viracocha Inca, Apo Maytac Inca, Urco Inca and twin daughters who died, as well as many bastards. Maytac and Urco bravely accompanied their father in his campaign against the tribes of Cuntisuyu, whom they conquered as far as Arequipa, the capital. On their return to Cuzco, to the great grief of their father, they died and were buried with full honours.

The Eighth Inca

Viracocha Inca, who was a handsome man, was remarkable for his white skin. He wore a beard which was really no more than a few hairs on the chin. By nature he was good-hearted.

He was a devoted worshipper of the god Viracocha and it is told of him that he wanted to destroy all the other idols and shrines in the country. It was his wife who dissuaded him from such a course, telling him that he would put himself in danger of death if he so far forgot the laws made by his predecessors. The Inca accepted her advice in spite of his commitment to the divine Viracocha.

He believed in another world in which Viracocha reigned as the supreme god. For this reason, and because he himself was white-skinned and was destined for the throne, he was given the name of Viracocha by his father. When he came to power he imposed a severe form of justice. He was particularly rigorous in his treatment of adulterous women and rapists, whom he invariably sentenced to death.

But there was a lighter side to his character. He enjoyed giving great banquets in the public squares in honour of the god whom he worshipped and he liked to make merry with the guests.

His Queen, Mama Yunto Cayan Coya, was inclined to melancholy and rather timid, but also physically attractive. She never attended her husband's feasts or joined in songs and dances, being too shy to do so. She kept few servants; and those that she did keep were usually female dwarfs and hunchbacks. Slaves were more welcome to her than friends of her own sex.

She was likely to burst into tears at the slightest excuse, her temperament was miserable and she was over-fond of eating. With her, the bad habit of chewing coca leaves had reached the point where she actually fell asleep with the pellets of coca in her mouth. She was inordinate in her love for treasures of gold and silver. Her children who survived into adult life were Pachacuti Inca Yupanqui, three other sons and Mama Anahuarque Coya. When she died in old age in Cuzco she left all her property to her dwarfs and cripples, the only beings for whom she could feel real affection.

Her husband, who had in his lifetime subdued various provinces, died at about the same time and left a fortune in massy gold to the Sun.

The Ninth Inca

Pachacuti Inca Yupanqui is depicted as holding a sling with golden projectiles for use against the enemy.

He was a handsome, tall man with a round face. Whenever something stirred his anger, his eyes became as terrible as a lion's and he lost all control. He was a glutton and a heavy drinker. His chief pleasure was the making of war, in which he was invariably victorious.

His sister-wife Mama Anahuarque Coya had a round face like his. She was beautiful, with small eyes and mouth, her hands and feet always well cared-for, and graceful in her bearing. Whether in a good or a bad temper, it was her habit to strike herself on the breast and exclaim: 'God help me!' or call upon Viracocha, the creator of mankind, by name. Moreover, those who tell this story maintain that when they heard the name of the god all those present prostrated themselves on the ground.

She was meticulous in her obedience to her husband and when he flew into one of his rages she lowered her eyes to the floor and did not dare to raise them until he called her by name.

The bravest of Pachacuti Inca's sons was Apo Camac Inca. He resembled Pachacuti in his leonine appearance and flashing eyes. His strength was such that with a single blow he could knock a man unconscious for an hour.

He accompanied his victorious father in the invasion of Chile at the head of 50,000 soldiers. It is said that they caused the death of 100,000 Chilean Indians. The Chaclla, Yaucha, Chinchaycocha and Tarma provinces were taken. But when, with reduced forces, they continued the advance and made war upon the Yunca Indians of the plains, several of the Inca's sons perished.

The defeat of Chile was made possible by the ravages of plague, which lasted for ten years. Disease and famine, even more than force of arms, brought about the downfall of the Chileans, just as civil war between Huascar and Atahuallpa was later to facilitate the Spanish conquest.

Peru itself suffered terribly from plague, famine and drought. For a decade no rain fell and the grass withered and died. People were reduced to devouring their own children and when the stomachs of the poor were opened it was sometimes found that they had managed to sustain life by eating grasses. Earthquakes and violent storms were frequent, so that weeping and burial of the dead became the usual occupation of the people. It was for these reasons that the Inca was given the name of Pachacuti, which means 'cataclysm' or 'disaster'.

But the Inca was also responsible for building temples to his gods and setting up convents of sacred virgins. He founded religious houses for both sexes and provided the new cult with magicians and priests. He instituted feast-days for each month of the year, specifying the exact days on which they should be celebrated and the dances which should be performed at each one. Also he set aside private property for each of the temples and shrines.

He was severe in his treatment of offenders. False magicians, highwaymen and adulteresses were put to death and any public act of immorality was punished. Pachacuti Inca Yupanqui died in Cuzco, a rich man, at the age of 88.

The Tenth Inca

Tupac Inca Yupanqui, who succeeded to the throne, wore a blue helmet and carried a shield. His cloak was shot with different colours and his tunic was criss-crossed all over with squares of ornamental wool.

He was good-looking, tall, very learned, something of a martinet, on friendly terms with the nobility, courteous in his manners, fond of parties and banquets and attentive to ladies of quality. He had a particular dislike of liars, whom he punished with death. Making war was his chief occupation.

It was on his orders that the royal highways and bridges were planned and constructed. He organised the system of express runners and ordinary runners to carry messages; and he had inns and relay stations built along the way. It was on his initiative that magistrates, constables and annual inspectors were appointed. He also created judges and counsellors. On his own staff he had an official spokesman known as 'he who speaks for the Inca', a protector of the poor, a secretary to look after the archives, another to record commands, an accountant, and others who were necessary for good government.

The Inca was also active in marking boundaries, classifying various kinds of land and concentrating the people in villages. The administration of the whole country was carefully controlled by means of the system of knotted cords.

Under his rule the conquests made by his father were extended to Huanuco and to the mountain range above Lima. 1,000,000 more Indians were brought under Inca rule.

One of the young princes, Auqui Tupac Inca, lost his life during the invasion of Huanuco at the head of 100,000 men.

Another of the Inca's sons, Urco, was given the task of moving huge stones from Cuzco to Huanuco. The story is told that one of these stones became tired and refused to move any further, so it is still there today. Yet another son, the future Inca Huayna Capac, was responsible for moving stones towards Quito in the north.

The Queen, Mama Ocllo Coya, inspired awe and respect in her subjects.

She was good-looking, plump and short in stature. Her face was very small. In character she was gay and usually peaceable, but she was capable of jealousy when her husband's affections were concerned.

In her retinue the Queen kept 80-year-old ladies as maids and attendants, and old men as servants and lackeys. She had affectionate names for them and liked talking, eating and drinking in their company.

Huayna Capac, who was chosen as Inca, was the youngest of her sons. She had several daughters including Rava Ocllo and my mother Curi Ocllo, but three of them died as young girls.

She was fond of possessions and when she died she left her riches and many golden vessels to be divided between her old servants.

Her husband, Tupac Inca Yupanqui, died of pure old age and without ever having fallen ill. He hardly noticed the moment of death. Until it came he was eating and sleeping well.

The Eleventh Inca

Huayna Capac Inca wore a tunic divided like a chessboard into squares.

He was handsome and charming, white-skinned, widely esteemed by the people and friendly in his manner. At first he intended to be on visiting terms with all the gods and shrines in his country. Then, when they failed to respond to his advances, he ordered the idols to be broken and destroyed and the priests put to death. Only a few of the gods, including the Sun and Moon, survived this destruction and continued to be worshipped.

It seems that Huayna Capac was the youngest of all the legitimate members of his family. When they entered the temple of the Sun to compete for election by their divine father and thus obtain the title of Inca, the others were ignored as they made their sacrifices. But each time he came forward his name, Huayna Capac, was spoken aloud. Thereupon he took possession of the imperial fringe, stood upright and ordered the death of two of his brothers as his first act of authority. He was instantly obeyed.

The new Inca made a number of warlike conquests including all the cities, villages and dwellings of the north. He marched at the head of an army of 50,000 Indians, divided into different commands under their own officers. Challcuchima, the Captain-General, Quizquiz and Atahuallpa Inca were some of those who accompanied him in his victorious advance.

The Queen, Rava Ocllo Coya, was beautiful and well-proportioned, with an abundant head of hair. She was prudent in her conduct, charitable towards the poor and also merciful. She fed at least 200 of the needy every day. Her possessions were on a great scale, consisting of estates, houses, flocks of animals, servants and vessels of gold and silver. She moved about surrounded by lackeys and guards. The company which she kept was that of the most powerful nobles and their ladies and entourage; and she was fond of receiving rich presents. She was used to entertaining during certain months of the year. Sometimes as many as 500 guests were invited and there were 1,000 Indians to do her bidding: some to dance, some to sing, some to beat the drums and some to play the flute. She gave lodging to numbers of singers in her palace.

For listening to music she favoured particular places according to their nature: one place for songs and others for the flute.

She bore her husband two children named Huascar Inca and Chuquillanto. Her husband also fathered many bastards including Atahuallpa Inca,
whose mother was Chachapoya; Manco Inca and Ninan Cuyochi, the
children of Caya Cuzco; Illescas Inca, the son of Chuquillanto; Paullu
Tupac the son of Azca; Titu Atauchi the son of Cari; and many others
including a relation of my own.

Huayna Capac died near the city of Tumi as a consequence of measles
and smallpox. In his fear of these illnesses he fled from human company
and hid in a rocky cave where he spent his last hours alone. He had given
orders that in the case of his death it should be given out that he was still
alive. In conformity with this order his corpse was carried to Cuzco in a
lifelike posture. In this way a rising of the Indians was prevented.

His wife Rava Ocllo Coya also died at about the same time in Tumi,
aged 90.

From the time of Huayna Capac's death onwards there were many dis-
turbances, risings and civil wars, especially between the half-brothers
Huascar Inca and Atahuallpa Inca. These struggles cost the country a great
deal in treasure and blood. Justice became a dead letter and looting and
pillage took its place. At last the Christians came and conquered the
country, bringing death to the Incas.

The Twelfth Inca

Huascar Inca came to the throne by the process of election and religious
ritual. He was invested with the helmet, the fringe, the axe and the shield
which were customary.

He was swarthy, long-faced, graceless and ugly, with an unpleasant
character. He governed the country from his residence in the valley of
Xauxa among the Huanca Indians. His miserable nature was relieved to
some extent by bravery. Although he was married to his sister Chuquillanto
Coya he had no children by her, nor any bastards. He died at the age of 25
at the estate of Andamarca, as a prisoner of his mortal enemies. Those who
judged and sentenced him were the generals Challcuchima and Quizquiz
acting under the orders of Huascar's bastard brother Atahuallpa Inca.

Once he was in their power they made cruel sport of him. They gave him
human and dogs' excrement to eat and human and sheep's urine to drink.
They also concocted a mixture of human filth with medicinal herbs and
made him chew it instead of coca leaves.

When finally they had put Huascar to death, these generals moved into
the city of Cuzco, where they massacred every member of the legitimate
line of descent, without even sparing the princesses who were pregnant at

the time. The only ones who escaped death were those who fled and hid themselves until the danger was past.

Another traitor, although a clever and courageous one, was Rumiñavi, the son of an ordinary commoner from the provinces. He put to death the youthful Illescas Inca. This occurred in the city of Quito where Illescas had been left by his father Huayna Capac Inca. Rumiñavi, who was ambitious for power, did not hesitate to kill the 20-year-old boy. But he died himself in Quito at the hands of the local Indians, who had suffered sufficiently from his misdeeds in the past.

With the death of Huascar Inca the dynasty of the Peruvian Kings came to an end. His downfall was due to his own criminal folly. Atahuallpa, his bastard brother, wished to honour him and sent an embassy with rich presents. But instead of receiving the visitors kindly, Huascar had them treated as women and dressed up in skirts, cloaks, girdles, brooches, combs and sandals. With this excessive and presumptuous action Huascar initiated a succession of cause and effect which involved dispute, civil war, battle and murder. Noblemen, officers and common soldiers were done to death and the whole wealth of the country was destroyed. The Spaniards were able to walk in as if by an open door, because our Indians in their confusion and disunity failed to defend themselves as the Chileans did; and this was especially true of our leaders.

The Queen, Chuquillanto Coya, is known to have been beautiful, fair in complexion and without any blemish on her body. She was lively in temperament and fond of singing. Her favourite occupation consisted in keeping and breeding small birds. It was her misfortune that her husband was extremely parsimonious and she had to satisfy herself with one daily meal, which she took at midnight. On the following morning she had to be content with chewing a wad of coca leaves.

With her goodness of heart and her gaiety she was able to keep her husband happy, although he was perverse in his habits. His reign was a short one and on his death she was overwhelmed with grief. The sad life which she led under the Conquest ended with her death at Yucay at the age of 59. There is no evidence that she ever gave birth to a son or daughter.

According to Inca law the proper title of the King was *Capac Apo Inca*. The word 'Inca' by itself does not mean 'King'. Indeed it can be applied to people of low rank. In combination with other words, it can be used to designate a potter, a cheat, a gossip or liar, or an executioner.

Capac Apo Inca is the expression which corresponds to 'King', just as *auquicuna* and *ñustacuna* are used to designate the high nobility of either sex. To become *Capac Apo Inca*, it is necessary to be the legitimate son of the former King and Queen, who are themselves brother and sister or son and mother.* The election is confirmed by a ritual of nomination in the temple

* Huamán Poma has exaggerated what was only an occasional practice, by making incest invariable within the dynasty.

of the Sun, who is the ancestor of the ruling dynasty. The question of whether a candidate is the elder or the younger brother is unimportant, provided that his legitimacy is established. Bastards of the ruling line are comparable in status with half-castes, so the dynasty can be said to have ended with the death of Huascar Inca.

When an Indian uses the term *Viracocha*, he usually means to describe a white-skinned foreigner, whether Castilian, Jewish, Moorish, Turkish, English or French. All these nationalities are in his view *Viracochas* or Spaniards, just as he uses the expression 'Inca' in a general sense. So, when Huascar Inca died, he was succeeded in the government of this country by the Viracocha King of Spain.

OTHER RULERS

My grandfather, Capac Apo Huaman Chava, was the second person in the State after the Inca and was also Captain-General of Chinchaysuyu. He was one of the bravest of the conquerors of Tumi and Quito. Until the end he was the loyal comrade of Huayna Capac Inca.

His wife was Capac Huarmi Poma Huallca, who was decended from Queens who had reigned before the coming of the Incas. She herself was a beautiful and high-spirited woman, equal in dignity to her husband.

The province of Antisuyu was represented in the conquest of Tumi and Quito by Capac Apo Ninarua. Some of the Anti soldiers who were enlisted by Huayna Capac Inca, in order to demonstrate the vastness of his empire, were naked savages in the habit of eating their enemies. They fed themselves during the campaign on the flesh of defeated nobles, who were often condemned to this grisly fate.

The Antis still live in their mountains and forests beyond the rivers among poisonous snakes, beasts of prey, monkeys and parrots, and are rich in gold and silver.

Their women of high rank are extremely beautiful and fairer in complexion than many Spanish ladies. But it is their custom to go about clothed very scantily in animals' skins. Both the men and the women are fierce by nature and inclined to cannibalism. They prefer death to conquest.

Capac Apo Mallco, Powerful Lord Condor, the ruler of Collasuyu, was another ally of Huayna Capac. Many of his officers died during the wars of conquest, but the descendants of others are still to be found today as colonists in Quito and Tumi.

He was married to a noble lady called Capacome Tallama, but although high-spirited and beautiful in her fashion she appeared ugly because of her grossness. Like all the Colla people she was lazy, inefficient, weak-minded and interested mainly in eating and sleeping. The Collas, however, are important and powerful because they have the silver of Potosí and the gold of Carabaya, which is the finest that exists. They also possess great flocks of llamas and alpacas. They grow potatoes, but are deficient in maize, wheat and vines.

Capac Apo Mullo, Powerful Lord Coloured Shell, the ruler of Cuntisuyu, was prominent in the wars, laying waste whole areas and putting to death famous enemy leaders such as Apo Pinto. His wife, Mallco Huarmi Timtama, came from Arequipa, which is very poor and exists on the trade in chilli pepper and cotton.

LAWS AND STATUTES

Since the earliest times there were primitive laws in Peru, which were later amplified by the Incas. Their purpose was to regulate religious ritual, holidays and feast-days, fasts, initiation ceremonies, sacrifices, selection of virgins, stores of food and clothing and other matters.

The laws and statutes formulated during the reign of Tupac Inca Yupanqui are as follows:

Whatever is lawfully commanded must be carried out on pain of death. Those who resist an order of the Inca shall be scourged, condemned to death and executed. The whole of their families shall be exterminated. Their dwellings shall be destroyed and the ground sown with salt. Only wild beasts and birds of prey shall inhabit these places.

Such penalties are imposed for all time. Dispute and controversy can never occur, since the operation of justice is immediate and irrevocable.

Magicians shall be appointed as high priests: one in this great city of Cuzco and one in each of the provinces of Chinchaysuyu, Antisuyu, Collasuyu and Cuntisuyu.

The temples of the Sun and other shrines shall be served by ordinary priests, who shall live in their precincts and devote themselves to the establishment and proper conduct of the ceremonies.

The Council of the Realm shall consist of two Incas of Higher Cuzco and two of Lower Cuzco, four nobles of Chinchaysuyu, two of Antisuyu, four of Collasuyu and two of Cuntisuyu.

6 *Tupac Inca Yupanqui*

There shall be an official spokesman called 'he who speaks for the Inca', who shall be chosen from among the principal nobles.

The Inca shall have a deputy or Viceroy, who shall be granted the privilege of being carried in a litter of the royal grey colour on his visits to the provinces, as if he were the Inca himself. (This was the post and dignity held by my grandfather Capac Apo Huaman Chava.)

In each province a magistrate shall be appointed to administer justice. He shall be named *tocricoc* or 'he who sees all' and shall be chosen from among the nobles entitled to wear ornaments in their ears.

Justice at the Inca's Court shall be administered by an official of high rank with power to arrest and detain the great nobles. He shall wear a specially deep fringe as an emblem of his authority.

The Inca shall be provided with informants in every part of the country. There shall also be constables of higher and lower rank.

Secretaries skilled in the use of the *quipu* shall attend upon the Inca and the Council of the Realm. Others with the same skill shall visit each settlement and send back their records to the Inca. The settlements shall also have their own clerks entrusted with the use of the *quipu*.

Registrars shall travel through the country to count the population and record to the nearest month and year the birth of all children, and especially the descendants of chiefs. This and the other dispositions which have been made are for the purposes of good government and justice.

No person shall utter any slander against the Inca's father, the Sun, against his mother, the Moon, against the Day-Star and other stars, against the sacred idols and shrines, or against the Inca and the Coya. Any violation of this ordinance shall be punished with death. Slanders against the Council, the principal nobles and even against persons of humble position shall also be punished.

Although other cities exist such as Quito, Huanuco, Hatun Colla and Charcas, the capital city of them all shall be Cuzco, where the representatives from the provinces shall meet together to form the Council and watch over the laws.

Women shall not be permitted to give evidence before the law because of their propensity for tale-bearing, lying and dissembling. People without property are similarly debarred as witnesses, because they are capable of being bribed or suborned.

No fruit-tree, timber, woodland or straw shall be burnt or cut without proper authority on pain of death or some lesser punishment.

All deer and the Peruvian sheep bearing wool of high quality, called *huanaco* and *vicuña*, shall be protected against hunting, capture and wanton killing so that their numbers may increase. By contrast it is lawful to kill foxes and wild cats because of the damage caused by these animals.

A woman who is widowed shall not show her face uncovered or go outside her house until six months have elapsed since her husband's death. She shall wear mourning for a full year and shall not know any man for the remainder of her life. She shall be chaste and circumspect, occupying herself with the upbringing of her children and the care of her property and orchards. She shall resign herself to weeping and the misery of her condition.

All people are required to bury their dead in special vaults and not inside their houses, on pain of banishment. The burial shall be performed according to local custom. Vessels, food, drink and clothing shall be provided for the corpses.

Children and young people are required to obey their father and mother, their elders and those set in authority. They shall be flogged for a first act of disobedience and banished to the gold- and silver-mines for a second act.

Thieves and highwaymen shall not be permitted to live. For a first offence they shall be given 500 strokes of the lash. For a second offence they shall be stoned to death and their bodies left unburied, so that they are eaten by the foxes and condors.

Those who find lost property and restore it to the owners shall be recompensed for their service. If they are not treated as robbers, the property is more likely to be discovered.

Upon the death of any person, his debts contracted in life shall not be recoverable. Neither wife nor husband shall be required to pay on behalf of the other; neither son for father nor father for son; nor any person for any other person whatsoever unless the debt is claimed in the daylight of life. Thus the suspicion of false claims shall be avoided. Even if it is provided in a will that payment is to be made from the property of the deceased, the creditor shall not be paid if the deceased was a poor man.

Men and women who are banished or removed from office for any fault of theirs shall be punished with hard labour. In this way they shall both purge their own guilt and act as an example to others.

No person shall make use of poison or magic for the purpose of killing. Anyone convicted of such an act shall be flung from a cliff and then quartered. Should the act be committed against the Inca or any of the important nobles, the culprits shall be declared rebels and traitors. After execution their skins shall be made into drums, their bones into flutes, their teeth into necklaces and their skulls into vessels for drinking fermented maize. This punishment, which is the invariable one for treason, is to be carried out in public. The traitors are to be described as 'having two hearts'.

Any person who kills another shall in general be killed in the same manner, whether by stoning or beating to death. The sentence and execution shall be exactly matched with the crime.

No woman shall enter any shrine or temple during her menstrual period. Any such action shall be punished.

If any woman procures an abortion of a male child, she shall be done to death; if of a female child, she shall be given 200 strokes of the lash and then banished.

Women who are immoral, those who allow themselves to be seduced and those who become whores shall suffer a living death by being suspended from a rock by their hair and hands and left there to perish.

A man who deflowers a virgin shall be given 500 strokes of the lash and shall also undergo a torture which consists in dropping a weight from a height of nearly three feet on to the back of the culprit. It is usual for death to ensue, but there are some known cases of survival.

A man who rapes a woman shall suffer the death penalty. If the woman consents to an illicit relationship, both partners shall be suspended by the hair until they die.

A son shall inherit his father's property, including house, farm and orchard. If the only child is a daughter, she shall inherit half the property and the other half shall be divided between the close relations of the deceased person.

A father with one son shall be accepted as an honest man; the father of two shall be treated with favour; gardens, pasture and other land shall be given to the father of three; the father of four shall be considered as a person of consequence; the father with five sons shall have the standing of a foreman; ten children shall entitle a father to authority in the community; and in the case of even greater numbers the fathers shall have the right to choose estates for themselves, either in the village or in untilled land, and establish themselves there.

Lazy, dirty and lewd people shall be forced to drink the household slops and the water in which others have washed their faces, hands and feet. This punishment shall be imposed throughout the country. Gourds shall be used for the drinking of the dirty water.

The principal chiefs shall be entitled to 50 women each for service in their households and for the procreation of children. Lesser chiefs, according to their rank, shall be entitled to 30, 20, 15, 10 or only a few women. Indians of humble position or colonists shall be entitled to two women each. Soldiers in wartime, after a victorious battle, shall be awarded a woman each to encourage an increase in the population.

Nobody shall marry his sister, or his mother, or his first cousin, or his aunt, or his niece, or other close relation, or his godmother. Offenders against this law shall have their eyes gouged out, shall be quartered and shall be exposed on the hillside, so that their punishment shall long be remembered, for only the Inca can legally marry the sister of his own flesh.

Captains in the army shall be of noble blood. Soldiers shall be required to be loyal, vigorous, strong and disciplined. They shall be liable for service until their fifties.

Nobody shall spill maize on the ground or peel or mutilate vegetables such as the potato, for if these foods were capable of understanding they would weep tears at being used in this manner. Those who commit such faults are to be punished.

During times of pestilence, tempest, starvation or drought, or following the death of the Inca or another great ruler, or during an uprising of the people, all festivities shall be discontinued. There shall be no dancing, singing or playing of the drum or flute. Men shall not even touch their women. In token of true penitence nobody shall eat salt, chilli, meat or fruit, but only blanched maize, and no spirit shall be drunk.

During times of frost, hailstorms and failure of the maize-crop the people shall pray for rain to the creator of man. As a sign of their affliction they shall paint their faces with red plum-juice and lampblack and run about the mountains weeping and invoking the name of Pachacamac. All the people, including women and children, shall utter this prayer: 'Ay! Ay! Let us weep and grieve! Your poor sons are sick of heart. We can offer only our tears in exchange for your showers of rain.'

Idleness and laziness shall be discouraged, particularly among those with important duties such as administrators, counsellors, priests, artists, tradesmen, joiners, stonemasons, potters, jewellers, upholsterers, embroiderers, farmers, shepherds, weavers, tailors, dressmakers, bakers, cooks, stewards, caterers, clerks, secretaries, singers, flautists and soldiers. Any failure in their duties among these categories of people shall be punished as if they were thieves.

There shall always be abundance of food throughout the country. Maize, potato, yacca and other crops shall be sown on a large scale. Root vegetables shall be preserved by drying and freezing, and maize by blanching. The crops, including green vegetables, shall be arranged in sequence so that the people have something to eat all the year round. The sowing of maize, potatoes, chilli and cotton shall be the responsibility of each community. Flowers and leaves of certain kinds shall be collected to make dye for woven fabrics. *Llipta* for chewing with coca leaves shall be prepared by the burning of grain.

The magistrates called *tocricoc* shall superintend the completion of these measures and any backsliding shall be punished severely.

Twice a year an inspection shall be carried out of every house and property to control the volume of clothing, pots and pans, animals and work in the orchards. Those found to have failed in their duty shall receive 100 strokes of the lash. The inspectors shall ask for an account of the garden produce, taking care that there is abundance of everything and that the warehouses are full, for the service of the Inca or any other visiting notability. The posting-houses shall be properly looked after, the royal highways kept clear by the runners and the bridges repaired when necessary, so that journeys can be made at all times and the usual ceremonies can be observed.

Doctors and surgeons shall be obliged to use herbal medicines for their cures. Midwives shall relieve the pains of women in labour. Nurses who have charge of orphans, either giving suck to them or bringing them up, shall be exempt from all other work and shall be entitled to assistance.

No member of any tribe shall wear clothing other than what is customary in the tribe, on pain of 100 strokes of the lash.

Communal meals shall be arranged in the public squares of the towns, at which the important chiefs can meet on equal terms with those of humble rank and which the poor, the orphans, the widows, the old and sick, the blind and paralysed, strangers and travellers can attend without any sense of accepting charity but as part of the custom of the country. This tradition has been handed down by the earliest inhabitants of the country and was continued by the Incas.

Virgins shall be chosen for service in the temples and shall be obliged to keep their virginity intact until death.

All of these laws and statutes were imposed by Tupac Inca Yupanqui and his Council of the Realm. On the advice of the Viceroy, who had informed himself about this code, the best laws were revived under authority of your father King Philip II of Spain. The meals and ceremonies in the public squares, for example, were still held after the Conquest.

GENERAL INSPECTION

A visit or general inspection used to be made by the Inca and the nobles belonging to the Council of the Realm. The people, whether male or female, were separated into ten categories in order to facilitate counting them. Each person was employed in the calling for which he or she was best suited and laziness was discouraged. In no other way could the bare subsistence of the Indians, the greater state kept by their nobles and the majesty of the Inca have been maintained.

As soon as the males had been counted, which took three days, it was the turn of the females to undergo their inspection. The ritual of the visits occurred unalterably every six months, and it was then that the people moved up from one age-group to another and adopted their new duties.

The official in charge of classification of any group of Indians thus had two visits in each year to deal with. These were ordered and announced by the Inca in the proper form, namely 'to our children, in order that they should be counted and recorded on the *quipu* in accordance with their ages'.

The first category consisted of newborn babies up to the age of a month or two and still being rocked in the cradle by their mothers, who are the proper source of milk and affection for these tiny creatures. The relations might assist, but it was on the mother that the full load of responsibility was placed by the law. This load was all the heavier if the baby was nobly born or if it had lost its father in war.

To the second category belonged the children who were feeding at their mothers' breasts and learning to walk. These beings in their first years of life were incapable of looking after themselves and were often put in the care of elder children so that they should not fall or burn themselves or come to any other harm. They were still considered as the responsibility of their mothers, but special provision was made for twins. A law, which was a happy survival from primitive times, obliged both the father and mother to care for these personally for a period of two years.

If the little children were orphans, from the moment of birth they had a right to a certain area of cultivated land. Thus the whole community, and not just the parents, was concerned about their support and supervision.

The children aged between five and nine, who made up the third category, began to be disciplined by their parents with frequent beatings. When they were not playing for their own amusement, they were used to look after the younger children or to rock the cradles of the newly born.

The girls of the same age were sometimes able to do jobs about the house or to learn a skill such as spinning fine thread. Some of them gathered herbs, helped to make maize spirit or looked after babies. It was an important part of their education that they were taught to be clean in person and useful to their parents.

The fourth category was composed of boys and girls between the ages of 9 and 12. The boys were employed in trapping small birds which were sometimes brilliantly coloured, like humming-birds, sometimes ash-coloured, and sometimes linnets or ring-doves. The skins of these birds were treated as leather, the flesh was prepared for eating and the feathers were used to decorate shields or make tufts round lances for the Inca and his warriors.

Boys got their education in the fields and were not sent to any other school. It was considered inadvisable to train them for a job, since they would only have treated the job as a game until they were grown up. Only small tasks like watching the flocks, carrying wood, weaving and twisting thread were entrusted to them.

The main occupation of the girls in this category was picking the large variety of wild flowers in the countryside. These flowers were used for dyeing the fine cloth called *cunbe*, among other purposes. The girls also gathered nutritious herbs which were dried and stored for a period of up to one year.

It was part of their ritual duty to assist in sacrifices and invocations to the Sun. The turban which the Inca wore, the *llautu*, owed its delicate colours to their ministrations, as did other clothing such as headbands, sashes, belts and sandals.

In the fifth category were all those between the ages of about 12 and 18. The boys' main duty was to watch the flocks of mountain sheep. Whilst so occupied, they learned to catch or kill a wide variety of animal life with the help of lassoos, traps and catapults.

Even before the Incas took power, boys of this age were employed in the personal service of the rulers and their divinities.

The young girls with cropped hair, who belonged to this age-group, performed various useful jobs in and out-of-doors for their parents and grandparents, such as cooking and cleaning the house or helping about the farm. Being submissive and respectful, they quickly learned whatever was expected of them. Along with their short hair they went barefoot and wore short dresses without any pretence of elegance until they reached the age of marriage. Even then, they continued to lead the same life of poverty and service until the change from the single to the married state was ordered by the Inca or someone acting in his name. It was forbidden on pain of death for any of these girls to anticipate the order by giving themselves to a man and this was so well understood that punishment seldom had to be imposed.

In the sixth category, the young men between the ages of 18 and 20 were given the name of *sayapayac*, which means 'ready to obey commands'. They served as messengers, travelling between villages or places within the same valley. They also looked after the herds, carried the rations for the army and attended upon the chiefs. They kept to a simple diet, avoidance of alcohol, and chaste habits. All they needed was a little tea, some boiled maize, a shirt and a warm coat. The boys of noble birth lived all the more austerely, were harshly treated and seldom allowed to rest, and were deprived of women until they were older.

Their female counterparts were the girls who were ready for marriage. These young and pretty creatures were still expected to remain virgins until the actual ceremony. Indeed, some of them were chosen to be perpetual virgins in the service of the Sun, the Moon, the Day-Star and other divinities. Some were also distributed among the Inca and the great nobles, or people of special merit. The distribution was carried out with absolute impartiality, even when the Inca was concerned. Nobody was permitted to take a woman according to his own will or desire. Even the Inca was subject to the penalties of the law, including death for crimes against the virtue of girls and women. This respect for virginity was one of the noblest features of our country. Some women, while living a perfectly free life in their homes and fields, were never touched in their whole lifetime and died as pure as on the day when they were born.

It was a wonderful provision of our law to separate those girls who were to marry from those who were to remain intact all their days.

The seventh and most important category included all the brave men capable of service in war and aged between 25 and 50. On reaching the age

(a) 9 years

(b) 12 years

(c) 33 years

(d) 80 years

7 Age categories of the General Inspection

of 33 they were regarded as fully trained and kept in readiness for battle or whatever other duties might be assigned to them. Some of them were designated as *mitimaes* or settlers. They were sent to populate other provinces where they were allotted farms of a size big enough for the support of a family. Local girls were enlisted as wives for them. This policy enabled the Inca to assure the security of distant and uncertain provinces, where the settlers acted as his trustworthy informants.

Members of this category, who were in general called *aucacamayoc* or men of war, were also employed in agriculture and the mines, and in duties at court. Likewise girls of the same age were primarily regarded as suitable wives for fighting men, but in their girlhood they were given the task of making clothes for the nobility. They had to weave the thick cloth called *auasca* and spin the fine and delicate *cunbe*. They were not regarded as free agents at the inspection because they were already firmly destined to become soldiers' wives. As soon as a particular man was designated as the husband, the girl passed under his control.

Girls of good family were carefully shielded against marrying men of no consequence or adventurers. If any girl succeeded in breaking this rule she was degraded to the same level as the man. Once properly married, a woman received the title of *Mama* and was honoured in her capacity as a mother of children.

The sick and handicapped, who were in the eighth category, included the dumb, the blind, the chronically unfit, the crippled and deformed and those lacking a limb. Some of them, especially the dwarfs, hunchbacks and those with split noses, made a pastime out of their skill in telling jokes and stories. Others were employed according to their actual capacities. If they had legs they were used for coming and going. If they had hands they were trained to weave; or they might be given jobs as stewards and accountants.

The female unfortunates were usually very skilful in handiwork of all kinds, such as the making of fine cloth, cooking and fermenting. As with the men, the amusing ones found a place as entertainers of the nobility. In return for the affection and help of the community they often did more work than able-bodied Spanish women seem to be capable of.

In all cases the handicapped were encouraged or obliged to marry their counterparts. A blind man was paired off with a blind woman, a dumb man with a dumb woman, a cripple with a cripple, a hunchback with a hunchback and a dwarf with a dwarf. In this way, under a dispensation made for them by the Inca, they were allowed to multiply their own kind. Handicapped women who failed to find husbands took lovers so that they should not remain childless.

These sick and deformed Indians owned their own houses and property and stood in need of no charity, being adequately provided for under the law.

The ninth category was composed of those beyond their prime but still fairly active, who worked on the farms, carried wood and straw or acted as servants to the nobility. After the age of 50 they were relieved from military service and from any obligation to live away from home, but remained at the beck and call of the rulers.

The women over 50 often resumed their old occupation of weaving. Others attended upon great ladies or upon the sacred virgins, carrying out whatever duties were entrusted to them including carrying a *quipu* for the keeping of accounts.

Not all the women in this class were advanced in age since widows were included, however young, on the grounds that they were not virgins any more. Such widows were considered as lost lives and of no particular value to the community, although later they might be respected for their old age.

The tenth and last category was left for the dull and sleepy old people, usually deaf as well, over the age of 80. Being so very ancient, they were not expected to do much more than eat and sleep. Some few of them were still able to make ropes, weave blankets, spin thread, act as doorkeepers and look after rabbits and ducks. A number of old women might be more or less usefully occupied in a household of some consequence.

The aged were greatly respected and honoured. Value was attached to their influence over the young, their advice and their capacity to hand down the knowledge of religion with their little remaining understanding. They were clothed free of charge and allowed to have their own garden plots, which were cultivated under a communal system called *minga*. One couple, a man and a woman, undertook to take care of each old person, to whom they made many gifts. Thus it was unnecessary to maintain any hospitals for the aged.

Such were the details of the general inspection originated by Tupac Inca Yupanqui and his Council of the Realm. It had the effect of grouping the Indians in their own villages, where they bred with one another. It was possible to avoid the multiplication of half-castes, which is such a feature of the present time. The result is as unfortunate as the mixture of the *vicuña* and *taruga*, two kinds of Peruvian sheep, which produces an offspring resembling neither the mother nor the father. Thus a degenerate race is created.

THE MONTHS AND YEARS

Under the rule of the Incas time was divided into years, months and weeks. The sages and astrologers of an earlier period had determined that the week should contain ten days and the month thirty days, with occasional extra days. The duration of the year was reckoned on this basis in accordance with the movement of the heavenly bodies.

It was well known that the Sun was more distant than the Moon and that when one was exactly behind the other, as occasionally happened, an eclipse of the Sun was produced. As the Sun became blood-red and then dark, the people feared that it was going to die and fall down upon the Earth. Similarly, if there was an eclipse of the Moon, they believed that it was going to fall down. At these times the people shrieked while the dogs howled and all the drums were sounded. It was their belief that by making the greatest possible tumult they could forestall the death of the Sun or the Moon.

Not only the day of the month, but the exact hour was calculated at which crops should be sown. Observations were made of the way in which the Sun's rays illuminated the highest peaks in the morning, or how they penetrated into the windows of the rooms. The direction and intensity of the rays provided a reliable clock to regulate the sowing and harvesting of crops.

Capac Raymi Camay Quilla (Supreme Fast of Penitence Month)

The first month was named after the great fast which was held during its course. Sacrifices were offered up and the people sprinkled ashes on their heads and in their doorways, as they still do nowadays. Processions were formed to visit the temples of the Sun and Moon and various other deities and idols. From temple to temple and from hill-top to hill-top the priests and sorcerers led their congregations forward. The ceremonies went on for days without a pause, with much weeping and kissing of holy shrines.

It was a time of heavy showers of rain. It was also the time for pruning maize, potatoes and other crops while the plants were tender. The young maize and new potatoes were ready for eating. People were employed to watch over the fields, to prevent the destruction of the plants by partridges and other birds, polecats and deer.

In this month the volume of the rivers increased. The animals were lean. Green chillies were ready for picking, but not coca. It was a bad month for the sick, for pregnant women and for giving birth.

Paucar Huaray Hatun Pucuy (Flowers, Breeching and Great Rain)

The Inca set an example to the people in this month by presenting great sums in gold and silver and by sacrificing animals to the Sun, Moon and stars. Visits were made to the shrines in the high mountains above the snow-line, where the Huancavilca idols were kept.

It was a time of floods and downpours, when vegetation and especially green weeds sprang up everywhere. As food was scarce and the people were hungry, there was no choice but to eat these weeds, called *yuyo*, and the fruit which was still green and unripe. The result was a severe diarrhoea, which carried off many old people and children. Death was actually caused by a conjunction of this stomach trouble, near-starvation and the noxious fumes which rose from the wet ground and infected the human body.

The wearing of breeches was traditionally associated with this month. They were worn for the first time by the young men as a symbol of their growing up and ceasing to be boys. It was also customary to cut the hair short, but these were heathen practices.

All the time the rain was falling and turning the earth into mud. In the mountains it was snow that fell, because of the cold, and travellers could easily fall into drifts. It was best to work alone in the house and not sally forth into the outside world where so many dangers lurked: lightning, flood, storm and earthquake. It was impossible to cross the rivers except by high bridges, such was the fury of the waters, and any attempt resulted in drowning.

Pacha Pucuy (Season of Rain)

Black llamas were sacrificed to the gods in the third month. The Incas designated particular places for the ceremonies, which were conducted by the priests and magicians and often personally attended by demons.

It was usual to fast for a certain number of days during the month. Salt was not taken and no fruit was eaten, there was no intercourse with women and singing was forbidden. The Inca set the pattern for everyone by his attention to the ceremonies and to the worship of the idols.

By this time the crops were beginning to ripen and there was enough to eat. New potatoes and young maize were available and the *yuyo*, which was now ripe, no longer upset the people's stomachs. Hunger ceased to be a problem and the livestock could be quickly fattened on the abundance of fodder. The whole earth was covered with vegetation.

During this month it always rains in bucketfuls and the earth is moist with water. It was the proper time for preparing the ground for sowing.

Maize and vegetables of various sorts were sown and were watered by the streams coming from the mountains. A watch needed to be kept against little parrots, which went after the green ears. During this month of ripening crops it was thought necessary to appoint special judges to punish any Indians who consumed and wasted food before it was ready for eating.

From this month onwards, various foods were dried and preserved so as to be available throughout the year. *Yuyo* weeds, fish, prawns, potatoes, mushrooms, snails, lamb and fresh-water grapes could all be stored away.

During *Pacha Pucuy* the mountain sheep brought forth their young.

Inca Raymi Quilla (Inca's Feast Month)

The Inca's own festival was marked by the sacrifice of brindled sheep. People of all ranks of society were invited to the celebration in the public square, where the Inca ate, danced and sang with them. He performed what was considered as his special song. This began with an imitation of the bleat of the llama, a rhythmical repetition of the animal sound 'yn' on low and high notes, and continued with the song of the rivers, which was a more melodious representation of the sound of running water.

The guests drank their fill of the Inca's maize spirit. As the crops were ripe and the harvest was at hand, they could eat and drink as much as they liked at their ruler's expense. Food was in such plenty that even the birds and mice had enough.

At this time of year the nobility occupied itself with various sports and games such as pitch-and-toss and the throwing of dice. Those who were classified as 'Incas from outside', 'powerful Incas' and 'poor Incas' had their ears pierced during the month, thus giving rise to further celebrations to which both rich and poor were invited.

It was the month of beautiful flowers and happiness. All the fruit was now ripe and wholesome. People who had become ill in the difficult months were now on the road to recovery. Beasts, birds and even fishes became fat and sleek and there was abundance everywhere.

Hatun Almoray Quilla (Great Storage Month)

This was the month of the harvest, when beasts of all shades and colours were offered up for sacrifice. Apart from the main harvest festival there were other small celebrations for different occasions, as for instance when the harvest was actually gathered, or brought in from the fields, or stored away. It could be stored in granaries dug out of the ground or in buildings plastered with mud or made out of the stalks of the maize. These, and many more, were all opportunities for the people to get drunk and sing songs like the *harauayo*, which had the words: 'I beg you to watch over the maize so that it will never cease to be nourished by the full breast of its mother, the Earth'.

It was also the season for collecting the prickly cactus and burning it to make *llipta* for mixing with coca leaves.

Inspections were carried out in the various communities during this month with the object of counting all the livestock and the stores put away in the warehouses. Anyone who failed to give an exact account of the quantities was punished. Attention was paid to the stocks of dried meat, partridge, fish and fish-roes, edible roots, preserves, rope, wool from different kinds of sheep, blankets and slippers. Once the count was over, the shepherds had their own festival of rejoicing over the full stores and the abundance of food in all the homes.

By this time the *yuyo* had been dried and it was specially noticed in the inspection as it would keep the poor from suffering the pangs of hunger during the coming months. Grasses and herbs were plentiful, and some of them were used as medicine.

During this month rivers could again be crossed without danger and the Indians could circulate freely with loads of provisions and clothing. It was a good time for both men and beasts. They worked well and were well fed. Children born in this month were likely to be successful and fortunate.

Cusqui Quilla (Hard Earth Month)

During this month the earth was dried up by heat and drought and the festival of the Sun, called *Inti raymi*, was celebrated at enormous expense. In the course of the sacrifice known as *capacocha* 500 innocent children, much gold and silver and a lot of coloured shells were buried in the ground.

Meanwhile the officials and judges were conducting an elaborate survey of the contents of every house in the country. Their purpose was to ensure that each man and woman, down to the last orphan and whatever his or her station in life, had a sufficiency of dried *yuyo*, rabbits and ducks in the yard, coca to chew, wood and straw. When their task was at last complete they had to be ready to start over again six months later.

Cusqui Quilla was the month when edible roots were in their greatest abundance. A kind of mashed potato, made from the peeled and cooked vegetable, was eaten during the *minga* or rotation of work for the community. Small fish were plentiful. Hunting-parties were arranged so as to provide plenty of game. During the decrease of the Moon trees were felled for timber.

Chacra Conacuy (Farm Allotment)

This was the month in which the land was parcelled out among the poor for cultivation, all the boundaries being clearly marked. The gardens were dug with manure and the farms put in order. Any unappropriated land was set aside to be sown at the expense of the *sapci*, the whole community.

During this month 100 llamas of a brownish-red colour, like blood, and 1,000 white rabbits were burnt in the public square. The purpose of this sacrifice was to prevent the Sun or the water from damaging the crops while they were growing.

Sowing was always started first in the mountain regions of the Andes. It was the season in which the peaks are hidden by cloud. The heat is beginning to moderate, but all sorts of disease break out among high and low, men, women and children. At the same time the livestock is attacked by the mange and many animals die if the shepherds do not take good care of them.

Chacra Yapuy Quilla (Farm Sowing Month)

The whole population was employed in breaking the ground and ploughing, so that the maize could be sown.

Sacrifices were made by the people at their shrines in keeping with their limited means: rabbits, or coloured shells, or dough made with maize flour, or fermented maize or llamas. In some places it was the custom to sacrifice a son or a daughter and each inhabitant might expect his family to be affected in this way once in a lifetime. When it fell to the lot of somebody to contribute one of the victims, he gave up his child at the shrine to be buried alive and followed weeping in the procession to the appointed place of death.

A triumphal song called the *haylli*, which varied from place to place, was sung to make sure of a good harvest and everyone from the Inca downwards celebrated the ploughing of his own land. Maize spirit and food were consumed in great quantities when the work for the community was being done, because this was the way in which the labour was paid for. The dance which was usual on these occasions was called the *aymaran*.

The seed was put into the ground as the Sun was rising. Plants are the creatures of the Sun and the air, which together convert them into nourishment. So the maize needed to be cultivated in the Sun's time.

The time of sowing the maize was spread over nearly half the year and the actual date depended on the climate, rainfall and sunshine in each region. In the lower valleys and the Yunca territory the sowing was a good deal later than in the mountains. In Cuzco it began very early.

There was little *yuyo* or fruit available, but meat was abundant. It was a healthy month, in which outbreaks of disease never occurred.

Coya Raymi (Queen's Feast)

This month was so-called because during its course the great festival of the Moon was held and the Moon, the bride of the Sun, was the Queen of all the planets and stars in the sky. Women of high station, including the Inca's family and the virgins of the Moon, took a prominent part in the entertainments. It was they who issued the invitations to the men.

It was during this month that steps were taken by the Inca to drive disease out of every village in the country. The men presented themselves fully armed and formed up in companies, as if they were going into battle. They fired their sling-shots into the air or simply flung burning torches. At the same time they shouted to the diseases at the top of their voices, telling them to go away and leave the villages in peace and quiet. They also washed out the houses and sluiced down the streets, which had the effect of a general cleansing operation. The diseases which they were anxious to get rid of included one caused by sports and amusements, the marsh fever, the maize sickness or smallpox, a disease produced by the rainbow and other fatal ones caused by the earth and the wind which blows over the sea from Egypt.

During *Coya Raymi* more maize was sown and it was the first month for growing potatoes. It was time to start the watch against birds and polecats on the farms, since otherwise these creatures would scratch up the seed and remove it.

A scarcity of food began gradually to be felt in the whole country. It was necessary to use the *yuyo* and other products in the warehouses. Prudent souls who had planted early potatoes would be well provided for, while the lazy ones might suffer from some hunger.

Uma Raymi Quilla (Hill-top Procession Month)

This month was distinguished by its ceremonies and prayers for rain. A sacrifice of 100 white llamas was made to the gods and another 100 black ones were tethered in the public square and denied all food, so that their sufferings would add to the people's tears. In a similar way, dogs were tied up and left to howl and bark when they heard the cries of the people. Those that failed to bark were beaten with sticks.

Men and women, accompanied by a concourse of the sick, crippled, blind and aged, wept and groaned in the hope of attracting water from the sky. They prayed to Runa Camac, the creator of mankind, in these words: 'Ay, we are weeping. Ay, we are groaning. We, your children, are afflicted and we can do nothing but weep. O God, creator of mankind, ripener of the crops, origin of the world, where are you hiding? Let loose your waters and send down rain upon us.'

Uttering these words and groaning aloud, weeping and giving convincing demonstrations of their grief, the people went in procession from hill-top to hill-top. They called upon Runa Camac with all their heart to give them water.

In the fields the guardians had to be on duty at all hours, with sling in hand. A crop of potatoes was harvested and stored. The mountain sheep also needed to be shorn and treated for mange.

Aya Marcay Quilla (Corpse Carrying Month)

This was the month in which reverence was paid to the dead. It was the custom to take the corpses out of their tombs and put them on show in the open air. Food and drink were placed beside them, they were dressed in their best clothes and feathers were stuck in their heads. The people danced and sang in their company.

Afterwards the dead bodies were put in litters and carried from house to house by way of the streets and squares. Then, when the procession was over, they were put back in their tombs. Quantities of food were provided in gold and silver dishes for the noble corpses, and in earthenware dishes for the remains of the poor. Also, domestic animals and a variety of clothing had to be provided for the use of the dead, so that this ceremony was liable to be extremely costly.

During the month the Incas carried out further rites of ear-piercing and preparing boys for manhood. In the case of girls, their first menstruation was an occasion for feasting and drunkenness, when water was symbolically tapped from the springs. Other ceremonies were concerned with dressing-up in adult clothes for the first time and with lifting the babies out of their cradles.

A general inspection was held during these days and a census was taken. Potential officers and soldiers were put into training and the women were allotted in marriage. Walls were repaired and roofs thatched. A count was made of the livestock in private hands and in the possession of the community.

New virgins were also chosen to fill up the houses in which they were taught to spin and weave, so that they could make fine clothes for the Inca and his Court.

8 *Festival of the Dead*

   Meanwhile the watercourses dried up under the heat of the Sun. Special officials distributed the available supplies in a fair manner. It was time to plant vegetables and fruit-trees so that when the rains came they would already have roots and be able to grow quickly.

Capac Inti Raymi (Supreme Sun Feast)

This name was given to the last month of the year, because it contained the great feast and solemn festival of *Inti*, the Sun, just as the Moon was celebrated in the month of *Coya raymi*. The word *Capac*, which means

9 *Festival of the Sun*

'supreme' or 'powerful', indicated that this was a more important occasion than the mere *Inti raymi* celebrated earlier in the year. The Sun was now worshipped as the all-powerful ruler of the sky, the planets and the stars.

Gold and silver in large amounts and valuable dishes were buried in honour of the sun. Also, 500 innocent boys and girls were buried alive in an upright position along with the precious metal and an assortment of coloured shells and animals.

After the sacrifice a great deal of eating and drinking at the expense of the Sun took place in the public squares of Cuzco and other towns. Any excesses committed by the guests in their cups were immediately punished with death. The offences in question were quarrelsome brawling, scandalous talk, attempts on the virtue of women and disloyalty. Sentence was pronounced in the words: 'Put him under arrest and do away with him as a brawler, a lecher or a traitor. Look well at him and observe that he deserves his fate.'

However much he had consumed, it was prudent for the drunkard to hold his tongue and go virtuously to bed because if he made any slip, and it was reported, that was the end of him. As a result, there was less drunkenness than there is today.

The great effort of seed-time shared the month of *Capac Inti Raymi* with the onset of the rains. The rivers rose in level until they became threatening to all travel. Bold spirits who insisted on continuing with their avocations suffered hunger, loss of their possessions and sometimes death. Saturated with water and without even a candle to light them in the darkness, they tried to continue on their way in vain.

Conclusion

The division of time into years, months and weeks was not very different from the present practice. Each month began with the new Moon and ended with the waning of the Moon.

Not only were sowing and harvesting regulated by the calendar, on the advice of astrologers. The system of recording on the *quipu* was also co-ordinated with the passing of time and increases and decreases of stocks were noted month by month and year by year.

In order to fix the exact hour and day, the rising and setting of the Sun were observed through a crevice. It was found that the shadows thrown by the rays of the Sun from morning onwards turned round like the hands of a watch, never missing a single hour. For six months the shadows revolved to the left and for the other six months to the right, thus constituting the full cycle of the year.

IDOLS AND SHRINES OF THE INCA

It is well known that Tupac Inca Yupanqui carried on conversations with stones and demons, and by this means knew the secrets of the past and the future and everything that was happening in the world. He was aware in advance of the arrival of the Spaniards to rule his country in the semblance

10 *Idols of Antisuyu*

of Viracocha and he even had some idea of the existence of God as one great and powerful lord.

By means of their demons the Incas were kept fully informed of everything within their own dominions from Chile to Quito. They needed only to consult the magicians who were mouthpieces of these powers.

Huayna Capac, the successor of Tupac Inca Yupanqui, was as anxious to be informed as his predecessor, but the magicians refused to tell him anything. So the Inca killed them all and destroyed the less important shrines, saving only those which were of great importance.

It is said that only the shrine of Pariacaca was able to satisfy his curiosity. From this shrine the Inca heard that it was useless to inquire any more about problems of internal policy. The godlike beings from across the sea were already on their way to rule over Peru in the name of their King-Emperor. This disturbance would occur during the period of his own reign. On hearing this prediction the Inca went away in great sadness.

There were various places where the Incas were accustomed to make their sacrifices, consisting usually of a stone embedded in the ground on which the ruler seated himself, or a heap of stones beside a mountain road. But on particular occasions the Inca chose the temple of Coricancha, where the walls were decorated with the finest gold from top to bottom, where there were huge crystals above the gate and there were sculptured lions on either side. There he made presents of gold and silver to his father the Sun and offered up the lives of children of 10 years old, selected from the whole of Peru, none of whom had any spot, blemish or mole on their bodies. As the Sun set, its rays shone into the temple. The assembled Indians expelled their breath so that a rainbow was formed in the air. In the midst of them the Inca knelt with his face and hands stretched forward to the Sun and the golden image of the Sun. He prayed and the demons answered the prayers which he uttered. Behind him were his priests and magicians; and the great nobles, stationed at the windows, joined in the Inca's worship of the Sun.

At another shrine, called the Lion's Tail, the Queen led a procession to pray to the Moon, as the deity which presides over women's intimate lives. The various princes and princesses went to make their devotions to the Day-Star.

In the reign of Tupac Inca Yupanqui it had been decreed that the Indians coming up from the hot valleys and the Indians descending from the mountains should all of them perform an act of worship to Pachacamac at one of the shrines beside the road, which were called *apachita*. Every traveller was obliged to bring a stone and add it to a heap and also to leave flowers and twisted straw on the left-hand side of the shrine.

A law of the first Inca, Manco Capac, laid down that fingernails, eyelashes and hair were suitable objects for sacrifice and should be kept intact for this purpose. This is the reason why the priests generally had very long nails like dogs or demons, and the same custom was followed by their wives and families.

Something has already been said of the great festivals of the Incas and their insistence on religious ritual. From their familiar demons they knew of the existence of mines of silver, gold, copper, tin, lead, mercury and various pigments. These mines could not be properly worked because of the lack of tools. Enormous riches still lie concealed in them.

In Chinchaysuyu

The people of this province worshipped Pachacamac and other gods, to whom they made sacrifices of coloured cottons, coca, fruit and maize spirit.

The Yauyo Indians preferred coloured shells, a dough made of flour and various foods. They and some other tribes also sacrificed the dogs which formed their usual diet. They had to implore their idol not to be alarmed at the sound of barking made by these miserable animals. Although dog-eating is now considered barbarous, some of these people still risk punishment by carrying on the old custom.

The Aymará Indians offered up gold, silver, lodestone, alpacas, coloured wool and chillies in an annual sacrifice.

In Antisuyu

The Indians living in the forests beyond the Andes worshipped the tiger. Snake-fat, maize, coca and the feathers of various birds were burnt as a sacrifice.

Apart from the tiger, the coca tree was also an object of adoration and was known as *Coca Mama*. It was customary to kiss the coca leaves before putting them in the mouth and chewing them. Sacrifices of white rabbits, coca, coloured shells and animals' blood were also offered to the hill-top divinities called Savaciray and Pituciray and to other idols.

The inhabitants of the virgin forest itself did not have any developed system of worship, but this was replaced by the great fear which they felt at the prospect of being devoured or attacked by tigers and snakes. In order to propitiate these savage creatures, they gave the tiger the name of 'grand-father' or 'father' and the snake was addressed by them as 'powerful lord'.

In Collasuyu

The Colla people made their sacrifices with sheep, either black or white according to the particular shrine, baskets of coca leaves, rabbits, earthen-ware, dried potato, coloured shells and fish caught in the lake of Puquina. The feathers of a bird similar to the ostrich were burnt in order to perfume the holy places.

At the shrine of Titicaca it was the custom to present gold, silver and valuable clothing. But the Pomacanche Indians offered up various sorts of filth which were burnt and then buried on a hill-top at Canchi Circa.

In each town or village the proper sacrifice had to be carried out once a year in the presence of the Inca's representatives. Full reports of the proceedings were sent by runners to the capital.

In Cuntisuyu

Gold, silver, heron- and duck-feathers, coca leaves, coloured shells, raw meat and blood were offered up at the shrine of Coropona Urco. The blood was mixed with maize-flour to make a food which was relished by these Indians. The Inca gave the force of law to such local customs, which have therefore survived to the present day.

It was also the Inca's will that the sea should be worshipped under the name of *Mama Cocha*. The Yunca Indians, for the most part, had their shrines on the sea-shore and these were attended by all the fishermen.

MAGICIANS

One class of magicians which used to be found, and still is found, in Peru consists of evil characters who use poison for killing. These quacks sometimes do their work quickly and sometimes more slowly, so that the victim takes a whole year to dry up until he becomes as thin as a bean-pole and expires. Originally only the Inca retained the services of this sort of magician.

Another class of magicians was skilled in making men and women fall in love, or making men generous in their treatment of women. This spell was worked by burning grease and nameless dirt in a brand-new pot which was exposed to intense heat. A demon then materialised and carried out the required sorcery. Similarly, married couples or lovers could be estranged from one another with the help of the demons.

Curses and maledictions were made effective by blowing upon maize-flour mixed with the burnt hair of those to whom harm was intended. Thus the hair had first to be stolen and burnt, before the mischief could be carried out. Maize-flour was also mixed with powdered human bone. It was believed that by blowing this compound in the direction of their pursuers thieves and murderers could escape from justice. As the dust blew away, the pursuers perished.

When maize or potatoes are stolen from the fields, it is an old custom to take the leaves of the plants and fasten them on posts or trees along the highway, at the same time uttering a curse against the thief. The idea is that he should see the leaves and be ashamed.

Another form of witchcraft, still used today, consists in poisoning people with the venom of toads and snakes. Alternatively, a toad is caught, its

11 *Magicians*

mouth and eyes stitched with thorns and its feet tied together. It is then buried in a hole underneath where an enemy is in the habit of sitting, with the idea that he should suffer and die in the same manner as the buried toad. Some magicians keep toads and snakes in captivity so as to make use of them in this way.

Other magicians have adopted the custom of taking black and white threads and twisting them in a left-handed direction. The twisted yarn is stretched across a path which some enemy is expected to use and serves as a lassoo or snare. Because of the spells which have been cast, the victim who falls into the snare is in danger of becoming ill or even, if the thread breaks, of a painful death. It is necessary to set this snare at the last moment before the enemy passes and the magician therefore has to lie in wait beside the way.

A special sort of magic is made with the aid of the *huacanqui*. Some say that these are little birds from the Andes; some that they are thorns, or water, or stones, or leaves from the trees, or colours. They are used as love-charms by Indian women who work for the Spaniards and by innkeepers and their servants. Some Spanish ladies, too, have taken up the use of the *huacanqui*. Their lovers, under its spell, make over all their property to them, become penniless as a result, and commit suicide.

When the magicians take refuge for the night in a cave, they say a prayer: 'Cave, do not eat me. Watch over me and make me sleep sound tonight.' While uttering these words they plaster the walls of the cave with chewed maize and coca-leaves, as a way of giving them food.

If twins are born, or a child has a cleft nose, or if a baby is born feet first, the priests and magicians talk about them as children of Illapa and Curi and refuse to visit them. The fathers are obliged to abstain from salt and women for a time.

The same penance applies when there is a death in the house. Ashes are heaped in the doorway. That night, all night, a vigil is kept. The people drink until they are intoxicated. For five more days and nights they dance and live on raw meat and blood. As this custom is still extant I have often experienced it. The usual excuse of people discovered in the act is: 'If we are blamed, it's simply because people are against us.'

The most important of the magicians formed part of the Inca's retinue and these high priests were adored and respected for their supernatural powers.

According to all accounts, it was their custom to take a new stewpot and first of all warm it while empty. Then they put into it fat, maize, coca and other foods, with some gold and silver. The contents were heated up until they were burnt and charred. At that stage the priests were able to talk to demons who remained inside the pot. They asked questions and received answers about how to make men and women fall in love and how to poison enemies. This was also the means by which they knew of future events. The male and female priests, once they had talked to these demons out of Hell, were able to divine everything which existed or was about to occur in the whole of the world.

These high priests of the Inca carried out sacrifices with llamas and rabbits, exactly as their ruler dictated. They blew the ashes of the sacrifice towards their shrines and in this way were able to make the special demons of the shrines enter into conversation with them.

During the time of the Incas ghosts and evil spirits circulated freely among the Indians. The phantasms of Chinchaysuyu and Antisuyu embraced at Anllaypampa and those of the other provinces, Collasuyu and Cuntisuyu, had their separate rendezvous. In these places the souls of the dead were to be seen, suffering from hunger, thirst, heat, cold and fire.

The claim of some magicians was that they could suck diseases out of the body and they went through the motions of extracting from their victims such various objects as silver, sticks and stones, maggots, toads, straw and maize. They cheated both the people, from whom they took money, and the demons. It was part of their false doctrine to spread a belief in imaginary diseases.

Some of the magicians talked to demons in their sleep, between one dream and another, and revealed all their desires and wishes in exchange for information. At dawn, when they awoke, they performed sacrifices and then set about deceiving the people with the help of the subtle secrets which they had learnt.

The highest priests of all, who officiated in the shrines of the Sun, Huanacauri and other important divinities, were personally appointed by the Inca. The second grade, officiating at the lesser shrines or at the volcanoes, were maintained at the Inca's expense and were under his protection. There was a third grade of priests, who acted as the guardians of local places of worship. They had an easy job persuading the people that the idols could eat, drink and speak. Such a form of religion was obligatory in the whole country and anyone who failed to comply paid for it with his life.

The reason why I am well informed about the priests is that I was for a time in the service of the Inspector-General of the Church, Don Cristóbal de Albornos. This Christian judge travelled about the country destroying every trace of magic and witchcraft that he could find.

SUPERSTITIOUS ABUSES

From the earliest times until the present, faith has been placed by our people in auguries and forebodings of disaster. These were thought to occur when snakes came indoors or when owls were heard hooting or when bats appeared in the twilight. Even butterflies and nightingales were considered unlucky. Phrases in common use were: 'They have called for me'; 'The bat has paid me a visit'; 'The glow-worm* is dragging me towards the grave'; 'Maybe one of us is marked for death'; 'The demons have sent a fox'. The mere sound of a certain animal was enough to cause fear in both men and women.

* The 'maggot of fire' is the native expression.

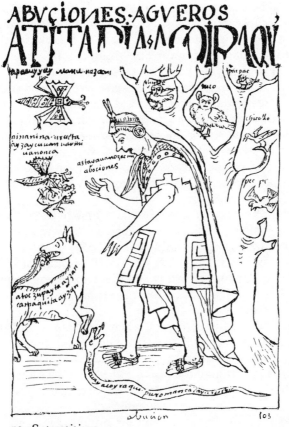

12 *Superstitions*

The Indian fortune-tellers maintained that the head, arms, legs and intestines of certain living people could be seen going out and walking about on their own. This, according to the charlatans, signified that those concerned were about to die or quit their homes, leave their husbands, wives or families, drown themselves in the river, throw themselves over a precipice or into a fire, or hang themselves in the manner of the Chanca people, who commit suicide while in their cups in the expectation of being carried off by the demons.

As with the entry of certain animals into the house, the presence of fungus or a plague of fleas in a room was regarded as a sure sign of approaching death. Even nowadays, the result of such a visitation is that the family eats up all its provisions and gets deliberately and continuously drunk.

A special credence has always been placed in dreams. If a glow-worm appears to the dreamer, he is thought likely to fall ill. If certain birds are seen, there will be a quarrel in the household. If by ill fortune, in the course of sleep, the eclipse of the Sun or Moon is witnessed while crossing a bridge over a river, this announces the death of either a father or a mother. The dreamed loss of a tooth means the death of a father or a brother. The decapitation or shearing of a llama is a presage of widowhood.

In dreams a black dress, burial, the sight of toadstools and the breaking of a calabash are variously interpreted as warnings of the death of father, mother or brother, an unhappy separation, a journey or absence from home.

Other superstitions attach importance to the left eyelid as an indicator of something or someone to be seen, or of weeping; and to a pain in the foot as a sign that people are coming on a visit, or of going for a walk. A sudden chill means a meeting with strangers. A buzzing in the ears points to ill-health, slander, a slap or a blow.

It was common practice for our Indian people to curse each other, using some of these phrases: 'The demons take you' ;'May you die of grief'; 'May you be reduced to living like a wild animal'; 'May you have to beg for your living or work as a servant'; 'May you wander like a lost soul'; 'May you starve, shrivel in the sun, go astray and die in misery as a penniless, miser-able, cowardly, thieving, lousy son of a whoring mother.' Similar ex-pressions are still in common use.

It was regarded as an unlucky sign when two plants or tubers were found growing together as one, or if they had reached an unnatural size. Those who had witnessed these monstrosities, feeling themselves threatened with death, would dance through the whole of the night, be careful never to close their eyes, sing 'Harauayo, harauayo, harauayo', drink all the next day, chew coca leaves and eat raw meat without salt.

Similar vigils, which were of ancient origin, were kept for the sick, especially when pestilence was raging.

THE DISASTERS OF THE INCAS

A number of calamities afflicted our country during the time of the Incas. For instance, fire rained down upon the town of Cacha in the Collao. The volcano of Putina erupted and caused a rain of dust. Also the city of Arequipa and the surrounding district were levelled to the ground.

There were epidemics of measles and smallpox. Enormous casualties were caused by earthquakes. Once there was no rain for ten years and the very stones exploded with the heat. Agriculture was often disturbed by frosts and hailstorms. A plague of maggots destroyed the gardens and fields. On top of this, moths and mice consumed everything indoors. In the high plains of the Andes a disease broke out among the wild life and birds, cats, foxes and deer all perished.

There is a story told by the old people that during these times the figure of a poor hermit was observed begging for clothing, food and drink. He was particularly apt to appear during feasts in the public squares. If charity was not shown towards this apparition, terrible punishments were inflicted on the people by Pachacamac, creator of the world. Their town was swallowed up by the earth, buried under a hill or converted into a lake. This was the explanation usually offered for such phenomena as the natural stairs at Pariacaca and the destruction of Cacha.

THE BURIAL OF THE INCAS

Before their burial the Incas were embalmed and care was taken to avoid any damage to the body. The eyes and face were arranged to look exactly as they had done in life. The dead rulers were then dressed in their richest clothing. Their bodies were referred to as *Illapa*, the divine name for lightning, to distinguish them from all the other corpses, which were called *aya*. It was the custom to bury the Incas with a quantity of gold- and silver-ware and with the pages, servants and women who had been their favourite companions in life. The best loved of the women was designated as Queen for this purpose and was killed with the others before burial.

The manner of their killing was that they were made drunk and then their mouths were forced open and they were choked with coca-leaf which had been ground into powder. Their bodies were then embalmed and placed by the side of the Inca's 'lightning' in lifelike postures.

The bodies were kept on show for a full month while in the whole country there was a period of mourning celebrated not only with tears but with music, singing and dancing. At the end of this time the bodies were carried to the vault called a *pucullo*.

The solemn ceremonies, with presents of gold and silver and other valuables, continued up to the moment of the burial. This procedure, or something like it, was also observed on the death of rulers of provinces with the title of *Capac Apo*, but no other Indians were considered worthy of such respect.

During the month after burial a fast was kept by all the legitimate sons of

CAPITVLOPRIMEROENTIERODELĨGA
INCAILLAPA·AIADEFVTO

pucullo

yllapa·
defunto

in tierro   como

13 *Dead Inca or 'Lightning'*

the Inca, his bastards and the important nobles. Then, in the third month, the legitimate sons went to offer their prayers and sacrifices in Coricancha, the temple of the Sun. Whether they were one or two or three or four in number, their mission was to discover which of them, an elder or a younger one, would be elected by their god, the Sun, to succeed the dead Inca.

The one who was designated miraculously by the Sun, even if he were the youngest of the brothers,* put on the imperial fringe and became from that moment the supreme ruler. The others remained only princes of the blood royal with the same duty of obedience to the chosen one as the rest of the nobility.

* *The Incas attached no importance to primogeniture. The many sons of a dead ruler were equally capable of assuming power. Even if one of them were designated by a supernatural event or by his father, he had to justify this choice by competence in office.*

OTHER BURIAL CUSTOMS

The Indians of Chinchaysuyu remained unburied for five days after their death. A fast was observed during the first night, when salt was particularly avoided. Then a llama was killed and eaten without salt or chilli. The blood, either as a drink or mixed with mashed potato, was offered to the corpse. The higher the dead person's rank, the greater was the abundance of food and drink which was provided.

The qualification for taking part in these banquets consisted in weeping, shrieking, singing, dancing and making music in the noisiest possible manner. The one who cried most was the one who got drunk quickest, because he got the most liquor as well as the biggest ration of meat. The reward of the champion singer and mourner was a leg of the animal all to himself. In fact, these wakes were simply an excuse for having licensed orgies.

Once the corpse had been washed, it was dressed in its best clothes and adorned with feathers and jewellery; then placed on a litter and paraded with song and dance and lamentation among all the families related to it.

When five days were past the corpse was carried to the tomb in procession. At the end of ten days there was a further ceremony when the widow went there, covered in mourning so that her face could not be seen, and all her hair was cut off. The ritual was repeated after six months and again after a year. A pious widow might even keep up these practices for two years.

In Antisuyu the whole of one day was spent in weeping and singing in company. Unlike the mountain Indians, the forest people observed no other ceremonies. According to reliable reports they were cannibals and set about eating the remains until only the bones were left.

Apparently the procedure was that, as soon as the breath had left the body, it was dressed in feathered garments specially made for the purpose. At the end of the wake this plumage was stripped off, the naked corpse was washed and then the butchers set about their business. There was no weeping once the meal had begun. The sole remaining duty of the relations was to bestow the bones in a tree called *uitaca*, making use of the worm-eaten holes in the trunk. The holes were carefully stopped up and from that moment onwards nobody ever came back to look at the remains, or thought of the dead person, or took part in ceremonies as the mountain Indians did.

The mountain people from the upper part of Antisuyu used to put gold, silver and coca in the mouths of their corpses. They buried them in their clothes and their sandals, with meals to eat: with everything down to the big silver brooches that the women wear. They still believe the dead can take their possessions with them. The father has the task of closing the eyes and wrapping the bodies up. If there is no father, the people do without him and wrap up the bodies in the old style which has never been forgotten.

When the Colla Indians die, the corpses are dressed and the period of mourning goes on until the fifth day. Then they are buried in a sitting position in all their finery and with their most precious possessions. Poor Indians used to receive gifts of food, drink, plate and clothing after their death, which were accepted by the relations and buried with them.

At the end of ten days the Colla people return to the tomb, bringing with them other gifts to be burnt. It is their belief that when the flame of the fire crackles and makes a noise the spirit of the dead is expressing thanks. For that spirit can now go directly to Puquina Pampa and Coropona, where the souls of the Colla Indians are united with those from Cuntisuyu. It is said that they talk and entertain each other, but then are exposed to terrible sufferings. That is why the living bring them consolatory offerings.

The ceremony is repeated in six months' time, and again after a year, but the corpses are never taken out of the tomb in the fashion of Chinchaysuyu. They are left in their village of the dead, where they are provided with whatever they need.

In Cuntisuyu the procedure for burial is much the same, as regards the period of fasting, but the intestines are removed. The bodies are embalmed and dressed in their best clothes, whereupon they are wept and drunk over by the mourners.

Before the actual burial silver is placed in the corpse's mouth, as is the general custom in our country. There is an idea that salt corrupts in the same way that death corrupts the body, so salt is avoided by those fasting in the hope of avoiding death for themselves.

The tombs, which are built out of stone, resemble ovens and are white-washed or painted in different colours. Some tombs are hollowed out of the rocks or hillsides.

The large bones which are sometimes discovered in ravines are those of the earliest inhabitants of the country. Tombs were only introduced at a later stage, during the warlike period before the coming of the Incas. In those days, as soon as a person died, a llama was sacrificed so that it could carry in its load the food which was needed for the journey. On the fifth day another beast was killed, and others after ten days, six months and a year. I myself have witnessed with my own eyes that traces of this custom survive into the present age. Such survival is connived at by the present parish priests, who accept money for turning a blind eye.

The Yunca Indians from the coastal plains towards Quito in the north shared the tomb with their dogs, which were sacrificed exactly as if they had been sheep. This was also the case with the inhabitants of the valley of

ENTIERO
DE AVTISVIOS

vitaca
arbol

yquima

aya

entierro

io mi

Yauyo, who were notorious as dog-eaters. The Yunca Indians of the plains used to set up a doleful chant of '*Nanu, nanu, nanu*'. Following this, they ate and drank until they lost consciousness or became crazy. They preferred meat for their feasts, but fish and prawns were more readily available.

It was their custom to remove both the intestines and the flesh from their corpses and deposit these in a new earthenware pot. The remainder, which was mainly skeleton, was shrouded in cotton and tied up with sisal rope of the kind used for lassoos. The tops of the shrouds were painted with bright colours. The corpses, with the pots containing their flesh, were seated in the tomb in a family circle presided over by the father and mother.

It was the custom under the Incas, after the burial of the head of a household, for the widow and other relations to take all his remaining clothing and wash it at a place where there was a confluence of two rivers. Afterwards a test was made to determine whether the widow was to die soon or not. There was a tunnel with two openings for water: one for going in and one for coming out. If there was any delay over the water emerging it was considered as a bad omen and a sign of early death.

In other places the test was made with several water-conduits leading to a single stream at a lower level. The widow poured in the water above and if it all came out together below this was taken as a sign of long life rather than death; but if the water was slow in passing through one of the conduits and arrived late, it was thought that death was at hand. As a sign of having taken the test, the widow left her belt, hair-ribbons and sandals behind. In some villages the test was made in the watercourse where the dead man's clothes had been washed. The widow took some twisted white and black threads to the left bank and stretched them across to the right bank in the form of a loop which could be seen by everyone passing. The following night was then spent in revelry.

VIRGINS

During the time of the Incas certain women, who were called *accla* or 'the chosen', were destined for lifelong virginity. Mostly they were confined in houses and they belonged to one of two main categories, namely sacred virgins and common virgins.

The so-called 'virgins with red cheeks' entered upon their duties at the age of 20 and were dedicated to the service of the Sun, the Moon and the Day-Star. In their whole life they were never allowed to speak to a man.

15 *Virgins*

The virgins of the Inca's own shrine of Huanacauri were known for their beauty as well as their chastity. The other principal shrines had similar girls in attendance. At the less important shrines there were older virgins who occupied themselves with spinning and weaving the silk-like clothes worn by their idols. There was a still lower class of virgins, over 40 years of age and no longer very beautiful, who performed unimportant religious duties and worked in the fields or as ordinary seamstresses.

Daughters of noble families who had grown into old maids were adept at making girdles, headbands, string-bags and similar articles in the intervals of their pious observances.

Girls who had musical talent were selected to sing or play the flute and drum at Court, weddings and other ceremonies and all the innumerable festivals of the Inca year.

There was yet another class of *accla* or 'chosen', only some of whom kept their virginity and others not. These were the Inca's beautiful attendants and concubines, who were drawn from noble families and lived in his palaces. They made clothing for him out of material finer than taffeta or silk. They also prepared a maize spirit of extraordinary richness, which was matured for an entire month, and they cooked delicious dishes for the Inca. They also lay with him, but never with any other man.

Thus chastity was greatly prized in our country. It was the Inca who received our girls from the Sun and who allotted them, always as virgins, to his subjects. Until that time the man did not know the woman nor the woman the man. The man might be in Quito or Chile and might be assigned a woman from quite a different region but a contract of marriage was made with the help of the woman's brother.

PENALTIES

Justice was enforced by the Incas with all the severity of the law. The chief prisons in the country were the one in which 'two-hearted traitors' and other serious criminals were exterminated; and the common prisons.

The prison designed for extermination was hollowed out of the ground so that it resembled a dark cave. In it were kept toads, lizards, snakes and all sorts of poisonous reptiles, lions, tigers, bears, foxes, dogs, mountain cats, vultures, eagles and owls. The animals were provided in large numbers to torment the criminals committed to the prison, who included traitors, thieves and highwaymen, quacks and those convicted of presumption or insulting behaviour towards the Inca. These were regarded as grave offences, for which the punishment was to be eaten alive by the wild beasts.

If by some miracle one of the condemned was found to have survived, he was left in the cave for two days more. Cases were known in which a criminal somehow succeeded in fighting off the animals and keeping alive. When this happened it was reported to the Inca, who set the man free, pardoned his offence and removed any stain on his honour. There was no other possibility of escape from the dungeon.

Such a prison could only be maintained in a great city under the personal supervision of the Inca, who was the source of all justice. The harshness of the punishment could be justified as a deterrent against civil risings, which might well have been instigated by nobles of more ancient lineage than the Inca had they not been kept quiet by fear of the consequences.

If necessary, torture was applied by binding the hands and feet with a rope which was twisted until the victim confessed.

People of high rank who were arrested were lodged in special apartments with a courtyard for exercise. They were amply provided for and the Inca himself would sometimes pay them a visit. But it was only in these lodgings for the captive nobility that visits were permitted. The poor, imprisoned in various city gaols, had to manage without.

Disobedience was punished even in the nursery by pinching the children's ears. As old people grew their finger-nails long, the little ears were often pierced through from side to side. Then the children's eyes started out of their heads, tears came to them and they cried with the pain.

The crime of adultery was punished with exceptional severity. The couples, who were executed together by stoning, remained unburied, so that their remains would be eaten by vultures and foxes and only the bones left scattered on the ground.

The virtue of unmarried men and girls was similarly protected by the law. If a couple became known as illicit lovers, they were sentenced to be suspended by their hair and left to die. The place where they were executed was called the 'copper rock'. Some of them died in a very pitiful manner, singing this song: 'Take me with you, father condor. Guide me, brother falcon. Tell my mother that for days I have eaten or drunk nothing. Father and messenger, who can remove all troubles, take my grief and my affection to my mother and my father. Tell them what has happened to me.' And with these words they died swinging on the air.

If one of the partners violated or seduced the other, only the guilty one was condemned to death. But a girl who had lost her virginity in an illicit way had no future except as a public whore and was considered as a disgrace to her whole family.

The sacred virgins were liable to be suspended by the hair even if they were seen speaking to a man or if they just sent a message with the intention of making an assignation. The immediate punishment of any slight transgression acted as a warning to others to stick very strictly to their vows of chastity.

Members of the nobility, judges and high officials were open to prosecution, torture and execution if they rebelled against the Inca's authority or give false evidence.

Any privileged officials with authority over 500 or more Indians who committed offences faced the penalty of having a heavy stone dropped from a height on to their backs. The same treatment was also applied to seducers, drunkards and brawlers.

Drunkards who tried to kiss a woman by force, or vomited, or talked in an objectionable way were laid on the ground and done to death by trampling, so that all their gall was spilt out with the liquor.

Liars and perjurers were flogged with a rope's end shaped out of two

CASTIGOIVSTICIA
SAVICASIIOVICIO

yaya pacha cama c
uana zacyaya
coy soncay
poyusys
canmi

zomcay
suella mi
cuuay huya
3apa son cuyta

compacchoyayayu
ma uau canqui ma
ma uaycuan
conqui

maypim
canquisu
yazapapa
camachic quic
pitihuay runa
canba Dios

castigos

16 Dungeon

DEL IVGA
AVTCACACARAVALCAS

equico yun

antaca ca
lota puna

TIGOS DE VIRGENES
tasyona uacllispa yaya
 utiec. cuna

17 Fornicators

thicknesses of softened leather like a child's shoe. Twenty strokes with this were enough to cause internal damage.

Dirty, lazy and disreputable people were punished by being compelled to drink a disgusting concoction in public.

Gambling was discouraged by a severe whipping applied to the hands and arms. This was an uncommon event, because the hard work imposed on the whole community left little or no time for play. Poisoners, quack doctors and charlatans who made use of snakes and toads to cause suffering or death were dragged off to the so-called 'field of blood', where they and their descendants were clubbed to death. The only ones to escape were babes-in-arms, on the grounds of their presumed innocence. The corpses were left exposed to the attentions of condors, vultures and foxes. These killings were carried out by the Inca's executioner, who reported to the ruler on the completion of his task.

Murderers were stoned to death on the site of their crime. If somebody wounded a fellow-creature, causing the loss of eyes or teeth or breaking a leg or an arm, he was condemned to suffer precisely the same penalty himself.

FESTIVALS AND SONGS

The songs and dances of our people do not involve any element of magic or witchcraft. If it were not for the drunkenness associated with them, they would be a pure expression of relaxation and joy. The popular songs called *aravi* and *taqui* are brimming with happiness. The *haylli aravi*, which celebrates victory in war or success in the harvest, is sung by girls to the accompaniment of flutes played by young men. The shepherds have their own special song called *llamaya* and the farm-labourers have one called *pachaca harauayo*. There is also the *aimarana*, a dance on going out to the fields; and the *huanca*, on the return, which is sung by the girls while the boys play the instrument called the *quena quena*. There is no cause for any criticism or censure of these entertainments of the people. It is simply a case of the poor mitigating their hard work by singing and dancing among themselves.

The words of the *huanca*, translated from the Quechua language, are as follows: 'Queen, we are kept apart by misfortune. We are separated by an illusion of the senses. You are my darling *Cicllallay*, the flower of Chinchircoma. I shall always carry you with me in my thoughts and in my heart.

18 *Harvest Song*

You were a lie and an illusion, like everything which is reflected in the waters. You were a deception, like the images which disappear when the waters are stirred. Your mother is a false friend, who wants to separate and destroy us. Your evil father is the cause of our misfortune. Perhaps, if God approves, my Queen, we shall one day meet and be together for ever. Remembering your smiling eyes, I feel faint; remembering your playful eyes I am near to death. I have been seeking you everywhere with a heavy heart, looking among the rivers, mountains and villages. As a last hope, I shall wait for you in my despair on the edge of the flowery ravine, my beautiful *Cicllallay.*'

The version in the Aymará language runs: 'The two of us shall go together through snow and ice. For me there is nobody but you, you. Brimming with tenderness, you hold me in your power. Our cup is full of sweetness. Yet your mother and your wicked father have kept us apart. Come to me all alone. I am waiting with happiness in my heart. Presently we shall saddle a horse and a mule and ride together by day and night like two lost orphans, nourishing ourselves on grass and roots like the sheep which you used to tend. Whoever tries to deprive me of your songs shall die at my hands and be put to sleep for ever; and his life shall be like a broken thread. I implore you to listen to me in this icy cold of the night. Come in one movement into my arms, where I shall hold you for eternity; but if you say "No", my heart will weep.'

There is also a gay song called the *cachiva*, the words of which run: 'I am waiting, my Chanca girl. Come from wherever you are hiding and join me, because I am waiting. Put on your elegant clothes for the ceremony and then, Chanca, put on your oldest things for the long journey we shall take together. I am waiting, my Chanca, as you will be waiting too. When we are together it will be time to be gay. Put on your ribbon and sash and let us be together. I shall carry you, carry you everwhere and hide you away, my gentle maid. When your linnet sings you will come to me. When my linnet sings, linnet, linnet, you will be with child.'

The Inca's song, called 'the song to the creator', was sung at the festivals which he sometimes gave. The *puca llama*, or red llama, took part in the slow, rhythmic incantation which lasted for half an hour. The Inca himself joined in, imitating the llama's bleat, and verses were contributed by the ladies in attendance, starting on a high note and gradually descending with an agreeable effect. The words *aravi aravi* were alternated with improvisations delivered in the same tone of voice. Typical of the improvised verses were these: 'You have chillies in your garden. I shall come on the excuse of picking chillies. You have flowers and my excuse will be picking flowers.' When the women came to an end, a man would answer: 'Yes, there is a Queen.' And the men, singing in the same tone as the women, would continue: 'There is a lady. I have sown the seed. There is a princess. There is a girl as lovely as the *ciccla* flower.'

The *aravi* was a sad and pitiful song, as it was intoned by the ladies to the accompaniment of boys playing on the flute. Here are some more of the words: 'My dear, tender love, isn't your heart painful and don't you want to cry? You, who are my precious flower, my Queen and my princess. See how justice has laid hold of me and keeps me imprisoned, as the current carries water when it rains. When I look at your cloak and your dress, everything goes dark before my eyes and the day no longer exists. When I awake at night, it seems to me that the dawn will never come because you, my Queen and lady, no longer remember me. I am in prison, where I shall be devoured by the lion and the fox. I am forgotten and discouraged. I am lost, my lady.'

In Chinchaysuyu there was a song called the *huauco*, which was performed by young girls to the beat of the drum. The words ran: 'I don't

see the sheep called *taruga* with you, although you seem to be looking after
it. I don't see the venison in your load, although you seem to have loaded it,
dear brother, dear brother.' To this the men replied by blowing the horn of
the stag which had been killed and beating the drum with a sound of
huauco, huauco.

There was a song in which the women sang first and the men replied:
'In the place of pleasure, where the chosen virgins are displayed, I have
seen you, and I have seen you in the square of the llama.'

The words of the shepherds' song were these: 'My llama, dear llama,
you are something of my own, my llama.' And there were also warlike songs,
of which the most important one went as follows: 'In the warriors' square,
in the place of pleasure of the mighty Inca, you were accustomed to receive
your orders. Where are you now, noble and strong falcon and powerful lion
of the race of Yarovilca, counsellor and confidant of the King.' This
invocation was addressed to my own ancestor, whom I greatly revere and
honour.

In Antisuyu, which extends from Cuzco to the jungles of the Amazon
and as far as the northern sea, there are songs and dances performed by the
warlike women who abound in those parts. The Anti and Chuncho Indians
like to sing to the accompaniment of the flute and dance with linked hands,
wheeling in a ring with cries of joy and merriment. In the so-called 'dance of
the fighting woman', the men dress up in women's clothes and hold arrows in
their hands. To the sound of the drum they intone the words: 'Brave warrior
and singing dove, I shall carry you off like the spider, my warlike dove.'

The songs of the Colla Indians, who live to the south of Cuzco, are
addressed to their *curaca* or chief. There is the song to the chief and the
song to the powerful of the Earth. They begin with a drum-tap and then
the women sing: 'Let us salute the powerful ruler. Come, Colla people, and
be gay because the King of our land is with us, the supreme ruler of the
Collao. Rejoice with him. Dance with all who have come from town or
country. Let us sing, play and dance with our womenfolk and make merry
in the square of Collaypampa.'

Each community had its own verses and songs as far as Tucumán and
Paraguay, and especially in the region of Potosí.

In Cuntisuyu and around Arequipa there was a song and dance of the
death-masks. The women sang: 'You have the face of a dead man.' To this
a man answered with a cry of 'Aao'. And the women maintained: 'You
can't terrify us with your mask, because it's only a mask. When you take it
off we shall see you as you are. When you drop your mask we shall know
you.' And the man answered once more: 'If you can do what you say, then
do it, but it's certain that you can't.' And the song ended in a tremendous
burst of laughter from the man.

PALACES, CUSTOMS AND DIVERSIONS

The Inca possessed a number of residences and offices: the royal palace itself, various places of retreat, a circular dwelling, a house open on one side, another which contained only two rooms, guest-houses, a store or warehouse, a distillery, quarters for the servants and almshouses. Other great lords had similar arrangements, but in scale with their lesser importance.

For hunting deer and partridge the Inca made use of his private estates, where he and the Coya were the only people entitled to kill the wild life. Their weapons included a noose, a special lance, a bituminous substance for spreading on the ground and a kind of net.

Hunts were often made an occasion for feasting and pleasure, in which all the nobility joined. The estates were like immense gardens in which the animals ran wild for the pleasure of the ruler.

A sure source of entertainment were the clowns and jesters, some of whom specialised in verbal foolery. There were also actors and mountebanks, grotesquely masked and garbed; plainsmen with a gift for comedy; and Colla rogues with woollen earpieces. All of them contributed with their jokes and tricks to the amusement of these occasions.

The Inca bestowed honours on Indians who had distinguished themselves in some way, but were of lower rank than the nobility. These honours given to comparatively humble people could not be inherited, but perished with the death of the recipients. Some were given the title of *curaca* and had authority over people like farm-workers, shepherds and stone-masons.

The Inca occasionally disguised himself as a poor man and went out from his palace on foot in order to find out what was happening and see how other people lived. And he, the supreme ruler, often humbly obeyed the advice given to him by magicians and other counsellors.

When he went to war the Inca travelled in a litter with Indian bearers. Sometimes he fought from a red litter, as was the case when Huayna Capac conquered the province of Quito. The weapons which he used were slingshot made of gold.

Our rulers were undoubtedly responsible for the widespread custom of chewing coca. This was supposed to be nourishing, but in my view it is a bad habit, comparable with the Spanish one of taking tobacco, and leads to craving and addiction.

It was usual for the nobility, on coming before the Inca and the Coya, to bring presents with them; and the nobility in their turn were accustomed to expect presents from Indians of lower rank than themselves.

19 *Inca couple in litter*

Specially delicious food was prepared for the Inca. He used to eat maize which was as white and soft as cotton, a delicate sort of potato, the meat of white llamas and rabbits, wild duck and a lot of fruit. These foods were reserved for his own use and ordinary mortals risked the death penalty if they touched them.

Perfumes made of musk and civet were not only used in Court circles, but often among the people. Pearls were worn by the ruler and the nobility, as were also brilliants, rainbow-coloured stones and others, and coloured shells from the sea-shore.

Every two days the Inca took a bath, except when the moon was in a particular phase of waxing or waning. At such times it was believed that illness was near and that the body was likely to fall sick and die as a result of wandering currents of air.

When the Inca travelled abroad he took with him a large retinue of servants and bodyguards, the royal standards and the musicians. There was dancing and singing along the road. Naked tribesmen were exhibited in the procession as a mark of ostentation and power. The Inca and the Coya travelled in their litter which was decorated with precious stones.

Among the musical instruments used in the Inca's festivals were the great lion-skin drum, the trumpet, the spiral shell, the calabash, the flute, the pipe and the *quena quena*. In the various provinces there were also local instruments which were produced on the occasion of the Inca's visits.

In his amorous tastes it was usual for the ruler to favour the Colla, Canchi and Pacage girls. He therefore often visited those parts of the country, but took much less interest in Chinchaysuyu. It was usual for the Coya to be extremely jealous of these activities of the Inca.

At one of his palaces he had a courtyard full of monkeys, parrots, hawks, doves, thrushes and other birds of the Andes. He also coursed hares; and he had water-gardens with fountains and fishes, and other gardens with flowers.

The Inca kept drums made out of the skin of chiefs who had rebelled against his rule. Their whole body was made into a human drum which seemed to come to life and quiver grotesquely when the belly was slapped with the hands.

ADMINISTRATION

Warehouses were maintained by the Inca in all the four provinces. Frozen, dried potato, cooked potato, cooked cassava, dried meat and wool were usually stored in the Collao. Maize, sweet potato, yacca, chilli, cotton and dyestuff were kept at scattered points throughout the rest of the country. Each warehouse corresponded to a particular farming area. Some of them belonged to the local community, some to the Inca and some to the Sun and Moon. They were all under the control of the central farming administration.

In the same way in which he supervised the value of goods and stores, the Inca assessed the courage and endurance of his subjects, both male and female. He was specially interested in their aptitude for fighting in battle and he identified this in the Indians of Chinchaysuyu above all others. Although these people are small in stature, they have an amazing vitality which is derived from their diet of fresh mutton, maize and maize-spirit. By contrast, the Colla Indians are corpulent and greasy. They have no

20 *Administration by runner*

spirit in them and have a feeble physique, since they eat quantities of starch
and drink bad liquor made from potatoes.

The most nimble of the Indians were trained under the Inca's orders to
become runners and to jump with the agility of young bucks. They were
put through a difficult course of cross-country running, and those who
excelled in these tests had the speed of sparrow-hawks. It was possible for
one of these runners to cover the distance between Cuzco and the coast
in four days, arriving at his destination before lunchtime.

The chief fortresses of the Incas were Sacsahuaman at Cuzco, which
communicated by a tunnel with the Temple of the Sun; and Pucamarca,
Suchona, Callis and Pucyo Chingana.

No taxation or tribute in the form of money was payable by the people
to the Inca or anyone else. The individual's obligation to the State was
expressed in the form of work and service. The artisans and their families

could count themselves free people; and domestic service was confined to those who waited upon the small class of the nobility.

Porters for short distances were drawn from the Indians of Callahuaya and for long distances from my own tribe of Lucanas. They were known as 'the feet of the Inca'.

OFFICIALS

The Viceroy, who was called *Incap rantin*, was second only to the Inca and his position at court was comparable to that of the Duke of Alba in Castile. He was never of humble birth and neither wealth nor wisdom had anything to do with his selection. His position derived solely from his descent from an ancient dynasty of Kings. Lesser chiefs, who were not even entitled to be carried in a litter, were never entrusted with such a high office.

He was the person with whom the Inca usually dined, drank, amused himself and held conversations. Being the next in power, he was also sent on important missions to Chile or Ecuador. His rank and lineage procured obedience from even the greatest of the nobility, who would have rebelled against any lesser person. As Viceroy and Captain-General, distinguished by the grey colour of his litter, he held authority under the Inca in all of Tahuantinsuyu from the last mountains of Chile to the northern sea and from the jungles of the Amazon to the sandy beaches of the Pacific Ocean.

My own ancestors long held this dignity of *Incap rantin*.

There were also mayors of the palace with the power to arrest members of the nobility in the Inca's name if they took part in a rebellion. As their badge of rank these officials wore a fringe similar to the Inca's so as to impress powerful offenders with the absolute nature of the authority delegated to them. They had precise instructions how to make their arrests and bring their prisoners in front of the Inca and his Council of the Realm, so that sentence could be pronounced and punishment carried out in a fitting style. Only the most loyal, impartial and truthful candidates were selected; and poor ones as well as dishonest ones were rejected, on the grounds that they were capable of being suborned. The object was to find officials who would rigorously prosecute the guilty, but if they encountered innocence would proclaim it without ambiguity. As the death penalty was involved, their responsibility was all the greater. To ensure that they would carry out their task faithfully and that justice would be done, they were chosen from the court nobility of Higher and Lower Cuzco or other important nobles who had demonstrated their loyalty to the Inca.

21 *Man with* quipu

The constables of both higher and lower rank, who were also used for making arrests, were picked from among the bastard sons and close relations of the ruler. Sometimes the sons of the Huanuco chiefs were also chosen since they had a tradition of service to the Crown, but this privilege was never extended to other tribes. The Huanuco Indians from Chinchay-suyu, over whom my grandfather ruled, were comparable in their loyalty with the Basques in Spain and they were richly rewarded with grants of land and office. By contrast the Chachapoya and the Canari Indians, who were notorious rebels and traitors, were never given such authority.

When they were making an arrest the constables carried as their symbol of office a bag or pouch of the type used for holding coca leaves; and they also wore sandals similar to the Inca's own. In this way their warrant was recognised and respected in the whole of our country.

The *tocricoc*, who was appointed to rule over a town or province, corresponded to the present royal administrator, just as the *michoc* was the equivalent of the Christian judge. These dignitaries too were recruited from the ranks of the royal bastards and it was quite usual for them to have some physical defect like a split ear or damaged teeth or a missing hand or foot. They invariably had the distinguishing mark of 'big ears', but had been barred from religious ceremonies in the capital because of their unlucky appearance. They were accordingly sent to the provinces to make their career. The Incas were specially averse to having one-eyed or squinting nobles at Court since they were useless in the arts of war, which require good health and normality for their practice.

The immediate subordinates of the *tocricoc* were not themselves members of the Inca caste. Rather they were the leading natives of the town or province in question.

The *tocricoc* were mostly fair-minded rulers, who kept aloof from all corruption and intrigue. It was customary for them to hold their office until removed from it by death.

The next step down in the provincial administration was occupied by the sons of the native nobility. The jobs entrusted to them were concerned with the community, local worship and the land. They had to administer the provision of food, fruit-growing, garment-making, flocks and mines, whether the owner was the community, or the poor, or the Inca and nobility, or the Sun. The shepherds were under their control and they had to see that the valuable Peruvian sheep were counted and cared for. They had to record on the *quipu* the available stocks of pond-weed, dried fish, pigeon, duck and partridge; the stocks of knives, ropes, distaffs, bobbins, and forks for digging, which all had to be wrapped and tied; and further stocks of medicinal herbs, straw and wood.

In addition, these would-be rulers were charged with preventing theft and keeping the peace.

The communications of the whole country were secured by the messengers, called *chasqui*, of whom some were called 'higher messengers'and some 'messengers with a shell trumpet'. They were usually of good family and were famous for their loyalty. They wore a sun-bonnet of white feathers so that they could be seen from a long way off by other messengers. The purpose of the trumpet was similar: to alert the next runner at the relay station by a blast of sound from the approaching *chasqui*. They were armed with a cudgel and a sling and were maintained at the Inca's expense, being authorised to draw food and other stores from his warehouses all over the country.

The messengers with a trumpet worked in relays, one *chasqui* relieving another after a distance of just under two miles. In this way the rate of progress of the message could be kept astoundingly high. It was said that a snail picked off a leaf at Tumi in the north of the Empire could be delivered to the Inca in Cuzco still alive. As for the higher messengers, their task was to carry heavy loads on a whole day's journey at a time.

All the messengers were under the authority of an official chosen from among the Inca's children. This person kept a keen eye open to detect any breakdowns in the system and remedy them when they occurred. Under the Inca's authority, he also regulated the issue of rations from the warehouses. The messengers were treated as a permanent force, the members of which were never moved to other employment. Reliance was placed on their fidelity, devotion to duty and speed of travel. It was unheard-of for a *chasqui* to let down his relief.

The wives and families of messengers were allowed to provide them with whatever comfort could be arranged. The messengers were also allowed to own land and beasts, but only in the vicinity of their work, which might require their presence at any moment of any hour of the day or night.

The roads trodden by these runners were under the control of an administrator who was always chosen from among the Anta Incas. There were six important highways and a much greater number of interconnecting roads. The first highway went along the coastal plains and sandy beaches of the south. The second one led to Urupampa and the third one through Huayllacucho. The fourth passed through Huamanga on the way to Xauxa. The fifth penetrated into the jungles and the sixth followed the chain of the Andes up to the northern sea.

These highways were all carefully measured and marked with the distances to their destinations. They followed a straight course some eleven feet wide, the edges being contained by evenly placed kerb-stones. Their rectilinear form was so accurately carried through that no other authority on Earth could have matched the achievement.

Control-posts and inns were placed at intervals along the highways and administered by the province concerned. Travellers could find lodging, service and food there, important officials paused there on their journeys and the messengers were always in a state of readiness. The highways were kept in perfect order. Where they passed through marshes, stone causeways were laid down to make a firm footing.

Long bridges over the river-gorges existed at a number of places and there were many smaller bridges. The strength of the construction varied with the size of the rivers. Sometimes fibre ropes and timbers were used and sometimes floating rafts. These last were contrived by the ferrymen of the Collao.

Under the Incas, all the bridges came under the control of a single official. When the Spanish Viceroys took over, they ordered the construction of stone bridges, thus saving the lives of many poor Indians who used to be employed in mending our own hazardous contraptions. It would be a mercy for our people if all the bridges could be built of stone.

Two high officials presided over the placing of landmarks and boundaries in the Inca Empire. One of them, who was always a member of the Higher Cuzco nobility, had the responsibility for dividing the land into separate allotments. The other, who was an Inca of Lower Cuzco, had charge of the actual demarcation. Their writ extended to the whole area, both mountainous and littoral, which Tupac Inca Yupanqui had ordered to be parcelled out. Even if there was only one Indian, or one woman or child, in any particular place there was still a division of the land and an allotment of pasture and water for irrigation. Straw and wood was also shared out and such tact and fairness was shown that there were seldom any grievances. Everybody, from the Sun and Moon down to the poorest Indian, received enough to live on, without disturbing the rights of the community which had been passed down from generation to generation. The decisions of the two officials, acting together, were obeyed without question because they were seen to be impartial and helpful.

Both the Inca and his Council of the Realm were served by secretaries, some of whom belonged to my family in past times, and my ancestor the *Incap rantin* or Viceroy also had his own secretary. Such people were highly esteemed because of their ability to use the *quipu*. The secretaries calculated dates, recorded instructions, received information from messengers and kept in touch with their colleagues who used the *quipu* in all parts of the country. They accompanied the rulers and judges on important visits, recording decisions and contracts with such skill that the knots in their cords had the clarity of written letters.

There was a chief treasurer, who kept the accounts of the whole Empire and received the Inca's share of the country's wealth. His ability was so outstanding that on one occasion, in order to try him out, the Inca is said to have ordered an exact count of the entire population of Tahuantinsuyu. Using grains of quinoa, an Indian cereal, the treasurer represented one Indian with each of these grains. Then he recorded the total on a special *quipu* which had cords made from the wool of three different animals, so that he was able to demonstrate the accuracy of his calculation as ably as any Christian clerk.

With the help of a colleague, the treasurer was able to do sums according to the decimal system. *Uc* was the name for the figure one; *chunga* for ten; *pachaca* for 100; *huaranga* for 1,000; *huno* for 1,000,000; and *pantacac huno* for infinity.

Inspectors used to be sent to all parts of the country to examine the inns and relay stations, check the level of the stores in the warehouses and visit the communities, the shrines and the houses of the sacred virgins. Some of these inspectors acted additionally as spies and tale-bearers for the Inca. They were commissioned to investigate alleged crimes and if they could discover no proper evidence they sometimes went back to the Inca with a pack of lies and fabrications which they poured into his ear. For this reason, whenever the inspectors came on the scene our people were careful to keep themselves to themselves. The saying went round among them: 'Keep quiet and you won't get into trouble'.

The Council of the Realm had its seat in the capital city of Cuzco in the middle of the Empire. If ever one of the great nobles lost his place in the Council, all his relations were deprived of office at the same time. Only members of the hereditary ruling caste were eligible, for the eminence and majesty of the office could not be reconciled with mediocrity or humble birth. If these nobles had been of less than the highest rank, the Inca himself might have been brought into contempt.

Common Indians, of whichever sex, were never allowed direct access to the ruler, but had to submit their petitions for justice through an intermediary. But the Inca himself felt much sympathy for the poor and unfortunate. Sometimes he sent for one of them and said in a kindly way: 'My son, tell me your story'.

AUTHOR'S DECLARATION

I, Huamán Poma, chief of Lucanas, have opened the secrets of the *quipu* to my readers. I have recounted what has been told me by descendants of the Incas and the other dynasties of rulers. I have traced our history from the arrival of the first Indian sent by God to these shores through the various ages which followed. Everything has been conscientiously set down in this book and now I am able to proceed further and tell what I have personally observed and experienced from my years of service with the Christians.

Your Majesty, in your great goodness you have always charged your Viceroys and prelates, when they came to Peru, to look after our Indians and show favour to them, but once they disembark from their ships and set foot on land they forget your commands and turn against us.

Our ancient idolatry and heresy was due only to ignorance of the true path. Our Indians, who may have been barbarous but were still good creatures, wept for their idols when these were broken up at the time of the Conquest. But it is the Christians who still adore property, gold and silver as their idols.

THE SECOND PART OF THIS CHRONICLE
Conquest and Spanish Rule

22 *Spanish conqueror and conquered Indian prince*

THE CONQUEST

The first inhabitant of the Old World to discover our country was St Bartholomew, who arrived from Jerusalem during the reign of the Inca Sinchi Roca.

It was much later that the way across the sea was opened up. Alexander VI, a Spaniard, was Pope and Maximilian I was the Holy Roman Emperor. Queen Joan was on the throne of Spain.* Already it was known that another ocean existed to the west of the Indies.

Our countries were properly discovered by two men: one of Columbus' companions and Pedro de Candia. When the former died he left his papers to his friend. Candia returned to Castile and reported that he had been ashore at Santa.

The way it happened was that the Inca Huayna Capac, who was in Cuzco, was told that some men with long beards and the appearance of corpses had landed in his Empire. He immediately gave the order that one of them – who turned out to be Candia – was to be brought by his messengers as freight to Cuzco, so that he could see him with his own eyes. In this way the two of them, the Inca and the Spaniard, got to know one another.

They communicated by signs. When Candia was asked what he ate, he replied that he lived on silver and gold. The Inca thereupon gave him some silver and gold-dust and a quantity of gold plate and had him returned by the messengers to Santa, where he found his companion lying dead. Candia travelled back to Spain alone, taking with him the precious gifts which he had obtained.†

He spread the news of the wealth to be found in Peru and reported that our people were dressed and shod in gold and silver, wore ornaments of these metals on their heads and hands and even walked on gold and silver floors. This was true to the extent that our Indians decorated themselves for their feasts and entertainments with bracelets, diadems and brooches made of the precious metals. And Candia added that a small kind of camel was to be found in our country, meaning the llama.

The greed for gold which was awakened by Candia's story caused a number of Spaniards to enlist themselves for the Conquest of our country. They were assisted by a Peruvian Indian who had been brought back to Spain as a captive and who was given the name of Felipe or Felipillo. This Indian learnt the Castilian tongue in order to be able to act as interpreter. The Spaniards could hardly wait for their arrival in Peru, so anxious were they to lay their hands on our treasures.

* *Ferdinand and Isabella were the Sovereigns in 1492.*
† *Candia met, not the Inca, but an Inca nobleman at Tumbes.*

Francisco Pizarro and Diego de Almagro were the two officers in charge and they had recruited some hundred or two soldiers of Castile for their enterprise. All of them were stirred by the prospect of wealth and adventure. Even in their dreams they muttered about the Indies and the gold and silver of Peru. Their songs and poems were composed around the same theme. The personal concern of the Spanish monarch and the Pope was so great that they sent their own representatives to join the military force.

During the reign of Queen Joan of Spain, Vasco Nuñez de Balboa was able to confirm the existence of the Pacific Ocean. At this news, all of Spain seethed with excitement and if the Queen had allowed it the entire population of Castile would have come to see for itself, driven on by the greed which the news about gold and silver ornaments and floors of solid gold or silver had aroused.

Soon afterwards came the discovery of the River Plate and Paraguay by Juan Díaz de Solís, the pilot and native of Lebrija in Spain.

The captains of vessels began to collect their stores for the voyage: ship's biscuit, salt pork, salt beef, a stock of presents and suitable clothing. The adventurers took few possessions of their own, but devoted all the space available to arms and ammunition. Their hope was that on the return voyage their vessels would be weighed down with the treasure of the Indies.

Santo Domingo and Panama were already taken. Only one leap was needed to bring the invaders into Peru. Although the first discovery of our country was made when Huayna Capac was Inca, the Conquest took place at a period when the next Inca, Huascar, was fighting a civil war against his bastard brother, Atahuallpa.

Pizarro and Almagro, with Martín Fernández Enciso, the factor Illán, Friar Vicente de Valverde, the Indian interpreter Felipe and a number of soldiers, set sail on a course for Peru. They kept on their way unwearyingly and without wasting any time in the intervening ports. By now they were completely obsessed by thoughts of the treasure of the Indies. They felt that they had this treasure in their power in the same way that a cat keeps a mouse within reach of its claws while it plays with it and, if the mouse escapes for a moment, lies in wait, pounces and gives all its attention to catching it again and always returns to the same place until the game is finished. The conquerors reached a point where they had lost the fear of death in their greed for riches.

As soon as they landed on Peruvian soil, differences broke out between the leaders of the expedition. They were ready to kill each other or be killed. As their quarrels continued, the ordinary soldiers became terrified and alarmed.

In 1532, when Charles V was King of Spain and also Holy Roman Emperor, Pizarro and Almagro, acting in their capacity as his ambassadors, received an envoy from the legitimate ruler Capac Apo Inca Tupac

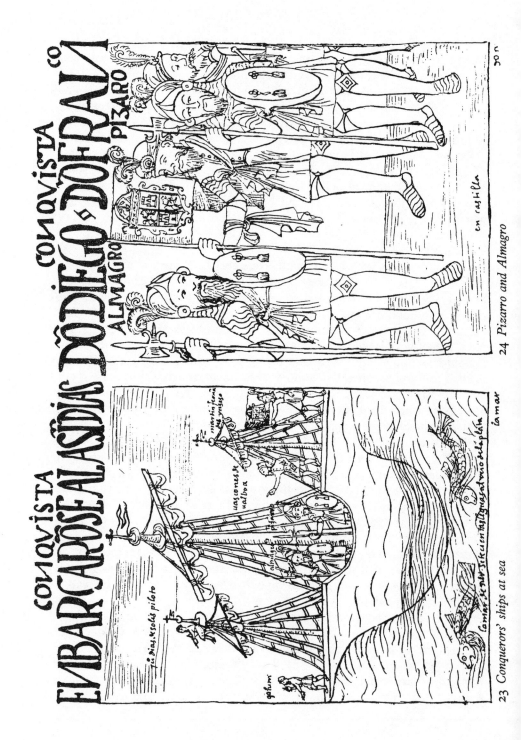

23 Conquerors' ships at sea

24 Pizarro and Almagro

Cucihualpa Huascar, who came with a message of peace to greet them at the port of Tumbes. This envoy was my father Huaman Mallqui, who carried credentials from the capital city of Cuzco.

The Spaniards Pizarro and Almagro and my father Huaman Mallqui all knelt down and embraced one another. Professions of peace and friendship were delivered in the names of their respective masters and the usual compliments were paid. The three of them dined together at the same table. They talked at some length and presents were exchanged. This was the first embassy sent to the Spaniards and arrived at the port of Tumbes before the one sent by Atahuallpa.

During this time of doubtful fortunes between the two rivals for the throne, the body of the Inca Huayna Capac was being brought from the province of Quito to be buried in Cuzco. Atahuallpa, with the support of his generals, claimed the division of the country into two parts. The area between Xauxa and Quito in the north was in his power, while the legitimate successor Huascar ruled over the provinces south of Xauxa as far as Chile. When the litter of Huayna Capac started on its journey to the capital, nobody knew that the occupant was a corpse, or a 'lightning' as the Inca's remains were called. So there was no rising or commotion in the country as the embalmed body, which was thought to be a living one, continued on its way towards the imperial vault in Cuzco. When it reached Xauxa, however, it became known that the Inca was dead. On the arrival of the news in Cuzco there was universal sorrow and weeping, but also apprehension because the demons had long ago prophesied this event. The prophecy had been to the effect that men in the likeness of Viracocha would land in the country; and it seemed to have been fulfilled when the Spaniards disembarked at Tumbes.

The second ambassador to be received by the Spaniards was Rumiñavi, the commanding general of Atahuallpa. He presented himself with great ceremony before Pizarro and Almagro and requested them to remove their troops from the country. In exchange for their departure he offered them a large amount of gold and silver. The Spaniards refused the request, saying that they wished to meet and kiss hands with the Inca in their capacity as ambassadors of their King-Emperor and that they could not leave the country until they had done so.

The presents which Atahuallpa sent to Pizarro and Almagro and the factor Illán consisted of male servants and sacred virgins. Some of the virgins were also offered to the Spaniards' horses because, seeing them eating maize, the Peruvians took them for a kind of human being. Until that time, horses were unknown to our people and it seemed advisable to treat them with respect.

Pizarro and Almagro advanced to the town of Caxamarca with 160 soldiers, who faced the 100,000 Indians under the command of Atahuallpa. Hearing of the Spaniards' arrival, the Inca deputed his general Rumiñavi to renew the request that the Spaniards should leave the country, but this was again refused.

Once the Spaniards had occupied Caxamarca, which Atahuallpa had abandoned to them, they did not settle down in their lodgings but turned the place into an armed camp.

Atahuallpa and his nobles were amazed at what they heard of the Spaniards' way of life. Instead of sleeping, these strangers mounted guard at night. They and their horses were supposed to nourish themselves on gold and silver. They apparently wore silver on their feet, and their arms and their horses' bits and shoes were also reputed to be of silver, instead of the iron which they were really made of. Above all, it was said that all day and all night the Spaniards talked to their books and papers, which were called *quilca*.

To our Indian eyes, the Spaniards looked as if they were shrouded like corpses. Their faces were covered with wool, leaving only the eyes visible, and the caps which they wore resembled little red pots on top of their heads. Sometimes they also decorated their heads with plumes. Their swords appeared very long, since they had to be carried with the points turned in a backward direction. They were all dressed alike and talked together like brothers and ate at the same table. Only one of them seemed to have powers of command and he had a dark face, white teeth and flashing eyes. He often shouted at the others and they obeyed his orders.

The Inca was astonished and put out by the news about the strangers and he abused the messenger. The same alarm was felt by the nobility at the unprecedented nature of what was happening. It was hoped that the gift of women would appease the Spaniards and their horses. But some of these girls made a joke of it all and said that the swords were part of the Spaniards' bodies. Atahuallpa had them killed at once and replaced by others. In answer to his request that the strangers should leave the country, they insisted all the more strongly on a personal meeting.

Atahuallpa Inca was at the baths close to Caxamarca when Hernando Pizarro, the general's brother, Hernando de Soto and Sebastián Benalcázar rode out to visit him on their prancing horses. They were in full armour, magnificently mounted, with plumed helmets and jingling bells. With the pressure of their thighs they caused their horses to curvet in front of the Indians and soon made a sudden charge towards the imperial party. The sound of bells and the hoof-beats produced the utmost consternation. The Inca's bearers fled in terror at the sight of the huge animals and riders careering towards them and the Inca himself fell to the ground from the litter on which he had been sitting.

The Spaniards, on the other hand, were delighted by the panic of the Indians, which was increased still more by another mock charge. On his return to Caxamarca Hernando gave an account of the visit to his brother, Francisco Pizarro. The opinion brought back by the mounted party was in favour of an immediate attack upon Atahuallpa. They measured the terror of the Indians by the fact that the Inca had been left lying on the ground while the attendants ran off in all directions; and they regarded this as a sign sent to them by the Virgin Mary and St James, promising them success.

Pizarro, Almagro and Friar Vicente de Valverde waited for Atahuallpa, who was carried from the baths to the town of Caxamarca on the *usno*, a golden throne with steps which was mounted on his open litter. He arrived in great state surrounded by his officers and about 100,000 Indians, many of whom were crammed into the public square around him.

Then Francisco Pizarro, speaking for himself and Almagro, explained through the Indian interpreter Felipe that he was the messenger and ambassador of a great ruler who desired friendship with the Inca and that this was the only object of his mission to Peru. Atahuallpa listened with close attention to the words spoken by Pizarro and then by the interpreter. He answered with great dignity that he had no reason to doubt the fact of the Spaniards' long journey or their mission from an important ruler. However, he had no need to make any pact of friendship with them because he too was a great ruler in his own country.

After this reply Friar Vicente joined in the conversation. He came forward holding a crucifix in his right hand and a breviary in his left and introduced himself as another envoy of the Spanish ruler, who according to his account was a friend of God, and who often worshipped before the cross and believed in the Gospel. Friar Vicente called upon the Inca to renounce all other gods as being a mockery of the truth.

Atahuallpa's reply was that he could not change his belief in the Sun, who was immortal, and in the other Inca divinities. He asked Friar Vicente what authority he had for his own belief and the friar told him it was all written in the book which he held. The Inca then said: 'Give me the book so that it can speak to me'. The book was handed up to him and he began to eye it carefully and listen to it page by page. At last he asked: 'Why doesn't the book say anything to me?' Still sitting on his throne, he threw it on to the ground with a haughty and petulant gesture.

Friar Vicente found his voice and called out that the Indians were against the Christian faith. Thereupon Pizarro and Almagro began to shout orders to their men, telling them to attack these Indians who rejected God and the Emperor. The Spaniards began to fire their muskets and charged upon the Indians, killing them like ants. At the sound of the explosions and the jingle of bells on the horses' harness, the shock of arms and the whole amazing novelty of their attackers' appearance, the Indians were terror-stricken. The pressure of their numbers caused the walls of the square to crumble and fall. They were desperate to escape from being trampled by the horses and in their headlong flight a lot of them were crushed to death. So many Indians were killed that it was impracticable to count them. As for the Spaniards, only five of them lost their lives and these few casualties were not caused by the Indians, who had at no time dared to attack the formidable strangers. The Spaniards' corpses were found clasped together with their Indian victims and it was assumed that they had been mistakenly trampled to death by their own cavalry.

Atahuallpa Inca was pulled down from his throne without injury and became the prisoner of Pizarro and Almagro. He was chained and guarded by Spanish soldiers in a room close to Francisco Pizarro's lodging. Deprived of his throne and all his majesty, he was left sadly and disconsolately sitting on the ground in his prison.

Once Atahuallpa was in their power, Pizarro and Almagro and their followers set about robbing him of all his enormous wealth. In Coricancha alone, the temple of the Sun, the walls, the floor, the door and the windows were all covered with solid gold. Anyone walking into that blaze of gold appeared like a corpse as his features took on the colour of the metal. The shrine of Huanacauri, which was also looted for the benefit of the Spaniards, contained incalculable quantities of gold and silver. To these treasures were added the personal possessions of Atahuallpa and the nobility. The Inca's travelling throne was constructed out of a block of gold which weighed more than 20,000 marks and the same amount of fine silver. The whole booty came to a value of 1,326,000 pieces of gold.

Great sadness of heart was caused to the Inca by the treatment of his Queen by the conquerors. Finding her weeping, he wept himself and for a time refused to eat anything.

Grief was also widespread in the city of Cuzco, where the Indians sang: 'Ay, ay, my Queen, a wicked adventurer has put us in chains. He has chained us up and plundered us, my Queen. Now there is nothing left for us except to die. Do not look on our affliction, but let us weep and shed tears, my Queen, for what is done to us.'

In his imprisonment Atahuallpa held conversations with Pizarro, Almagro and others of the Spaniards. He learnt to play chess with his captors and this game was given the Indian name of *taptana* or 'surprise attack'. The Inca's character appeared mild and peaceable, for he did his best to keep on good terms with the Christians. He gave away all his wealth to them, but still put himself out to please them. Meanwhile he lost much of the allegiance of his own nobility.

Atahuallpa's aim was to ransom his own life with the gold which he handed over to the Spaniards. Using Pizarro's sword as a pointer, he indicated a level half-way up the wall. The room in which the Inca was confined measured eight arms' spans by four and he promised to fill the entire space with gold. This promise was duly fulfilled, the gold being divided between the Emperor, Pizarro, Almagro and their officers and soldiers. Much of the treasure was shipped back to Spain.

In the meantime Atahuallpa sent his generals Challcuchima and Quizquiz, among others, to pursue his feud against his legitimate brother Huascar Inca. Huascar, after being taken prisoner, was abominably mal-treated. Rotten maize, bitter herbs and dung were given him to eat. His cap was filled with llama's piss; he was made to spend the night on rough matting; and his natural desire was mocked by putting him to bed with a long stone dressed up as a woman. After all these humiliations he was done to death in a place called Andamarca. The song of the dead – *poluya poluya huuiya huuiya* – was chanted by the executioners.

The motive for this killing lay in the inquiries which the Christians had been making about the legitimate ruler of Peru and his family. By Atahuallpa's orders, sent from his prison, all the princes and princesses were murdered and even unborn children were slaughtered in the womb.

At this time our Indians lost all sense of direction. They forgot their gods and missed the authority of their rulers; and no justice or religion was yet imposed by the Christians. Not only the Spaniards, but Indian leaders like Challcuchima, Quizquiz and Rumiñavi, set a bad example of looting and murder. The Canari, Chachapoya and Huanca Indians behaved in an especially treacherous and dishonest fashion. Hunger, thirst and disorder caused numerous deaths.

After a summary trial Atahuallpa was sentenced to death by Francisco Pizarro. There were some of the Spaniards who opposed the sentence on the grounds that the Inca had kept his promise and handed over his entire wealth in gold and silver. In their opinion he should now be taken before the Emperor, to whom he could apply for restitution if he wished.

Atahuallpa was informed of the sentence by the interpreter Felipe, who acted in bad faith by failing to pass on the Inca's plea for justice and clemency. This plea might have been effective in view of the lack of unanimity among the judges. Felipe suppressed it because of his infatuation with the Queen* and consequent ill-will towards Atahuallpa. So the Inca was executed in the city of Caxamarca.

Under orders from Pizarro a Spanish expedition set off to Xauxa, where the generals Challcuchima and Quizquiz were said to be in arms. Only Challcuchima was captured and executed. The other chiefs including Quizquiz and Rumiñavi were able to escape.

* *It was probably a favourite concubine. This was the cause of the Inca's sadness* (p. 110).

25 (a) *Atahuallpa being carried from the baths*   (b) *Atahuallpa on his throne*

(c) *Atahuallpa in prison*   (d) *Execution of Atahuallpa*

The arrival of the Peruvian gold in Spain awakened even greater greed than hitherto. Many priests, merchants and also ladies set out on the voyage to Peru, for Peru, the Indies, gold and silver were all that anybody thought about. The Emperor, when he saw the treasure with his own eyes, sent administrators, judges and bishops to Peru. From the 160 Spaniards and one negro from the Congo, who were the first to land on these shores, the visiting population increased rapidly. Traders and pedlars of all sorts arrived, and also numerous negroes.

At Lati, close to Lima, a number of Spaniards including Captain Luis Avalos de Ayala had a bloody encounter at this time with Quizo Yupanqui, the son of Tupac Inca Yupanqui, at the head of twelve chiefs and 1,000 Indians. Quizo Yupanqui was a fast runner and so agile that he was able to dodge underneath the Spaniards' horses. However, he slipped on some wet ground and was run through and killed by the Spanish Captain. When this happened, the other Indian chiefs did not pursue the battle but fled to their own villages with their men.

I myself was involved on both sides in this encounter, for Quizo Yupanqui was my uncle and Captain Avalos de Ayala was to become the father of my half-brother Martín, who entered the Church.

Lima was the first name of the place which was later called the City of the Kings because of its foundation by the Spaniards on the feast-day of the Magi. It became the capital of Peru and the seat of the Spanish Viceroy, under the patronage of St James.

The first conquerors of Peru, once they had settled down, dressed themselves differently from the present-day Spaniards. They wore thick doublets as a protection against the cold, flat red caps with a plume, close-fitting breeches and short capes with loose sleeves. As for the ladies, they wore long tunics and short capes in something like the old Indian style. It was only later that they cultivated neatness and elegance, exaggerating the cut of their clothes.

At first there was almost no mutual comprehension between the conquerors and the Indians. If a Spaniard asked for water he was likely to be brought wood. Then, as a new race of half-castes grew up, a mixture of the Quechua and Spanish languages became usual but was still not fully understood by either race.

The conquerors were able to take over Indian land and property by learning only a few words in the native language. For instance they would call out in a loud voice: 'Don't be afraid: I am the Inca.' At this, the Indians would flee in terror without offering any resistance. Bad Indians like the Canari and Chachapoya joined in with the conquerors for the sake of the loot rather than any loyalty to the Spanish Crown.

Even under the reign of the Incas there were highwaymen called *pomaranra*, who made their hiding-places in the deepest gorges and on the loneliest rocky hills. These ruffians, who had their own hierarchy of leaders, laid ambushes on the highways and lived by what they could steal and pillage. After the Conquest they became the willing tools of the Spaniards and were employed to rob their own Indian countrymen. They also moved into cities such as Quito, Huanuco, Lima, Huamanga, Cuzco, Arequipa, Potosí and Chuquizaca, where the pickings were good.

My ancestor Capac Apo Huaman Chava, who had been the second person to the Inca in his time and was now very old, was walled up in a small room with other distinguished people on the orders of Pizarro and Almagro. It was made clear to them that they should hand over all their treasures; and, when they refused, the infuriated Spaniards set fire to their prison and burned them to death.

Important rulers and officials in each of the provinces shared the same fate. Some died under torture and others were carried about in chains, or bound with ropes and halters of twisted leather. It came to such a point that the former rulers concealed their rank and passed themselves off as poor Indians, so as to escape from torture and forced labour.

Manco Inca led a rising against the Spaniards with the support of generals like Quizquiz and surviving members of the Inca Council of the Realm including the highest nobility of Cuzco. The murder of Capac Apo Huaman Chava was one of the causes which sparked off the revolt, but there was growing resentment at the ill-treatment and mockery of our Indian leaders, whose wives and daughters were often carried off before our eyes and in spite of our protests. Thus the insurgents acted in defence of their lawful rights.

The Spaniards were surrounded in the capital by such immense armies of Indians from all parts of the country that it was impossible to calculate their numbers. On their knees, the Christians begged for God's mercy and called upon the Virgin Mary and all their Saints. With tears in their eyes they prayed aloud: 'Bless us, St James! Bless us, Holy Mary! God save us!' Before every battle they humbled themselves and with their weapons actually in their hands appealed to their Holy Mary.

The Indians tried to set fire to the palace called Cuyusmanco, which the Christians had transformed into a house of God and which is now the cathedral of the city of Cuzco. A cross had been erected on the altar and another on the roof. The Indians began by setting fire to the Spaniards' lodgings. Then, when these houses were enveloped by the flames, they spread the fire to the roof of the palace. But according to all accounts the fire flew up to the top of the roof without burning it. The Indians were amazed that the flames could not touch the holy cross and recognised this as a miracle which Christianity had achieved in the New World. It was not the only miracle of the day, for as the Spaniards who were surrounded in the main square of Cuzco fell upon their knees and prayed to the Virgin Mary, the Mother of God actually appeared and floated before their eyes. She was seen by the Indians as a beautiful lady in a snow-white robe and with a face brighter than the Sun, who threw dust in their eyes to hamper their efforts.

Also St James of Galicia, according to those who were present, made his appearance in the form of a clap of thunder followed by a shaft of light which illuminated the Inca fortress of Sacsahuaman above the city. The Indians were terrified at the idea that Illapa, the thunder and lightning, had descended from the sky. And many witnesses testified that St James descended on a white horse with a plume on its head and jingling bells and trappings. The Saint was dressed in a red cape and carried a banner. He was armed with a shield and a naked sword, with which he caused great havoc and killed a multitude of Indians, breaking up the encirclement of the Christians and forcing Manco Inca into flight.

Manco and a large number of his followers retired to Tampu, where houses were built and new land put under cultivation. The young Inca ordered his own portrait and his arms to be painted on a rock so that his presence there would be remembered. However, he did not feel safe in the town of Tampu and opened up ways of retreat into the mountains around Vilcabamba. He had with him the generals Curi Paucar Manacutana and Atoc Rumi Soncco among others. In the heart of the mountains they reached a great river, across which they constructed a bridge with fibre ropes. The city of Vilcabamba was founded on the further bank and Manco Inca ordered a new Coricancha, or temple of the Sun, to be built there. He also armed the population of the place, consisting as it did of his assortment of followers. Since there were no gardens or farms or cattle, it was only a poor sort of a life which they were capable of leading in their new capital.

The Inca sent his generals to take possession of the gorge of the Apurimac at the point where the highway from Cuzco to Lima crossed over the river. Their mission was to attack all parties of Spaniards or Indians friendly to the Spaniards, who tried to pass the bridge with their herds of cattle or merchandise. The Spaniards were robbed and killed, and their attendant Indians taken prisoner. In this way, on the profits of highway robbery, Manco Inca and his family were able to survive in Vilcabamba for many years.

A half-caste named Diego Méndez used to visit the city of Vilcabamba with news and gossip intended for the Inca's private ear. His speciality was advance information about the movement of cattle belonging either to the Crown or some rich individual. These cattle were subsequently ambushed on the highway.

On a particular occasion the Inca and Diego Méndez got drunk together and began to play a game. An argument arose between them in the course of which the half-caste stabbed the Inca to death. The half-caste was immediately killed in his turn by the Inca's guards.

Manco Inca was succeeded by a son borne to him by Cuci Huarcay Coya. This son, the Inca Sayri Tupac, later died in Cuzco and was succeeded by Tupac Amaru.

After Manco Inca's time Quizquiz raised the flag of revolt against the Spaniards. He supported the claims of Inca Paullu Tupac, a bastard son of Huayna Capac Inca. Paullu Tupac began as a bitter opponent of the Spaniards, but later agreed to serve and help them. However, this help was never sincere and he remained under suspicion until his death in Cuzco, when he left a son behind him.

As for Quizquiz, he was indefatigable in his hostility to the Christians and never made peace with them. He was finally put to death by some of his own supporters, but there were others ready to carry on the battle.

Meanwhile civil war had broken out between the Spaniards. Francisco Pizarro, in his ambition to be the sole ruler of Peru and master of all its riches, fell into dispute with his comrade Diego de Almagro the elder. A battle was fought at Yauripampa below the city of Cuzco, in which Pizarro's army was led by his brothers. Almagro was taken prisoner and executed, whereupon Pizarro proclaimed himself Governor of the whole country. Having landed in Peru as an ambassador, he now hoisted his own standard and claimed absolute powers.

In the year 1541 Francisco Pizarro was killed by the supporters of Diego de Almagro the younger, who assumed the government. This new leader, who was a half-caste, was faced at the battle of Chupas with an army sent by the Spanish Crown and commanded by Vaca de Castro. Young Almagro had 800 soldiers, of whom 400 were mounted. Of the foot soldiers 300 were armed with pikes and 100 were arquebusiers. There were also 4 pieces of artillery under the command of Pedro de Candia, who was killed with a lance by Almagro himself in the course of the fighting, while he was firing too high and wide of the mark. On the royalist side there was a similar number of troops, but only 60 horsemen. There were 200 arquebusiers and 700 pikemen. My father was involved in the battle, being at the time in attendance on two Incas who supported the royalists.

After being defeated the surviving forces of Almagro the younger took to flight, while the corpses on the battlefield were stripped. The young commander was executed by the victors. His rebellion against the Crown was not motivated by greed or ambition, but by the honourable purpose of avenging his father's death. He faced his end with dignity.

Vaca de Castro, after the defeat of Almagro the younger in March 1542, was left in control of Peru. Under instructions from his Emperor he did much to check any further disorders among the Christians. However, in 1543 the first Viceroy, Blasco Nuñez Vela, arrived in Peru. He disembarked in Nombre de Dios on 10 January and proceeded to Panama, where he stayed for three weeks. This was enough time for his officials to learn that the colonists were antagonistic to his new policies: particularly those who had served in Vaca de Castro's victorious campaign against Almagro.

When the Viceroy with his four judges arrived in the capital, Gonzalo Pizarro, the brother of the murdered Governor, raised a rebellion and brought together 500 men. Diego Centeno, who was leaving Lima to collect taxes in the Viceroy's name, encountered a party of the rebels under Captain Almendras and was compelled to make a report on the situation in the capital. By such means Gonzalo Pizarro was kept fully informed of events.

The Viceroy in his alarm ordered the arrest of Vaca de Castro and other loyal officers and put them on a ship bound for Nicaragua and Panama.

Suspecting treason on the part of the factor Illán Suárez, the Viceroy had him murdered by his attendants.* Following this illegal act, an order for the arrest of the Viceroy was signed by the judges and Captain Martín de Robles took him into custody. He was not disarmed, but was deposed and sent under guard to a small island close to Lima. Precautions were taken to protect him against reprisals by the murdered man's family. Meanwhile the lawyer Cepeda took over as President of the Government.

The Viceroy Blasco Nuñez Vela was set at liberty by Juan Alvarez, one of the judges, and took up arms against the rebels. He was defeated, however, by Gonzalo Pizarro at Quito. In the course of the battle he was decapitated. His associates, Silva and Centeno, had their forces broken up and put to flight by Captain de Carbajal. This officer then returned from Charcas with his forces and a fortune in silver, and was received in Lima with great solemnity by Gonzalo Pizarro and the other rebel leaders.

In the hope that the Government of Peru would now be formally entrusted to him, Gonzalo Pizarro wrote a letter to the Emperor Charles V and also sent a full account of the recent actions of the Viceroy and the judges. The letter ran:

'Your Majesty,
'I have to report that your province of Peru has been disturbed by revolt and bloodshed as a consequence of rivalry between the conquerors. My brother Don Francisco Pizarro, Don Diego de Almagro and others have been killed. There can be no end to these troubles, nor can tranquillity and

---

* *Illán Suárez was probably first stabbed by the Viceroy's hand.*

peace return, until Your Majesty provides the remedy. On the contrary, these troubles and disasters are bound to increase as long as there are warring commanders with their various pretensions and claims, all of them doing as they want and refusing their duty as subjects of the Crown. The accounts which I have given to Your Majesty demonstrate the need for a solution before the situation deteriorates still further.

'In the meantime I have the honour to kiss your Majesty's hands and feet.

'Your humble vassal of Peru,

Gonzalo Pizarro.'

In return, the Emperor wrote a free pardon to Gonzalo Pizarro by the hand of Pedro de la Gasca, whom he appointed to Peru as President of the Royal Audience. Gasca in his turn sent Pedro Fernández Paniagua with this letter and one of his own to Gonzalo Pizarro. The Emperor's letter was as follows:

'Charles, by the grace of God Holy Roman Emperor, King of Spain and Germany, to Gonzalo Pizarro.

'We are advised by your letter and by other accounts of the rebellion which lately troubled our provinces of Peru, following the arrival there of our Viceroy Blasco Nuñez Vela and the judges of our Royal Audience. Their purpose was to put into execution our new laws. According to our information, your unwillingness to accept these laws was the cause of the uprising.

'We now freely extend our pardon to you and those others concerned, trusting that in future our commands will be unhesitatingly obeyed.

Charles.'

In view of Gonzalo Pizarro's assumption of royal powers, the real mission of Pedro de la Gasca was to uphold the Emperor's interests, bring the rebels to justice and pacify the whole country. His courier Fernández Paniagua carried letters from him to the Governor of Quito and others whom he wished to attract to his cause.

It was reported in Pizarro's camp that four ships had been sighted at Puerto Viejo, but had slipped past at some distance from the shore. The suspicion aroused by this incident was confirmed when the occupants of the ships were disembarked at Truxillo and turned out to be Gasca's supporters.

Gonzalo Pizarro began to put his forces in order. He appointed as his lieutenant Francisco de Carbajal, who had brought 100 arquebusiers with him from Charcas.

Carbajal carried the same colours that had seen victory in the battle against the Viceroy. Other officers adopted the images of the Virgin Mary or St James; or they caused to be woven into their banners the monogram GP for Gonzalo Pizarro, surmounted by a royal crown.

Pedro de la Gasca was prosecuted in his absence and sentenced to be beheaded. Lorenzo de Aldana, Admiral Hinojosa and other officers were to be quartered alive as soon as they were captured. However, the lawyers who were consulted about this legal instrument refused to sign it and advised against its promulgation. They argued that President de la Gasca, being a priest, was outside Gonzalo Pizarro's jurisdiction.

Lorenzo de Aldana had been sent by Gonzalo Pizarro to inform the Emperor of events in Peru, but had gone over to Gasca's side on the way. Now he was reported off the coast with some ships and a landing was feared. Moreover, the officer whom Pizarro sent to oppose him deserted.

Gonzalo Pizarro next ordered a detachment of 300 men to go and burn down Huanuco and punish its defenders, who were many of them in the service of the Emperor. My father, Huaman Mallqui, was in command of these Indians and did his best to defend the city. Failing in the attempt, he fled with four others to Caxamarca.

In Cuzco, Antonio Robles rallied the supporters of Pizarro. He was confronted by Diego Centeno with a number of loyalists. Centeno, on his approach to the city, used Indians to remove the saddles and bridles from his opponents' horses. By this ruse he succeeded in driving them out of Cuzco.

Pizarro's adherents began to suspect treachery at every turn. A certain Mejía, the Count of Gomera's son-in-law, was summarily beheaded on suspicion of treachery. The standard-bearer Antonio Altamirano, who was considered lukewarm in his attachment to the cause, was garrotted one night and the following day his body was hung up in public. The standard was put in charge of Antonio Rivera.

The leading citizens of Lima were called together by Gonzalo Pizarro, who thanked them for all the exertions and sacrifices which they had undergone in the interests of his brother, the Marquis Don Francisco Pizarro, and told them they were entitled to the honours of the Conquest. He then ordered Juan de Acosta with 300 men to go by the mountain road to Cuzco, so as to confront and defeat Diego Centeno.

At the same time the fleet commanded by Lorenzo de Aldana appeared a few miles off the port of Callao. Captain Mendoza and several of the most influential citizens of Lima took this opportunity of going over to the other side. Turning their backs on their former chief, they went about shouting 'Long live the Emperor' and 'Death to the tyrant Pizarro!'. It became known that all who resumed their loyalty, even at this late hour, would be entitled to a free pardon from the Emperor. Some left the city after seeking Pizarro's permission to join the expedition to Cuzco; and some of those who were already on the way to Cuzco went over to the Emperor's side. Juan de Acosta, however, continued on his way and in due course arrived at Arequipa with 100 men. Gonzalo Pizarro, who had abandoned the capital, joined him there by arrangement.

The loyalist Diego Centeno was now in the Collao with 350 men. To these need to be added the troops under Captain Mendoza who had deserted Pizarro for the Crown. The Emperor's side could also count upon a force which disembarked at the port of Tumbez. Admiral Hinojosa, leaving his ship there, marched to join the growing loyalist movement which extended to Charcas, Cuzco and Arequipa.

Before battle was joined at Huarina in the Collao there was some parleying through a priest. In all, Diego Centeno now had 1,000 men under his orders. Of these 150 were arquebusiers and 200 were cavalry. Gonzalo Pizarro, with his lieutenant Francisco de Carbajal, took the field with a lesser force including 300 arquebusiers and 80 cavalry, as well as the pikemen.

At the first volley of musketry from the rebel army 150 of Centeno's men and two of his best officers fell dead. The second discharge completed the destruction of his main column, which was put to flight. Meanwhile Gonzalo Pizarro had a near escape from death with the cavalry. But the battle had turned against Centeno, whose casualties included Luis Rivera and other distinguished captains. Thirty of his men including a friar of the Order of Mercy were summarily executed. Others only escaped by precipitate flight from the hands of Gonzalo Pizarro and Carbajal.

On Pizarro's side there were 120 fatalities. Carbajal himself with some of the horse had a narrow escape from death. In this battle, the greatest that had ever been fought between the Christians in our country, the Indians did not take sides but remained as spectators, whether their allegiance was to the Crown or to the traitor Pizarro.

Gonzalo Pizarro now entered Cuzco, where he recruited new followers. But the President of the Royal Audience, Pedro de la Gasca, continued resolutely with his preparations for the final encounter. He was able to bring together a numerous army, in which Marshal Alvarado held a high command. The President was accompanied by the Archbishop of Lima, the Bishops of Cuzco and Quito and other prelates.

It was in 1548 that Pedro de la Gasca offered battle to Gonzalo Pizarro in the valley of Xaquixaguana. The rebel captain attempted to parley, but the President was in mind for compromise and rejected the approach. Gasca's infantry numbered 900, his cavalry 500 and his arquebusiers 500. He also brought six cannon on to the battlefield, which was about 20 miles outside Cuzco.

Gonzalo Pizarro began the day in a confident spirit, but was disillusioned when his followers started to go over to the enemy's side. He is reported to have said: 'If they all go, I shall go too and perhaps I'll even be pardoned.' To this Captain Acosta replied: 'Rather than that, let's fall upon them and die like good soldiers.' But Pizarro maintained: 'It's better to give ourselves up and pray to God that we shall be allowed to die like Christians and not heathens.' With this, he surrendered to an opposing Sergeant-Major, Pedro Villavicencio, to whom he gave up his sword. He and the officers accompanying him were handed over as prisoners to Diego Centeno. Meanwhile Carbajal, in trying to escape from the battlefield, was seized among some reeds growing in a nearby river.

On the following day the prisoners were brought to trial before the Licentiate Ciancas and Alonso de Alvarado. They were sentenced to death and Gonzalo Pizarro's head, after his decapitation, was taken to Lima and exhibited in an iron cage with open sides. Carbajal was drawn and quartered and nine other officers were hanged. By means of these acts of justice the civil war was brought to an end.

In the year 1553, however, Francisco Hernández Girón led a rising against the Crown in the city of Cuzco. At the head of 70 soldiers he stormed into the Governor's house shouting 'Long live the King' and 'Liberty, liberty!'. He threatened with death any member of the household who dared to rise from the table. 'The Governor,' he said, 'is the only person we're looking for.' When some resistance was attempted he killed a captain and a local citizen. In the confusion the Governor was able to escape into the next room, where a wedding-party was being held.

Hernández Girón thereupon recruited and armed more men to serve under him. On the suspicion of loyalty to the Crown he ordered the execution by beheading of distinguished officials.

He thought of a clever ruse for a night battle in the Valley of Pachacamac, which might have won him considerable fame. His plan envisaged a surprise attack on the forces of the Royal Audience. Getting possession of a herd of docile cattle, he had a flaming torch tied to each horn of the beasts. The intention was to make a great din with fifes and trumpets and light up the standard as the cattle advanced. Then the enemy, thinking themselves under attack, would fall upon the harmless animals, whilst in reality Hernández Girón was preparing to assault them in the rear. Fortunately for the loyal cause, two soldiers succeeded in crossing the lines and gave away the plan as it was about to be put into operation. The battle was promptly abandoned and the rebels retreated.

Hernández Girón set about establishing his army in an ancient Indian fortress on the hillside above Chuquinga. This place was provided both with a main gateway and a false one which could not be detected. The rebel standard was hoisted over the garrison of 300 infantry and 100 arquebusiers.

On the other side, Marshal Alonso de Alvarado had at his disposal 400 cavalry, 300 pikemen and 300 arquebusiers. This much superior force followed up Hernández Girón and his men, who made a pretence of fleeing in disorder into their fortress. The Royalists pressed the attack, believing the small force of rebels to be at their mercy. At this moment the 100 arquebusiers of Hernández Girón emerged from the false gate and enfiladed the loyalists. It was claimed that one arquebusier had killed as many as 100 men. The casualties on the Marshal's side were enormous, while Hernández Girón lost only 50 men. Alonso de Alvarado fled with the survivors of his force towards the plains. In the course of pursuing them, Francisco Hernández Girón caused great damage to the property and animals of the leading Indians of the province, including my father.

The decisive battle between Hernández Girón and the forces of the Royal Audience was at Pucará. The rebel army was largely destroyed and some of its soldiers went over to the Crown. Hernández Girón took refuge in the mountains with 300 men.

My father and the other Indian chiefs, who were still smarting under their injuries, gave battle to the traitor and, although inferior in numbers, inflicted some 200 casualties.

The end of the story came with the traitor's flight through Hatacocha and Xauxa without either powder or ball, and with his being captured like a woman by the Huanca Indians. He and his six officers had hidden themselves away in a shepherd's hut. They were escorted to Lima, where sentence of death was passed on them. Hernández Girón was beheaded and the others were hanged, drawn and quartered. So justice was done. The heads were displayed in public and the rebellion was over.

It was 32 years since the outbreak of civil war between the two Inca brothers Huascar and Atahuallpa. During that period of time Francisco Pizarro, Diego de Almagro the elder and the younger, Gonzalo Pizarro, Carbajal and Hernández Girón had committed treason to the Crown and instigated disorder and unrest. They had all of them been driven by the ambition of poor men to make a fortune and become great lords in our country.

THE GOVERNMENT OF
THE VICEROYS

The second Spanish Viceroy, following upon Blasco Nuñez Vela, was Antonio Mendoza, Count of the Nieva, a knight of the Order of St James. He was an old man of 70, and had no fear of death or injury at the hands of the rebellious conquerors of Peru. It appears to me that he had every chance of success in serving his royal master, but unfortunately he died in Lima very soon after his arrival.

He was succeeded by Andrés Hurtado de Mendoza, Marquis of Cañete, the Elder, who enjoyed a peaceful reign and did no particular harm to anybody. In his concern for the safety of travellers he ordered the construction of the stone bridges in Lima, Xauxa, Angoyaco and Amancay, which are still standing. He also had the rope bridges repaired and the highways kept in good order.

It came to the ears of Sayri Tupac Inca, the legitimate son of Manco Inca, that the Marquis of Cañete was a Christian gentleman, in whom reliance could be placed. He accordingly emerged from the mountains of Vilcabamba with an escort of officers and savage Chuncho Indians in order to seek a meeting with the Viceroy. Without stopping at Cuzco, he pressed on towards Lima and was accepted everywhere along the road as the Inca ruler. His brother Tupac Amaru remained at home in Vilcabamba as his deputy.

Sayri Tupac was received by the Marquis with every ceremony and respect.* The Viceroy and his principal officers rode out from Lima to welcome him on the highway. A firework display and other entertainments were arranged. The Inca entered the city in his litter with all the state of an Emperor of Peru. He was received by the Royal Audience and the Court and on greeting these Spanish dignitaries he embraced them and kissed their hands in the traditional manner. Then he was carried to the lodgings which had been provided.

Sayri Tupac and the Marquis of Cañete seated themselves on two chairs and held a conversation through an interpreter. The Inca showed himself to be clever and circumspect, and at the banquet which followed he was soon on affectionate terms with the Viceroy. The Spanish conquerors, and even the Bishops, outdid one another in their compliments and flattery.

Soon afterwards Sayri Tupac Inca was accompanied by the Viceregal Court to the gates of Lima, where he took the road for the old capital of Cuzco. He was to be married under the name of Cristóbal to a bride who

* *5 January 1558.*

BVEN GOBIERNO
DÕANDRESMAR
ques·bizorrey ysayritopa ynga eray del piru brucibio y
lon rro y platico asen tado el dho marques y sayi topa—
enlos Reys deli ma

26 *The Viceroy Marquis of Cañete with Sayri Tupac*

was renamed for the occasion Beatriz. At Cuzco the couple were received
by the city dignitaries as well as the nobles of both the city's orders, the
Higher and the Lower.

Before the wedding came the ceremony of baptism into the Christian
faith. The bride and bridegroom were brother and sister, both of them
being the children of Manco Inca and Cuci Huarcay Coya. A dispensation
for their marriage was given by Archbishop Juan Solano as the representative of the Pope.

After his conversion Sayri Tupac was generally respected by Spaniards
and Indians, but a small group of Inca princes was unable to forgive his
emergence from the mountains and his new-found friendship with the
Spaniards. With the help of a certain Captain Chilche Canari they succeeded in giving him a fatal dose of poison. He left no male heir behind
him, but only a daughter who was called Beatriz after her mother and who

later married Martín García de Loyola. Sayri Tupac was succeeded as the legitimate Inca ruler by Tupac Amaru in his mountain city of Vilcabamba.

The fourth Viceroy of Peru was Francisco de Toledo, whose first step, after his formal reception in Lima, was to travel by way of Huamanga to Cuzco. There he gave orders for the building of new towns and cities, some of which were in suitable areas and others in wholly unsuitable ones, depending on the luck of the draw. In no case were the Indians consulted and some of them found themselves far away from their homes and sources of food.

During his journey, after quitting Huamanga and arriving at Vilcas Huaman, he mounted the *usno*, the travelling throne with steps which only the Inca ruler was entitled to use, and took the homage of the Indians of my province of Lucanas as if he were really their Emperor. As a gesture he invited the most senior of them, who was called Naccha Huarcaya, to take his turn on the *usno*.

The Viceroy's next action was to arm and equip an expedition against Vilcabamba with the object of seizing Tupac Amaru Inca and his generals Curi Paucar and Manacutuna. When this expedition was about to set out, the Viceroy appeared on a sorrel nag among his officers to carry out an inspection. The troops were well-disciplined and included a good number of arquebusiers. A piece of statuary was displayed which showed an Inca seated on his litter and shooting at the Viceroy, whilst around him on a mountain were clustered Indians with their lances and slings and a variety of wild beasts and birds.

The work of art bore some resemblance to the truth, except that when battle was joined at Vilcabamba there was a total lack of resistance. The Inca, who was too young to have learnt the skills of war, was taken prisoner beside the river to which he had fled on his own, without even an escort. As well as the ruler, the commander of the expedition brought the generals and the surviving princes and princesses of the Inca blood back to Cuzco in triumph.

Tupac Amaru Inca, the crowned and sovereign lord of our country, was made to walk barefoot with manacles on his wrists and a golden chain round his neck. One of his generals, who was still armed, went in front carrying golden images of the Sun and the idol Huanacauri. The little princes and princesses followed behind.

This procession was brought along the street in which Don Francisco de Toledo was lodging with a citizen named Diego de Silva, so that the Viceroy could witness the remarkable scene. At the same time the Christian-ised Inca princes living in the city of Cuzco, such as Carlos Paullu Tupac and Alonso Atauchi, were arrested and imprisoned.

The Bishop of Cuzco went down on his knees before the Viceroy to beg for the life of Tupac Amaru. Other priests, soldiers and citizens joined in the plea for mercy. The great ladies of Cuzco were unanimous in opposing the execution. Considerable sums of money in silver were even offered as a ransom. But Francisco de Toledo was extremely annoyed about a remark which Tupac Amaru was reported to have made at his expense. This was when the Viceroy had sent for him and the Inca, with youthful candour, had said that he could not comply with an order from the servant of another master. In his hatred and spite the Viceroy had Tupac Amaru sentenced to death. By this decision, it should be added, he caused heavy financial loss to the Spanish Crown. Apart from the ransom offered by the citizens of Cuzco, the Inca had declared his willingness to become the King of Spain's vassal and slave if the sentence were rescinded. He promised to hand over treasures of gold and silver which had been left to him by his ancestors and also mines still undiscovered by the conquerors. All this wealth was refused by the Viceroy because he was determined to exert power over the Inca, who was really his superior. Such an attitude amounted to criminal pretension. Neither he as Viceroy, nor the Royal Audience, had any legal right to order the execution of the Inca. Instead, the case should have been referred to Your Majesty's predecessor, the King of Spain, who as the universal ruler was the only authority capable of pronouncing either sentence or pardon.

As it was, Tupac Amaru was executed in accordance with the Viceroy's sentence. The Inca, who had been baptised a Christian, was only fifteen years old. The ladies of the capital wept as many tears for him as his own Indian subjects. Cuzco was all in mourning and the bells were rung for his passing. An immense crowd of the leading Spaniards and Indians attended his interment in the cathedral. Don Francisco had taken his revenge.

The Viceroy next gave orders for the appointment of royal administrators. These officials were responsible for many injuries and injustices to the Indians in their charge. The result was a general movement by the victims away from their homes and property. The fields remained untilled and the countryside came to have an empty and deserted appearance.

Not only the administrators were to blame. Everyone with a little authority plundered the Indian settlements. Wives and daughters, married or single, were carried off and used as concubines. According to the Viceroy's orders, children were to be given religious instruction from an early age. It was not expressly stated whether girls were included, but the parish priests took advantage of the situation to provide themselves with young mistresses and numerous families. These men of God sometimes fathered as many as twenty bastards.

Another of the Viceroy's measures was to preserve some of the old customs of the country such as holding celebrations in the public squares.

Also, many of the posts which he created bore a resemblance to those which had functioned under the rule of the Incas. Unfortunately, they were often badly filled. Young boys were appointed as mayors and were openly mocked at. One of them, who had been caught fighting, was whipped in public on the orders of the town-crier, who pulled up his chair to see that the punishment was properly carried out.

Among the posts which the Viceroy filled were those of inspectors, with the duty of ensuring the payment of taxes by the Indians. One was appointed for each province: among them Geronimo de Silva, Rodrigo de Cantos and Damian de Bandera. When Don Damian started on his inspection, many of the children and grandchildren of the Indian nobility were overlooked and no record was made of their existence. On the other hand, notice was taken of commoners, who were often promoted to being chiefs. In this way the existing hierarchy was broken up and the true ruling caste lost its influence.

By natural right, the Indian chiefs of Peru ought to have authority over the Spaniards. The newcomers from Castile have entered into the physical jurisdiction of the Indians who are the proprietors of the country and they owe obedience to our laws. If the Spaniards do not wish to be subject to the Indians, they can easily escape from their predicament by leaving Peru.

Once he had completed his long term of office in the New World, the Viceroy Francisco de Toledo returned to Castile and asked leave to kiss hands with King Philip II. But his application was rejected and the groom of the chamber refused him entry. Stricken mortally by this rebuff, Toledo went home and sat down in a chair. His appetite deserted him. Very soon he died of grief at being denied the sight of his King and of remorse for the troubles which he had brought upon Peru.

At about this time Martín Arbieto, the Inca Tomás Tupac Yupanqui and Father Gaspar de Zuñiga set out to conquer Antisuyu, the country of the savage Chuncho Indians. They succeeded in reducing the Amanari Anti to submission and this tribe was converted to Christianity, only to find itself cruelly deceived. The conquerors stopped at nothing in their efforts to extort gold and silver and proceeded to burn the chief of the tribe, Tanpulla Apo Hualpaca, alive. In their rage at this injustice the Indians rose against the oppressors and slaughtered them almost to the last man. One survivor of the massacre was my half-brother Father Martín de Ayala. He had joined the expedition in the hope of dying a martyr's death.

Toledo's successor as Viceroy was Count Martín Henriquez. During the two years of his term of office he sent great fleets of ships to complete the Conquest of Chile and helped to develop the city of Santiago. He was a good administrator who was missed here when he returned to Castile.

The next Viceroy was Fernando de Torres y Portugal, Count of Villar.

His rule was marked by an earthquake and various epidemics. He was followed by García Hurtado de Mendoza, Marquis of Cañete, the younger. This new Viceroy confiscated the property of Greeks, Flemings and Portuguese who had settled in the New World: a shrewd policy which brought considerable gains to the Crown of Spain. He also insisted on the proper collection of excise duty and thereby caused an abortive revolt against the Crown. In Quito some of the soldiers took part in a rising. In all cases the offenders were brought to justice.

Luis de Velasco, the next ruler, raised troops for the defence of our country against the English.

Count Carlos of Monterrey, during his short reign, showed some sympathy for the plight of the Indians in the mines, where they were dying of exhaustion, and he also took steps to curb abuses among the priests. However, before he could carry these reforms very far he died in Lima, while still in office. The Royal Audience took over the Government in the name of King Philip III, who had come to the throne.

The next Viceroy, Juan de Mendoza y Luna, Marquis of Montesclaros, visited the silver mines at Chocllococha and the mercury mines at Huancavelica and was accordingly able to verify with his own eyes the suffering and high mortality among the Indian workers. He realised that the country had been depopulated to provide labour in the mines and that the process was still continuing.

This brings to an end my account of the Conquest and the imposition of new forms of justice and government in Peru.

ROYAL ADMINISTRATORS

The so-called *corregidores* or royal administrators can usually count upon making 30,000 pesos in cash out of their term of office, and also upon retiring with an estate worth more than 50,000 pesos. It is their practice to collect Indians into groups and send them to forced labour without wages, while they themselves receive the payment for the work. During their term of office the royal administrators make all sorts of contracts and deals, embezzle public funds and even lay their hands on the royal fifth. They also raise loans from church funds. The Indian chiefs do not protest because they are accomplices in many of the malpractices. They are praised and commended by the administrators, who go about saying, 'What a good chief so-and-so is'. The chiefs sometimes prefer to keep quiet because they

27 *Royal Audience*

are afraid, or have no intention of losing their position in the community. They are well aware of how easily they could be dismissed on a trumped-up charge.

The royal administrators and the other Spaniards lord it over the Indians with absolute power. They can commit crimes with impunity because of the support which they can count on from higher authority. All complaint against them is stifled by fear of the consequences.

Of course, administrators exist who commit no crimes and make no enemies, but even these virtuous ones invariably leave office with a well-filled purse. Their good record comes in useful to get them promotion.

There is an opposite case of those who run into debt and are dunned by their creditors. Their expenses become impossible to meet and writs,

esta a son cristobal de
leon o traues porq̃ le rres
pondio en fabor delos y̅n̅s

por dios pasare este trauajo

COREGIMIENTO
COREG.º AFRENTAA
alcalde hordenario por dos guebos que no le da mi tayo

peobincias   cor

28 *Cristóbal de León in the stocks*   29 *Flogging an Indian*

petitions and complaints rain down upon them until they have to flee from office as poor and naked as on the day they were born. Their plight is due to being uncontrollable gamblers or womanisers, or squandering money on banquets for their Spanish friends.

In order to obtain the post of a royal administrator, ambitious candidates are often prepared to risk their entire fortune. Sometimes they succeed and sometimes not. The appointment is often made in accordance with the merit and record of the candidate, rather than what he has spent in currying favour. Once appointed, all their efforts to obtain the post are forgotten and they accordingly set about maltreating and robbing the Indians. Some of them have already pledged their future to the last peso. In order to become solvent, they have to depopulate their region by hiring out gangs of workers.

One trick which they practise is that of lending money at interest in the name of some other Spaniard. Then, under the pretence of safeguarding the other Spaniard's investment, they initiate legal action to confiscate the debtor's property and keep it for themselves.

The excuse which royal administrators always give for failing to carry out any benevolent instructions from above is that they themselves are poor men and need more money. They take the precaution of explaining their non-compliance with orders by a string of letters to the Royal Audience, the Viceroy and even the King, in which they pass on false information and conceal the true state of affairs.

Legal actions brought against them seldom succeed and in this way they avoid paying debts to the Indians for goods, property and services. Either influence is brought to bear on the judge, or the judge himself is aiming at a similar post and intends to commit precisely the same abuses when he takes over. There is an unwritten pact of silence and hypocrisy between the officials. Whenever they find themselves in financial difficulty they get together and award each other lucrative posts and commissions.

When taxes are being collected, the royal administrators demand more than is actually due, or they confiscate cattle under the pretext of taxation. Meanwhile their underlings simply take whatever they want by force. All such officials are understandably hostile to clever Indians, who have learnt how to read and write and, even worse from the officials' point of view, know how to formulate complaints to higher authority. Indians of this sort are capable of appearing in court and demanding an account of the wrongs and sufferings of their people.

One Indian who dared to oppose the Spanish rulers of his province was Cristóbal de León of the Omapacha tribe of Lucanas. He was one of several Christian pupils of mine who turned out to be clever as well as compassionate towards their fellow-Indians. Except for a certain tendency towards drunkenness, he was capable of matching his wits against any Spaniard. For some time he was able to defend himself against persecution and false accusations made against him. He refused to supply Indians for the transportation of wine from the plains to Cuzco or for making clothes for the Spaniards. Meanwhile other Indian chiefs were allowing their men to be treated like horses or donkeys, while the wives and daughters were kept busy spinning, twisting and weaving, or else debauched.

Cristóbal de León made up his mind to demand justice and set out on the road to Lima, taking his detailed complaints with him. But Father Peralta, a priest whose conduct with girls he had criticised, was warned of his departure and went in pursuit of him with two men. They arrested him and took away his papers. Then Father Peralta had him brought before the royal administrator, a fellow of his own sort, to whom he had lent 2,000 pesos. Between the two of them, they tortured León and fabricated evidence against him. He was put in the stocks and his property sold.

Even when a new royal administrator took over, Cristóbal de León was still kept in the stocks behind the house and denied any company, even that of his wife and family. His friends among the chiefs did not dare to come forward and defend him because of their fear of the consequences. As a last stroke, his house was burnt down. Finding himself stripped of his possessions and virtually naked, Cristóbal de León gave notice of an appeal. The result was that he was murdered by beheading in 1612.

A protector of Indian rights ought to be appointed by Your Majesty to be present whenever judgement is being passed or administrative decisions of importance being discussed. Such a protector should be immune from any fear of Spanish officials, being solely responsible to the Crown.

In general, Indians and Spaniards ought to lead separate lives, not just in the country but in the cities. At present the Spanish administrators and Indians of noble family sit at the same table, eat and drink and gamble with every sort of buffoon, thief and drunkard. Jews and half-breeds are allowed to join in as well; and of course they pretend to be just as good as the rest. Some of the guests only come as a formality; some want to drink; and others are motivated by fear or the desire to ingratiate themselves, in case they need support on some future occasion.

My own opinion is that people ought to have more sense of their own dignity. The high officials should invite each other to their tables; and the church dignitaries should do the same. Our Indian chiefs should hold gatherings of their own sort; and the Indians of lower rank likewise.

It is proper that one person of quality should entertain another, but this custom should not be confused with charity, which is a demonstration of love for a neighbour. It is an honour for a poor man to entertain his master or employer. And this same consideration applies when a woman of humble birth gives herself to a person of quality without insisting on marriage. Even if she has a bastard son, it is still an honour for her.

Why should there be any disrespect for people of quality? If you happen to be one, you can recommend yourself to God and his saints and angels, live a quiet family life and end up as a royal administrator with a valuable property in the country.

The good administrator is one who does not surround himself with deputies and officials. He is content with a fat hen for lunch and a chicken for dinner; keeps two horses, two Indian servants and a boy; eats by himself and does not play for money.

DEPUTIES, JUDGES AND CLERKS

The purpose in life of deputies is to imitate their masters, the royal administrators, and find similar opportunities for robbery and oppression. They usually have some 20 or 30 Indians at their beck and call, whom they find fault with for the slightest thing, including even scratching their buttocks. In many provinces there are half-a-dozen deputies and the same number of judges, which means that these places are effectively burdened with a dozen administrators instead of one.

In the town of Hatun Lucana in my province, in the year 1608, the royal administrator's deputy had no less than six single girls working in his kitchen, and a dozen female workers who were kept busy with spinning and weaving, making bread and preserves, distilling spirits and preparing coca. The Indian mayor, not to be outdone, soon engaged three servant girls of his own. Unfortunately, if a bad example is set, it is soon followed by everybody.

Here is another true story from the year 1608. An Indian chief called Pedro Taypimarca was very ill at his home in town. The deputy, who was a half-caste from Soras, got into the habit of roaming around in the chief's quarters at night. He went into the kitchen and larder looking for the Indian girls, under the pretext that he suspected them of being the chief's mistresses. In the larder he came upon a jar of butter flavoured with orange-flower water, which I had given to the chief for his own use. Without any scruple the deputy carried this off and gave it as a present to the royal administrator as coming from himself.

The so-called judges in commission are officials who are sent out from the cities to investigate disputes. Needless to say, Indians are invariably

30 *Bribes*

discovered to be in the wrong. As an example, one Indian killed a Spaniard in self-defence, with the result that ten Indians were hanged in the town of Ocobamba near Córdova.

The various kinds of clerk, secretary and treasurer are in the habit of taking bribes from Indians for getting them appointments, taking their side in disputes and procuring evidence of the payment of taxes. Often, when they are employed to collect evidence, their expenses amount to more than the money which is due. It would be better to take evidence from the local mayors, rather than sending out clerks to claim taxes owed by Indians who have left their villages. Also, a receipt should be given for the exact sum of money collected. What happens otherwise is that the Indian officials gamble and drink away more than the whole valuation for tax, and then declare that they have been given nothing. The poor taxpayers, who have already paid up, find themselves faced by yet another demand.

Clerks habitually deceive and misinform the royal administrators for whom they work. Their aim, of course, is to enrich themselves at his expense. When they succeed, the administrator is left penniless, immersed in disputes and carrying all the blame for what has gone wrong. Then it is often said that he was a fool to trust his clerk.

A clerk can count upon an annual income of 1,000 pesos in bribes and presents from the Indians, not counting perquisites like free service and firewood.

MINERS

At the mercury mines of Huancavelica the Indian workers are punished and ill-treated to such an extent that they die like flies and our whole race is threatened with extermination. Even the chiefs are tortured by being suspended by their feet. Conditions in the silver-mines of Potosí and Chocllococha, or at the gold-mine of Carabaya, are little better. The managers and supervisors, who are either Spaniards or half-castes, have virtually absolute power. There is no reason for them to fear justice, since they are never brought before the courts.

Beatings are incessant. The victims are mounted for this purpose on a llama's back, tied naked to a round pillar or put in the stocks. Their hair is cut off and they are deprived of food and water during detention.

Any shortage in the labour gangs is made into an excuse for punishing the chiefs as if they were common thieves or traitors instead of the nobility of the country. The work itself is so hard as to cause permanent injury to many of those who survive it. There is no remuneration for the journey to the mines and a day's labour is paid for at the rate of half a day.

In the mining towns the Indians are exploited over the supply of their food and drink, so that they easily get into debt. Their womenfolk are engaged as cooks and then raped or seduced; or the husbands are sent to the mines at night while the overseers make free with their wives.

Your Majesty must be aware that mine-owners who dress up in silk and brocade are spending a great deal of money.

The only way they can get it is by ill-treating their workers, who are not only overworked but whipped like children on their bare buttocks. There should be a general inspection of the mines every six months, at which a full investigation of these practices should be insisted upon.

Some workers escape from the mines and others do their best never to

31 *In the Mines*

arrive there. Instead of dying by inches, they would rather get it over with 'at one time', as they say. Once they inhale the vapour of the mercury mines, they contract asthma and gradually their bodies become as thin and dry as sticks. They cannot find any peace, either by day or night, until death comes to free them from their sufferings.

When these miners die at work, no compensation is paid to their families. Similarly, if they are crippled, they are not entitled to any payment from the employer. They are expected to provide their own tools and materials free of cost, but if they lose anything of the employer's they are overcharged for it. Sometimes they are able to purchase exemption from their service in the mines from a corrupt overseer. They are hidden away and then employed in the houses of the overseer's friends, where they end up as unpaid servants.

One piece of eight, with entitlement to a meal, is what can be earned by a day's work in the mercury mines; and half as much in the gold- and silver-mines, where the danger to health is less. Judges and priests are all concerned to encourage the work in the mines, and even the clerks are diligent in their paperwork.

Indians who go down the mercury mines, or heat the mercury in cauldrons, should be required to do only one turn of duty. Their only hope is to get through their time without being affected by the vapour or dying in some other way. Therefore mine-owners who put them to a second turn of work ought to be severely punished.

At present the owners take no account of whether their workers are Christian or not. There is no religious instruction, no confession and no rest on Sundays and holidays, and no solemn Mass is sung for the souls of the dead. Yet every worker, including the negro slaves, ought to be properly registered and remembered.

There should be some discouragement of the heavy drinking, on which the miners spend their meagre pay. The result of such improvidence is that when they arrive back in their villages they no longer have a single coin to contribute to taxes or to the support of their families.

Miners are often cheated out of the livestock which they bring with them to the mines, so that the great herds of our country are constantly diminished.

AT WAYSIDE INNS

Spaniards, including priests, who travel on the royal highways, are apt to arrive at the inns in a bad humour. They box the ears of the Indian servants, their tastes are finicky and they expect an infinite variety of foods and comforts.

The Spaniards impose excessive burdens on their animals, which often die on the road as a result. Then they demand replacements and ride off into the blue; or alternatively they load up five or ten Indians, who have to make do as animals.

The innkeepers are usually Spaniards, even if they have no legal right to possession of the inns. They sometimes employ as many as 20 Indians, who receive no pay whatever. It is quite usual for them to keep half a dozen whores on the premises, under the pretence that they are the wives of the Indian servants. In reality, of course, they are hired out to travellers who spend the night there. These women get no regular pay, but they are

32 *Indian kicked at an inn*

reasonably happy as long as they can spend their time dressing themselves up and painting their faces. Often they are put into the trade by their own mothers, while their husbands are sent off to the labour gangs and in most cases never return. Indians travelling on the highways sometimes have the experience that their wives, sisters or daughters are forcibly taken away from them and used for the pleasure of Spaniards.

I myself decided to stay for four days in a typical inn and observe the behaviour of both Spaniards and Indians. Because of its convenience I selected a place known as the 'burnt inn'. My attention was caught by the unscrupulous way in which even the priests among the customers behaved. As soon as a Spaniard enters the door he starts brandishing his stick at the nearest Indian, who for all he knows may be a chief or the local mayor. The customer demands service, food, firewood and other little trifles. He himself is the last person to keep any account of what he has had and is likely to go cheerfully on his way the next morning without enquiring about the cost. He probably carries off with him any blankets, mats or dishes which have taken his fancy.

Having observed a good number of the men and women who come to the inns for lodging, I believe there should be a stricter control on the use of titles such as Don and Doña, Maestro and Doctor. These titles have some meaning, whether they have been obtained by examination or by inheritance. It is precisely the class of people without any right to them which claims these titles and causes the worst damage and offence to Indians under Your Majesty's protection. Ordinary hawkers, tailors, cobblers and grocers promote themselves and their wives to the rank of Don and Doña and then half-castes and Indians of small consequence follow their example.

SPANIARDS

A large number of Spanish tramps and vagabonds are continually on the move along our highways and in and out of our inns and villages. Their refrain is always 'Give me a servant' and 'Give me a present'. The richest of them own no more than a negro servant, a boy, a beast to carry their own carcass and another for their mattress, a set of clothes for the road and another for wearing in the town. Every day of their lives they eat about twelve pesos' worth of food and ride off without paying, but still give themselves the airs of gentlemen. Although they are fit and healthy, they never condescend to bend their backs or do the hard work which they were used to in Castile.

All Spaniards travelling on honest business ought to carry passports, showing their rank and social standing. If they fail to produce these credentials on demand, they should be liable to confiscation of their belongings. But those carrying the proper papers and paying their debts at the inns would be allowed to pass without any hindrance.

As matters stand, there are more thieves in Peru than even in Castile; and the difference is that here they are provided with free meals and women.

The fat ones are perhaps the worst, but ironically it is they who eat most of the food and who drink the very best wines and spirits. They are slack, cowardly and lacking in judgement. Their stomachs are so distended that they can hardly walk and are useless for soldiering. In my experience a fat face or a big head is an infallible sign of ignorance, laziness and greed, whether in men or in women.

33 *Violence in the town*

Those who are broad in shoulder and hip are inclined to be more active. The little ones in this category, particularly, are as agile as monkeys. They have strong bones and a blow from their fists is like a sledge-hammer. You need to beware, too, of the dark-skinned, curly-haired ones with untrustworthy eyes.

Spaniards with honest eyes and well-proportioned bodies can usually be counted upon as friends. After all, if they are the rulers of a great part of the world, it is because they are in the main hard-working, able and decent. The men of this type are neatly barbered, with short beards. Their women have large eyes, small mouths and waists like ants; and they plant their feet firmly on the ground when they walk. It is fair to add that even the straightforward type of Spaniard makes a bad enemy and is quite capable of knocking you down if he gets annoyed.

Another type consists of the tall, desiccated men and the women with no calves to their legs, who are usually the lecherous ones and extremely jealous into the bargain.

But the people with most influence in the Christian world are often light in body, thin and narrow-chested. These are the ones who become learned doctors or men of great wealth and position, because of their energy. They are at the opposite end of the scale from the wastrels, liars, boasters, drunkards and lechers who can be trusted with nothing and seldom deserve even charity.

Spanish couples who are blessed with big families spend all their days and nights dreaming about the gold and silver which their children are going to earn. The husband says to the wife: 'You can't imagine how concerned I am, my dear, about our children's education. To give them a good start in life, we must put them into the Church.'

The wife answers: 'Well said, darling. Our son Iago can become a priest and little Francisco can do the same. Then they'll earn enough to let us have servants and give us lots of presents like partridges, chickens, eggs, fruit and vegetables. Later on, little Alonso can be an Augustinian, little Martín can be a Dominican and little Gonzalo can join the Order of Mercy.'

When some outstanding service is rendered to the Crown, Your Majesty feels under an obligation to provide lucrative posts not only for the person concerned but for his sons and grandsons and other relations, even if they happen to be babes-in-arms or bedridden old men, or women. But important and indeed essential posts, like that of royal administrator, ought to be given to the people who deserve them and the fact of race should not come into the choice. If a baby or an old man has a claim on the appointment, at least the actual job should be given to somebody of intelligence and goodwill who would represent the beneficiary and watch over his interests.

To sum up what I have to say, the Spaniards in Peru should be made to refrain from arrogance and brutality towards the Indians. Just imagine that our people were to arrive in Spain and start confiscating property, sleeping with the women and girls, chastising the men and treating everybody like pigs! What would the Spaniards do then? Even if they tried to endure their lot with resignation, they would still be liable to be arrested, tied to a pillar and flogged. And if they rebelled and attempted to kill their persecutors, they would certainly go to their death on the gallows.

One exception to the general rule of injustice in Peru was the case of a Spanish gentleman, who was hanged by the Viceroy, the Marquis de Cañete, for ordering the death of a poor Indian. The Viceroy would not eat a morsel of food until he had seen justice done.

There is still time for the others to mend their ways.

PROPRIETORS

Your majesty has granted large estates, including the right to employ Indian labour, to a number of individuals of whom some are good Christians and the remainder are very bad ones. These *encomenderos*, as they are termed, may boast about their high position, but in reality they are harmful both to the labour force and to the surviving Indian nobility. I therefore propose to set down the details of their life and conduct.

They exude an air of success as they go from their card-games to their dinners in fine silk clothes. Their money is squandered on these luxuries, as well it may, since it costs them no work or sweat whatever. Although the Indians ultimately pay the bill, no concern is ever felt for them or even for Your Majesty or God himself. Several of these big proprietors have been guilty of treason in their own person. Others had fathers or grandfathers who fought against the Crown under the elder or the younger Almagro, Gonzalo Pizarro or Girón. What has happened so many times before can certainly happen again.

Official posts like those of royal administrator and judge ought not to be given to big employers or mine-owners or their obnoxious sons, because these people have enough to live on already. The appointments ought to go to Christian gentlemen of small means, who have rendered some service to the Crown and are educated and humane, not just greedy.

Anybody with rights over Indian labour sees to it that his own household is well supplied with servant girls and indoor and outdoor staff. When collecting dues and taxes, it is usual to impose penalties and detain Indians against their will. There is no redress since, if any complaint is made, the law always favours the employer.

The collection of tribute is delegated to stewards, who make a practice of adding something on for themselves. They too consider themselves entitled to free service and obligatory presents, and they end up as bad as their masters. All of them, and their wives as well, regard themselves as entitled to eat at the Indians' expense.

The Indians are seldom paid the few reales a day which are owed to them, but they are hired out for the porterage of wine and making rope or clothing. Little rest is possible either by day or night and they are usually unable to sleep at home.

It is impossible for servant girls, or even married women, to remain chaste. They are bound to be corrupted and prostituted, because employers do not feel any scruple about threatening them with flogging, execution or burial alive if they refuse to satisfy their masters' desires.

The Spanish grandees and their wives have borrowed from the Inca the

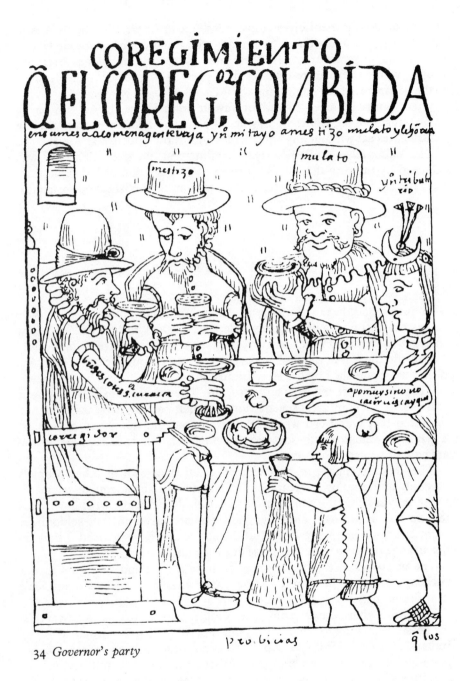

34 *Governor's party*

custom of having themselves conveyed about in litters like the images of saints in processions. These Spaniards are absolute lords without fear of either God or retribution. In their own eyes they are judges over our people, whom they can reserve for their personal service or their pleasure, to the detriment of the community.

Great positions are achieved by favour from above, by wealth or by having relations at Court in Castile. With some notable exceptions, the beneficiaries act without any consideration for those under their control.

The *encomenderos* call themselves conquerors, but their Conquest was achieved by uttering the words: *Ama mancha noca Inca*, or 'Have no fear. I am the Inca'. This false pretence was the sum total of their performance.

THE FATHERS

The priesthood began with Jesus Christ and his Apostles, but their successors in the various religious orders established in Peru do not follow this holy example. On the contrary, they show an unholy greed for worldly wealth and the sins of the flesh and a good example would be set to everyone if they were punished by the Holy Inquisition.

These priests are irascible and arrogant. They wield considerable power and usually act with great severity towards their parishioners, as if they had forgotten that Our Lord was poor and humble and the friend of sinners. Their own intimate circle is restricted to their relations and dependants, who are either Spanish or half-caste.

They readily engage in business, either on their own or other people's account, and employ a great deal of labour without adequate payment. Often they say that the work is for ecclesiastical vestments, when really it is for the sale of ordinary clothing. Managers are taken on, but seldom get themselves properly rewarded. And the native chiefs are blamed if they do not arrange the immediate purchase of the goods.

The usual practice is for a priest to have a man and two girls in the kitchen, a groom, a gardener, a porter, and others to carry wood and look after the animals.

Sometimes there are as many as ten mules in the stables, not counting the beasts belonging to neighbours, and they all have to be sustained at the Indians' expense. Herds of 1,000 cattle, goats, pigs or sheep are a commonplace and there are often hundreds of capons, chickens and rabbits, all requiring their own special arrangements, as well as market gardens. If a

35 *Priest trampling on Indian chief*

single animal is lost, the Indian held responsible has to pay for it in full. Since the servants are not even properly fed, it is no wonder that they avoid work. But there are always pretty girls attached to the household, who have been corrupted by the priests and bear them children. This kind of showy establishment is of course enormously costly.

A favourite source of income of the priesthood consists in organising the porterage of wine, chillies, coca and maize. These wares are carried on the backs of Indians and llamas and in some cases need to be brought down from high altitudes. The descent often results in death for the Indians, who catch a fever when they arrive in a warm climate. Any damage to their loads during the journey has to be made good at their own expense.

The priests make a practice of confiscating property which really belongs to a church, a society or a hospital and putting it to their own uses. In the same way they often overcharge for Masses for the dead. For a sung Mass they charge 6 reales instead of 3; and for spoken Mass 4 reales instead of 1. Some of them go so far as to extort 10 or 20 reales and then fail to celebrate Mass at all. Although the giving of alms is supposed to be voluntary, they insist on a contribution of 4 reales from each person. This is robbery and our Indians should have their money refunded to them. When a priest officiates at a wedding, he want 5 pesos to cover the earnest-money, the candles and the collection. Similarly the usual rate for a baptism is 4 pesos. It never seems to occur to the priest that he is paid his salary for performing these offices.

The amount of food of various sorts which these holy fathers put away in the course of a single day comes to a value of about six pieces of eight.* Usually they eat at our expense, but occasionally, to set their consciences at rest, they pay up half of one piece of eight in settlement of the account.

They are apt to go astray in the way they meddle in the process of justice, which is no concern of theirs. They give orders, countermand them, intervene in disputes, organise petitions and send reports to the authorities. The example which they set is nearly always bad.

A priest named Juan Bautista Alvadán, who was in charge of the parish of Pampachire, acted in so gross and cruel a manner that it is difficult to find words for what he did. A local Indian named Diego Caruas had refused to hand over some mutton to him, whereupon the priest had the man tied naked to a cross. He took a burning brand and thrust it into the Indian's body and private parts. He smeared one torch after another with pitch, set it alight and opened the man's body with his hands in order to push them in. And other atrocities were committed by this priest, which only God knows the whole truth about.

Their misbehaviour with girls, particularly, forfeits any claim which the priests might make to obedience and respect. Because they are obvious sinners, they are unable to give the sacrament of confession to their own mistresses or their mistresses' relations. Nor can they honestly claim their salary for absolving girls with whom they are committing mortal sin. The present practice is for them to get their fellow-priests to confess their Indian mistresses.

When these holy fathers are living as husband and wife with Indian girls and begetting children, they always refer to the half-castes as their nephews. With the aid of a little hypocrisy they make sin seem more attractive, so that it spreads and corrupts one girl after another.

Even though our former priests worshipped images of metal or stone, at least they sometimes set a good example in their lives. If they had not been heathens they would have made good Christians. But the present servants

* The patacón or piece of eight was equivalent to eight reales. The bill might amount to £15 in English terms but the priest would pay little more than £1.

of the true God have lost all sense of vocation and their children are as bad as they are. Abusive and bullying, they impose cruel punishments on their staff and helpers in the churches, who sooner or later take to flight. Then the priests have them arrested and put in irons, or even killed. The sacristy or the vestry is often fully equipped as a torture-chamber with stocks, shackles, chains and handcuffs. I know of such cases, but name no names in order to avoid giving offence.

Many of the priests live as grandly as our former rulers, offering banquets to their friends and wasting the substance of the people on these entertainments. If they have money to spare, it ought to be spent on the local hospital or church. At present, the church is often kept in worse condition than a stable for horses.

Our clergy, being obliged to provide wax candles, incense and soap, get the Indians to pay by confiscating the silver subscribed for charity. It would be more honest to use the fees from burials, weddings and baptisms, or the money left at the foot of the altars on holy days, to provide these stores.

There have been cases of such absolute licence among the clergy that Your Majesty's own orders are contravened. One particular Indian of distinguished family and great ability was entitled to the post of royal administrator among his own people. He was able to read and write and was well versed in all the regulations, so that he could defend his Indians against any injustice of the Spanish officials. For this reason they took against him and deprived him of his post. The Indian had been nominated for office, however, by Your Majesty. In these circumstances what did the local priest do? He gave orders in the village that nobody was to obey the Indian and those who remained loyal were cruelly punished. Then he summoned a meeting with other important Spaniards at his house for the purpose of inventing accusations against the Indian, who was taken to court and sentenced to banishment from the village. Afterwards, the priest boasted that as long as he remained in the parish the Indian would never return to his post. If it was possible to deal in this way with one of the leading chiefs, how much easier must it be to rob, burn and destroy the property of poor and ignorant Indians? Your Majesty never comes to hear about most of these injustices.

Indian couples are often married by force or under duress, against their will. The officiating priest invariably has some personal stake in the matter. Either the girl has refused herself to him, or is pregnant by him, or he wants an opportunity to sleep with her while pretending to prepare her for the responsibilities of marriage. Thus a ceremony which is regarded by the Church as a sacrament is disgracefully perverted and our Indians are prevented from living a Christian life by the sins of the priest.

When the women working in priests' houses are married, the husbands are sent away to deliver messages so that the wives can be enjoyed at leisure. Sometimes, too, the married women are put in charge of the girls whom the priests keep for their amusement.

In one case, a priest employed a native treasurer who was constantly demanding silver from people in the village, saying that it was needed by the priest or some visiting official. It turned out that this treasurer had been whipped and fined by the priest for living with a woman. The man's defence was that the priest kept a woman of his own and had several illegitimate children, so why should not he, the treasurer, do the same?

After fining the treasurer for immorality, the priest next demanded the man's daughter for his own bed. He argued that it was more honourable for the girl to be a priest's woman that an ordinary Indian's wife. Also he promised to help the treasurer with his fine and defend him against any action by the native chiefs or the mayor. The man's family would be kept supplied with wine, bread and meat, and the job of treasurer would remain his for life. If, however, he refused to hand the girl over he would be whipped, discharged from his post and sent to the mines. Out of fear for his future the man agreed to give up his daughter, whom the priest promptly deflowered by force. The insatiable cleric then demanded the girl's sister. This time the treasurer refused to part with her, with the result that he was flogged yet again for his alleged immorality. The sole conclusion which can be drawn from such a story is that women of whatever age should stay away from priests.

In another case, a vicar named Matamoros held religious classes for young women, whom he raped and made pregnant one after another. The resulting brood of half-a-dozen children had to be carried by Indian bearers from one village to another. When this vicar died, he actually left directions for everyone to wear mourning for him.

In the year 1600 I came across a similar instance in the Aymará village of Tiaparo. The local cleric simply declared himself to be the sole proprietor of the parish. Since he had helped to enrich one of the big employers, it proved impossible for either the Spaniards or the Indian chiefs to get him out of his post. He was always well-groomed and wore the most elegant clothes. Any Indian who took an interest in the girls of his household was rewarded with a flogging. In the secrecy of his home he behaved like an Inca, with his own collection of brides attending to his every want. It may seem astonishing that a priest like this can have up to a dozen children by different girls. One child or even two might be pardonable, for we are all human, but not such a number.

This man loaded his children on two mules, six on one and six on the other, to send them with a hired muleteer to the City of the Kings at Lima.

By divine Providence one of the mules fell over a precipice with the children before reaching the capital.

It is the custom at present for priests to hear confession in their houses, in the sacristy and in all sorts of dark corners which are well-adapted for love-making. The houses themselves are full of dark cubby-holes and they have easy communication with the kitchen and the alley-ways at the back. The kitchen is usually crammed with young Indian girls and the priests' own rooms are filthy, with bread and knives all over the floor. But room can always be found for the priests to take the girls to bed with them.

The normal period of service in a priest's home is ten years, without any payment in money, but it sometimes runs to more. If a servant leaves to get married, no provision is made and the servant has to return everything supplied by the employer and depart in a state of poverty.

Priests should never be allowed to advise on the siting of settlements of Christian natives. Since a priest is unlikely to stay long in the parish, he often gives bad advice and the settlement is put down in an unhealthy area where the settlers sicken and die. The Indians are not allowed to give their advice even when they can see that the site for a settlement is no good. Our people have special knowledge going back to the time of the Incas of the conditions which are favourable for the growth of population. They can detect bad water, which causes tumours on the neck, land which is too dry or too soggy, dangerous exhalations and also influences coming from the Sun, planets or stars. But the accepted practice is still to ask the clergy.

When they occasionally travel abroad, the priests insist on being welcomed home with a peal of bells. The villagers have to come out in procession with crosses and banners, just as if these clerics were Bishops, when in reality they are no better than the rest of humanity.

In setting down truthfully this account of the way of life of the priests, the goods which they possess and the evil which they do, I am hoping to bring it to the attention of Your Majesty and other important persons. Although I feel exhausted by the effort, I propose to continue with my task.

One particular priest in the Andamarca district was such an arrogant bully that he arrested both men and women for no other fault than having their hair combed or wearing new clothes. He had them stripped as naked as on the day when they were born, tied by the hands and feet and flogged until the blood came. Then he had them smeared with fat and scorched with the burning fibre of the maguey plant. Finally, a disgusting mixture of urine, salt and chilli pepper was used to bathe the wounds.

Once, during the year 1610, a poor soldier arrived at the inn of Apcara, where he found that no bread was available. So he sent his boy into the village of Cabana to buy some. The priest in question, noticing this boy, called him over and the boy kissed his hands in the proper manner. Thereupon the priest asked if he was a thief. Seeing that the boy was well-dressed, he ordered the native officials to take him to the flogging-pillar in the court-yard. There he had him stripped, flogged and tortured in the way which has been described. The boy was left for dead, but came to after a time and dragged himself away on all fours like a wounded cat. He succeeded in finding his master, the poor soldier, and showing the marks of burning and the flayed skin on his body. The Spanish soldier went in search of the priest and subsequently made a complaint against him to the royal administrator. But it was the soldier who found himself in trouble for causing annoyance to a priest.

Clerics of this sort are no better than common executioners, because they either perform cruel acts themselves or order them to be performed. When they hear our Indians' confessions they kick and hit them, and sometimes flog them. The result is that the Indians avoid confession and cover up their sins by making payments of up to 10 pesos.

Instead of performing their duties in the parish, the priests often go off to entertainments and banquets, where they amble about, break wind and take their pleasure. Meanwhile they put out the story that they are taking confession.

It ought to be obligatory for every priest, instead of a crowded sweat-shop, to keep a clean and decently furnished house, an oratory for his devotions, a bedroom, sitting-room and separate kitchen, and stables for the animals. Another house should be provided for official visitors, such as Bishops or judges, or for guests. These lodgings should be equally clean and newly decorated, with a key in the door. It is important that the houses should be well-lighted, without any hiding-places or dark corners. There should be no suspicion of misconduct, for these are houses of religion.

The priests overlook the injustices committed by their subordinates, because these people know too much about their wickednesses. The right sort of assistants for them would be Christian Indians of some intelligence, who could officiate for them during church festivals and look after the aged and the sick. They could keep the candle burning on the altar, arrange processions and say prayers.

But if ever an Indian assistant performs his duties in an honest and reputable fashion, refuses to rob the parishioners and tries to dissuade the priest from doing so, he is promptly removed from his job. The priest acts as if he were the Bishop, although it ought not to be within his power to revoke any appointment.

As a matter of policy, our Indians are hindered from learning to read and write. Schoolmasters are not encouraged. It would be dangerous for the clergy if the laws and ordinances were understood, because theft and other misdeeds would appear as what they are.

In front of other Spaniards the priests play the part of saintly, meek and charitable people, but once they are away from their Orders they display venom and cunning.

When an Indian makes a complaint or demands justice, it is usual for the priest to retaliate by accusing him of ignorance of the Christian doctrine. He says: 'Tell me the doctrine, you troublesome Indian. Start talking at once!'

I have seen a priest deceive Christian fugitives from justice, namely an Indian man and woman who took sanctuary in his church. When they threw themselves on his mercy he advised them to go out and give themselves up. The priest was therefore to blame when they were tortured and hanged. He might pretend to be on their side, but was ready to reveal their hiding-place and denounce them to the law. Yet as a priest he ought not to betray those in trouble, but protect them.

When the native chiefs want to clean and paint the sacred images in their local churches and buy decorations for them, it is usual for the priest to agree like a good Christian as long as other Spaniards are present, but subsequently to refuse in private and excuse himself. Because of this attitude the churches and holy places in the Andes, at least in my own province of Lucanas, have become empty and deserted. The sanctuary, where the holy sacraments are given, is not cared for any more, the ornaments are old and peeling and the images are broken.

During the Conquest the priests imposed the following catechism on the Indians: 'Are you a thief? Are you a fornicator? Do you kiss graven images? Have you loved women, and how many times? Have you used bad language? Do you eat raw meat? Have you taken another person's property? Are you a drunkard?' Then the priest would announce in the Indian tongue: 'Come and be baptised as Christians. Believe in God and you will go to Heaven.' As he said this, the congregation lifted their faces and pointed with their right hand towards the sky. The priest continued: 'If you do not worship God you will go down to Hell.' And the congregation lowered their heads and pointed downwards with one finger of their left hand. The service ended with the priest saying: 'Obey the command of the Son of God, who has the power to forgive sins and whose mercy is boundless, love your neighbour and believe in God the Father. Go with God. Go with God. Amen. Amen.'

The priests of that time collected Indians together every week in batches of twenty at a time and married them to one another. The result was that some of them got married to their own sisters, mothers, aunts or nieces.

In their eagerness to convert all the Indians to Christianity, the priests used to baptise them in herds as if they were animals. Some of the new converts never received the holy water, the oil or the chrism because of the priests' negligence.

If all these complaints against the priests are to be avoided, they must learn to discharge their office properly. If they cannot do so, they should not be employed in it for a single day. They should always be of mature age, because the actions of children and boys never result in anything good in this world. Indeed, their blunders soon become impossible to endure. Real priests ought to be learned, modest and charitable.

It is true that many clerics begin as men of considerable learning, but pride is usually their downfall.

Among the few kind and charitable priests I have known were Father Benavides, Francisco de Padilla and Father Yñigo. These ones at least did not run after girls or beget bastards, and they treated people of all sorts with respect.

Usually the priests have an inadequate knowledge of our native languages, Quechua and Aymará. This makes it difficult for them to hear confession and above all to preach a sermon every week. Of course, they still feel themselves to be capable of instructing the Indians when they only know a handful of phrases like 'Lead the horse', 'There's nothing to eat' and 'Where are the girls?'. Often they introduce into their sermons all sorts of personal matters and instructions about property and payments. One priest in Huamanga abused the congregation because a complaint about him had been sent to the Bishop. Another preacher maintained that sexual intercourse with Indians would result in animal babies being born to the parents.

The notorious Father Alvadán used to enumerate in his sermons the various things that he needed, such as starch, freshwater fish, wool and firewood. These were denied to him, he said, while the royal administrator and others with official posts got whatever they wanted. And he ended by threatening that a new priest would soon come who would strangle the parishioners unless they behaved in a more generous fashion.

A Dominican father recalled the promises to make clothing for him, which would be better than even the royal administrator wore, but he complained that nothing ever came of these promises. So he issued a warning in his sermon, in his capacity as God's representative, that he might be obliged to whip people whom he wanted to love with all his heart.

Morua, a friar of the Order of Mercy, used the pulpit for a denunciation of the Aymará Indians, who were accusing him of seducing the local girls. But these girls, he maintained, were working for the Bishop and the King, who had to have clothes to wear on their backs. Possibly he would be dismissed from his parish and he was not afraid to die, but first he would kill the Aymará chief and whip all the Indians to stop their slanderous tongues from wagging any more.

The eloquent Father Molina, who preached in Cuzco, had some skill in the Quechua and Aymará languages, but spoke them in a very old-fashioned way. 'Our lips', he used to say, 'shall open like the buds of flowers to invoke the name of Jesus.'

Father Loayza accused his parishioners of being senseless drunkards, thieves and whores because they avoided him and would not visit him at home. He assured them that he was more important than any Inca or than the native chiefs, who were not worthy to lace up his shoes and whom he was in a position to hang or skin alive if he so decided. But he was nevertheless full of love and compassion for his spiritual children, he asserted.

The sacrament of baptism ought always to be marked by a proper celebration attended by the godfathers and godmothers. The people should be well-combed and dressed as they carry the child through arches of flowers to the font in the church. Trumpets, clarinets and flutes can provide the music for our native songs and dances. No idolatry or drunkenness is called for. A table can be furnished with a holy image or a cross and a plate provided for gifts to the child, who as a new Christian is starting on the road to Heaven. Nor should the priest himself be forgotten at such a time.

The sacrament of confession to a priest requires some preparation in advance. The penitent requires to examine his soul and conscience for at least a week and count up his sins on the *quipu*. Our Indians need to be instructed which sins are mortal and which venial. For instance, fornication between unmarried people is a mortal sin. So is adultery between the married or incest between parents and their children. And so is the rape of a virgin of either sex. Sacrilege, which is the worst sin a Christian can commit, is a form of spiritual adultery. The distinction between these and other sins can be taught to our Indians in our own language. We have words for young men who sleep with girls, for rape, for sins among boys and even for the mortal sins committed by the priests.

It is typical of our Indians to confess the theft of four maize-cakes as if it were something important and overlook the fact that in the course of a year even a saint would commit more serious offences. A little thought would discover something far less trivial than taking the maize-cakes.

The sacrament of marriage, which is so important, needs to be celebrated with proper solemnity. The betrothed couple should be clean in body and soul when they come together at the altar, wearing silk, and carrying offerings of gold and silver. The priest's presence is essential, so that he can have the bells rung, perform the ceremony, preach the sermon and make a gift of money and fruit to the newly married pair. The chiefs and elders also have their duties in the way of advice and instruction.

The priest and the whole village ought to be invited to the house after the service and nobody should be allowed to stay away. In the streets there should be a triumphal song, and dancing to the music of trumpets and flutes. The people should enter the house through an arch of flowers.

The burial of the dead, when Christians are concerned, is a work of pity which requires care and attention from the priest. The body ought to be laid out in a clean corner of the house, with a sacred image before it, and a table arranged for the offerings of the mourners. The passing bell should be tolled and the people collected together in their mourning, with wax candles in their hands, while the priest carries the crucifix in its box with pennons. In all the Christian world the body needs to stay unburied for one day, so that the first Mass for the dead can be celebrated in its presence.

The priests should be obliged to keep a book with details of all receipts from Masses for the dead, prayers for survival and village ceremonies. Any charitable legacies should be entered with details of the day, month and year. It will thus be possible to discover any discrepancy. When the Visitor comes, he will only have to audit the account.

One particular priest, who arrived in an Aymará village to take it over as his parish, asked his clerk for whatever writing-materials were available. The clerk said he could have as much as he wanted and subsequently brought him a large quantity. Seeing this, and sagely reflecting that his own misdeeds would result in a flood of complaints from such an unusually literate village, the priest told his clerk: 'My son, I'm not looking for a parish in which so many people know how to write. I'm leaving at once. In fact I shall be gone by to-morrow.' He was as good as his word, for he left the parish without another word of explanation. The last thing he intended to do was to deal with clever Indians, who had learnt their letters.

THE VICAR-GENERAL

To hold the office of Vicar-General of a province a man ought to be advanced in years, learned, disinterested, modest, just and charitable. It is also an advantage for him to be rich and a gentleman. Good family and education are essential in those who seek to rule the Church, for without these attributes they could never be obeyed or respected. Our Lord may have been poor, but he was well-born.

The Vicar-General must imprison offenders when necessary, but also listen attentively to complaints from distressed Indians. If the complaints are justified, these Indians deserve compensation and their false accusers, even if they are priests, ought to be sent to prison. Their punishment needs to be exemplary so that they improve their conduct in the future. And those who make a mockery of justice by failing to appear in court ought to have to pay for the privilege. If the Vicar-General is not himself a just man his office should be taken away from him.

THE CHURCH

The proper payment for a sung Mass with organ music is 24 reales, and for a spoken Mass one piece of 8 reales.

Mass should be announced by ten peals of the big or little bells, followed by a single bell ringing for quarter of an hour. By this means all the people of consequence, as well as the old and sick who are only able to walk with difficulty, would get ample warning. It would also remove the necessity for town-criers and others to make a personal tour of the parishioners' houses, in the course of which they often find opportunities for theft and lechery. One way of punishing these offenders would be to get all the parishioners together in church, while a special party would lie in wait for clandestine prowlers and make them captive. These culprits might be allowed to get off with a caution the first time, but the second time they should be whipped behind the church. The same treatment would be appropriate for magicians who throw eggs at the church door. The surviving old people from Inca times are reaching the end of their lives and their children are all baptised Christians, so the whole population ought to respond to a summons to church.

Clerks and sacristans are inclined to exploit the Indians and particularly the girls. One of their tricks is to arrange services on Wednesday and Friday evenings when the priest is away, so as to arouse the interest of these young creatures and seduce them afterwards. When their priest leaves them in charge of the parish, they pay much less attention to matters such as ringing the bells for prayer, helping the sick to die well and burying the dead.

Fines are often levied on the Indians for such matters as immorality, non-attendance at church, failing to remove their headgear on entering the church and grazing their livestock in the cemetery.

Members of church choirs should be fairly paid for their services. The steward should supply them with meals; and the priest should contribute their maize and potatoes. They should be professionally competent and in good health, but can be quite old.

The education of the young is in the hands of the schoolmasters and choirmasters. The boys are usually taught in school and the girls in their homes. While they are learning to read, write and sing, the real object is to make good Christians out of them and get them to believe in Heaven. The cost of their instruction is borne by the parish out of its resources. But the teachers ought nevertheless to have some measure of independence. A teacher who does not resort to drink or drugs ought to be secure in his job for life, because this class of person carries the main responsibility for instilling principle, cleanliness and order in our society: more so in many cases than the priests.

36 *Priest uncovering woman*

There was a case of a schoolmaster in Santiago de Queros, a Chanca Indian named Damián, who made a contract to teach the children for 80 pesos and his board. By the parish priest's decision the salary was paid in advance. The result was that in the whole of a year the man never once taught in school and did not even know his Christian doctrine. He was blind drunk every day and played all kinds of tricks, while the parish priest turned a blind eye. To prevent such abuses, there ought to be an examination at the end of every year. If the pupils do well, the teacher should be paid his full salary and re-engaged for another period.

ARTISTS

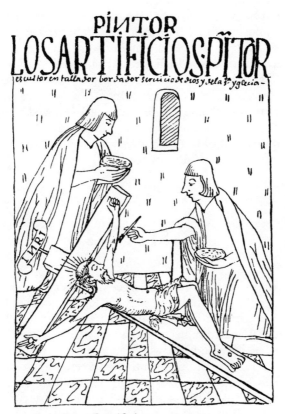

37 *Painting a Crucifixion*

Painters, engravers, embroiderers and other artists are employed in making images in the likeness of God. This practice is regarded as an important part of worship, which benefits both soul and body, and has therefore been adopted by our new rulers. Holy images are to be found, with other religious curiosities, in all our churches and temples. There is invariably a picture of the Last Judgement, showing the coming of the Lord, the joys of Heaven and the penalties of Hell, to serve as a warning to sinners. The artist should be properly paid for such work and get his meals free, but on no account should he be encouraged to join in drinking-bouts with the

Indian chiefs. Indeed, if he is addicted to drink or drugs he should not be allowed to continue in his vocation however great his talent. He should be sentenced by the court if he is tempted into heretical fancies under the influence of strong drink. The artist, however sinful, bears a responsibility. If his judgement becomes confused, demons are likely to enter into him and lure him into mortal error. The error is often irreversible because no Christian likes to alter or destroy a religious work, for fear of being charged with sacrilege. I came across such a case in the year 1613 in the village of San Pedro de Huarochirí. The Visitor himself was disobeyed when he ordered the destruction of a picture which had been painted under the influence of an uncontrollable lust for women. It showed a number of girls resisting the effort of a priest to have intercourse with them. The Visitor did his utmost, and even the Archbishop was informed, but any interference with the picture was successfully opposed.

VISITORS

Cristóbal de Albornoz, who held the office of Visitor-General, was fearless in his judgements and a stern opponent of arrogance on the part of the priests. He never accepted bribes or used physical violence. He was a plain and good man, but he had in his employment a certain Juan Cocha Quispe, an Indian clerk of humble birth who opposed other people's idolatry but practised the old religion of our country in secret. Thanks to his deceit he was promoted to being chief. He took bribes from all quarters and soon became very rich, unlike his Spanish master. To this day, with the assistance of his children, he rules over the Quechua people.

One of the Visitor's duties is to confiscate any arms carried by the priests, whether for self-defence or for aggressive purposes. Not only are such arms terrifying to the Indians, but they are unsuitable in the hands of men anointed and consecrated to the service of God, who should be performing works of compassion.

Even when the bad priests are cleared out of their parishes by the Visitor, they simply retire to the nearest inhabited place. Then they continue to make the rounds of their old village, insisting on all sorts of gifts and services and uttering menaces against the Indians. Usually they put it abroad that they will be returning to the parish after six months' banishment and that they will flay anyone alive who has not provided them with eggs, poultry and fruit in the meantime. They also make sure that their

VÍCÍTADOR
BECÍTADOR·PROVE

38 *Visitor-General*

animals are looked after and that young girls are still set aside for them. If there is any failure they are quick to write to their friends in high places, lodging an official complaint.

Visitors are not entitled to appoint vicars, preachers or learned judges. Such appointments are reserved by Your Majesty for the Bishops. If they are left to Visitors who have been well and truly bribed, as many as ten children may be nominated to livings in a single province.

Visitors ought not to be allowed to stay in any one place more than a day, because of all the obligations of service which they impose. Once they have given judgement on the cases awaiting them, let them go on their way and be heard of no more until the next occasion. If they are allowed to stay they pretend to be making a count of the Masses which have been celebrated, while they are really laying their hands on all the money which they can find: contributions, ticket-money, fines and even the bribes received by the clergy. Altogether, it is usual for Visitors to extort something like 100 pesos from every village on their itinerary. Yet there is very good reason why they should have to pay their own expenses.

In the year 1611 a Visitor-General was sent out by the Bishop of Cuzco to correct the arrogance of the clergy and it is worth relating what occurred as a lesson for the future. He punished some of the priests, but others he let off because he had become good friends with them. In contempt of his orders, he himself confiscated property and provisions from the Indians, insisted on unpaid service and assumed privileges which he was in no way entitled to. Over and above this he treated the Indians with manifest hatred, going to the limits of what the law permits.

As a learned judge once said, when he was concerned about developments in this country, the foot on its own is not capable of ruling the world or giving orders. It needs to be controlled by the brain and the senses. If this control is lacking, the foot should be cut off and prevented from making any movement.

Visitors usually imagine that they are being fed and entertained at the expense of their hosts, the parish priests, but in reality it is the Indians who have to settle the bill. Moreover, the Visitors put on an air of immense importance and dignity, travelling in style with a multitude of attendants and causing no end of a disturbance in the country. The Indians are so intimidated that they never dare to come forward and ask for justice, so the tangible results of the visit are often negligible.

Visitors also make a great fuss if they are not given presents of silver, fine clothing and valuable ornaments. Indeed, some Visitors are so arrogant and violent in temper that they try to trample both Spaniards and Indians underfoot. God preserve us from their attentions! Others are open to bribery in cash. And a Visitor will require 1,000 pesos where a clerk would be content with 100.

Once the visit is at an end, any Indians who have complained about the conduct of the priests are punished with hideous cruelty and even flogged to death.

No Visitor should be appointed who has not already proved his worth in some other high office in the Church. A Jesuit would be a good choice because he would know how to judge a dispute on its merits. If the Indians were in the right he would favour their cause, even against the parish priest.

Stiff penalties should be imposed on people who carry holy images, ornaments and bells belonging to the Church from one village to another. There are some sculptures worth 500 or 1,000 pesos, which can easily be damaged during the process of removal. Even excommunication is not too heavy a punishment in such a case. I have seen works of art cracked by the hot sun and damaged by showers of rain and our Indians sometimes play frivolous games with images of the Virgin Mary. The houses in which sacred works are kept should always be clean and newly painted. Since they are made in the likeness of God these works should never be touched by hand.

It is the Visitor's job to look out for any misdemeanour or oversight on the part of the priests: visit the church buildings and see that they are properly painted, check that the doors are provided with locks, notice whether the holy images have been treated with respect and whether the bells are in order, and inspect the stocks of wax, incense, soap and oil. The high cross for processions and the vestments of the sacristans and choirboys need to be inspected. The priest's house also deserves attention. Is it clean and proper, or is it full of women? Is the priest in the habit of roaming around at night, or visiting wine-shops during the day? Does he hoard food, own property or embezzle the funds encharged to him? If he has a pillar for flogging Indians in his back yard he is nothing but an executioner; and if his barns are stuffed with loot he is a thief. A large number of dependants and servants is bound to tell against him.

This is the right way to conduct a visit and nothing more can be expected of the occasion. The Visitor should never ask direct questions, such as whether the priest says his prayers or carries a rosary. Rather, he should notice the lack of the rosary and require it to be remedied. In the same way he should be aware of the tendency of the clerks to go out after women at night. This will be all the more obvious if they offer to bring girls to him in his lodgings. Any such offer should of course be rejected.

The main task of the Visitor is thus to discover and chastise bad priests. Of course the priests themselves will talk about 'a bad Visitor' when what they mean is a Visitor who knows about their misdeeds. Conversely, if the Visitor allows himself to be bribed, these priests will talk about him as 'a good Christian', meaning that he does not interfere in their affairs.

Visitors are sometimes guilty of imposing unjust punishments. One of them had an Indian foreman flogged for refusing to provide eggs and assistance in the kitchen, and the man died on the spot. In another case, when a pregnant Indian girl was whipped for immorality, the punishment was similarly fatal. Often, by a strange irony, our persecutors have to be kept supplied with liberal quantities of meat, eggs, and vegetables and girls are brought two by two to their lodgings at night while they are sitting in judgement on us.

NEGROES

The black men imported from Guinea are modest and decent-living. Once they become Christians they are faithful and obedient. Being affectionate in nature, they get on well with their neighbours and make excellent slaves. Their King in Africa is a strong ruler who defeated the Grand Turk but submitted to Your Majesty, bringing gifts of arms and provisions. San Juan Buenaventura was himself a Guinean. Admittedly, the Spaniards insist that all imported negroes are worthless, but they are mistaken. A little religion and education makes a Guinean worth two Creole half-castes and in an extreme case he is capable of sainthood.

All the negroes ought to be married, both for moral reasons and for the financial benefit of their masters. I say this because in many cases they are actually prevented from marrying. In others, married negroes are sold and separated from their wives. The negroes, man and wife, ought preferably to live together in one house. If this cannot be arranged, they should at least be brought together at night.

Also the sons and daughters of negro homes ought not to be sold or separated from their mothers, with the result that there is nobody to look after them in life or grieve for them in death. The children should be treated fairly. If they are needed for work on the farms, they are entitled in return to be taught to read and write and become good Christians.

On one occasion some slaves who had been put in irons entered into conversation and began quarrelling. One of them said to another 'You're carrying that load of fetters because you're a drunkard'; and the other answered: 'You're carrying yours because you're nothing but a thief'. When slaves go to the bad, the best way of dealing with them is indeed to put them in irons. Beating or smearing with tar is unnecessary, because the iron alone subdues them. Threatening them is unprofitable, because they simply take to the mountains. The best cure is good hard iron.

But the decent negroes, living in Christian marriage, show admirable patience in the service of their Spanish masters and mistresses. They have to work from morning until noon without eating, for they are fed only once a day. A man who is working hard needs to breakfast and lunch and dine, but these poor Christians are made by the mistresses to do without meat or treats of any kind. Yet they are only made of flesh and blood.

When mulattos – a mixture of negro and Indian – produce quadroon children, these children lose all physical trace of their negro origin except for the ear, which still gives them away by its shape and size.

Wherever there is a negro community of ten persons in any city, village, mine or farm, it should have the right to appoint a mayor, a magistrate and

NEGROS
COMOLLEBAEИTÃTA
paciencia y amor de jesu cristo los puenos
negros y negras y el vellaco de su amo no
tiene caridad y amor de progimo

so Coʋ bioso   como

39 *Negroes being beaten*

a clerk of its own race. If the community is still larger it will require constables, a lawyer and a town crier. These persons should be allowed to carry defensive weapons such as swords, halberds and coats of mail. Similarly the negro slaves of people of importance should be entitled to carry arms, but only when at their masters' sides or on active duty. Otherwise they should not even be given a knife or there is bound to be trouble.

Once a negro mayor has been elected to office, he should be given two days' leave of absence a week from his other work, in the interests of good administration. He should attend at council on Wednesdays and Thursdays.

The masters and mistresses of negroes ought to be prevented from punishing their slaves for any crime, even if their guilt is established, and should certainly never be allowed to punish the families. All accusations ought to be made through the proper negro official and in accordance with justice. The master and mistress should be consulted about the value of any goods stolen and if this is considerable the punishment should be exemplary.

A SCALE OF CHARGES*

A fixed scale of prices for foodstuffs is necessary for the convenience of travellers, because in some parts of the country there is an abundance of maize and in other parts none at all. Some areas are richer than others in potatoes, or they have more cattle brought over from Spain. Similarly chicken is plentiful in one region but not in another.

The highest officials, such as the Viceroy, do not travel widely enough to appreciate all the mischief that goes on. The fact is that royal administrators increase the price of food to suit themselves. They buy in order to sell at a higher price, retaining the difference as a sort of tax which goes into their own pockets. Thus, for instance, they will buy half a measure of maize for 1 peso and sell it for 3. Potatoes they will get for 4 reales and sell for 2 pesos a half-measure. Mutton costs them 4 reales and fetches 2 pesos. Chicken goes up from 2 to 8 reales. They buy twenty eggs for 1 real and sell for 2½. At the same time these Spanish officials charge the Indians 4 reales a league for the hire of a pack-horse, and 2 reales for a saddle. A llama for carrying goods costs 2 reales a league and if by chance the animal dies the Indian porter not only loses his commission but has to pay 30 or 40 pesos. In view of these abuses one of the Viceroys, the Marquis García de Mendoza, stopped entirely the hiring out of horses and llamas at inns.

The Indians have to buy all their household provisions, as well as hiring such necessities as blankets and rope. It would therefore be a valuable measure to have a scale of charges displayed in every shop in the inns along the highways, laying down the proper prices, which are as follows:

Maize: 6 pesos for a measure of one and a half bushels in non-producing areas, and 3 pesos in producing areas.
Potatoes: 4 pesos in non-producing and 2 in producing areas, with variations for the different sorts of dried potatoes.
A pound of bread should cost about 1 real in places where wheat is grown.
Meat: 2 pesos for beef in areas where it is not raised, and 1 peso in cattle-raising areas. 1 peso for imported mutton, and 4 reales if it is home-raised. 6 reales and 4 reales respectively for kid. 2 pesos for capon.
Cattle: 4 pesos for a cow, 6 for a young bull and 2 for a calf.
Peruvian sheep: The kind called llamas, if in good condition, 3 pesos, or

* The peso de oro was linked to the value of gold and the real to the value of silver. These values were subject to change, as they are now, but the peso and real could be related by means of the basic Spanish monetary unit, the maravedí. One peso was worth approximately fourteen reales. It can be reckoned, as an approximate guide, that the peso was equivalent to about £4 in English money and one real to about 30p.

40 *Clerk at the receipt of custom*

1½ for the ewe. The kind called alpacas, 1½, and 1 for the ewe. Wool of high quality, 4 reales, and of poor quality 2 reales.

Horses: a good horse, carefully selected, is worth 20 pesos; and if it has a turn of speed it may be worth 50. An ill-favoured horse cannot be expected to fetch more than 12. A colt or a mare is properly valued at 8.

Poultry: Where they can be reared, the right price is 6 reales for hens and 2 for chickens.

Cheese: The best quality is valued at 1 peso for a large piece. Small cheeses cost 1 real each, and milk also 1 real a measure.

Chilli and salt: 4 reales a pound. One cabbage, two lettuces, four onions, two cloves of garlic, four radishes, coriander, parsley and edible grass are all worth 2 reales.

Wine and spirits: Old wine is worth 4 reales a measure in the plains where it was grown, but in the mountains its proper value is 8 reales. Cheap wine can be priced at 1 real and vinegar at $\frac{1}{2}$ a real. A jug of fermented maize is worth 8 reales in the plains and in the Collao, but anywhere in the mountains its value is only 4 reales.

A measure of coca will vary between 2 reales in the plains and 4 in the mountains.

Wood and grass: A large bundle of firewood is worth 1 real in summer and 2 reales in winter. Grass is worth 4 reales a bale in summer and 2 reales in winter.

If an Indian is hired, the proper rate is 2 reales for the day and 1 real for the night. While being used as a guide, he can claim a rate of 1 real a league and his food as well. But this troublesome habit of hiring guides is unknown in Castile and should not be practised here in Peru, since the law is in principle the same.

ANIMALS

The Indians fear the royal administrator because these people are like snakes, which devour them and their property. It is no use struggling, for the administrator is bound to succeed. And if he is a snake the proprietor of Indian labour is a lion which savages the poor and has no compassion on them. By comparison, the priest is a crafty fox that uses its intelligence to get itself trophies and females. The clerk is a cat on the prowl, lying in wait for the mouse. Once it has caught its prey it never lets it go and sets about destroying it.

Spaniards who travel about the country, going from inn to inn, are like tigers. Having no pity even for themselves they are worse than all the other animals.*

Indians of low rank, who have first become foremen over gangs of five or ten Indians and then advanced themselves to the status of chiefs, resemble mice gnawing away at the property of their fellow-creatures, but so gradually that their attentions are scarcely noticed. With their special mixture of pilfering and tax-collecting they bleed their victims little by little of money and food and even embezzle the community funds. The damage which they

---

* However extreme Huamán Poma's account of the misconduct of royal administrators, employers, priests and newly promoted chiefs may seem, it is no more so than the observations of two Viceroys, Garcia Hurtado de Mendoza and Luis de Velasco, on the same theme.

cause is disastrous by reason of the fact that they never cease from their activities either by day or by night.

Thus these six animals, the snake, lion, tiger, fox, cat and mouse, constantly devour the substance of our poor Indians, who can get no rest, being at the mercy of the marauders who help and favour each other at every turn.

SOME GOOD EXAMPLES

Among the good Christians whom I have known in Peru were the following:

Don Pedro de Córdoba y Guzmán of the Order of St James, Captain of Cavalry, was the principal landowner and employer of our Indians in Lucanas. Neither he nor his family visited the villages or sent stewards to them as a rule, but lived all the time in Lima. He left half the tribute due to him in the hands of the Indians. The administration was conducted for him by an Indian named Diego Chachapoya and no Spaniards were employed on the estate. Once, when complaints were made against his son Rodrigo, he sent the young man to Chile as a ship's Captain. He also opposed any exploitation by administrators, priests and others. He was charitable and never abusive, an honest man who did not engage in business himself or demand presents in the customary style. If any of the Indians ever brought him a gift, he returned it eightfold, for he was really sorry for their laborious life. It is a pleasure for me to record the good example which he set during his term of office.

The royal administrator of the province of Lucanas, Don Gregorio Lopez de Puga, was a genuinely learned man whose influence was always exerted on the side of justice. He liked to travel alone, not even taking a clerk with him, and to judge cases and disputes on his own. Often his judgements reflected a sympathy with the native rulers and a distaste for vagabonds. On one occasion he sentenced two Spaniards, who held important positions, saying that Your Majesty had sent him to do justice and not to condone robbery and inhumanity. Such a person, mature and considerate, deserves to remain a long time in office.

Father Diego Beltrán de Saravia, who was Visitor-General of the province of Andamarcas, Soras and Lucanas, lived close to his church in the provincial capital of Vilcabamba de Suntunto. He did so much in defence of the Indians that it is impossible to record it all in detail. After thirty-five years of service he still died as a poor man, having given most of his

41 *Clerk of the Council*

property away. He had only one servant and one mule to carry him on his journeys. In the church he employed crippled Indians out of kindliness. He did not collect pretty girls, as others do, but regularly taught the 6-year-old boys. His name was never associated with any scandal and he was hard on those whom he caught misbehaving. He was considerate and generous towards the Indian workers, with the result that they had no need to take to their heels. He would have made a good Bishop.

Juan García de la Vega, of the mercury mines of Huancavelica, was the half-caste son of Don Juan de la Vega, a loyal servant of Your Majesty who even lent money to the Exchequer on one occasion when it was short of funds.

The son never allowed Indian miners to be flogged or hung up by the feet, as the custom was. He also ensured that they got their proper pay and gave them food and drink in his own house, free of charge. He was a wealthy man but he attended to the workers himself rather than hand them over to stewards. Invariably he had words of encouragement for them when they were going to work and he was a stout defender of their rights.

When the Indians were being divided up into gangs for work at the royal depot, and when Juan García's name was called, everybody wanted to work for him and there was a rush in his direction, even though the overseers were pulling these Indians back by the hair. Dead or alive, they were determined to join his gang. When, by contrast, the names of other managers were called, they went to any length to avoid service.

Pedro Sanchez, a native of Valladolid in Spain, walked from inn to inn along the highways in spite of his great age. He was a humble and peaceful person, who always paid for his own keep in advance and referred to the Indians as sons of Adam.

I must also mention again to Your Majesty the loyal service of Huaman Mallqui, my distinguished father.

Lastly, San Juan Buenaventura showed the path which even a negro can follow if he is a saintly man.

In this book I have set down both the good and the evil of life in my country, so that the next Government may be correspondingly improved. My hope is that my work will be preserved in the archives of the Cathedral in Rome.

THE READERS OF THIS BOOK

I can assure the hierarchy of the Church that what I have written in this book about the administration of justice is not malicious, but intended for the improvement of bad Christians. If I had set down all the misdeeds of priests and other Spaniards, I would long since have run out of paper. Therefore I have spoken mainly in generalities, which apply to a number of cases. Every Visitor or important churchman ought to carry my book with him, so as to know how to punish the guilty. Vicars and priests ought to have it too, to make them confess the Indians, learn the native language and control their own tempers. With its help, even His Holiness will be in a better position to impose excommunication and restore order and decency in our country.

I, the author, Huaman Poma, declare that every Christian reader will be amazed and astounded to read the various chapters of my book and will ask himself who taught me and how I ever learned so much. So I say that it has cost me thirty years of work, if I am not mistaken, or at least twenty years of toil and poverty. Leaving my family, my house and property, I have mixed among the poor and learnt the various dialects which they speak. I have studied with the wise and unwise and served in the palaces of government. I have acted as interpreter to Viceroys, royal administrators and Bishops. I have spoken with indigent Spaniards as well as Indians and negroes. I have seen the Visitors of the Holy Church come and go and been present when our Indian lands were divided up.

I treated with people as a poor man and so was able to discover their misery or else their arrogance. When I write down what has happened to me, and the atrocities I have witnessed, it is sometimes a matter for tears, sometimes laughter and often pity. What I have seen was seen with my own eyes, for the astonishment of Your Majesty and others.

Some people will argue that my aim has been to discredit those in authority, but rather it has been to protect the Indians. Now, reading my own words, I myself am amazed at the lack of Christianity in this country. I begin to weep tears and to wonder how God can pardon such wrongs.

My readers should not be annoyed by my accusations, but reflect that I have found some honest officials and some kindly priests serving in parishes. Good people will take no offence. It is the evil ones who will be angry and want to kill me. But surely everyone can remember a brother who has loved him and been able to relieve him of his care and sadness. My book should be read, word by word, in the same way. Tears will come, but the good will be separated from the evil. Once the book is finished, it will be possible for people to talk freely with lords and prelates. Readers of my book will be honoured and respected by great and small. Even Your Majesty will always have it in mind.

THE THIRD PART
OF THIS CHRONICLE
There is no Remedy

NOBLES AND CHIEFS

The dynasty of the Incas in the legitimate line ended with Huascar Inca and the Crown passed to the Emperor Charles V and his successors on the Spanish throne.

The surviving children and grandchildren of the Inca Kings are the princes Melchor Carlos, Cristóbal Suna, Juan Ninancuro, Cari Topa, Alonso Atauchi and Francisco Hilaquita. Through my mother, who was one of the daughters of the tenth Inca King Tupac Yupanqui, my family and I also share in the Inca heritage.

The nobles of Higher and Lower Cuzco are distantly related to the former Inca Kings. There are also Incas born outside the capital and living as ordinary taxpayers in the various provinces.

Since the ruling dynasty has come to an end, the remaining princes have a right to be awarded salaries by the Spanish Crown, as well as to own property and employ labour, so that they can maintain their state.

The nobles of Cuzco deserve exemption from all taxation. But the so-called 'big ears' from the four provinces are just ordinary Indians and are therefore obliged to pay tribute like anybody else. Only the princes and rulers are entitled to exemption.

The ruling chief of a province is the administrator of the Indian population and its community funds. His responsibility is to Your Majesty or at least to the Royal Audience. As for his salary, it should amount to one-seventh of the total tribute paid by the Indians of his province. When he travels, a married couple should be assigned to him as servants in each of the royal inns. Meat, bread and wine should be provided. He should wear his clothes in the Spanish style, but his hair should not be cut shorter than the level of the ears. He should wear a vest, collar-band, shirt, cape and hat, be booted and carry a sword or halberd. By virtue of his rank he should have horses and mules at his disposal and be carried in a sedan chair. To avoid being mistaken for a half-caste he needs to shave off his beard. It is also advisable for him to avoid wine, spirits and coca and refuse to take part in gambling. His behaviour should be modelled on the Spanish patterns of eating and sleeping. He needs to have a proper table service to hold his own with the leading Spaniards. Of course he must be a good Christian and know how to read, write and count. To know Latin is an advantage to him and so is some slight legal knowledge. On no account should he allow his children to marry either Spaniards or ordinary Indians. They should mate with their equals and preserve the purity of their caste.

At the top of the feminine hierarchy are the Queens; then the princesses who are the daughters of princes of the royal blood. The daughters of the nobles of Higher and Lower Cuzco have a slightly less exalted rank. These ladies sit on a dais when receiving visitors and are accustomed to carpets and cushions. They wear cork-soled slippers and, as a sign of their rank, special kinds of blouse, skirt, head-dress and jewellery. Other distinguishing features are a scarf over the hair and a small brooch pinned against the shoulder. They usually call themselves by names such as Doña Juana or Doña Maria, but if when they are widowed they marry a Spaniard, or if they marry their daughters to Spaniards, they lose the right to any such appellation and to the special style of dress, for they have chosen to abandon their high caste and become members of a mixed race.

The hereditary aristocracy of our country, descended from its ancient rulers, is noted for being open-hearted, kind, modest and clever. The blood imposes a high degree of loyalty and service. By contrast, Indians of lowly origin can be recognised as such by their appearance, their conversation and their bearing in a court of law. For this class of Indian is dependent on the Spanish administrator and therefore easy to intimidate. It would take only one word from the administrator to deprive the person in question of his office, whatever it may be.

Out of every ten Indians, five are petty officials who are supported by the other five. And the officials are usually swindlers and liars, wasting our taxes on drink and drugs. They learn to play cards and throw dice like Spaniards. Half-castes and negroes join in the various games, which lead inevitably to drunkenness and manslaughter.

A trick which the chiefs often play is to prevent Indians from paying for Masses for members of their families who have died. They themselves appropriate the money and spend it on extravagances. One case in point concerned an Indian called Don Gonzalo Quispe Huarcaya, a citizen of Chupi in Lucanas. He promoted himself from ordinary taxpayer to chief and made a practice of taking over property for himself on an owner's death. At the same time he found good use for the widows and any single

(a) *Melchor Carlos Inca*

(b) *Small overseer*

(c) *Mama Poma*

(d) *Chief and wife*

42 *Indian Types*

girls. One of his mistresses happened to live 20 miles away in Hatun Lucanas and he often sent Indian girls all the way to her with jars of maize spirit. This is just a single example of the pointless labour which can be caused by a drunken upstart.

The present chiefs fail to inspire obedience or respect because they neither show breeding nor set a good example to others. Their word of honour cannot be trusted in a business arrangement. In their homes there is such a state of disorder that a table cannot be properly laid for visitors. Too often they are drunk and their conversation consists of lies and boasting. They are lazy, dishonest, greedy, envious and immoral. Worst of all, they inflict cruel punishments on their Indian brothers, who detest them in consequence. In the old days the Indian chiefs were prepared to die for their own people, who wept for them if they fell into adversity. Now that they are Christians, the chiefs have all the more reason to sacrifice themselves and love their neighbours, but this is not what happens. There may be some of these new masters who have done something for the poor people of our country, but I personally have never witnessed such a case.

From my experience I would say that an Indian chief needs to have a mixture of gall and honey in his veins, or needs to be a mixture of lion and lamb, if he is to rule successfully. He needs to be bold and docile by turn with the Spanish authorities, according to circumstances. And a mixture of these qualities is also useful in dealing with the Indians, who may be deceitful but may equally well be honest. It is true, not everyone is against the chief, but unless he keeps his wits about him he can easily find himself made into a laughing-stock. Everyone is out to deceive him and ill-treat the people for whom he is responsible. If he is slack or careless, he is likely to lose everything down to his very testicles. His Indians will flee into the mountains and Your Majesty will be highly displeased.

Chiefs need to be examined in their knowledge of Castilian and to have a good command of Quechua, which is the general language of the country. As well as knowing their alphabet and their figures, they should be in a position to issue orders, write petitions and conduct inquiries.

Unfortunately many of the chiefs are addicted to spirits, wine, coca and gambling. Every day they can be found intoxicated or even quite unconscious, neglecting all their duties. When they come to, they set about extorting enough money for another drinking-bout. They are prepared to lay their hands on all sorts of funds, whether private or public, in order to gratify their appetites. In their drunkenness they return to their ancestral beliefs and take up their old relationship with the demons. They want to have nothing to do with priests or Christians of any sort, except to rob them. If this were only from greed or from necessity it would not be so alarming, but they commit theft simply because they are drunk or under the influence of coca. They chew coca leaves as horses chew grass. They chew all through the day and night. Even when they are asleep they have wads of coca in their mouths. This is an offence and those who are guilty of it have no claim on the respect of their Indians.

Don Juan Capcha is an example of a very ordinary type of Indian, a drunkard and a liar who has always kept bad company, but he puts on the airs of an important chief in his village of Santa Maria Magdalena de Uruysa, which contains no more than a handful of taxpayers and four huts. There he still lords it over the women, who have no option but to sleep with him and work for him without payment, their men having fled from home. It is his habit to invite the neighbouring officials to dinner and regale them with roast kid belonging to the community, just to hear them all call him by his title. He is never sober, for a jar of wine and jug of spirits are always within his reach. The poor people of the village are terrified of his goat's beard and sacrifice all their money so that he can dress himself up in a lace collar, a cape and boots. He is the bastard son of another impostor named Capcha, a self-styled foreman who is really a highwayman and attacks and robs strangers on their way through our part of the country. With the tacit approval of the royal administrator, to whom he pays bribes, this rogue has recruited a band of criminals who have all either been in irons or had their ears cut off for various crimes in the past. Whenever the judges come round, these thieves are hidden away out of sight in a ravine.

The son, Juan Capcha, is a practising magician as well as a drunkard. He is conversant with all the rituals and in his cups gets into conversation with a demon whom he refers to as his bosom friend. He is for ever stirring up trouble with the priests and making accusations against them which are sometimes taken seriously. One priest for instance, who was called Father Antón Fernandez de Peralta, wrote to this drink-sodden impostor as if he was a great lord and begged him not to continue to give false evidence against him. Father Antón took no pains to investigate the character of this common fellow, but paid him greater honour than he did to Juan Capcha's superior, the Indian chief Don Felipe Huancarilla, no doubt because the latter chooses to dress in a modest manner.

The following is the text of a letter written to me by Juan Capcha about his case against the priest:

'To Don Felipe de Ayala, nobleman, at his residence.

'Sir, the priest is already aware of the substance of my complaints against him, which have been duly signed by the other chiefs. They were put in the hands of Don Pedro Usco de Songochi for despatch to Cuzco, but as this chief was intoxicated at the time they were not sent off. Father Peralta is very unhappy and asks for my forgiveness. But I shall ensure the despatch of the documents either today or tomorrow, because this priest is a rude and turbulent fellow. I need say no more.

'Today, Wednesday, at Uruysa, Your Grace's servant, Don Juan Capcha, principal chief and ruler of Uruysa.'

It is an undoubted fact that our Indians, both great and humble, come together in their villages on holy days such as Corpus Christi, Maundy Thursday, Easter Sunday, Christmas Day and St John's Day. But their real object is to get drunk and under cover of Christian piety to celebrate the old Inca customs. These include piercing of the ears, putting-on of various garments and brooches, mourning for the dead by means of official mourners, ritual placing of infants in the cradle, symbolic washing, putting turbans on boys' heads, shouting at people in agony to prevent them from dying, calling on the dead to arise, celebrating deaths five days afterwards at the confluence of rivers, worship of gold, attendance at childbirths and adoration of the lightning.

Our people succeed in joining these ceremonies on to the Christian ones, even at a time when they are going punctually to Mass. Afterwards they sally forth into the square to enjoy themselves. Far from correcting them, the priests invite these Indians into the courtyards of their houses to give displays of singing and dancing, whereupon they all get drunk together. Anybody who objects to these proceedings is liable to be thrown out of the village so as to avoid any witnesses of the priests' orgies with Indians, which always follow.

It is essential to ration the consumption of spirits by our Indians on holy days and other special occasions. They should never exceed two glasses at breakfast, two at lunch and two at dinner. Then they will be able to dance without falling senseless to the ground and enjoy themselves without sexual licence.

A knowledge of the Castilian language ought to be regarded as part of the education of our Indians. They should be taught to read and write like Spaniards. An illiterate person is no better than a horse and hardly even Christian. But our Indians can improve with the knowledge of letters. They are by nature charitable, humble and patient. With some education they can learn the mastery of a number of professions and arts and thus become better servants of Your Majesty.

Our Indians have a clear right to perform their traditional dances and songs, such as the song of victory, the song of the masks, the shepherds' song, the war song, the song of the Grand Chimú, the dazzling and gay songs, the song of women led astray, the songs of shepherds and farmers, the song in praise of the creator, the triumphal song of harvest-time, the songs to the sound of fife or flute and the song which is sung whilst walking to and fro. Whatever was once performed in honour of the Inca deities, at the command of their heathen priests, can now be properly offered to the Christian God. But there should be no regression to false beliefs and idolatries.

It is only proper that everybody should be dressed according to his or her station in life, so as to be easily recognised and greeted. Indian chiefs who wear beards resemble boiled prawns and are indistinguishable from half-castes. They would do better to retain their natural style. The Spaniards, on the other hand, look like aging prostitutes in fancy dress when they discard their beards. They are used to taking care of the hair on their faces. If they were to wear it like the Indians they would look like wild animals. A Spaniard who dresses in the Spanish manner, wears a beard and keeps his hair cut short is making the best of himself.

It is the man who determines caste in marriage. A woman, even if she is able to call herself Doña Francisca or Doña Juana, takes the caste of any husband who is beneath her in rank. Her title of Doña, which is derived from the Emperor himself, is thereby cast into the river, carried away, drowned and lost in the sea, and it may never come back again. If she dies, she dies for ever and sinks in the sea without any trace. Her close relations, such as her father and mother, are as much responsible as she is. From that moment she is unable to use her title, even if she is Spanish by blood, because the honour which she possessed has become virtually irrecoverable. Not only she, but all who come after her, will be disappointed. She and her children and still more her grandchildren will have come down very low in the world.

It is important that the Indian chiefs, their wives and their children should enjoy respect. In church they can be placed a little apart, where they are to be seen handling their rosaries and turning the pages of their prayer-books. The ordinary worshippers can be grouped together, so that the two lots of Indians can be distinguished from one another by the authorities. But the chiefs' wives, sitting in the raised part of the church, may like to have some visiting ladies or even servants around them and they should not be prevented from this, since it enables them to instruct others in their own more admirable way of life.

It is customary for the chiefs to make presents to the leading Spanish officials. The poorer Indians are obliged to contribute their share of these gifts, just as if they were themselves part of the chiefs' property. Of course, the beneficiaries imagine that the chiefs have paid for them and never realise that their thanks are due to the ordinary people. They talk in a fatuous manner about 'how kind it is of Don Juan or Don Francisco', and do not think for a moment of the Indians who have actually provided their pleasure. The situation is all the worse because some of the chiefs spend only a real or two on a present for the authorities, but collect 20 or 30 pesos from the Indians for this purpose, or else simply embezzle the money from the community funds. The royal administrators, on their side, are liable to demand money if they do not get generous gifts of chicken, capon and mutton.

JUSTICE TO INDIANS

I shall now try to describe the various sorts of mayors, magistrates, constables, town criers, executioners and others concerned with the administration of justice.

The mayors and local justices are chosen from among the farmers and are exempt from forced labour. The best of them come from the class of overseers of 500 Indians. It is an advantage if they are also capable, well-educated people, free of vices and with the proper Christian principles. Indians chosen in this manner are preferable to Spaniards, being prepared to carry out their duties without bribes, presents and privileges. They assist the royal administrator as well as the chiefs of their own race.

They are elected or nominated by the municipal council, which meets for this purpose every year. It would be a useful reform if Your Majesty made the appointment for a whole lifetime. But in any case the number of such officials in any one province ought to be controlled by the Indian chief. They should never be appointed by the administrator, because in such cases there is a tendency for them to be used as mere agents and negotiators and to be deprived of the wand of justice which is the essence of their office.

The mayor's duties include keeping an account of expenses incurred and damages caused by the authorities, collecting taxes from the Indians, sending off labour gangs to the mines and elsewhere, watching over the interests of the local Indian chief and acting as custodian of the community and church funds. At the beginning of each year he is obliged to prepare a signed record of his stewardship, itemised by days and months, and present it to the court at the moment when the new mayor takes over. This record can be consulted during any subsequent proceedings or visits by higher authorities.

The lesser officials of the municipality are paid at the rate of one chicken for every house which they visit in the course of their duties. They go constantly from town to town and village to village, calling on the married, the unmarried and the widowed and inspecting the stores of foodstuffs kept

CONZEDERACION
COMOLEMALTRATA

miento dellos corregdes y P̃ es
los yn̄s yn̄s pobres esta
ensu tierra sinconcidera
cion dello y no temea dios
niala justisia desumag̃d

espanoles deste reyno a

soberbia   como

43 *Beating of Indians*

in barrels and underground cellars, which are often sealed with clay. These foodstuffs usually consist of dried sugar-cane, dried vegetables, grasses, edible flowers, chillies and salt. People also store little cakes of ash for chewing with coca, plants for use as dyestuffs and three varieties of water-eggs. They keep their possessions in all sorts of jars, pitchers and casks in order to avoid running short of something important. This might equally well be firewood, straw, water for washing, corn-husks, rope or clothing. It is usual to keep about ten laying hens and ten rabbits about the house.

Supervision is needed to ensure that the Indian families keep themselves and their possessions clean. Each house ought to have its own larder, an enclosure for animals, a kitchen garden and a place for the members of the family to pray.

Although the mayors and lesser officials are a part of Your Majesty's judicial establishment, they themselves are often victimised for trifling offences by administrators, landowners, priests and even ordinary Spanish travellers. They find themselves accused of stealing two eggs or failing to provide firewood or fodder for horses, and punished outrageously. Abuses of justice occur because of the arrogance and immunity from arrest of such people and it is no wonder if many of the Indians come to the end of their patience as a result.

The truth is that some officials are great rogues, who have an eye on the main chance. Their distinguishing sign is a pendulous belly, so that they resemble ugly great horses. Both body and face are distended by their indulgences. They roam around the villages by day and night, going from house to house in search of strong drink and women. It follows that they cease to lead a decent life with their own wives and become incapable of dispensing justice properly, since their reason is always disturbed. Once they are deprived of office it is seen that they soon lose their bulk and become as thin as rakes, and they look as if they had a year's illness behind them. The lesson to be drawn is that care should be taken to prevent the election of such officials, if justice is ever to be done.

It would be a good thing to destroy by fire all the buildings that have been erected on the high table-land and in the ravines, because these places are used for idolatry and the worship of demons. Instead, chapels should be set up with a good path leading to them and several houses nearby, forming a small village with its own farms, orchards and livestock. All these villages ought to come under the jurisdiction of the nearest city, which might have as many as four of them to look after. This is a system which apparently works well in Castile, but the villages need to produce large quantities of mutton, chicken, duck, rabbit, figs, peaches, apples and pears. An industrious labour force is necessary and any drunkard or waster should be expelled immediately.

The Spanish authorities ought to be kept from meddling in these communities, because they only want to snatch the profits. By the same token the Visitors of the Church should help and not hinder village life.

Even the less important Indian officials ought in future to be empowered to arrest Spaniards who are manifestly guilty of insolence and arrogance, give evidence against them and see that they are dealt with. After all, the greatest and most beautiful of the angels was justly punished by God for excessive pride, and it is only right that the Spaniards should be subject to the same treatment and taught some humility.

All officials, on quitting their posts at the end of their term, ought to come before the courts and be forced to make restitution for any injustices committed by them, or else acquitted if their conduct has been blameless.

A watch needs to be kept on church and municipal buildings, as well as ordinary houses, to ensure that the roofing is in good order. Vandalism and arson need to be punished severely. All dwellings, squares and churches ought to be kept clean.

Constables should be active in enforcing the law, but never exceed their powers. Their duty is to go in pairs and visit the farms twice a year, at the times of ploughing and sowing. They need to see that the ground is manured and kept clear of weeds; carry out levelling operations; have the paths cleared; and attend to the irrigation of all the maize, potatoes, other edible roots, beans, chick-peas and various sorts of fruit. They should be no respecters of persons, however elevated, in their efforts to assure supplies of food for everybody throughout the year. The provision of clean water is in their particular charge.

Their remuneration should be at the rate of a measure of grain or potatoes for a certain acreage of land, payable by all concerned including the local chief. But they themselves have an obligation to join in the work on the land and spread manure without extra pay; and at the same time keep an eye on the other Indians and tinkle a small bell in the Inca style as a reminder to the lazy.

The executioners and those responsible for floggings can get their payment from the recipients of their attentions, but no Christian person ought to be made to disgorge more than the smallest coin, called a maravedí. It is from the ranks of the executioners and also the town criers that people are chosen to tend the former royal gardens, which used to be sacred to the deity of lightning. All kinds of herb, vegetable and fruit are grown there, and also carnations and similar red flowers, which are sold to those able to afford them.

Stewards who have the custody of church or community funds should in general only claim a fixed sum, or food or livestock to the same value. If such a standard could be kept, thefts of grain and wool would come to an end. A dishonest or inefficient steward ought to be dismissed from his job, but a faithful and capable one should be retained for his lifetime.

There needs to be some control over the appointment of stewards. It should not be at the whim of judges and dignitaries of the Church, but an administrative choice based upon the candidates' ability to make a success of the job. If the candidates are drunkards, drug-addicts or gamblers, it is obvious that they are going to waste on their private celebrations all the funds entrusted to them for lay or clerical purposes. The whole lot will be spent on drink or on the payment of their own taxes. Such people have no intention of acting as honest stewards and they simply dissipate everything which comes into their hands.

Thus a considerable responsibility rests upon the Indian administrator, who may well be the hereditary chief, holding office immediately under the Spanish administrator. He is likely to have a special responsibility for the inns along the highways, where all the food and wine will be in his care.

The person who holds this office in Lucanas, Soras, Andamarca and Circamarca is myself, in my capacity of protector of the Indians and deputy to the royal administrator. Others are installed in similar positions in the different provinces of our country. They are obliged to visit all the people under their jurisdiction and select the ones destined for public works, labour in the mines, repair of the bridges or the messenger service along the highways. It is also their responsibility to register deaths, marriages and liability to taxation, as well as absence due to illness. To help them in this task, it is the priests' duty to supply them with signed statements of the names of everyone whom they baptise, marry or bury in the course of the year, complete with the exact dates of these ceremonies.

Once any place in the country reaches the standing of a town with its own mayor and municipal council, it ought to be linked with other towns by runners, whose salaries should compare with the mayor's. By this means a postal system can be established which resembles the one which existed in the time of the Incas. At the same time ordinary people, including even paupers and half-castes, will be able to send off letters, correspond on business matters or forward legal documents. Any such communication, once it is entrusted to the runner, will be safely carried to any part of the country. If any loss or theft should occur, the culprit should be punished by the death penalty. This extreme measure is justified by the consideration that the post is rightly regarded as sacred in every part of the world where it has been introduced: in China, Mexico, India, Portugal and also other parts of this Continent.

The clerk of the municipal council is an official to whom the community pays a salary of 12 pesos, as well as 12 measures of food and 12 sheep every year. In the provinces a senior clerk is always stationed in the same centre as the Indian chief who acts as administrator; but there are junior clerks, who pay no taxes and are free from all other duties, in every inhabited place however small. This is essential because their records and depositions form the basis of any review or decision made by higher authority.

These clerks ought not to live in constant fear of the royal administrator and visiting officials. They should have full discretion to assess and receive the taxes on silver, clothing, cereals and livestock.

Full records should be kept of the details of all farms: how big they are, whether they belong to private persons or the community, where they are located, how they came into the hands of the present owner, who the incumbent is and how old he is, and what trees, animals and crops the land supports. It is important that records should be kept of all the springs, waterways, wells and ponds, with details of the properties irrigated by them and the priority of claims on the water. Enough clarity should be aimed at to allow the Indians to fix their boundaries without any chance of error and also enable them to give away their estates as dowries or in their wills, or sell them to other Indians. Spaniards and half-castes should not be allowed to intervene in any such arrangements. All sales of land ought to be conducted according to the principle that our Indians have a legitimate and preferential physical right to the country in which God settled them in the first place.

Indians should be allowed to draw up their wills without any witnesses. They should be guided by their own conscience and leave their property to whomsoever they wish, without interference from outside. But there is an obligation on them to declare the names of all their children, including illegitimate ones, with their sex and age. If he wishes, the testator can divide his property between all these children. As a rule, during his lifetime any legitimate son is unlikely to bring him so much as a jug of water and may even attack him on occasion, whereas a bastard will serve him like a negro slave and comply with every order. Whatever the father decides, his will should not be opposed and should be executed as it stands. It should bear the confirming signature of the Indian chief, whose duty it is to have its details copied by the clerk into a special book. The original should then be returned to its owner, but the copy will serve as a safeguard that all the provisions are carried out.

All judges, whether lay or ecclesiastical, are obliged to receive petitions and inquiries in either spoken or written form. These can be in the Indians' own language and, if written, may take up only one line of space. In each case the answer should be written below and the document returned to the petitioner as a demonstration that justice has been done. Those who are involved in the administration of the law should try to dissuade petitioners from oral statement and get them to express themselves in writing if possible. But the text of the petition should never be altered by a literate clerk, and the true meaning concealed by this means. It should be accepted in the form in which it is received, otherwise serious grievances can arise.

If petitions were not allowed, it would be impossible for our Indians to get their due and the authorities would be inadequately informed. That is why the Viceroy Don Luis de Velasco imposed a fine of 100 pesos on any royal administrator refusing to accept a petition and gave orders that justice was to be done in each separate case brought forward by an Indian.

It is right and proper that the figure of justice should be represented as blindfolded, holding a pair of scales and in her right hand a sword with a cutting edge. Justice should never look to see whether the suppliant is rich or poor, but should weigh the evidence with impartiality. The judge himself cannot be a witness, but must listen to the testimony of those who were on the scene of a crime. All witnesses need to swear on some sacred emblem, and if they tell a lie upon oath they are committing perjury. A judge who has any suspicion that this is the case cannot pass sentence. On the contrary, he is bound to look for some further clarification which will lead to the truth. He must always show favour and charity towards the accused and ensure that there is a competent lawyer to conduct the defence; and he must insist that the prosecution is based upon factual evidence.

The love for religion and justice, together with respect for Your Majesty and charity towards the poor, needs to be stimulated in every Christian. The priests in particular are under an obligation to love and assist the wretched, as part of God's work in the world. Poor people are like miserable sheep, which would otherwise be devoured by foxes and serpents. A good example in the way of service to the poor was set by my father, who in spite of his high rank worked for thirty years in the hospitals of Cuzco and Huamanga, and by my mother with her direct descent from the Inca dynasty. They both of them preferred to die in God's service rather than lead selfish lives. My father was no Spaniard, but an Indian like other Indians, and my mother was an Indian and no lady from Castile. But theirs is the path which the humble people of our country ought to follow.

A POOR GENTLEMAN

Now let me say something about my vocation as an author. There is some merit in writing books, even if they are mainly based upon legends, as long as their object is to improve the conditions of life as well as entertaining the readers. Therefore authors, such as myself, should be entitled to call themselves Doctors just as much as Doctors of Medicine or Law.

The fact is that there is little justice in the life which we lead nowadays. The usual motives for conduct are self-interest, interference in other people's affairs, disloyalty and aggression. If some citizen were to start an insurrection against the Crown, and if the city in question were to remain faithful to Your Majesty and defend itself against the rebel, this would be a mark of eternal honour for the city. But this is seldom the case. The general rule in our times is one of fraud and violence and a great deal of infamy would need to be removed or buried deep in the earth in order to avoid occurrences like the one I am about to relate. This is the case of a poor gentleman who was martyred in spite of being a Christian and no infidel. His name was Don García de Solís Portocarrero: a Knight of Santiago, royal administrator and judge of the town of Huamanga and the mines of Huancavelica. He was arrested on Your Majesty's warrant at the hour of vespers in the square of the parish of Santa Ana, just as he was descending alone and unarmed from the hill where the mines of Huancavelica are situated. His house was searched but nothing incriminating was found. Then he was surrounded by soldiers, taken to Huamanga and handed over to some enemies whom he had made in that town. He was held under close guard in the public prison, as if he had been a poor wretch who had got himself into trouble.

For two months he was kept locked up in the jail without receiving any privilege or even kindness, for everybody was against him. There was not even anyone willing to bring him a jug of water or a crust of bread except for a local lady called Doña Inez de Villalobos who was afterwards arrested for her acts of charity. A judge who was known for his hostility to the unfortunate gentleman was brought all the way from Lima, the City of Kings. When Don García was told about the arrival of this emissary from the capital he realised that his very life was at stake. In due course false evidence was laid against him by three of his former servants, who were named Peralta, Orejón and Urbina. These three had robbed a shop in order to have enough money to gamble with, and for this offence had been punished by Don García. Now, in order to revenge themselves, they stated on oath that their master had been planning an insurrection against the Crown. They also took pains to spread this accusation far and wide amongst all those who had any grievance against Don García. This was the same method of slander which had been used against Melchor Inca, who was shipped off to Spain, and Alonso Gutierrez Hovero, who was garrotted and his body quartered.

Don García was found guilty and sentenced. He was able to face death with tranquillity because he knew himself to be a loyal subject and his conscience was clear. He was dressed in the manner of an ordinary male-factor and lashed on the back of a mule.

A scaffold, entirely covered in black, had been erected in the public square. Don García made his confession and then placed himself in all humility in the hands of the executioner, who decapitated him.* His severed head was displayed in the square with a placard written by the negro executioner and a half-caste, which repeated the slanders of the accusation against him. This sign was a disgrace and dishonour to the town in which it was displayed. Later, the false witnesses were unmasked and punished and that was the end of the affair.

ORDINARY CHRISTIAN INDIANS

The Indians in our country are just as gifted as Castilians in their artistry and workmanship. Some of them are excellent singers and musicians. They make themselves masters of the organ, fiddle, flute, clarinet, trumpet and horn without any difficulty. They also become capable municipal clerks. It is quite usual for them to deputise for royal administrators and mayors and they sometimes perform the duties of constables and accountants. They can use a gun, a sword or a halberd as well as any Spaniard. Often they are first-rate horsemen and trainers of animals, with a special aptitude with bulls. Some of them know Latin and study literature. If they were allowed to, they could perfectly well be ordained as priests. Above all they are loyal and admirable servants of the Crown, with no taste for rebellion.

Indians are skilful at all the decorative arts such as painting, engraving, carving, gilding, metalwork and embroidery. They make good tailors, cobblers, carpenters, masons and potters. Also, by simply watching the Spaniards, they have learnt how to do well in trade.

In the same way the Indian girls learn reading, writing, music and needle-work at the convents which they attend. They are just as clever and accomplished as Spanish girls at the domestic skills.

The clever ones among the Indians get themselves jobs with the Church, either as singers or clerks. Because of the incompetence or absence of the priests they soon find themselves burying the dead with all the proper prayers and responses. They take vespers and look after the music and singing, as well as intoning the prayers. On Sundays and holy days they

* *The execution was in 1601.*

44 *Feeding the poor*

conduct the ceremonies as well as any Spaniard. In default of a priest they baptise the babies with holy water, reciting the proper form of words, and this is allowed by the authorities in order to avoid any of the small creatures going to limbo for lack of baptism. On Wednesdays and Fridays Indians conduct the early morning service, these being the obligatory days, and they say the prayers for the dead. However, they get nothing but interference from the priests themselves, who usually refer to them dismissively as 'clever children'.

The Indian barber-surgeons have a considerable knowledge of bleeding, the cure of illnesses and the healing of wounds. Mostly they make use of herbs and purges, but they also have a theory of medicine as other doctors have. They believe that all sickness proceeds from one of two causes, namely either from heat or cold. There are also good women with some medical knowledge, who mostly assist at confinements but are proficient in dealing with ailments such as stomach troubles and dislocations. The authorities make difficulties for such people and even the Indians regard them simply as magicians. But it is right that they should be allowed to continue practising, because they contribute a great deal to the well-being of the poor. To take one example, they know the proper treatment for workers affected by mercury vapours. They know, too, that tobacco acts as a poison to the feverish, but is excellent if taken in small quantities as a remedy against cold. Too much of it is liable to upset the stomach, so it is best to sniff it up the nostrils in the form of snuff. With a doctor's advice, a man's life can be preserved to a great old age. I will write no more on this subject of medicine, since I have told all that I know.

It is the duty of the shepherds and herdsmen to watch over the community's livestock. In early times these *llamamiches*, as they are called, guarded the Inca's herds and they had the secondary occupation of making ropes, blankets and slippers out of the animals' hides. Twice a year they were obliged to hand over 100 boxes of dried and preserved meat taken from different parts of the carcass, such as the leg, shoulder, loin, ribs, liver and offal, which was used to make little sausages and other delicacies. Any of the Peruvian sheep could be used, but the *llullucha*, which has unusually tender flesh, was favoured. The shepherds also treated and preserved the meat of the sacred bird of the Incas, which lived among the lakes on the high table-land. It was yet another part of their duties to collect firewood and animal foodstuffs, which were added to the community stores, and to fashion various implements such as bobbins, spindles, ladles and spikes. A report was required from them of any foxes or wild cats which they destroyed. In this manner the shepherds kept count of everything, to the advantage of common people.

But nowadays the system no longer operates. Indeed, matters have gone to the opposite extreme and although the shepherds have plenty of meat they refuse to part with it in the cause of charity. They act the part of bandits, rather, and try to kill innocent travellers and merchants passing through their countryside. I know this for certain because I saw some Aymará Indians assaulting a Spaniard named Correa; and at a place called Urupampa, near Apcara, the shepherds assaulted an Indian and when he tried to defend himself they knocked him unconscious, tied him up and took all that he and his wife possessed. I myself was attacked on the road at Otoca above Concepción and robbed of 500 pesos and the suit of clothes I was wearing. One of the thieves was the self-styled chief from the village of Uruysa, Juan Capcha.

Usually the Indians are incapable of such armed assaults unless they are put up to it by somebody. I should recall that Juan Capcha kept his own place of worship and his demons on the heights above Otoca. To prevent me from discovering this, he and his gang made their attack on me. They wanted to go on worshipping at their shrines and making love to their women. And of course, like other shepherds, they dressed themselves in the clothes which they stole from travellers.

Many of the shepherds bury or hide away the money which they make by selling their animals. Meanwhile they are content to go about in rags and feed off rotten maize. I came upon an example of this behaviour when I visited a certain Juan Yuto of Hatun Lucana, who owned 500 beasts. On my arrival I told him for the love of God to let me have a handful of corn. He did not want to give me any, however, and I finished up by having to buy a full measure for 4 reales. Apparently this was how he treated anybody who came his way.

The coca-growing Indians who live along the entire length of the Andes have a reputation for ill-treating those who are unfortunate enough to work for them. What they save by underpaying their labour, these mountain Indians spend on bribes and presents to the Spanish authorities, for they are undisciplined and dishonest. The *huarco*, which is the measure in which coca is sold, is priced at 2 reales where it is grown, but 4 reales in the mountains. This higher price ought to be reflected in the wages and meals provided.

Another category of Indians consists of the old, blind and crippled ones who have no other means of livelihood. They are entitled to a licence to beg in public on Sundays and holy days, and also to go from house to house on other days. Those who are unable to walk have to depend on charitable visits from their neighbours or on collections taken for this purpose on Sundays. However, it is only right to utter a warning that some of these cripples own a great deal of property in the form of flocks of sheep, farms and precious metals. They nevertheless prefer to play the lucrative role of paupers.

Among our Indians from the earliest times until the present there has been a tradition of mutual assistance involving both rich and poor. This has extended to sowing of seed, watering, making dams, growing coca, weeding, preparing the ground and other agricultural tasks. No other race of people has developed such compassionate customs, which favour the old and infirm and regard work for the community as a means of earning the food necessary for life. Our Indian pattern of hospitality involves the giving of food and drink to workers at midday, more in the afternoon and a last meal and drink at night. This custom is called the *minga*.

It needs to be explained that the Indians of our country are divided into three main groups, the Yuncas, the Indians of the Andes and those who live in the forests of the Amazon. Each of these groups has its own attitude of mind, its own style of dress and its own way of expression. Their food, ceremonies, dances, songs and music also vary from one group to another. There is a marked difference between them in appearance and bearing. The

Chunchos of the forests are as white-skinned as the Spaniards. The Aymará and Canari Indians have pale skins as well as gentle natures. But the Yunca, Quechua, Cunti, Colla and Charca people are swarthy as well as tall. The inhabitants of Quito and its vicinity are dark-skinned as a rule. They are ugly in physique, thick-set and untamed in the same way as the negroes of Guinea.

The Indians living at the ends of the mountain range of the Andes, whether in the extreme north or the south of our country, hold on to their old religion even when they have been baptised as Christians. They have retained all their old ceremonies, as I have been able to confirm. I have spent a great deal of time in those distant places and suffered from hunger, thirst, cold and illness in order to collect my information.

These people bury their dead in vaults and their churches have long since fallen into disrepair. They never pray on Sundays and indeed they are quite unaware on any day whether it is Wednesday or Thursday. I was told by a local painter and sculptor that no images of the saints were ever ordered from him, even though he offered to provide them free. The people would never agree to this and there were no Christian images to be seen in their houses. They still worshipped their old idols, fasted in the ancient style and carried on drinking bouts among themselves.

In contrast, the Indians of the Collao and the inhabitants of the whole central part of the mountain range are for the most part good Christians, as I have witnessed. It is only in certain areas of the Cordillera that I have come upon a lack of faith and charity.

Some Indians are properly employed as hunters, going in search of pigeons, partridge and other fowl. They mostly use falcons and they train dogs to retrieve their game for them. Others go after the mountain sheep called *vicuña* and *huanaco*, which are rounded up by mongrel dogs of the sort developed by the Incas. The hunters need lassoes for animals like deer, sheep and rabbits, snares for catching small birds and nets for fish and prawns. All this equipment needs to be provided, so that they are able to earn their living.

At seed-time the Indians have to attend to their duties on the farms, because by daylight the birds are already at their destructive work, eating up the seed. It is essential that sources of food should be guarded and preserved.

Breaking the virgin soil has to be done at the proper time, since later it becomes impossible. Similarly, sowing and ploughing have their special seasons. If the seed is not sown on the right day of the right month it may be lost. Then, from that time until the crop ripens, vigilance is required whether it consists of maize, potatoes or fruit; and the same vigilance is needed with animals.

Big and little dogs are both needed by the Indians, but the little ones are better for guarding houses and farms. They have a louder bark and they set up a continuous din which frightens away the thieves who circulate at night. The worst of these thieves are runaway negroes, but their number includes Spaniards and Indians. Guard-dogs are therefore necessary in the cities as well as the country. The killing of a dog ought accordingly to be made illegal and the offender fined. At least, a substantial reason for such an act needs to exist and to be explained to the owner of the dog. The tendency is for dogs to be killed for the merest trifles.

In every village in this country there are watercourses, constructed in ancient times, into which the water is diverted from rivers, lakes or ponds. So much labour was involved that if it had to be paid for nowadays the sum involved would amount to 10,000 or even 20,000 pesos. These works date back to the time before the Incas, when there was a large population under a single King. Not only watercourses were constructed but also terraces for the planting of crops on the hillsides. These were built up laboriously by hand, without tools, by Indians who each placed a single stone at a time to make long heaps. The number of workers was so vast that these projects were rapidly completed. Thus the terrain was made to bear cereals to feed the people, even in the sandy coastal plains and the rugged scenery of the Andes. Bridges and aqueducts were built and the marshes drained by order of these early Kings.

Then came the Incas, who ordained that existing custom and law should be preserved. There was to be no interference with the irrigation of the orchards and pastures which reached as far as the mountain peaks and gorges. They knew that these works, constructed by so great a labour force, could never in all probability be repeated. So the penalties which they prescribed for those removing stones or damaging the watercourses by incursions of their animals were not subject to any appeal and were stringently enforced. In later times the Viceroy Don Francisco de Toledo admired these laws and Your Majesty approved and confirmed them, since the failure to do so would have resulted in loss of cultivation, destruction of property and incapacity to pay the royal fifth and the tithe demanded by the Church. Despite all this, the Spaniards of today are in the habit of turning loose their cattle, mules, goats and sheep. Damage is done to the watercourses which no money can retrieve or repair and what little water is left the Spaniards keep for themselves and deny to the Indians.

Certain boundaries were fixed by the last Inca rulers to separate the territory of the mountain Indians from the lands belonging to the Indians of the coastal plains. This was important from the point of view of determining their respective obligations, which are now owed to the Spanish Crown. The boundary marks fixed by the authorities of that time still exist

45 Bird-scaring

46 Lazy couple in bed

and they lie partly in the foothills and partly in the flat country. Thus in some cases the mountain people have access to fruit and coca plantations. The people from the border valleys are under an obligation to go and work as miners in the mountains, but in practice they remain free by claiming that they are unable to report for duty. There is some truth in the claim for they often die from the change in climate, if they go.

Whether a person works in the mines or in an office, as a schoolmaster or in service, the compulsory working day consists of eight hours. This needs to be invariable for men and women and ought not to be affected by whether the rate of payment is high or low.

At present our Indians are overloaded and oppressed, being obliged to pay excessive taxes, which may amount in one year to more than 100 pesos or virtually all they earn, so that they have nothing left to spend. They are constantly forced to work for nothing, run errands or carry heavy loads, and seldom have any chance to rest. The women are kept busy twisting thread and making clothes, or preparing meals in the inns for any Spanish official who comes along. Meanwhile their daughters are similarly occupied with clothing, curtains and bedspreads and their sons are working for private employers in the fields. Their work does not benefit the community. They just waste their lives in poverty and misery for the benefit of the Spaniards. Among the causes of their distress is the corruption of their morals. Indian women often arrange for their husbands to leave home with another woman, because they themselves are pregnant by or interested in someone else. They even prepare dried meat for the departing couple to take with them. Also, when their husbands are away looking for jobs to earn enough money to pay their taxes, the women soon become transformed into whores. It usually happens that the royal administrator or some other official comes along to take advantage of the husband's absence, using force if necessary. More likely than not, the Spaniard is drunk on these occasions. Then, after such an initiation, it is the women who go off to the inns in search of Spanish lovers, or even half-castes. When the husband returns, he is admitted to his own house at midnight and hands over the money due in tax and the drugs and spirits which he has brought with him. The couple get drunk together and then the husband goes on his way without any of the local authorities, or even his own mother, knowing about his visit. The money which is handed over is then spent on the wife's love affairs. When the Indian chief comes to demand the payment of tax, the wife refers him to her husband and says it should be collected from him. If the chief looks like investigating the matter, the wife pretends to borrow the money and gives it to him. Although she may say it is a loan, it is really the money which her husband has handed over. These women are the ones who cause Spanish travellers to stay four or even ten days at a time in the inns, so as to have ample time to make love to them, and in the intervals the Spaniards demand servants and presents from the local population.

Some Indian men, as I know from my own experience, feel a sort of pure shame at the way in which their wives behave like whores and have children by other men, and they leave their villages never to return. Otherwise they would have to kill the women or become their accomplices.

It is impossible to accept some Indian women as witnesses in any sort of legal proceedings, for the reason that they are lazy, deceitful trollops, seditious and hostile to men. They easily resort to tears and think nothing of giving false evidence. The poor wretches are simply and solely an object of charity. They are incapable of supporting punishment or imprisonment, and if it is necessary to put them under restraint they should be entrusted to the care of some lady of consequence. If ever they are convicted and condemned in court, the sentence should be read over privately to them and then set aside. The just punishment inflicted on Eve, the first woman, is quite sufficient in their case.

Creoles are the children born of unions between our native Indians and Spanish settlers. They are capable of turning into good Christians and obedient citizens. If they work hard they can even become rich and well esteemed in the community. Unfortunately, many of them are simply hangers-on of the Spaniards, always ready to commit some act of treachery with the aid of a knife or dagger, a noose for strangling, or a stone. These weapons are often turned upon each other when they are drunk, with fatal results. Picking a pocket is more in their line than herding cattle. They take pains with their appearance and go about in the manner of gipsies in Spain. Looking for new adventures, they are always moving on to the next place.

Drunkenness transforms for the worse even the best-educated and most Christian Indians with their rosaries and Spanish clothes. If only they could hold their celebrations without getting drunk and taking drugs, there would be nothing to say against their dances and traditional songs. But I have to admit, because I have seen them with my own eyes, that in their cups they are capable of committing incest with their own sisters and mothers. The women themselves look round for a man and hardly care if it is their own brother or father. For this reason drunkenness was strictly forbidden by the Inca and the drunkard was treated like a brawler, lecher or traitor, who deserved to die. As a rule he was killed like an animal.

Among the worst drinkers are the Indians of the plains, who stab or strangle one another to death. They consume quantities of new wine, followed up by maize spirit and vinegar. Their addiction to spirits is such that they die without confessing, like animals. They often forget to make a will, but there is nothing to leave to their heirs since they are invariably in debt.

No effective punishment has been discovered by the Spaniards for this weakness in the Indian character. The Viceroy Francisco de Toledo tried to put an end to drunkenness without any success. The Marquess of Cañete gave orders that all implements and jars required for the making of maize spirit should be destroyed, but even this had no useful result.

Our Indians have adopted another custom which is contrary to Christian behaviour and was unknown in the time of the Incas. Parents allow their daughters to go out with boys every night, giving some such excuse as collecting firewood or looking for manure, when in reality they are acting like common prostitutes. The result is that virgins over a certain age are nowadays practically unknown. For this the parents are greatly to blame.

The Indians ought not to be allowed to make water and filth in their houses, or even in the doorway or the courtyard, but should have a special place for relieving themselves. The rest of the property should be kept clean and well-swept, so that it shines like a mirror. Drunks who urinate in doorways, whether by day or night, should be penalised.

The Indians ought not to be allowed to prepare spirit by chewing the maize in their mouths, so that it is mixed up with saliva, as this practice is a filthy and degraded one. All spirit should be made from germinated maize. The filters and jars should be kept clean.

No sympathy should be shown with Indians who follow the customs of eating lice and chewing coca leaves, who omit to cut their nails, who let their hair grow over their ears, who do not launder or mend their clothes, who refuse to wash their hands and faces and go about in a filthy state, who keep their hair in plaits, paint their faces, wear clothes reaching down to their feet or pluck out the hairs of their beards. They should be made to go about in clean clothes, wearing underclothes and proper shoes or boots.

There is no good reason why our Indians should have to act as unpaid agents of the royal administrators or the big proprietors. Nor should they need to satisfy the personal wishes of a great number of different chiefs, any of whom are capable of punishing them for not complying. An example of this state of affairs is the village called San Cristóbal de Chupe, where there are fifteen taxpaying Indians and exactly the same number of chiefs. The leading figure of another village, Chunga, has no right whatever to his title and his fellow-chiefs, who are mostly related to one another, are ordinary taxpayers who have promoted themselves to the dignity of hereditary rank. Without exception they are guilty of robbing the Indians under their rule. Faced with such injustice, it is small wonder if the Indians move to the plains. Once they arrive there, they are apt to change their appearance by putting on cotton clothes, with the object of deceiving the new chiefs whom they may encounter.

Respect for authority was greater in this country in the old days than it was in Spain, France, Rome, England, or among the Jews and negroes, or anywhere else in the world including China. Our Peruvian Indians rivalled the Franciscans and Jesuits in their capacity for obedience. They kissed the hands of their chiefs and gave a truthful account of all that had happened in their day's work. When they returned from a long spell of labour they brought with them a present such as they might give to their father: a bird which they had shot or caught or a freshly picked flower. It was their way of showing respect to their master, the Inca. But all this submission and love has been abused and thrown away by the Spanish authorities.

It is unsuitable for the Indians to show grief by uttering cries, either in their homes or out-of-doors. Their belief is that the dead walk abroad and return to their own houses. So they set up their wailing and bellowing in order to communicate with the spirits, just as the old magicians did in Inca times. It is necessary to discourage them.

Also, our Indians still adhere to the practice of killing their sheep, whether for eating or for ceremonial purposes, by opening up the heart with the right hand. According to the old magic formula, a boy says to an old man: 'He has been killed on the side of the heart, father.' And he receives the answer: 'All will be well, my son. We shall eat cakes baked with blood, and drink fresh blood.' This was always the superstitious practice: to consume raw blood and meat and afterwards to eat the meat cooked. From now onwards the sheep should not be killed by this method, but should have their throats cut.

Our people believe that if they do not take ashes from the fire they are allowed to eat meat during the whole of Lent. If they do impose some discipline on themselves, they keep count of this on their knotted cords and believe themselves entitled as a result to indulge themselves during Holy Week. They also regard drunkenness as a form of administering punishment to themselves. If they go to Mass, they find it necessary to record each visit on the *quipu*. All these false beliefs are admittedly encouraged by wrong or careless teaching, but they still occur when the people concerned are living in wild country, where there are no priests to mislead them.

Among the Indians there are various wise men and astrologers who know the exact times for sowing and harvesting the crops. For example, Juan Yumpa of the village of Uchuc Marca Lucana was an expert on the movements of the Sun and Moon and the stars and could calculate hours, days and months with the accuracy of a clock. He had all sorts of names for the different measures of time which he used. The span of summer and winter could be predicted from his observations. This thinker declared that, beginning with the month of January, the Sun seats himself on his royal throne and regulates his future course. Then again, in July, he seats himself on another throne and remains there without stirring because it is his day of rest. But on the third day he plans the remaining part of his journey in the space of a single minute, little as this interval of time may seem. From that point he goes on day after day for six months without resting, but every half-hour he looks over his left shoulder at the sea and the mountains. So he travels each year between his first and second thrones, which stand in the houses of which he is lord and master. But he also has a chair corresponding to each month of the year. As he moves between them, he is followed at a respectful distance by the Moon, who is his wife and the Queen of the stars. In this manner the months of the year are indicated as if on the face of a clock, and also the hours and minutes of every day. In the astrologer's view the Sun fixes the time with his rays during the morning. This can be proved by observation of the penetrative power of the rays through a window, or a careful study of how the Sun makes a sortie, then returns and sits down on his throne. The exact path which he follows can be calculated. Some Indians go out and watch the sunrise from ravines in the mountains. It is said that from the beginning of January the day is longer and the night shorter, whilst from July onwards the day is shorter and the night longer. The Moon, being his wife, is depicted as one degree lower in the sky than the Sun, who for his part is represented as having a beard like a man. And the people say at harvesting time: 'We're going to clip the Sun's beard for him.'

When there was an eclipse of the Moon the women used to utter loud cries and call out: 'Do not weaken, do not die, Mother Moon. Our men will scold us and punish us if you do.'

The astrologers believed that they could distinguish in the stars the figures of a man, several women, sheep and lambs with their shepherds, partridges and their hunters, a cloth-mill, a lion and a herd of deer. Among the planets they knew which ones brought success and which ones disaster. They used to say: 'The comets with long hair bring sickness,' and they could recognise the pole-star and the morning-star.'

The Indian whom I have mentioned, Juan Yumpa, was extremely old but his eyesight was still good and he had not lost any of his teeth. He had also kept the appetite of a young man.

The use of the fast and some other ceremonies from the time of the Incas is still kept up in the village of Asquem. The local people continue to worship the lightning, which used to be called *Illapa* but which they now confuse with St James. A child was born with a cleft nose in this village and the mother and child were shut up, because the Indians said that the child was the son of St James. An old watchman was the only person allowed to speak to the mother who was prevented from eating salt, chilli or meat and kept in darkness on a diet of blanched maize. When a month had gone by, the whole population came together and set about making ropes out of straw twisted in a left-handed direction. These were set on fire at the tip and used for flogging the poor woman, who was told: 'Get out of this village,' and was expelled from its shelter with her son into the hills. There it is said that she remained for another month, after which time the child died. The villagers came to bury the corpse and covered it in the grave with a living black llama and a number of unclean offerings. They made a sacrifice to the lightning and carried the mother, dressed in her best clothes, back to the village to the accompaniment of songs and dances. There they started a drinking-bout which lasted for five days and reached the stage where they all fell senseless to the ground. The parish priest was absent at the time and a member of the choir told me the story.

The *huarachico* is one of the old customs surviving into modern times. On the day when the maize is handed out for fermenting into spirit, all those present get well and truly drunk. They get drunk again on the day when the spirit is declared to be mature. All through the night, without a wink of sleep, they keep up their songs. The eating of salt and any contact with women are avoided. Then at daybreak any boy who has come of age is dressed by his uncle in the breeches which are called *huara*. The boy's ears are also pierced and the ceremony ends with some good advice to the young man. In much the same way a girl is invested with the coarse skirt called *cusma*, or the dress known as *anaco*, for the first time. These customs with their family meals, heavy consumption of maize spirit and drunken singing are part of the un-Christian past and ought to be discouraged.

Another case in point is the *ruto chico* or cutting of hair, which still goes on. Men and women all come together in the public square or else they meet separately in their houses. A young boy is put in the middle of the circle. Then each person in turn takes a pair of scissors and cuts off a lock of the boy's hair, at the same time offering him a present, until all the hair is gone. Afterwards the parents invite the others to a feast. Once again everyone has too much to drink and more dubious ceremonies may follow.

Convalescence from illness is similarly celebrated with a bout of heavy drinking.

In a place called Tuca Huasi there is an Indian called Francisco Alcas who sleeps with his own brother's wife. He and his mother and the brother never attend Mass or go to confession. As I heard from a person of negro blood who had been a good deal in the man's company, he used to have a retreat in the mountains in a so-called village of the dead, where funerals were held in the time of the Incas. Francisco Alcas buried in this place the Christians whom he succeeded in murdering and robbing of their possessions. According to the account which I heard, he had killed three women and an unspecified number of Indian men. On a further occasion he assaulted a half-caste of the name of Perales, who just managed to escape with his life. Perales made a complaint, but because the Indian Francisco Alcas had become rich through his robberies he was able to bribe the authorities to leave him in peace. So as to be certain in my own mind that the facts of this case were as they had been reported, I travelled to the place and made inquiries.

In their homes, our Indians should keep a dinner-service, if not of gold and silver, at least of wood or clay; and they should have fresh water, clean jugs, tables and stools of the kind which is normal for a Christian couple. It is right that they should put aside some money during their lifetime: say 1,000 or 2,000 pesos. They should be able to dress decently and wear a little jewellery. Also they should own some livestock, whether Peruvian or European. Their aim must be to support their families and leave enough at the end to defray Masses for their souls.

It is usually the fate of these ordinary taxpaying Indians to remain in their humble category, whatever their advantages of understanding and experience, or however much money they may earn. They can hardly be entrusted with responsible rank or honorific duties. Even after the passing of a generation it would be impossible to regard them as gentlemen, capable of meeting on equal terms with the ruling class. If they were sent on some diplomatic mission, they would make a bad impression in the city or anywhere else. So it is necessary for these people to remain in a subordinate capacity.

The food available to our Indians is as follows. Besides wheat, there are several different sorts of maize, such as the white, the hard and yellow, the dark, the dried and the frozen. Potatoes can be large or small, new or early-maturing, flat in shape, white and delicate, frozen or preserved. There are edible roots which can be dried by the Sun or frozen, called *oca*, and also the calabash and the yacca. Among fruits there are cherries, bananas and pineapples. Cucumbers and sweet potatoes are also abundant. Then there are a number of fishes, both from the sea and the rivers, and prawns. Fresh water is the source of various grasses and weeds, some of which are shaped like grapes. The kinds of Peruvian sheep are named llama, alpaca, *huanaco*, *vicuña*, which is smaller than the llama and bears superior wool, and *taruga*. Among the varieties of game are deer, rodents, partridge and other birds. And mention should be made of the foodstuffs which the Spaniards brought to our country: not only wheat but barley, beans, figs, sugar-cane, limes, oranges and lemons. From Castile also came cattle, goats, European sheep, pigs, chickens, pigeons, rabbits, wine, oil, vinegar and bread.

Our people are used to distilling spirits from maize, which can be strong and pungent, smooth and mature, freshly made, agreeable to ladies or specially adapted for sacrifices, as the case may be. Immense labour is involved in the manufacture of these different varieties.

The system of land tenure in Peru is derived from the former rulers and people still talk about the Inca's farms, the warriors' farms or the shepherds' farms. Then, at the time of the Conquest, the right of possession was usurped by the Spaniards and their Indian followers, who took away the lands and titles handed down from previous ages.

On the question of arms, the negroes are forbidden to possess either defensive or offensive weapons, including even knives and bludgeons; and a similar ban applies to half-castes of known evil character. In any case a royal licence is necessary for the carrying of arms. Even Spaniards ought not to be allowed them until they reach the age of 20 and can claim the title of gentlemen in their own right. And these arms ought only to be used in self-defence or in a righteous cause. Such a provision is specially necessary in the case of primitive people who are lawless by nature and being so underprivileged hardly care whether they live or die. The only reason for them to be armed is if they are in the service of some important person whose safety they are required to ensure. Arms ought also to be withheld from Spaniards who have a reputation for being mad or violent, possibly because of their debts or jealousy of their women, or because they are mutinous by disposition. Nor is there any excuse for priests and others who follow a religious career to go about armed to the teeth. As for the Indian chiefs, a distinction should be drawn between drunkards and wastrels on the one hand, and those who have earned the right to bear arms, together with their family and servants, on the other. This latter category is recognised by the title of Don as being loyal to Your Majesty and worthy of confidence.

It ought to be recalled that our Indian clothing, livestock and food were regarded as cheap and inferior at the time of the Conquest. The newcomers from Castile lived on their own stores and our Indians did the same, both sides feeling some repulsion at the thought of unfamiliar food and clothing. But nowadays there is a better sense of values and our Indian products are in just as much demand as the Spanish ones.

And here is a further reflection for Your Majesty. Someone who has given his toil and sweat to the acquisition and preservation of a flock of sheep is bound to feel for them and try to shield them from death or sickness. He looks after his animals because he knows that he and his family are dependent upon them; and he wants to increase their number so as to become rich. If the sheep are good, fat, healthy ones, they will give him a fine return on his investment. Now let us compare this flock with the sheep of God, in other words the people of our country. They were handed over to your care by your father, and to his care by your grandfather. They have brought you considerable wealth and added greatly to your fortune. But God is going to demand an account of how they have been looked after, since he has placed them under your protection. Therefore Your Majesty needs to look into all the ills from which these poor human sheep are suffering.

RULERS OF PERU

In our religion, it is the poor sinner who ought to be favoured above all others. Yet we have often seen such wretches condemned by choleric judges for no fault of their own. To put it more plainly, they have been dispatched by madmen, fools and irresponsibles to execution by hanging, beheading, shooting with arrows or strangling, innocent as they were of any crime. There was the case of the Viceroy Francisco Toledo, who took it upon himself to execute the Inca ruler, Tupac Amaru. Toledo was nothing but a soldier of fortune, diseased with pride, but he killed a King. Then there was the fate of the blameless Portocarrero. There was Don Melchor Carlos Inca, who was exiled without reason. Some princes of our race have been stripped of their possessions and others have been murdered. Nobody even knows what became of Juan García de la Vega, the unlucky mine-owner.

The Spaniards in this country have tricked themselves out as gentlemen and usually paid no more for their elevation in rank than a fee to a clerk for a document of doubtful legality. Often they have the further blemish of Jewish, Moorish, Turkish or even English blood. They would do better to content themselves with the claim to be Christians, for the right to a title would need to have come by inheritance in their own country, confirmed by their ruler's signature. If they possessed that, they could indeed call themselves fine gentlemen. And I have made it clear that all proper respect is due to a gentleman, even if he is a poor man, as long as he is a true servant of the King. But whether he holds high office or is simply a person of some learning, he should never claim more importance than his blood and lineage entitle him to. Least of all should he permit himself to be insolent or arrogant.

I have told how Don Francisco de Toledo sentenced the Inca prince Tupac Amaru to death by execution. This sentence was unacceptable according to any principle of right and justice; and so was the punishment of the leading nobles. The title of Inca is such an exalted one that, even if Tupac Amaru had really rebelled against the Spanish rule, it would have been wrong to affront or punish him in any way. If he was going to be kept in custody he should have been attended by kneeling servants, provided

47 *Governor and Priest Gambling*

with water for his hands and suitable food to eat, until it became possible to hand him over to Your Majesty for judgement. With all his ability and his wisdom in drawing up ordinances, Toledo was mistaken in setting himself up as a judge over a King of Peru. How would he have liked it if he in his turn had been sentenced by a judge from Spain and executed on the same scaffold? Your Majesty sent no such judge, preferring as a good Christian to leave the Viceroy to the pangs of his remorse. These pangs did indeed bring Toledo to the death which he deserved and only God knows where his soul is today.

Having read accounts of the various princes, Kings and Emperors of the world, I am sure none of them had the majesty or the power of Tupac Inca Yupanqui or Huayna Capac Inca. The monarchs of Turkey and China, the Roman Emperors, Christian and Jewish rulers, the King of Guinea: none of them enjoyed such esteem or wore so lofty a Crown. So exalted was the

Inca's position that he seldom talked, never dined with ordinary people and never laughed or cried in front of his subjects. His only companions at table, with whom he was ready to exchange toasts, were other Kings of unquestionable antecedence. When he travelled in person, he was accompanied by the chiefs of the Chunchos, naked savages who ate human flesh, so that his greatness would inspire awe and leave a lasting memory in any beholder's mind.

At regular intervals the great officials of the country were compelled to make their submission to the Inca, so as to dissuade them from instigating a rebellion. Such a rebellion sometimes occurred, but was suppressed. There was for instance one noble whose importance was emphasised by his enormous girth, who would never travel to Cuzco to pay his respects to the Inca. Whenever he was summoned he asked for leave of absence, which was always courteously conceded. This noble of the highest rank, whose name was Cullic Chava, had the reputation of being a great glutton. At every meal he consumed a vast quantity, almost a bushel, of bread, meat, vegetables and fruit. He also drank from sunrise to sunset. For this purpose he had his maize spirit put into a huge jug, from which he scooped it out with the aid of a gourd. On some days he even drank directly from the jug. Living in this lordly fashion, one day he took it into his head to lead a rising against the Inca's power. Equally foolhardy was Capac Apo Huari Callo, the ruler of Hatun Colla, who joined the same rebellion. Their fate was that the Inca ordered their skins to be made into drums, so that it was possible to play a tune on the huge belly of Cullic Chava. Drums of this sort were common at the time and were called *runa tinya*.

Although the Incas may have begun as barbarians, and although their lineage was derived from a woman, Mama Huaco Coya, their dynasty developed over a very long period of time. My grandfather serves as the model of a great King reigning over the Four Quarters. In a similar manner Your Majesty ought to preside over the four parts of the World, with four lesser Kings under your sway. As one of these I offer my son, who is a true prince of Peru. The second prince would be the black one of Guinea, the third of Rome and the fourth of Grand Turkey. These four princes, each with his own emblems of sovereignty, would be grouped round Your Majesty. If Your Majesty went out on foot, they would go on foot as well; and if Your Majesty rode a horse they would be mounted too under their different canopies.

Our Indians ought not to be thought of as a backward people who yielded easily to superior force. Just imagine, Your Majesty, being an Indian in your own country and being loaded up as if you were a horse, or driven along with a succession of blows from a stick. Imagine being called a dirty dog or a pig or a goat. Imagine having your women and your property taken away from you without any semblance of legality. What would you and your Spanish compatriots do in these circumstances? My own belief is that you would eat your tormentors alive and thoroughly enjoy the experience.

The Spaniards, hardly less unfortunate and just as poor, ran all sorts of risks in their voyage across the sea from Castile. Their aim was to compensate themselves by stealing all we had. But it ought not to be forgotten that when the Emperor's ambassadors arrived on our shores they asked for peace and friendship. From that time to this the Peruvian Indians have remained broadly loyal to Your Majesty. By contrast, the Indians of Chile have fought for their lands and the Christians have been unable to conquer and settle them; nor are they likely to succeed, because of the immense effort which such a settlement would involve. In view of all this, Your Majesty ought to favour the claims of Peru and give support to our Indian chiefs, who can be counted upon as faithful subjects. Apart from Your Majesty, they are the people with most right to the possession of the country. After all, the ambassadors who were sent by the Emperor to the New World rebelled against the Crown out of sheer greed for riches, and tried to make themselves into independent Kings.

So, to conclude this argument, it is not the Spanish administrators and employers who are the rightful owners of Peru. According to the laws of both God and man, we Indians are the proprietors. With the exception of Your Majesty alone, the Spaniards are only foreign settlers. It is our country because God has given it to us. We are the masters.

THE KING'S QUESTIONS

Your Majesty may wish to ask the author of this book some questions with the object of discovering the true state of affairs in Peru, so that the country can be properly and justly governed and the lot of the poor improved. I, the author, will listen attentively to Your Majesty's questions and do my best to answer them for the edification of my readers and Your Majesty's greater glory. This is an important service which I am able to render, for Your Majesty hears many lies as well as truths, and much of what is reported is simply a means of obtaining preferment for the writer in Church or State.

In my capacity as a grandson of the Inca of Peru I would like to speak to Your Majesty face to face, but I cannot achieve this because I am now 80 years old and in frail health. I cannot take the risk of the long journey to Spain. However, I am ready to pass on the observations which I have made

48 *Author with King Philip III*

in the last 30 years, since I left my home and family to live the life of a poor
traveller on the roads of my country. We can communicate with one another
by letter, with Your Majesty asking for information and myself replying,
as follows:

'Tell me, author, how is it that the Indians were able to prosper and
increase in numbers before the coming of the Incas?'

'Your Majesty, in those days there was only one King. He was well
served by his nobles, who superintended the mining of gold and silver, the
work on the farms and the herding of the Peruvian sheep. Although the
population was considerable, enough was produced to provision the fortresses as well as feed the women and children at home. The smallest
settlement possessed 1,000 soldiers and some could put an army into the
field.'

'Tell me then, Don Felipe de Ayala, how was the population maintained
after the Incas came?'

'Your Majesty, the Inca himself was a supreme ruler although there were
nobles of different ranks, similar to your Dukes, Marquesses and Counts,
under his sovereignty. But all these nobles were tireless in their obedience
to the Inca's laws and commands. So the people as a whole remained
prosperous and never went short of food.'

'Tell me, author, what is wrong nowadays? Why is the population
declining and why are the Indians getting poorer and poorer?'

'I'll explain to Your Majesty. The best of our girls and women are all
carried off by your priests and the other Spanish officials. Hence the large
number of half-castes in the country. Usually the priests give the excuse
that they want to stop our women living in sin, but their next step is to
appropriate them for themselves. As a result, many of our people give up
hope and want to hang themselves, following the example of a group of
Chanca Indians who collected on a hill-top at Andaguaylas and decided to
finish with their miserable lives for once and all.'

'Tell me, author, how can the population be made to increase again?'

'I have already written, Your Majesty, that priests and others ought to
try living a decent Christian life for a change. Indians ought to be allowed
to enjoy their married lives and bring up their daughters in peace. Above
all, the number of would-be Kings ruling over us ought to be reduced to
one, namely Your Majesty.'

'And how can the prosperity of the ordinary Indian be raised?'

'Well, Your Majesty, a lot depends on the community, the *sapci*, which
is responsible for growing maize, wheat, potatoes, chillies, coca, fruit and
cotton. There are also the mines to be worked. Young girls and widows can
be put to spinning and weaving, with ten of them engaged on a single

garment. Castilian cattle and Peruvian sheep are another source of wealth to the community, but individuals need to have their own livestock as well. Usually the *sapci* keeps one third of all produce. Another seventh can go to the local administrator and of course Your Majesty is entitled to one fifth at any time. Within these arrangements the community ought to prosper.'

'And tell me, author, how can the Indians who have fled from their homes be persuaded to return ?'

'The young ones can be tempted back to the abandoned villages if they are provided with fields and pastures with clearly marked boundaries. They should pay taxes, but the collection should be the responsibility of one salaried official only, and any money left over should go to the Crown. This official could well be the Indian chief. For it is a fact that we chiefs have never joined in rebellions and have proved ourselves to be remarkably loyal subjects. We handed over ourselves and our vassals to Your Majesty, together with the silver-mines of Potosí, the gold-mines of Carabaya and the mercury-mines of Huancavelica. For all this Your Majesty ought to show us some mark of gratitude. It ought to be recalled, too, that twelve learned men and four clerks of your own Council, as well as issuing a pronouncement against slavery, forbade the payment of taxes to the clergy. Thus the parish priests are no longer entitled to earn money as tax-collectors. They must live on the contributions which are left at the foot of their altars. These usually amount to between 1,000 and 2,000 pesos a year. They are made up of payments for Masses, voluntary offerings, responsories for the dead, presents, Christmas-boxes and alms. The quantity is adequate to provide them with enough to live on, dress and feed themselves decently. To go beyond this and arrogate to themselves the rights of landowners and employers is an offence against their calling. They ought to be content with our people's offerings and what they get from the Spaniards.'

'But tell me, author, why are you so much opposed to parish priests getting proper salaries ?'

'Your Majesty, the first priest of our religion was Jesus Christ, who lived on earth as a poor man, and his Apostles did the same. None of those holy men asked for salaries, but they were content to live by the charity of others. By the same token parish priests can manage quite well without collecting taxes or setting themselves up as men of property. If they do not care for such a way of life, Your Majesty should consult with the Pope in order to admit Indians to the priesthood. Being good Christians our people will not require any salary and the savings which Your Majesty will make can be used for the general good of the Church.'

'Tell me this, author. What can be done to prevent so much death, suffocation and hardship in the mines ?'

'The first point, Your Majesty, is that a stop should be put to the practice of hanging miners up by the feet and whipping them with their private parts openly displayed. Also the miners are forced to work day and night and paid only half of what is owed to them. Finally they are sent off to the high plateau where they die of exposure. The remedy would be to be more selective in the choice of labour and to allow any particular locality a six months' rest in between recruiting visits. It would also help if experts could be appointed and paid, who know how to cure the condition caused by poisonous fumes. That would alleviate much of the present hardship. Your Majesty should give orders that a store of provisions and water should be kept on the premises at every mine. In the case of miners being trapped by a collapse of the roof it would be a godsend to have food and drink available whilst day-and-night operations were in progress to free the trapped men.'

'And tell me, author, how can we discover all the hidden mines in Peru?'

'Very well, I'll tell Your Majesty. In these times, whenever an Indian reports the discovery of gold, silver, mercury, lead, copper, tin or even pigment, the Spaniards at once take over and the Indian is maltreated. So naturally enough no Indian is keen to make any such report to the authorities. But if Your Majesty were to enter into personal relations with the discoverer in each case, and treat him well, all the best mines would soon be brought to light. The result would be that Your Majesty would indeed be the richest and most important King in the world, and this would benefit Peru. As matters stand at present, the Indians are in the process of dying out. In twenty years' time there will be none of them left to defend the Crown and the Catholic Faith. The Emperor, who is now in glory, was great because of his possession of the Indies and the same was true of Your Majesty's father. I dare to say that it is also true of Your Majesty, and yet it is possible that Peru will lose all its value and your Indian subjects will no longer exist. Where once there were 1,000 souls, now there are hardly 100 left. Those who remain are many of them old and incapable of having children. The young men cannot find young brides to bear them sons. The girls and women, whether single or married, are all removed into the Spaniards' homes. It is impossible to remedy this state of affairs because the Spaniards support one another in all circumstances. They not only treat the Indians as slaves or servants, but dispossess them of their land and property. Even to set these facts down on paper is enough to make me weep tears. And the worst of it is that nobody dares to tell Your Majesty what is going on. If I were asked to put a price on the Peruvian Indian, I would put the figure very high and I would draw the conclusion that he or she ought to be treated with care and kindness, in the interests of the country. If by any chance one of our girls bears a child to an Indian man, the parish priest and the other authorities treat her like a criminal. Then the priest takes her into his kitchen so that he can sleep with her whenever he likes. She starts to bear him children and finds this style of life much to her taste. Other Indian girls, too, notice the privileges which she enjoys and want to share them. As I say, the real indignation is aroused when an Indian woman bears children to an Indian man. It is as if the sky had fallen on the earth. The father is tied to a pillar and flogged, and the mother has her hair cut off. If I ever started telling the story of such cases in any detail, I would never stop.'

'Tell me, author Ayala, now that you have recounted all these sad things, tell me how it is that the Indians are being exterminated, their women taken from them and their property stolen, when I never intended my judges and officials to do any wrong or damage. On the contrary, I expected them to treat the Indian chiefs with honour and allow the common people to lead useful and productive lives. Tell me, my good Ayala, what can be done to put things right?'

'All I can say, Your Majesty, is that the Spaniards ought to live like Christians. They should marry and be content with ladies of their own race and class, and allow the Indians to keep their own women and property. Anyone who has used his power to steal property from others should be made to give it back, and should also pay for what he has enjoyed. These penalties should be imposed summarily, without room for delay.'

'Tell me, author, how should I deal with the problem of Indian labourers who fail to report for duty?'

'Your Majesty should have a list kept, in which their names are all inscribed. Then the chiefs should be given the order to have them tracked down and discovered, wherever they may be. The cost of pursuing and arresting these Indians can be diminished if the inns provide free board and if the authorities put horses at the disposal of the agents employed in the task.'

'Tell me more, author, about these fugitives.'

'Your Majesty, they can be divided into three categories. First there are the runaways who leave their villages to become thieves and highwaymen. The second category consists of strangers within any particular community, who feel themselves to be outcasts, abused and ill-treated by everybody, without any living soul to whom they can turn in their trouble. They are so poor, too, that they are unable to pay their taxes. In the third category, finally, are the unfortunates who are employed as servants in the households of the landowners and administrators and who wish to escape. If things continue as they are now, Your Majesty, you are likely to lose all your Indian subjects, indeed to lose everything you possess.'

'Go on, author. Tell me what you mean by these remarks of yours.'

'I say with all frankness that the Indians provide much of Your Majesty's revenue. I am an Indian chief and I stand up for their interests. If they are allowed to perish, the land will become barren and inhospitable. That is the reason why Your Majesty ought to impose heavy penalties for any interference with the rights of the chiefs and also of the ordinary Indians.'

'And what other measures do you propose, author ?'

'If the Indian birthrate is to be kept up, Your Majesty, it is essential that parish priests should be made to pay a sum of money as a guarantee when they enter upon their duties, whether it is for the first or second time and even if their term of office is only for a single day. The reason is that these priests are in process of destroying the whole country.'

'Tell me this, author. Don't I send my Bishops to every large city with the mission of defending the oppressed and seeing that justice is done ? And don't the Bishops send out Visitors with power to punish offending priests and remove them from their parishes ? Why don't you Indians go to them or write your complaints to them, or else complain to the civil authorities ?'

'Let me explain the truth of this matter to Your Majesty. It's perfectly correct that Your Majesty sends all sorts of eminent persons with instructions to show special favour to our Indians. No doubt these people let you have reports on all the favour they have shown and the justice they have done. But the fact is that from the moment when they disembark in the harbour they forget your instructions and change into different beings. From then on, their only object is to keep on good terms with the richest of the Spaniards.'

'Tell me, author, how would you define service to God and the Crown, which I wear ?'

'I will explain to Your Majesty. A servant of God is someone who obeys His laws and cares for the poor. But such a person is also rendering service to your Crown, because he is protecting the Indians who are a valuable possession acquired by your grandfather.'

'Tell me this, author. Since you are the grandson of Tupac Inca Yupanqui and the son of the former second person in the State, why can't you do more in my name to favour the cause of the poor Indians and look after their interests ?'

'That is the purpose of my presenting myself now before Your Catholic Majesty. My conclusion is that Your Majesty ought to appoint a Visitor-General with power to remove unjust prelates from their posts and return them to Spain, if this becomes necessary. This Visitor-General should have his seat in Lima and send out his visitors to all parts of the country. Possibly his appointment could be agreed with the Pope, who would choose a Cardinal for the purpose. In particular, this Cardinal would supervise the various chapters, orders and monasteries and attend by this means to the wants of the Indians. Honest judges ought also to be appointed in the big cities for a period of five years at a time, at a fixed salary, to give their attention to wills and bequests of property, whether in the form of silver, clothing, livestock, farms or dowries. The judges should watch over the appreciation of property from year to year and make sure that the rights of minors in regard to legacies are upheld. In this way an advance in their living standards can be achieved for the poorest people.'

'Are there any other measures, author, which you can propose in the interests of good order and for the relief of suffering?'

'Yes, Your Majesty. The authority of the genuine Indian chiefs ought to be upheld. It has unfortunately become usual for petty overseers to assume the title of *Apo* or important chief. On payment of a small consideration, they can ensure that they are addressed in this fashion. To avoid any such trickery in the future, it is important that all petitions to higher authority should pass through the hands of an important chief who is able to give evidence about the petitioners' true standing. In this way cases can be avoided like the one which occurred in a place called Sancos, when an ordinary Indian declared himself to be a chief and proceeded to exempt the entire local population from work of any kind. The real chief of the place was not even consulted.'

'And how can such deceit be avoided, author?'

'The proper procedure is for me, as a writer and a prince of the Indian race, to give evidence upon all claims to titles and send it to Your Majesty, duly signed. When I am gone, my descendants would be empowered to continue in the same office for all time to come.'

'What do you regard as the prime object of policy?'

'The restoration of the Indian population, Your Majesty, and the ending of the flight of the Indians from their settlements. This would be easy and inexpensive to achieve if Your Majesty were determined to punish without appeal anybody who obstructs the necessary measures. The principal one of these is that no officials, or their wives, should continue to have Indian boys or girls in their power, or be allowed to detain them for even a single hour by force or against their will, or have the right to force them to work for nothing. No category of Indians ought to escape the liability to pay taxes and render services to the Crown. For this purpose a census ought to be taken of the whole population. It would also be a wise precaution to prevent any Spaniard or half-caste of any sort from living in a purely Indian settlement. Your Majesty would do better not to employ half-castes at all, since they only cause uproar, dissension, crime and scandal. They are the sworn enemies of their own uncles, the Spaniards. Moreover, those who have been ordained as priests are the worst of all and should never have been approved by Your Majesty, if you have any concern for the success of your rule in Peru.'

'And how should I rule, in your opinion, author ?'

'Only by virtue of your power and authority as monarch of the world. No other person should intervene between you and your people, except for your Viceroy and Council of the Realm, who should have the right to appoint the necessary officers such as mayors, judges, constables and clerks. No power of appointment whatsoever should be vested in your royal administrators, who are in the habit of retaining ten deputies, twice as many mayors and a number of judges to conduct their private business for them. Either they should be fined and suspended from office or they should be made to work on their own without any deputies or assistants. And the same procedure ought to be adopted in the case of the Church. The Pope, Your Majesty, the Cardinal and the Bishops ought to be the only authorities capable of appointing vicars in the capital cities of the various provinces. Those who are selected, and confirmed by Your Majesty, need to be learned Doctors who have reached a respectable age. At the present time there are as many as ten vicars in each province, many of whom are still boys, like chicks which have just emerged from the eggshell. Others are lecherous fools on the look-out for pretty girls to seduce. If all the girls are rounded up and kept in the priests' houses on the pretext of religious instruction, children are bound to follow. Now ask me, Your Majesty, what the remedy is for this state of affairs.'

'Tell me, then, author, what is the remedy for this state of affairs ?'

'There is no remedy, I can assure Your Majesty, other than compliance with the following principles. First, no priest should also be a proprietor. Secondly, he should put down a guarantee in money for his good conduct. Thirdly, the young girls should have their religious instruction at home and only the young boys should be taught in church. Fourthly, no Indian, great or small, should be forced to work for nothing for the Spaniards, since the service which he owes is to the community.'

'Is there any other improvement, author, which you have in mind ?'

'Yes, Your Majesty. Your most excellent Viceroys should be granted a term of office of twenty years at a time, or twelve years at least, so that they can impose an equitable and righteous form of government and come to know who are the bad people in the country and who are the good ones. This is the proper way to level out inequalities and bring to justice those who ill-treat your Indian vassals. If necessary, the Viceroys must punish and even banish the priests for the greater glory of your Crown.'

'What is your final conclusion, author Ayala ?'

'My conclusion is that you, King Philip III, should bear our wretchedness in mind and cease to send us so many punishments, misfortunes and disasters as in the past. Do not allow us to be exterminated, Your Majesty. Send us your Visitor and after he has departed let the Indian chief and the other authorities join together in a tour of inspection of each town and village in the region, so that they can discover exactly what the Visitor has done or left undone. Did the Visitor ask the priest for money? Was he rude, irascible and insulting in his manner? If he deprived the priest of his living, was this punishment deserved? And if the priest was actually a good Christian, ought he not to be restored to the living? On all these questions Your Majesty and the Bishop can be informed, so that the right solution can be found and Your Majesty's conscience set at rest. The Visitors need to be visited and the judges judged, if good government is to be installed in your Kingdom of Peru.'

THE MAP OF THE INDIES

The reader knows that our country was formerly divided into four parts under separate rulers. These were Chinchaysuyu, Antisuyu, Collasuyu and Cuntisuyu. The Incas also made a further distinction between Hanan Cuzco in the West and Lurin Cuzco in the East, with the dividing line falling through the centre of the capital city and Court of Cuzco. The contours of the country are irregular, with as many folds as a starched shirt. There are precipices and gorges more than a mile deep with rivers flowing at the bottom. In the various provinces there are big cities, towns and villages settled by the Indians. But there are also large areas, amounting to half the country in the north, which have never been subdued. The Spaniards have not tamed the tribes of Chile in the south, and the Arauqua and Mosquito Indians, although they were subject to the Inca rulers. There is a great wealth of gold in the possession of these natives. In the part of the mountain chain which is inhabited by female warriors there are also un- discovered silver-mines. These Indians are often resourceful and clever, but at the same time aggressive. Sometimes it is almost impossible to reach their territories because the rivers are swarming with poisonous snakes and the harsh mountains ranged by tigers and bears, but the Incas succeeded by their cunning in conquering them.

MAPA·MVNDI·D
·VUREINO·LLAMADO·ANTIS

OTROREINOLLAMADOCHINCHAISVIOPVNISOLO

OTROREINO·LLAMADO·COND

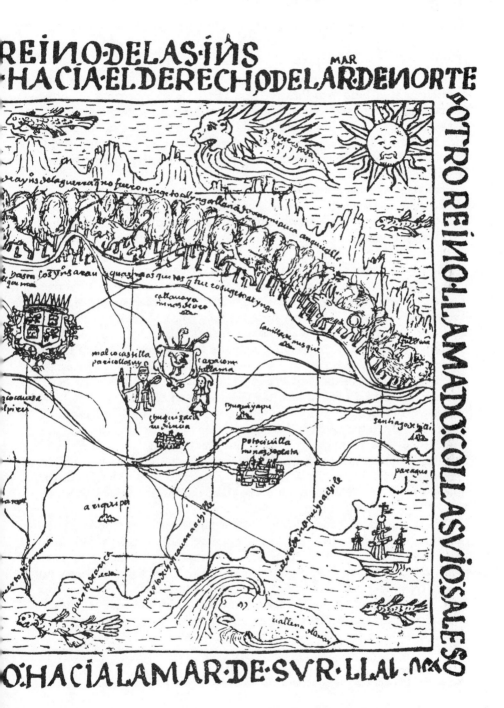

REINO·DELAS·INS
·HACIA·EL·DERECHO·DELAR DE NORTE
MAR

CITIES AND TOWNS*

Of the cities of Peru, some were founded by the Incas. Others owed their creation to Don Francisco Pizarro, Don Diego de Almagro and the other Captains who were sent out by the Emperor Charles V. Some were only started by the Viceroys at a later stage. They vary in size from an importance such as Potosí or Ica possesses, which would be considered remarkable even in Spain, to the humble condition of a Castilian village. Some of them are inhabited by Spaniards only.

Peru is only one of a number of territories governed by Viceroys, such as Mexico, Santo Domingo, Panama, Paraguay and Tucumán. Each country has its own race of Indians, who may have come from China in the first instance. Through the Viceroys Your Majesty rules the whole of the New World.

The city of Santa Fé de Bogotá, the capital of Novo Reino, was founded in 1536. It possesses an excellent climate although the country is a hot one. There is plenty of bread, wine and fruit, but only a small supply of meat. This, however, never fails. Very little silver or gold is found, but there are some precious stones. Pearls and coloured shells abound on the shores of the province, where there are also harbours from which ships can sail to Spain. The inhabitants are good Christians and the Church is well established. The loyalty of the province is attested by the fact that it has never since its foundation risen against the Crown. The people are peaceful and orderly, so that there is no need for much coming and going of judges.

The city of Quito, which is the capital of the province and diocese of the same name, was founded by Don Francisco Pizarro. Like the cities of Trujillo, Cuzco and Huamanga it has been a centre of rebellion. The inhabitants refused to offer service or pay taxes to Your Majesty in the time of the Viceroy Mendoza. They also killed the Viceroy Blasco Nuñez de Vela.

The various parts of the province produce little silver, but food with the exception of meat is plentiful. The people are bad Christians with little sense of charity in their dealings with one another, although they have plenty of religious institutions. Because of the high incidence of crime and disloyalty, judges are constantly coming and going in the city. But ever since its foundation Quito has been notorious for its mistrust of government. Spaniards and negroes alike are all too often engaged in brawls and disputes.

---

* It can be deduced from this chapter that the author knew little of Tucumán and Paraguay, which he imagines to be close to or even in the middle of the sea. Cuzco, Castrovirreyna, Huamanga and Callao, on the other hand, are evidently described from experience.

50 *Cuenca*

Where the city of Cuenca now stands, Huayna Capac Inca had some of his palaces. Its foundation as a city dates from the time of Pizarro's governorship. The inhabitants have a reputation for tranquillity and attachment to Christianity, and they have never been rebellious.

The temperate climate produces a good yield of fruit of all kinds, but meat is in scarce supply. Precious metals are also rare in the district.

Cuenca can be compared with the city of Seville in Spain, especially because of the law-abiding and friendly spirit within the community.

Caxamarca can be called the city of Atahuallpa Inca, the bastard brother of Huascar the legitimate Inca. In this city Atahuallpa was captured, tried and executed by order of Don Francisco Pizarro.

The city, which was re-established by the conquerors, enjoys good weather and its inhabitants are law-abiding and peaceful. Food, including fruit and meat, is plentiful. There is little silver but an adequate amount of gold. Clothing is manufactured in the place itself.

Caxamarca is well endowed with churches and convents and its people have always been faithful to the Crown.

The town of Paita was founded during the time when Don Francisco Pizarro was Governor. It has a small population of decent and loyal people, who are always ready to fight for what they believe in.

The weather is favourable and bread, wine, meat and fruit are always in good supply. The inhabitants have shown themselves to be generous towards poor Spaniards, whom they often help on their way along the high roads. They are serious in character and do not indulge in gossip or tale-bearing but follow the teaching of the Church. They are seldom in trouble with the law.

The foundation of Puerto Viejo was decreed by the Emperor Charles V and it appears that it was the first town or village to be founded by the Spaniards in this country. It was given its name by virtue of being the oldest port of the Conquest. From the beginning it was the place from which all the treasures and riches of Peru were shipped to Spain.

The townspeople are modest and charitable in character, with a particular loyalty to Your Majesty's rule. The climate is favourable and the supply of food adequate, but there is a scarcity of meat. Not much gold or silver is found in the place itself, but any amount of these precious metals passes through the port. The community lives at peace with itself and has no need of judges and prosecutions.

The city of Guayaquil was founded at the same time as the city of Huánuco when Pizarro was Governor. It enjoys a warm temperature and produces an abundance of fruit. Horses and mules are present in great numbers and precious metals are also found in the area. The inhabitants are known for their loyalty and their honesty in all dealings between themselves. Some of them own big estates, but give away much of their fortune in charity to the poor.

The city of Cartagena owed its foundation to the time when the Spaniards crossed the Atlantic Ocean and established themselves in Panama, Santo Domingo and Cartagena itself. It enjoys a hot climate and produces fruit and other food in plenty. It is also gold-bearing, but there is little silver. The ships from Spain lie alongside the quays and there is a wealth of fine churches, although no Bishop has yet been appointed. The loyalty of the local people has never been questioned; nor do they make a practice of quarrelling among themselves. Even the priests behave well.

It is at Cartagena that clothing from Spain and negro slaves of both sexes from Africa arrive in ships and are sold at the cheapest prices.

Panama, which is the seat of a Royal Audience and has its own Bishop, was explored in the time of Columbus and his companions Juan Díaz de Solís, the pilot, and Blasco Nuñez de Balboa, who discovered the Pacific

Ocean. It is close to the Equator and therefore similar in its climate to Guinea, from which the negro slaves are brought. Fruit and trees of all sorts are plentiful and the negroes soon feel at home there and begin to rear families. But amidst all the abundance of other food there is little meat. There is a lot of gold to be seen about and also the silver from Potosí passes through the port on its way to Castile. Conversely, clothing is brought from Spain by the arriving ships.

The people of Panama are influenced both by the Castilian and the Indian style of living, but they are good Christians and loyal servants of the Crown. When the Spanish settlers raised the flag of rebellion, it was in Panama that the fleets were assembled to subdue them in Your Majesty's name and that the Viceroy Blasco Nuñez de Vela and President La Gasca received popular support in your name.

The city of Huanuco used to bear my own family name of Huaman Poma, which means 'falcon puma' or 'eagle lion'. This name was changed into Royal Lion of Huanuco by the conquerors. Nowhere else have all the inhabitants of a city been so completely loyal to their ruler, ever since the time of the Incas. In this respect the people of Huanuco can be compared with the Biscayans in Spain. Just as the Biscayan family of Ayala, whose name I have taken, has been specially honoured, my own family in Peru was found worthy of the highest confidence and authority by the Inca's Council of State. My ancestors were the royal lions and eagles supporting the ruler in the same way as the Duke of Alba has served the Crown of Castile.

Huanuco is fortunate in possessing a climate which is neither too hot nor too cold. Its countryside produces ample supplies of bread, maize, meat and fruit. It lies in the foothills of the Cordillera and the mountain Indians are often to be seen there. Behind the city is the broad River Marañon, which flows down to Cartagena and is said to be full of lizards and snakes. The population of the city is rich and peaceful. Lies and deceits are virtually unknown in the old royal city of Huaman Poma.

The City of Kings, also known as Lima, was set up by the conquerors as the Court where the representatives of the Crown and men of learning were all to be found.

The site of the city was captured in spite of its being defended by Prince Quiso Yupanqui with 1,000 Indians behind him. This Inca leader was killed by Captain Luis Avalos de Ayala, who was to be the father of my own half-brother and who pierced him with a lance-thrust as he was crossing a watercourse leading towards the valley. The Captain's action gave the Spaniards possession of the place.

The valley of Lima produces all kinds of food, and a large quantity of silver circulates in the city. Here is also the seat of the Archbishop, who ought properly to be the second person in the Church after the Holy Father himself. Other dignitaries who reside in Lima are the Holy Inquisitor with his staff, the Vicar-General and the heads of the religious orders.

Lima knows well how to punish rebellion and abase false pride, and it knows too how to honour and reward excellence.

The town of Callao acts as the port of Lima, but it was founded before the city itself. Through Callao pass the official communications between the Indies and Castile. The town is also a fortress for the defence of Peru, and it successfully resisted the English when they attacked it during the time of the Viceroy Don García. These English were taken prisoner by the Spanish forces.

The rich merchants of the town send silver to Spain and receive in return clothing and other goods at favourable prices. Food is also cheap and it ought to be possible to lead a good Christian life.

The coastal area consists of a flat plain which is hot in summer and cold in winter. There is no fruit, but a good deal of fish; and there is wine, but little fresh water. News is constantly arriving in Callao from all over the world. Money is either sent abroad for safe keeping or dissipated in wild living. Some people go naked and others, the fortunate ones, are richly dressed. Some weep and others sing. And they all come and go in this great port of the Indies.

The town of Ica, built in the time of the Viceroy Don Antonio de Mendoza the elder, is a large place with jurisdiction over Hanan Yunca and Lurin Yunca. It is rich and powerful, producing an abundance of fruit of all sorts. There is plenty of bread, maize, meat and fish. As for the wine, it flows like water and is outstanding in the whole of Peru, as well as being cheap at the price of 8 reales a jug. Not surprisingly, there is a big market for this wine.

The climate is excellent. A lot of silver is always in circulation, but there is no gold. The leading townspeople are both charitable and loyal. They sustain no less than seven important religious institutions which are all of them active and prosperous.

It remains to be said that, because of the cheap wine, the Indians of Ica are notorious for their drunkenness. In their cups they often kill each other and some die from their overindulgence in the must called *auapi*. The local negroes are no better than the Indians, being appalling scoundrels who live by theft and violence against their neighbours.

Nazca, or as it is sometimes called Santiago de Nazca, was first started during the Viceroyalty of Don Luis de Velasco, who belonged to the Order of Santiago or St James. The actual founder was an Indian chief who went by the name of Don García de la Nazca. He chose the site and was concerned in the setting up of the Convent of St Augustine. He also welcomed the Spaniards, who soon established themselves in the town.

Nazca produces the finest wine in the whole country, comparable with the wine of Castile. It is golden in colour, very clear, smooth on the palate and with a delicate bouquet. The grapes from which it is pressed are fleshy, pure white in colour and the size of cherries. There is a considerable trade in this wine with other communities.

Bread and meat are plentiful in Nazca, but water is scarce. The good climate is responsible for a high yield of fruit. The highroad to Potosí, Cuzco and Arequipa passes through the town. People come down from the mountains and bring with them everything that is necessary for life. There is also a port at which ships from Lima arrive. Thus there is a lot of coming and going in the town. The royal mails pass through it and herds of live-stock are always on the move. As for the inhabitants, they are mostly law-abiding and peaceful.

The town of Castrovirreyna, also called Coyca Pallca, administers the two silver-mines of Chocllococha and Orco Cocha. It was established during the Viceroyalty of the Marquess of Cañete. One of the mines, the better of the two, is far from giving up its richest treasure. As its recesses are ex-plored, new veins of silver are always coming to light.

The town is supplied by neighbouring regions with plenty of bread, maize, meat and wine. The bread comes from Huamanga, the maize from the valley of Xauxa, fruit from the plains and wine from Ica. A lot of silver is in circulation, but gold is unknown. Some of the supervisors at the mines are notorious for their harsh treatment of the Indian workers.

There has never been any rebellion in Castrovirreyna and crimes of violence are rare.

The so-called Rich Town of Oropesa, the site of the mercury-mines of Huancavelica, was founded in the time of the Viceroy Don Francisco de Toledo. The mines were actually discovered by an Angara chief from the village of Acoria on the estate of Doña Inez de Villalobos de Cabrera. It was Cabrera who took possession of the mines and succeeded in enriching himself with their spoils. Later, during the reign of three different Vice-roys, the mines came gradually into the ownership of the Crown. When the local chiefs complained about the way in which the Indian workers were perishing, the Marquess of Montesclaros paid a visit and tried to remedy the situation, but he was unable to find any effective course of action. So matters were allowed to remain as they were. The Indians continued to be worked to death and only the women remained in the villages, which be-came desolate.

Oropesa is a cold place, situated on the bleak table-land. Gold is found in the form of powder and there are gems representing all the riches of the

Earth. If the problems of administration could be solved it would go ahead and become richer from year to year.

The bread for Oropesa comes from Huamanga, the maize from Xauxa and the wine from Uayuri. Fruit is brought from the plains and the mountains. But the poor Indians are constantly trying to escape from the deadly work in the mines.

The city of Huamanga was originated by officers of Don Francisco Pizarro, among them Lorenzo de Aldana.* In the first instance they sited it on the other bank of the river, in the place called Quinua. When the time came for the city to be erected where it now stands, my father and Don Hernán Cacya Marca could be considered as the founders. They built the first houses and farms in the part called Santa Catalina de Chupas and from there my father went with Don Juan Tingo to serve on the loyalist side against Don Diego de Almagro the younger at the Battle of Chupas. As well as fighting, they helped to provision the army.

In the beginning my father was one of the absolute owners of the present site of Huamanga. Then the people from the Quinua side came over, leaving their former homes empty. But they made no attempt to evict the earlier possessors, and indeed if they had done so they would have been strongly resisted.

It has to be admitted that some of the leading citizens of Huamanga have on occasion rebelled against the Crown, even if others have remained loyal. The nature of these people is apt to be uncharitable, quarrelsome and mutinous. The judges and priests enforce their own brand of justice, as is exemplified by the case of poor Don García Portocarrero, whose severed head was put on display in the main square.

The religious houses of Huamanga are very poor, but there are many rich people in the place. The climate is as good as any in the whole country and there is an abundance of bread, meat, fruit and wine. The only fault lies in the human beings, who in the opinion of the Viceroy Don Francisco de Toledo were to be compared with lustful horses.

Huamanga is a centre for other prosperous towns. It is situated on the royal highway which links Potosí with Cuzco and Quito, and also on the road to Lima. Law and order cannot be said to exist within its bounds. If some people are treated well, others are robbed of all their property, banished and even murdered. Some of the wealthiest citizens possess fortunes of up to 100,000 pesos. The very shopkeepers and soldiers are well off, perhaps because they have profited from so many rebellions.

The foundation of the great city of Cuzco, or Santiago del Cuzco as it is also called, goes back to our primitive Indians and their rulers Tocay Capac

* *It was founded by Vasco de Guevara in 1539.*

(a) *Bogotá*

(b) *Quito*

(c) *Cuzco*

(d) *Lima*

51 Cities

and Pinau Capac. At a later stage it became the capital and the Court of the twelve successive Inca Kings. It was famous for its splendid temples and palaces, its gold and its white flowers. Then, after the destruction of the Inca dynasty, it was turned into an important Spanish city by Pizarro and Almagro and became a bishopric. There was a last movement of Inca power when Manco, the descendant of the old kings, raised his standard, but his army was destroyed and he had to take refuge in the mountains of Vilcabamba.

There have been a number of other rebellions against the Crown in Cuzco. Francisco Hernández Girón revolted and paid the price of treason. Others, who took up arms to avoid paying excise, were Carreño, Olmos and Bustinza, and they too were punished.

A huge quantity of silver is constantly circulating in the city, but ordinary people have to live sparingly. Food and wine are expensive, and so is clothing. The climate is so cold that food can be frozen simply by leaving it out-of-doors. Whatever their race, the inhabitants tend to speak the general language introduced by the Incas and the old titles are still used.

Arequipa, which was founded by order of Pizarro, has a reputation for good order and tranquillity. The moderate climate produces plentiful food and wine, but there is more fruit than meat. Many of the citizens become rich from the silver of Potosí and the gold of Carabaya and they act charitably towards the poor.

Arequipa, the neighbouring town of Arica and a considerable area around them were devastated when a neighbouring volcano erupted in flashes of fire and clouds of smoke. A fall of ash and sand covered the whole area and there were numerous deaths. The vineyards and farms were all buried. Evil spirits appeared in the gloom, which lasted for thirty days and nights. Meanwhile processions were held and the image of the Virgin Mary, dressed in mourning, was carried by the survivors. In this way peace and order were gradually restored and the Sun appeared in the sky again. But all the farms in the valley of Majes were ruined and the livestock had all perished either from the ash or from disease.

Arica is the port of Arequipa and the outlet for the silver of Potosí. The climate is variable, with intense heat being succeeded by fresh breezes off the sea. It is a rich town because of the passage of gold and silver through the port. Much of its food comes from Cochabamba. There is plenty of fish, fruit and wine, but little meat.

The people are loyal to the Crown and know how to deal with the English, whom they have never permitted to set foot on their shores. Nor have they ever given refuge to traitors. They are known for their Christian feeling and for their good priests, who avoid interfering in any matters of justice. Murder and denunciation are virtually unknown in Arica.

A rich town, which can claim to be the flower or eye, or even better the heart, of this country is Potosí. Its name comes from the Indian word Potocchi, meaning 'member of the world'. This indeed it is, for its wealth sustains both the Catholic Faith and the Crown. For centuries past Potosí has ceaselessly been pouring out its silver. Just as it enriches Your Majesty today, formerly it made Tupac Inca Yupanqui powerful.

The high hill on the right-hand side of the mine is called Apo Potocchi and the lower one standing close to it is called Huayna Potocchi, meaning 'the powerful' and 'the young' respectively. The higher hill contains five veins or lodes of silver metal in the slope just below the summit, which is marked by a golden cross. On the lower hill there are six furnaces over which the silver is melted by Indian workers. Another hill, standing on the left-hand side of the mine, is called Porgo Uroro.

Along with the mercury-mines of Huancavelica, the gold-mine of Carabaya and some other silver-mines, Potosí is the greatest source of wealth in Peru. The Spanish discoverer, who was acting on the order of Don Francisco Pizarro, was Captain Pérez Suárez. The coat-of-arms of the town contains the royal emblems, four castles, a white flag with a red cross, ten severed heads of traitors and four lions as defenders.

In a certain sense Potosí dominates the whole of the Collao from Cuzco and Arequipa to Chuquizaca and Chuquiyabo, since Indians from all this area can be summoned to work in the mines. In such a rich town there are many rich people, so an abundance of food, wine and clothing is brought from all sides and offered for sale there. Silver is as common as stone and gold as common as powder in other places, yet there are thousands who never pay their taxes.

The city of Chuquizaca, which is now the seat of a Royal Audience and a bishopric, was founded by the Incas and later taken over by Pizarro. It has formal jurisdiction over the city of Chuquiyabo, the town of Potosí, the town of Misque and the province of Chucuito, so all the wealth of the silver-mines of Potosí and the gold of Carabaya lies within its orbit. There is ample bread, meat, wine and fruit. A speciality is the honey which comes from the mountains near Misque.

Chuquizaka itself is in the mountains. The climate is fairly warm. There are tigers, lions, bears and snakes as is usual in mountain country. The journey from there to Santiago de Chile requires two months: one month in the sandy desert and another month through the mountains, where there is a risk to life because of the savage Indians living there. In the country beyond rise the River Marañon and the watercourses which flow towards Tucumán and Paraguay.

The local citizens, who are usually loyal, were deceived into supporting the traitor Captain Carbajal, but they quickly discovered their mistake.

The country around is fertile, producing many good things to eat and drink.

Misque is the home of a large number of hermits and holy men, who dress in the style of John the Baptist in animals' skins. When the first one of these appeared in the town the people tried to undress him, but he resisted and finally they left him alone.

Santiago de Chile was built during the Viceroyalty of Don Francisco de Toledo. The climate and produce are comparable with what is found in Castile or the Holy Land, which this part of Chile much resembles. Thus there is excellent bread and wine, fruit-trees are plentiful and there are fat animals on all the farms. A lot of gold circulates and the people are prosperous, although there is little silver. All sorts of food are available, with the effect that health is generally good and the population is increasing. Even octogenarians succeed in remaining physically fit.

The cooking of the ample meals is usually done on hot stones. There is also good natural water, so that in most respects this can be called the best place on Earth. But the Chilean Indians are exceedingly brave and warlike. They never allow themselves to be finally defeated, all the more so when the Spaniards are concerned, who are in the habit of confiscating all their possessions including even wives and daughters. The Chileans prefer death to subjection, because it can only be experienced once. It is true that they submitted to the rule of the Incas, but then they were well-treated in return for handing over their gold.

The city only has jurisdiction within its own boundaries. It has a Bishop, but he and it are in constant danger from the Indians, who are never far from some act of violence.

The Fort of Santa Cruz, which has a good climate, is the fortress which the Christians built against the heathen Indians of Chile who confronted them from their own fortress nearby. The first Spaniards to reach Chile did their best to tread the Indians underfoot as they had done elsewhere in the New World. That is to say, they took away the Indians' property and their women. To begin with, the Indians seemed to allow these offences, but after a while they took to armed resistance. As I have mentioned, the Chilean Indians do not appreciate giving up their belongings to Spaniards. In this they resemble the Chuncho Indians of the mountains, who not only kill Spaniards but eat them alive. The Spaniards will never succeed in suppressing the Chileans in all the days of their life. These people have become distrustful as a result of their experiences and the losses they have suffered. Now they are defending themselves and are prepared to defend themselves to the last. Your Majesty has lost, or stands to lose, a great and rich country because of the bad treatment of the Indians by the conquerors.

The city of Tucumán has no bishopric and no jurisdiction over the neighbouring regions. It is separated from Paraguay by a huge river. It enjoys a mild climate, but there is a certain scarcity of food except for fish and fruit, which are plentiful. Good clothing is also scarce and the people are generally poor.

From this city the chain of mountains descends to an ocean dotted with islets. In these waters there are said to be sirens, and certainly there are swordfish and whales. These last-named are the biggest and most terrible fish which inhabit the seas between Spain and the New World.

Tucumán is a law-abiding place, which has always prided itself on its loyalty.

Paraguay is the seat of a bishopric, but it has no jurisdiction outside the boundaries of the city itself. It is in the middle of the sea, on a great river. By going upstream the Indians can also vanish into the mountains.

The climate of the Yunca plains is favourable and produces an abundance of food, especially fruit, and wine. Meat is scarce and so is clothing. There is little gold or silver in the region.

Paraguay has remained loyal ever since its early conquest, when the Spaniards coming by sea from Castile entered the River Plate and sailed up-river to these two cities which are now called Paraguay and Tucumán.

The cities which have been described are all of them peopled by races of Indians which are subject to the Spanish Viceroy and the Church of Rome.

From the central city of Cuzco a traveller can make a journey to Charcas, Potosí, Santiago de Chile, Tucumán, Paraguay or other places, passing from one inn to another along the roads. I am able to supply a list of all such inns and hostelries, showing their respective importance and the services which they can supply, and also details of the calendar which may be useful in planning the journey.

PREVIOUS HISTORIES

The works of Agustín Zárate and Diego de Fernández, who both wrote about our country, contain a great many errors and failures of verification. These writers were unaware that eye-witnesses of what had occurred were still alive. My father, who took the name of Don Martín de Ayala, was in earlier times the close companion of Tupac Inca Yupanqui, Huayna Capac Inca and Huascar Inca. He died, after many years of service to Your Majesty, at an extraordinarily old age, still able to testify to the events of the Spanish Conquest. And he was not the only one. Another survivor from the old days was Don Diego Zatuni, the chief of the Yunca Indians of Hacari.

Later, another history was written by Father José de Acosta, Rector of the Society of Jesus and author of some approved religious works. Other books came from the pens of Juan Ochoa, a Prior, and Brother Domingo de Santo Tomás, a lexicographer. But none of these writers were properly informed about the Indian races of the New World. Two Franciscan fathers who wrote on confessional matters never referred to the Conquest at all. Brother Martín de Morua and Father Cabellos both touched upon Inca history, but the latter particularly fell far short of his task. He failed to reveal where the Incas came from, or how they were able to take over the government of this country, or the way in which their dynasty came to an end. He said even less about the older rulers, from whom I am descended. Instead, he contented himself with expressing horror over the religious errors of these great figures of the past. It never seemed to occur to him that, if they had been mistaken, so had the Spaniards on numerous occasions.

As a writer, it has been my rule whenever possible to consult the learned in order to confirm the truth of my observations. Often I have simply set down on paper what I know to have occurred, without presuming to comment in the manner of a professional historian.

I have never been in a position to study any documents or texts and that is one reason why it has taken me thirty years to complete my work. During that time I have lived the life of a poor man, sometimes even a shivering and naked one without a grain of maize to eat. Now it is my honour to dedicate the record of this long and painful labour to Your Majesty and indeed the whole world.

THE AUTHOR'S TRAVELS

I, the author of this work, went out into the world among other people just as poor as myself. I wanted to compile a record for the benefit of Your Majesty and also the Indians. Leaving my house in my own town, I have worked for thirty years at this task. My first step was to dress myself in sackcloth so that I would really seem to be a poor man as I looked around at what the world had to show for itself. I did not take this action because I actually lacked the necessities of life, like food and clothing. Indeed I had been happy in receiving many favours from the Crown and my father, as I have related, held an important position. He stood by Your Majesty in

CAMINA EL AVTOR

52 *The Author on his travels*

the rebellions headed by Almagro, Gonzalo Pizarro and Girón. In this last emergency, while helping to destroy the traitor he was taken captive by some Indians at Xauxa. Finally he was rewarded by the Viceroy Don Francisco de Toledo with the title of Captain of Vilcabamba. His rank and salary were confirmed by the succeeding Viceroys, Don Garcia de Mendoza and Don Luis de Velasco.

Because of the authority which I wielded as a result, the poor found it difficult to meet me face to face and also nobody dared to ill-treat them in my presence, as they do if they are unaware of who I am and mistake me for a pauper. This was the reason why I adopted my disguise and in consequence I was a witness of the way in which the Indians are robbed of their property and their wives and daughters. I moved among the animals who prey upon the poor. Seeing me in the same condition as their victims, they attempted to make a similar meal out of me. I for my part, to strengthen my position as a writer who wanted to see and hear as much as possible, made myself the willing object of their persecutions. I was able to confirm that the poor are utterly despised by the rich and highly placed, to the extent that they never experience the charity which our religion enjoins, or even common justice. As proof of the truth of what I write, I propose to tell the full story of my vagrancy, my toil and my misadventures. If all this could happen to me, how much more would be suffered by feeble, inept and shiftless Indians? The Spaniards are pastmasters at robbery and seduction, but they go further and try to make horses or slaves out of our people. When they talk about taxpaying Indians, what they mean is slaves, and in face of such an attitude our people are unable to prosper. They are bearing a burden without any longer having an Inca to defend them. And the only person available to undertake their defence is Your Majesty.

Let me recount what happened to me at the time when I disguised myself as a pauper. I handed over some little property which I possessed to the Spaniards, believing that it would be in safe hands. But the person to whom I gave the money spent it on himself and I never got it back. This proved to me that these people are both bad Christians and dishonest. It is impossible to rely on them, whether you have a receipt or not. Another time a comparatively rich man named Miguel Palomino asked me for a loan of 200 pieces of eight, for which he gave me a receipt. When I asked him to repay the debt he refused point-blank. I tried to invoke the law, but inevitably I discovered that it was on the side of the rich man. The clerk and the lawyer whom I consulted advised me to draw up a petition, but I realised that this was more likely to be my perdition than a petition, for the lawyers are more like robbers and justice is as deaf as a post. On yet another occasion I had to go to court in order to defend my right to some lands which had belonged to my family since the Incas and indeed since the foundation of our country, long before the Spaniards ever came here as conquerors. Our title to the property was duly established and formally confirmed by the court after a review of the evidence; and was later upheld by the Viceroy. The lands in question were situated in the valley of Chupas, where the battle took place between Diego de Almagro the younger and the forces of the Crown including my father. The legal case was concluded by a visit to the scene and Judge Montalvo inspected our boundary marks. These had been erected by order of Tupac Inca Yupanqui and enclosed most of our property, although there were some houses and farms elsewhere.

At this stage the deputy of the royal administrator, a certain Pedro de Rivera who lived at Huamanga and who was unable to read or write, sent two of his clerks to stir up trouble and oppose the judgement pronounced in Your Majesty's name. I for my part lost all faith in the Spaniards and began to make friends with other Indian chiefs, thinking to myself that these were my brothers or at least relations, but I soon discovered my mistake, for these people steal from their own community and people. Nor are the holy fathers, who are supposed to represent God on Earth, any more reliable. On one occasion when I was going away I left some clothing in the keeping of a priest called Francisco Caballero. I had not even started on my journey when the priest began disposing of my shirts and some felt garments, which I have not seen again from that day to this. This was not my only unlucky experience with the clergy. A priest named Martín de Artiaga took two horses away from me, which were worth 50 pesos each or 100 for the pair, and a number of other valuables.

Because of these bad experiences, I decided to leave a locked box containing some of my belongings with a poor Indian in the village of Santiago de Quirauara. But during my absence the parish priest got hold of my box, forced it open and disposed of my property. When I wrote to him to claim its return, he made up a story that he believed I was dead and so had said Masses for my soul, which accounted for the value of the contents of the box. He also resorted to threats in the letter which he wrote to me. What hypocrisy, this taking credit for Masses whilst enriching themselves at our expense! The fact is that the very people who are paid to cherish the Indians are the ones who band themselves together to exploit and deceive them.

I suffered all these troubles in my own person, including even an attempt to seduce my wife away from me, which was made by a friar of the Order of Mercy named Morua in the town of Yanaca.

At last I decided to return to the world, namely to my own home among the Andamarca, Sora and Lucana Indians of central Peru. The biggest villages in this region are called San Cristóbal de Suntunto, Nueva Castilla and Santiago de Chipao. The local heraldic emblem consists of an eagle and a lion. The church was once a beautiful building, but it has since been destroyed. After the thirty years of my travels I also found my town and my province laid waste and the houses of my people in alien hands. When I came back, I discovered my own kin in a near-naked state, acting as servants to common taxpaying Indians. They did not even recognise me because by that time I was 88 years old, grey-haired, feeble, tattered and barefoot, whilst in former times it had been my custom to dress in silk and the finest wool, as was only proper for the grandson of the tenth Inca King.

I expected to find the houses and gardens which belonged to me still intact. I had after all been the local chief, principal figure in society, protector of the Indians and deputy of the royal administrator. I first visited the villages, which I have mentioned, of San Cristóbal de Suntunto and Santiago de Chipao. There I encountered an Indian who had once been just a foreman in charge of ten people, but had assumed the rank of lord or chief and taken the name of Don Diego Suyca. This man, an ordinary taxpayer, had been punished with his sister for the crime of witchcraft by the former Spanish administrator, Don Martín de Mendoza. Two snakes, named Suliman and Mata Callo, and other filth had been found in his possession and burnt. Suyca was a great favourite with Don Juan de León Flores, who was now the administrator, and with the priest Father Peralta, because he had made them a present of fifty pieces of the finest woollen cloth and various other considerations.

My own house and my gardens at Chinchaycocha had been handed over by Suyca to Pedro Colla Quispe, Esteban Atapillo and some other Indians, who had profited in this manner from my long absence. On discovering all these misfortunes, I and my Indian companions began to weep. At the same time the self-styled Don Diego Suyca and his Spanish friends were understandably upset by my arrival. They had formed a settled habit of robbing and maltreating those who were at their mercy, and the priests especially were merciless.

I resolved to appeal to Your Majesty and demand that ordinary Indians who had made themselves into chiefs by force and priests who abused their position should be dismissed. I also made an approach to the royal administrator. This person, Juan de León Flores, summoned me to be questioned in the presence of his predecessor in office Pedro López de Toledo. I made it clear that I had proof of my claim to be the principal chief of the whole province and I recited the high distinctions earned by my father and grandfather. Finally I expressed my abiding loyalty to Your Majesty.

The administrator said nothing for the moment, but his predecessor called out that all I had said was a pack of lies and deserved punishment. If he were still in office, he said, I would get my desserts. But Juan de León Flores opposed him and promised that I would be treated with honour and restored to my former high position on condition that I agreed to help him in all his affairs.

I told the royal administrator that there would be no honour for me in swindling the poor by making them provide more cloth and taxes than were actually due. For instance, in his own village of Santiago de Chipao I knew he had caused 80 rolls of cloth to be woven for him, and no less than 500 rolls in other places round about. Also he was engaged in selling provisions on his own account in all the villages under his control and he employed 100 men to transact his personal business, to the detriment of the local population. But I added that if he were to stop exploiting the Indians I saw no reason why we should not be good friends.

The administrator said in reply that he had no intention of altering his conduct. He was on good terms with the Viceroy, who was considering marriage with one of the young ladies of his family. He also enjoyed the favour of the Secretary to the Government, so he had nothing to fear from any quarter. Accordingly he had no interest in restoring my old authority and title to me, or in the return to me of my houses and gardens. In an entirely illegal manner he had me expelled from my own province. Thus, after registering a protest with him and the clerk, I set off for the City of Kings to complain to Your Majesty, accompanied by my son, my horse Giado* and my two dogs Amigo and Lautaro. I had to walk through the mountains in deep snow and intense cold. Luckily I encountered two Christians named Pedro Mosquera and Francisco Juarez, who helped me to reach the silver-mines at Chocllococha. There I fell in with another good man, Miguel Machado, and his wife, who looked after me, and I was able to pray at their local chapel.

From the silver-mines I went on to Castrovirreyna. The royal administrator, who was called Don Fernando de Castro, gave me some money for my onward journey and I also received money and kindnesses from other Spaniards and a half-caste priest. But the so-called protector of the Indians, Juan de Mora y Carbajal, was responsible for the theft of my white horse, which had cost me 50 pesos. Naturally I complained to the authorities but I got no satisfaction. I thanked God that I had come off so comparatively lightly.

Whilst I was in this region a disturbance occurred in Huachos. It seems that a priest demanded Indians to work for him and especially girls for weaving cloth. The local chief, a certain Don Pedro, refused. Out of spite, the priest accused him and his people of idolatry and proceeded to manufacture evidence that they had been worshipping rocks and stones. He did this by hanging up Don Pedro, some old people of both sexes and some children one by one, torturing them until in their agony they admitted the offence and produced stones which they said were their idols. Then a hundred Indians were taken to Castrovirreyna, stripped, cruelly flogged in the presence of the judge and kept in prison without food until eighty of them, including Don Pedro, had died. The priest and his friends then appropriated all the ornaments, silverware, scarf-pins, feathers and garments of coloured wool, which are worn by our Indians at their celebrations, from the houses of the dead and those nearby. These priests even took the bedspreads.

Your Majesty ought to feel pity for these eighty lost souls and their chief, if only because they represent so much lost property and wealth. I have seen the torments of such people and I have also heard a sermon preached by a Theatine Father, in which he said that all the Indians had to die, whether in the mines or at the hands of the Spaniards and their priests. This indicates that the Spaniards wish us ill and really want all of us to perish like the eighty Indians of Huachos.

* Guiado *seems more likely.*

I next visited the village of San Cristóbal, where I fell in with a foreman of ten Indian labourers called Juan Quille. This man employed me at a wage of 50 pesos, part of which was paid in the form of a light chestnut horse valued at 10 pesos. He had an Indian wife and therefore his legitimate daughter was a half-caste, whom he kept in his kitchen with other girls and used for baking bread and tilling his fields. The deputy to the royal administrator came on a visit to the village and the local priest complained to this official about girls who were living with men without being married. The deputy and the priest put their heads together and sent off three of the most beautiful girls to Huancavelica, ostensibly to work for the deputy's mother but really so that they could sleep with the Spaniards.

Juan Quille and I felt ourselves impotent to prevent these particular girls from being removed from the village. We discussed with one another the tendency of the priests to take advantage of the religious instruction which they impart to the young and we agreed that it would be advisable to limit the priesthood to men of over 70 years of age, by which time their passions were likely to have cooled. It so happened that we were talking in front of Juan Quille's daughter, who promptly went off and reported what she had heard to her mother. The mother then went at midnight to call on the parish priest and passed on the gist of the conversation. On the following morning the priest sent for me and ordered me to leave the village. I was to say nothing to anyone and do nothing which would put heart into the Indians. Otherwise he would have me tied over the back of a llama and flogged. The interview ended at this point and I was escorted out of San Cristóbal.

In another village called Chinchay Yunca the parish priest was engaged in the fabrication of false evidence about the local chief, presumably with the aim of destroying both him and the community. It would be a good idea to follow the custom of Castile and lock the friars up in their convents and the priests in their houses, to stop them propagating lies, as they do in Peru.

This priest whom I have mentioned kept the Indians in a state of terror. Even I was appalled at his conduct towards these feeble and defenceless people. I felt I had no option except to join them in their misery. This happened when I was in the village on Ash Wednesday and I heard a dreadful sermon preached by the priest. He told his parishioners he was going to have them all 'killed, skinned and salted down like mangy llamas' and made other similar threats, until I found myself obliged to leave the church to avoid witnessing Indians in such a state of terror. I have seen enough of the evils of this world and if I recount the incident now it is because I keep thinking of the fate of those eighty Indians whose murder I have described.

My next step was to return to the city of Castrovirreyna. There, not for the first time, I had to endure a good deal of misery. An Aymará Indian from the village of Uaquirca, who went by the name of Juan de León Cautillo, robbed me of a saddle and some other useful equipment. Also my eldest son Francisco, who had accompanied me hitherto, thought fit to leave me, poor and hungry as I was. I found nobody who was prepared to lend me a single real.

During the time when I was at San Cristóbal I made the acquaintance of a Spaniard from the town of Pisco. He was going to dine with Juan Quille, the foreman whom I have already mentioned, and took me with him. Over the meal I said to Juan Quille:

'Why don't you marry your daughter to an Indian? Wouldn't that be better than letting her be seduced by the parish priest?'

The Spaniard in his turn asked me: 'Why do you tire yourself out going around as you do, you who are such an old man? You could make a good living by making clothing and selling it to the Spanish authorities, couldn't you?'

I replied: 'None of the Viceroys have obliged me to make clothing or go into trade. The salaries of these high officials amount to a third of everything produced in our country, so they don't have any need to compel me to work for them.'

The Spaniard went on: 'A big employer in Chinchay wanted to get a new Indian appointed in place of the proper chief, who didn't get on well with the Spaniards. The old chief was told that if he didn't leave quietly he'd be flogged to death. That's what happens to trouble-makers, who don't bother to keep in with the authorities.'

'I'm not a trouble-maker,' I explained, 'but I happen to be a hereditary chief and landowner, descended through my mother from the tenth Inca King. Prince Melchor Carlos Paullu Tupac, who has travelled in Castile, is one of my uncles. My father served God and the King all his life. My Indian name Huaman Poma indicates the King of the birds and the King of the animals and my Spanish name Ayala gives proof of my loyalty to the Crown. Like the condor, which can smell carrion a hundred miles away, my family have smelt and avoided every treason in fifty years. My grandfather was called Chava, which means "the cruel", but all his cruelty was against traitors and usurpers.'

At this, the Spaniard said: 'Go to Castile, my son. The King is bound to show favour to someone of your birth and quality.'

'I'm well over 80 years old,' I replied. 'There's nothing I can do any more. It's up to His Majesty, who's the ruler of the country, to do something for our people.'

As I have related, I went on to Castrovirreyna and spent one night there. Poor and alone as I was I resumed my journey. Along the way I passed a number of Spaniards and Indians. On seeing me they usually asked who I was travelling with or whose servant I was. To this question I always replied that I was in the service of a man of importance called Cristóbal. The person I meant to refer to was Christ but I added the syllable 'bal'. Later I took to saying 'Cristóbal of the Cross'. When people asked me who this man was and whether he was rich and a mine-owner, I told them:

'My master used to be a great miner and now he is rich and powerful.'

'And shall we see this man?' they wanted to know.

'He's coming to join me where I'm going,' I said. 'You'll meet him if you look out for him, gentlemen.'

Once again I met my Christian friend Miguel Machado at Chocllococha and visited the chapel, for it was a Sunday during Lent. At the works nearby I came across twenty Indians from my home town. Recognising me as their old chief they encircled me, men, women and children, and recounted all their sufferings. But they also wept over me and could hardly believe that they had found me alive and reasonably well. According to their account, during my absence they had done nothing but make huge quantities of clothing for the Spanish officials. It was just as bad in the mines at Chocllococha, for the overseer punished them cruelly and kept back part of their wages. The mines at Huancavelica were the same.

In answer to these tears and complaints I explained that despite my advanced age I proposed to complete my report to Your Majesty.

When I left my Indian friends and rode forward, I was accompanied only by the two dogs who guarded me. The skies opened and it rained without ceasing. Then the rain turned to snow, which lay so thickly that I could hardly advance. Also the road passed through a treacherous marsh, so that the horse on which I was mounted trembled from fear as well as cold. In a pitiable state I at least reached the estate of a Señor Sotomayor. My dogs, meanwhile, had left me and run back to Castrovirreyna.

At the estate I made the acquaintance of three old Indian women, who told me about their sufferings in Atun Xauxa, the village from which they had fled. Their persecutor was a priest, Dr Avila, who came as a Visitor from the Bishop of Lima to the valley of Xauxa. He accused these women of practising as witches, worshipping idols and bowing down before stones. They had done none of these things, but in order to oblige them to confess Doctor Avila had them crowned, ropes tied round their necks and wax candles put in their hands. In this fashion they were made to walk in procession. It was explained to them that, if they confessed, the Visitor would be satisfied and they would be left in peace. But the three women, who were good Christians, protested that they had nothing to do with idols and only worshipped the true God. Thereupon they were tied upon the backs of white llamas and whipped, so that their blood dripped on the fleeces of the animals and dyed them red. At that stage, to avoid further torment, the three women agreed to confess to worshipping idols.

They also told me about an old man from their village who, to avoid being tortured, swallowed a powder made from softened coca leaves and suffocated himself. He was at first buried in consecrated ground, but the Visitor ordered the body to be exhumed and burnt. The ashes and fragments of bone were then scattered in the river.

Finally one of the old women said to me: 'It's true that our ancestors worshipped idols, but that applies to the Spaniards and other peoples as well. Nowadays we're baptised as Christians. But thanks to people like Dr Avila we're likely to return to our old forms of worship in the mountains, which have become our only place of refuge. There's nobody to grieve for us any more, except perhaps the Inca, and Don Melchor who belonged to his family is dead. We can look forward to nothing but pain and trouble.'

The old women were all weeping and praying for death and I was shocked by their pitiful story.

Next I entered the Rich Town of Oropesa, where the mines of Huancavelica are situated. I went into the church and, on coming out into the square, was amazed to see a number of chiefs and other Indians slapped and beaten. At the same time they were being abused as dogs and animals. I had the impression that all the demons had been let out of Hell to torment our wretched people. I saw these events in the square at close range, because I mingled with the Indians who were being maltreated. Among the crowd were a number of my own people who recognised and embraced me. Some of them carried me off to their homes, where they told me about their sufferings in the mines. They were part of a labour gang which had been enrolled by order of the royal administrator Don Juan de León Flores and his clerk Don Andrés Valle. When the lists were checked, 26 Andamarca, 30 Lucana and 10 Sora Indians were found to be missing and replacements were duly hired and paid for by the captain in charge. When an explanation was asked for, why so many Indians were missing, my people answered that 100 labourers had been requisitioned by the administrator for the porterage of his wine. Chiefs and other Indian officials had been pressed into service to handle and dispatch the wine to customers for the administrator's profit. An office had actually been set up for this purpose at a place called Uatacocha.

From Huancavelica I continued my journey towards the valley of Xauxa and arrived at a place called Llallas. There, while I was sleeping in a cave, two Huanca Indians tried to assault me. Fortunately there were half-a-dozen other Indians in the cave, who were descendants of the survivors of Challcuchima's army. They were inveterate thieves themselves, but on this occasion they were of some service since they scared off the others.

I pressed on as rapidly as possible, as I was anxious to celebrate Easter in a populated place. On my way I passed a great number of Spanish muleteers and traders, who seemed to have no thought of attending Mass. Yet the custom of stopping work on the eve of Palm Sunday and staying away over the four days of Easter is an excellent one.

I arrived at the village of Huancayo in a state of some distress, because of poverty and ill-health, but I attended the evening service and heard a good sermon from the priest who happened to be officiating. On Good Friday I heard an even better one preached by the incumbent. I did not succeed in finding a room at an inn since I had so little money; nor did I receive any charity although the local people seemed to be loaded with crucifixes and rosaries. Finally I found a lodging as the guest of an Indian called Caruarinri, who was in the choir and had been treasurer of the church for some years. I then returned to the streets and squares to observe what was going on. To excuse my misery, I explained that I was fasting, but on the second day of Easter I was invited to a meal by my host, with others who were equally unfortunate.

The next stop on my journey was at Concepción de Lurin Huanca and from there I went on into the valley of Xauxa. My impression was that in these villages the masculine half of the population lived off the Spaniards. These men wore shirts, engaged in dubious sorts of business, talked a great deal and ingratiated themselves with the local priest. The feminine half of the population consisted of Indian prostitutes dressed up in petticoats, long sleeves, buttons and blouses. Few of them had less than half-a-dozen illegitimate children and none of them had any intention of marrying the men of their own race.

The injustice with which Indians are treated is well illustrated by the case of a chief, Don Juan Apo Alanya, who was married to Doña Maria Manco Carua. Don Juan's mother, a woman named Maria Alta, made a second marriage with a half-caste, Francisco Serrano, who thus became the chief's stepfather. This Serrano, knowing that Don Juan was serving in the mines of Huancavelica, took the opportunity of violating Doña Maria, his own stepson's wife. Hearing of this, Don Juan came home, caught the couple together at night and killed them both. For this so-called crime he was punished by the royal administrator with the confiscation of all his property. Then Francisco Serrano's sons Juan and Miguel, a certain Diego López and another man called Villegas armed themselves with pistols and went to look for Don Juan Apo Alanya. They were four armed men and he was alone in the country, but these enemies of the Indians treacherously murdered him.

The four Spaniards went free and paid no penalty whatever, whereas they deserved to be quartered alive and have all their goods confiscated.

The one who suffered was the murdered chief's son, Juan Huayna Alanya, who was still a child and left destitute.

Another example of injustice which comes to my mind is the experience of some Yauyo Indians close to the town of Córdova. On the road a Spaniard attacked these ten Indians and tried to rob them of their possessions including the food which they were carrying. When the Indians defended themselves against him, the Spaniard drew his sword and wounded three of them. The Indians, to save their own lives, killed the Spaniard. On hearing of the incident the judge neglected to call for any evidence or verification, but had all ten of the Yauyo Indians hanged on the spot.

I crossed the wide river Huambo on a raft and reached the villages of Chongo, Chupaca, Cicaya, Urcotunan, Mito, Hinco and Huaripampa. There I came across the Huanca Indians, who are very cunning and deceitful. It is their habit to rob women whenever they can and to drive ignorant people out of their homes and farms, which these Indians then keep for themselves. They also succeed somehow in enlisting the support of the friars for their malpractices. The girls wear petticoats and cause a lot of trouble by becoming the mistresses of the priests. The married ones go so far as to give evidence against their husbands so that they can be free to sleep with the Spaniards. This actually happened to Don Diego Chuquillanti, the chief of Cochangara. His wife laid false information with the authorities to the effect that he was violating his daughter, sleeping with his sisters and practising witchcraft. The sole object of this woman was to get her husband hanged, so that she could play the whore.

The Indians of Lurin Huanca are special offenders in this way, as well as being thieves and liable to walk out of church in the middle of Mass.

I left Santo Domingo de Cicaya and was accompanied on my way by an Indian of excellent character who had joined me in the village. We discovered some hot springs close to the high road. We also heard tales about a provision merchant who made raids on the property of the local Indians at San Felipe.

On our way we encountered various herdsmen and travellers, who were sometimes accompanied by Indian girls of bad character. It was quite common to see Indian men loaded like animals and driven along the road by a horseman.

Among the people of San Felipe who spoke to us on our arrival was a man reputed to be over 100 years old, Don Pedro Puyca Caxa. The old Indian wept as he showed us the once beautiful church, the hospital, the priest's house and the chapter-house, all of them now destroyed. Indeed, the village itself was in ruins. I calculated that the cost of the damage must have amounted to 5,000 pesos for the church and public buildings, and as much again for the private houses. The Indians were obliged to walk six or seven miles to work in the neighbouring village of San Pedro. During this journey their wives and daughters were assaulted and the food which they brought with them was stolen. The notorious Visitor, Dr Avila, and the royal administrator enriched themselves by accusing innocent Indians of idolatrous practices and then confiscating their property. The priest did not even stop short at stealing the property of the poor in San Felipe, but proceeded to appoint his two sons as his representatives in the village of San Lorenzo. There they raised the price of food and increased the amount of service required of the Indians. Knowing themselves to be secure from prosecution, these two virtually flayed the villagers alive.

Perhaps this is the right place for me to say that the Yauyo Indians are a selfish lot, including those who come from the mountains along the Pacific coast. Far from behaving in a neighbourly fashion, they are vicious to the point of insanity. Their only abilities lie in the direction of eating and drinking.

At the top of the hill at Huarochiri I met a party of men and women who had arrived from the inn at Chorrillo. I inquired why these people had no Indian porters with them and was told that they would rather carry their own baggage than use Indians as beasts of burden. In Castile, they pointed out, horses rather than Christians were expected to carry heavy loads. Indeed, the horse had been created for that very purpose. Forced labour could not be demanded in Castile and Indian 'guides' were unknown, they told me. To my astonishment, these were the actual words that were spoken.

Seeing at a glance that I was old and poor, the strangers offered me some bread rolls and quince cheese from the provisions they had brought with them from Lima. I remarked that until now I had received no charity whatever from any Spaniard on my travels. Yet these people were certainly not half-castes of any sort. Indeed, they had every appearance of having been born in Castile and when I challenged them they confirmed that they were Spaniards who had been in Peru for the last ten years.

I arrived at the inn at Chorrillo and was served by some old Indians of both sexes. They told me in the course of our conversation that it was usual for the people of the valley of Xauxa to wear several layers of clothing, which they were prepared to strip off and sell for a few pence for each garment. In some cases the clothing was stolen from elsewhere and often it was exchanged for a meal of toasted maize, even when the clothing was brand new. This had occurred in the villages through which I was passing. It seemed that litigants were constantly on the move from the provinces to the capital to obtain justice. Some were seriously ill and many others were short of food, so it was easy for the local inhabitants to cheat them and rob them of their poor belongings. The Yauyo Indians had little understanding of Christian charity.

I arrived at the inn in the village of Cicicaya, but the local chief, who was known as Don Martín, was not waiting to welcome me. I was told that he was superintending some cleaning operations by his Indians in the neighbouring chapel. Upon my presenting myself he received me with much affection, entertained me and provided me with what I needed for my onward journey.

I made my way across a marsh and up the hillside of Aysabilca, where I fell in with a poor man called Diego de Aguayo, who was a native of Chuquizaca. We were crossing some sandy ground on the way to Lima when we were confronted by a muleteer who was elegantly dressed and very grand in his manner: someone from whom may God preserve us! He pretended to be sitting in judgement and uttered threats against my poor companion to induce him to part with his mule. First he asked where my companion came from, and then how long he had owned the mule. As there was no harness-sore on the beast, by which it could be distinguished, he claimed that it and his own mule were as alike as two peas. But all these arguments were just pretexts for trying to steal the animal.

Finally he gave up the attempt and we continued on our way until we arrived very late in the evening at Lima. Because we were obviously so poor, no inn would take us in and nobody offered to help us. We had to sleep in a gateway without even a mouthful of supper, and our beasts went without any hay or grass, so desperate was our situation. In the morning we crossed the walled road that encircles the city and called at a house close to a monastery. But the people set about us with sticks and drove us away in spite of our appeals for charity.

I was compelled to sell my horse and saddle to make enough money to live on. After praying in several of the churches, I rented a hut for 20 reales a month and shared this lodging with some poor friends.

The city of Lima was full of Indians who had fled from their own villages and were living on their wits or acting as servants in Spanish houses. The humblest taxpayers dressed themselves up and wore swords as if they came from Castile. Others tried to avoid taxes or service in the mines by disguising themselves. It was as if the world were turned upside down. The worst of it was that more and more Indians were following the example of the fugitives and leaving their villages. Nobody was left to pay the taxes and work in the mines. I saw also a great number of Indian prostitutes, encumbered with their half-caste babies and wearing petticoats, boots and elegant head-dresses. Even the married ones sold themselves indiscriminately to Spaniards and negroes alike. These women had no intention of giving up their vicious trade. The lowest quarters of the city were full of Indian whores.

It was to remedy these ills of my country that I had changed myself into a poor man, endured many hardships and given up all that I had in the way of family and property. Among the Indians I was born as a great lord and it was indispensable that someone of my rank should communicate personally with Your Majesty, whose dominions are illuminated in turn by the Sun. Who but I, the author, could dare to write and talk to you, or even approach so high a personage? It was this consideration which made me venture upon my long letter. I have written as your humble vassal in the New World but also as a prince, or *auqui* as we say in our language, the grandson of our tenth King, Tupac Inca Yupanqui, and the legitimate son of Curi Ocllo Coya, a Queen of Peru.

REÍ

CVRONAREAL

EGOLVLCIOCVLLVMASEIŎS
F

PLVS

VLTRA

.S. .C. .R.M.

53 *Endpiece to the 'Nueva Corónica': arms of the Spanish Crown*

INDEX